D1087923

HARRY BLOOM

TRANSVAAL

Episode

Second Chance Press
Sagaponack, New York

Jay Landesman Limited
London

Originally published in Great Britain 1956 by Collins,
London.

First republication 1981 by Second Chance Press,
Sagaponack, New York.

Published 1981 in Great Britain by
Jay Landesman Limited, London.

Library of Congress Catalogue Card Number: 81-51098
International Standard Book Numbers:
    (U.S.) 0-933256-24-8 (Clothbound)
           0-933256-25-6 (Paperbound)
    (U.K.) 0-905150-36-8

Printed in the United States of America

To
Beryl, Bram, Guy and Trevor,
who in various ways helped
me to write this book.

AUTHOR'S NOTE

Nelstroom has no existence outside this book; it is a fictional town. It is necessary to state this in case some readers, from the description of streets, landmarks, locale or climate will believe that they recognise Nelstroom as being a town they know. But Nelstroom has no real-life existence; it is meant to be merely a depiction of a typical, middle-sized Transvaal town. It is indeed, like so many such towns, that there is perhaps a temptation to try and identify it with one of them. Hence the need for this explanation.

The people of Nelstroom, both in the white town and the location, are similarly, imaginary people. That such *Types* exist, indeed are prevalent in South Africa, is of course true —otherwise I should not have written the story. But the people in this book are not modelled on real people, and if it should happen that a description of a character seems to fit a real person, that would be a purely accidental and unintentional consequence of writing a work of fiction that is intended to picture and typify a segment of life in South Africa. No particular living persons were in my mind when I wrote this book.

There have been many race riots in South Africa—they form part of the scene, like floods or droughts. Some of them occurred after I finished writing the book, and one of these bears a striking similarity to the events of this story. But these events were not modelled on any particular riot. Every riot has its own features. I have merely tried to describe the kind of things that *do* happen when, in the peculiar setting of South Africa, racial tensions reach breaking point.

1953 *was a quiet year. The previous year had been one of upheaval and violence, but in 1953 everything quietened down, as if exhaustion had forced a rest upon the contenders. Nobody had won and nothing was decided, but an hour of uneasy quiet settled on the land. And then the flames leapt up, briefly, in a town called Nelstroom.*

CHAPTER ONE

THERE IS an air of activity about Nelstroom, especially in the mornings. White-bearded old farmers arrive early from the districts for a day's shopping. A man takes delivery of a brand-new tractor and drives the gigantic bright-coloured toy away up the street. Lorries from the canneries rumble through the town carrying massive loads of canned tomato juice. Cars and trucks with a variety of licence plates fill up at the petrol stations before making the long trip down to the bushveld. A bell rings on the market square where a cattle sale is in progress. Hit tunes from café juke boxes blare out into the street. A clangour arises from the railway repair sheds and hangs in the air, a background for all the other noises.

A national road drives eastwards out of Johannesburg, over the flat plateau of the highveld, down the escarpment into the lowveld, and on to the coastal towns. Nelstroom lies about half-way along, within sight of the mountain kingdom of Swaziland. From the streets of Nelstroom one catches glimpses of the silvery road sneaking down the mountainside, cautiously stalking the town from the cover of a pine plantation, before coming out on to the floor of the valley. It makes a last dash across the little apron of flat land, enters the town by a back street and joins finally with Potgieter Street, Nelstroom's main thoroughfare.

All up and down Potgieter Street are filling stations and cafés. There is a haze of colour from cigarette, beer and petrol advertisements, and a bright shine of chromium about the shops. There are new hotels, banks, building societies, and a cinema with the flags of some recent jubilee still flying. Nelstroom, like many Transvaal towns, is old and new, old-fashioned and modern, a market town, a mining town and an industrial town, all at once.

9

There are some rich people in Nelstroom now, though still not many, and their houses look fine standing in the new wooded suburb overlooking the town. Most of its white people, however, live inside the town, in neat brick cottages with peach trees and rose bushes in the gardens. The whole town has a clean and tidy look, and with the mountains behind and the green valley rolling out below, it is pretty and sheltered and peaceful.

This is Nelstroom as the passing traveller sees it. This is the town that the visitor likes to remember. But there is another town, a submerged half, an ominous counterpart that lives within its shadow. The people of Nelstroom seldom speak about this other town. They would prefer not to think about it. But it is always present, somewhere, in their thoughts. Like captor and captive chained together, the two towns are never free from one another.

The curious thing is that one has to adjust one's eyes to see this second town. The people of both towns walk in the streets, but somehow one pays attention only to the white people. The black people seem to have a way of effacing themselves. When they meet a white man on the pavement, they slide out of his way, out of sight. They go about their business, very earnest, and apparently very anxious not to involve themselves with the white town more than necessary. They are always hurrying—or waiting. They wait in the shops until all the white people are served : they wait at their special window at the railway booking office until the clerk decides to notice them. They sit in silent, patient groups on the lawn of the Magistrate's Court, waiting for hours, days, for news of a case. They are always there and they seem to be a part of the natural surroundings, like shrubs. Somehow their presence in the town is shadowy and unobtrusive. Mostly they are very poorly clothed, often in tatters.

The place where they live is something different from the poor quarter of a town, something different from the usual segregated district. It is a special kind of living arrangement that cannot be compared with anything outside this country. They call this place the location, which is itself a significantly unique use of the word, for it denotes not a place where people live, but one where something is to be found.

There are no signs showing the way to this place. One finds

10

it by following the stream of a distinct kind of traffic that runs among the ordinary traffic of the town—ramshackle taxis, donkey carts, bicycles, women walking with bundles on their heads. It skirts the shopping section, goes past the high school, the park, through the factory section, alongside the fence of the railway yard, and across the railway line.

There, sloping away towards the river and stretching for more than a mile, lies an area crowded with poor houses. Nowhere does it touch the white area, for the two are kept apart by the railway line. And it is surrounded by a barbed-wire fence in which there are no gates except one at the southernmost end, which is the point farthest from the town.

A sand road runs parallel with the fence and straight down to the gate, and driving along the road, one sees the different styles of houses in the location. First, nearest the railway line, are wattle huts with peaked thatched roofs. They stand in clusters, like families, behind reed fences, and this part is like an old bush village, except that each house has a large, clear number above the door. They are the oldest houses, and were there even before the fence was erected.

Then comes an area of square cement houses with sheet-iron roofs held down by rocks. Each house is exactly like the next, and each has a number, like a badge, above the door. There had once been a housing scheme in Nelstroom but it was killed by mismanagement and a famous political feud in the Town Council, and the tenants completed the houses themselves. There are several acres of these tiny toy houses, laid out like white boxes in a factory yard.

Then the geometrical neatness suddenly ends and a desert of shanties commences. All the rest is a sprawling wasteland of mud-and-stone walls, unpainted wood, flattened paraffin tins, rusted corrugated iron, and flapping sackcloth. This makes up more than half the entire location. Here everything is dry and bleached, the exhausted sepia colour of hard, stamped-down earth. The surrounding veld is fresh and bright, there are blue mountains beyond, but here, inside the fence, is an area quarantined against the green things of nature. For an hour or two in the morning it is even shut out of the sunlight by a

11

curious atmospheric effect. A pall of smoke from the night fires hangs, reluctant to rise, a few feet above the plateau of rooftops, holding to the exact shape of the location.

*　　*　　*

The inhabitants of the location live like a captured people. They are bound and tethered by laws that have no application to the inhabitants of the white town. There is a mass of prohibitions—and what is not prohibited has to be specially permitted. Wherever a man goes, whatever he does, he runs the risk of breaking a law. There is a multitude of papers—pink papers, green papers, buff papers—for everything must be written and authorised. Life in the location is stifled by the dense web of bureaucracy. A man in the location goes about with the superintendent's signature all over his person. He becomes a piece of paper, his family becomes a cluster of papers, his house a number in a register, his job a yellow form; and his life and security exactly as valuable and durable as the scraps of paper that fill his pockets.

The work of the police is all too easy, for every man is a likely wrongdoer. No one can hope to obey all the laws—indeed it would be a catastrophe if everyone did, for many institutions, the farms particularly, are run on convict labour. The police stop any black man they see with a good chance of making an arrest. If things are too quiet in town, they raid the location and find the wrongdoers in their beds.

They call their Black Marias " pick-up vans," a name which implies all too clearly that their function is to roam the streets like dogcatchers, on the lookout for the daily bag of chance offenders.

The location people live in desperately close contact with the police. Any knock on the door might be that of a policeman. Any day might be the one when a husband fails to come home from work and is found to be in gaol, arrested for an irregularity in his pass, for possessing a spiked stick, for sitting on the wrong bench in the park, for leaving his tax receipt at home, for disobedience, impertinence, trespass, nuisance, disturbance—for any one of countless possible crimes; the day when money must be

12

hurriedly found for bails, fines, and lawyer's fees ; the day when a man is last seen before disappearing for weeks, months, sometimes years, while in his absence his house is sold and his family uprooted. Any night might be that when the police stage a raid on the location for beer or spirits, dangerous weapons, passes and permits, stolen goods—bursting into houses at random, ordering father, mother, and terrified children, lodgers and visitors at the point of a gun to stand in the street while they ransack the rooms.

Life in the location has a hovering uncertainty and unsafety, from hour to hour, day and night.

But it works out well for those sections of the white people who live by the labour of convicts. The farmers, who are the main support of the government, even co-operate with the police by building their own gaols, with their own money, and with the blessing of the Minister of Justice, to accommodate the constant flow of convicts from the location.

*　　　*　　　*

The location superintendent is a man with a peculiar job. He, more than any other official, is responsible for enforcing apartheid. Yet apartheid is not for him. All day long he works in an office surrounded by location people. His office in the location is a white frontier post in the black town.

Because of his daily contact with untouchables, people are inclined to consider his job a dirty one, and so it is not the kind of job to attract efficient or talented men. Even the government, despising the black people, tends to despise the official it employs to handle them—he is underpaid and overworked, promotion is slow.

Yet he is a man vested with extraordinary power. Everybody in the location lives by his goodwill. With a bang of his rubber stamp he can alter the course of a man's life. The medieval prince seldom had so much power over so many.

His job is a dirty one in another sense, too. He has to administer the hateful and obnoxious laws. And the location people hold him responsible for them, because he is the man they see in the office. He is the law and the government.

13

Yet his work brings him daily into the lives of the location people, and there is always a danger that he might become involved too closely. When this happens, his job is destroyed, for it cannot exist when the barrier that he is paid to maintain on behalf of the white town is down for him. So he must be constantly on guard. He must avoid being drawn into the affairs of the location people; he must not allow himself to grow fond of them or sorry for them. He must find a way of shutting his mind to all the life going on around him. And he must find a way to justify himself, to convince himself that he works for the benefit of the location people, or else too many disturbing ideas are let into his mind.

It takes a special kind of madman to do this. The ordinary white man does not have these strains and dilemmas. But the location superintendent is the exposed nerve of the apartheid system. Many superintendents begin to break up after a few years: they become uneasy, touchy, vindictive, callous, hasty, and frightened.

Nelstroom once had a famous location superintendent. His name was Hendrik Du Toit and he was a serious and hard-working man who tried to make a good job of the location. He did not stay long—a little over two and a half years in all—but in that time he made the location into a model of smooth and efficient management.

The Town Council were so pleased with his work that they bought him a new car, something they never did for any other superintendent, before or since. They were unanimous in saying that he was the best superintendent they ever had.

He did not set out only to please his employers, the Town Council. He tried to please the location people, too. He wanted them also to feel that he was the best superintendent they ever had. So although he enforced the laws strictly and without favour, he was always busy with welfare schemes and reforms to improve the lot of the location people.

He liked to speak of himself as the father of the location, and he meant it, too, in a certain sense. He considered the location people to be like children, incapable of managing their own affairs, and therefore in need of his services as superintendent.

Therefore, too, in need of the laws that stemmed from the idea that they had to be protected against themselves, such as that they could not be trusted with anything sharp or potent, and that all decisions had to be made for them.

He saw in the fact that they were black, God's design to make them different, and in the story of Noah's doomed and unfortunate son Ham proof that they were bound to remain inferiors for ever. But he did not despise them for it. He was very patient with them. He even had a perverse kind of love for them. He was a religious man, in a narrow Calvinist fashion, and he saw it all as part of a vague but divine plan that had a place for the location, the white town, the police, and himself.

He would have been amazed to know that his honest, earnest, and elevated motives made him into a tyrant in the location.

Hendrik Du Toit was not a typical superintendent, but then there is no such thing. Every superintendent works out his own problems in his own way, and Du Toit's way was about as good as any man's attempt to handle the dilemmas of his peculiar job.

CHAPTER TWO

ONE DAY in the hot, dry November of 1952 a new man came to live in the location. He came to take up a job in a garage in the town, but his arrival was somewhat unusual because it was keenly awaited by a certain section of the location people. He travelled by train from Johannesburg and it was late afternoon when he reached Nelstroom. He stood on the platform with a battered fibre suitcase in his hand and an old khaki trench-coat slung over his shoulder, and he peered about him, screwing up his eyes as he caught the glare of the huge sun that was going down behind the mountains.

There was something about this man that drew eyes to him, but it was hard to say just what it was. He was tall, heavily built, about forty-five years old. He had a strong-growing black beard and a shrewd, wide-eyed face and he wore a weather-beaten black leather cap. Perhaps it was that, the beard and the cap, for the two went perfectly together and gave him the jaunty, seasoned look of a barge skipper. Or perhaps it was the feeling of casual strength about the huge body, or perhaps the air of self-assured style. It was hard to say. He wore an old brown lumber jacket with the zipper gone, a yellow shirt, black patched trousers, but brand-new yellow shoes with half-inch treaded soles. His clothes were too heavy for so hot a day, and he sweated freely.

He put the suitcase on the ground, and the coat on top of it. and stood and watched the other passengers leave the station. There were subdued welcomes, hurried arrangements about luggage. He saw the three women who had travelled in his compartment hoist their heavy cloth-wrapped bundles on their heads and run with bent legs to the dilapidated taxis standing outside the station. He put his hand in his back pocket and felt his money. But he knew without doing it that he could not take a taxi. There were only a ten-shilling note and some coins, and that money had to last until the first payday.

He looked over the station fence into the town. Changed, he thought. Yet the same. Many new buildings, shops, the town more spread out, the spaces filled in, more trees, more traffic. But somehow the same. The feel of the air, the warmth, the smell of the grass and bush, the particular pitch of the insect sounds—slight things—these had not altered. The sensation of them instantly returned to him over the years and brought in their wake a host of dim and almost forgotten memories.

He saw a man hurrying through the gate, pushing against the stream of people leaving the station. He started to go to him but he suddenly checked himself and frowned. He watched the man coming, studying him, and unsure until there was no longer any doubt that the man was making for him. Then he picked up the suitcase and slung the heavy coat back over his shoulder.

" You are Walter Mabaso, I take it ? " the man said, offering his hand while still several feet away.

" You are—you must be Elliot Nkomo ? " Mabaso said. They shook hands.

" So—we meet at last," Nkomo said, not letting go of the hand but covering it with his other hand.

" Yes—at last." Mabaso felt embarrassed and could not think of anything to say. He looked down at the large head, the wide unequal shoulders, the squat figure, and tried desperately to bring himself to ease.

Nkomo said, " There was some holdup about your permit. So I'm sorry I wasn't here when the train came in. The train came in and I was nowhere to be seen. You must have got a bad impression." He spoke in English, with that stilted elocution that was common among clerks and schoolteachers. He had a deep, rough voice, but one with a curiously boyish and affectionate note.

He tried to take the suitcase from Mabaso, but Mabaso tugged it angrily away and moved it over to the side away from Nkomo. They walked out of the station and Mabaso purposely fell back and walked behind Nkomo. As he stared at the built-up boot,

17

the sprawling gait, the shoulders revolving with every difficult step, he tried frantically to think what this could mean. How could a man write so much and not mention a thing like this? For some absurd reason he felt hurt, as if he had been deceived. He had formed a picture of Nkomo from the letters, and now the man was nothing like the picture. It made him wonder how much else was going to change in the intense complete picture that he had built up in his mind.

They reached the street outside, and Nkomo took Mabaso's arm and steered him past the taxis.

"I have transportation," he said.

He went into a lane between two buildings while Mabaso waited in the street. Mabaso studied the row of shops now locked up for the day. One he recognised—the Dagbreek Kontant Winkel, with its sagging iron roof hanging far over the sidewalk and supported by thin, fancy-worked iron poles. He looked up and down the street hoping to find the Cross-Roads Garage, but could not see it. This was the quiet time of early evening; there were only a few people about although many cars were still parked in the street.

Nkomo came out pushing a bicycle. "Jump on," he said, holding it by the saddle and one handle grip.

Mabaso hesitated. "No. Let's walk."

"It's a hell of a way. Come on, jump on."

"Let's walk. I've got good legs." He wanted to bite the words back. It flabbergasted him that he had said it. He felt the heat come into his cheeks and ears. He looked away from Nkomo in confusion and then he felt his anger rising. He flung the suitcase violently into the carrier and began stuffing the trench-coat all around it.

"So have I. You'd be surprised," Nkomo said. "But they're better on a bicycle than on the ground. So jump on." He had gone over to Swazi now, and somehow this was a rebuke for Mabaso.

Mabaso stood with his back to the bicycle, placed his hands behind him on the cross-bar, and hoisted himself up. Nkomo held the bicycle firm while he did it, and Mabaso could feel the great strength of this gnarled little man transmitted through the steel frame. Nkomo ran a few clumsy, tottering steps pushing the bicycle, then hurled himself into the saddle with a distorted leap and began to pedal very fast. So they rode down the main street. With every stroke of the pedal Nkomo had to shift his whole weight and his knee came up and bumped Mabaso on the thigh and his head came down on Mabaso's shoulder. Each time Mabaso felt Nkomo's warm breath tickle the back of his neck. They went much too fast, taking the corners with wide, frantic curves, and Nkomo had to drag his boot on the road to avoid capsizing. When they reached a traffic light that was against them, he put on a burst of speed and went right through. Soon they came to the end of the town, and they dismounted to cross the railway line. As they were walking across, they suddenly stopped and looked at each other, and at the same moment both laughed.

They mounted again and now Nkomo rode at a slow, sensible pace down the flat road that ran alongside the location. " We call that Old Look Location," Nkomo said, pointing with his chin as they passed the area of thatched huts.

" This is New Look," he said when they came to the area of square white box houses. And when they came to the shanty-town, he said, " This is Jubilee City. You will see that we have some fancy titles in our location. It no longer seems incongruous to use these titles. In fact, we couldn't use any other." He was speaking English again, choosing his words delicately, like a man holding up some rare and treasured objects for admiration.

" I was born in Old Look," Mabaso said. " I grew up there until I was thirteen. But we didn't call it Old Look in those days. There was no New Look. We didn't even call it a location."

Nkomo said nothing, and something made Mabaso look back ; he saw Nkomo shaking his head in bewilderment.

" Strange, very strange," Nkomo said sadly.

" What's strange ? "

" That you never mentioned it, that's all."

" Didn't I mention it ? "

" No, not once."

Mabaso began to feel vaguely uncomfortable. He felt once

again that he was being rebuked. He could see now that there must have been speculation and anticipation on both sides, and he felt that in overlooking this he had been unfair and overbearing towards Nkomo in some way.

"It *is* strange. I can't think why I never mentioned it."

They rode on and Mabaso studied the shanty-town. It looked something like the location in Heidelberg, which he knew well. But it looked a little newer, flimsier, as if it had grown up in a bigger hurry.

"You know, I thought you would be altogether a different type of chap," Nkomo said.

Mabaso laughed. "Did you?"

"Yes. I thought you'd be younger. Somehow your letters seemed to be those of a young man. And then I thought I'd see a more intellectual type. I must say I was surprised to see a big, beefy two-hundred-pounder."

"Two hundred and fifteen pounds," Mabaso said.

"Well, anyway, you are the heaviest freight I ever had on this bike."

"Shall we walk the rest?"

"No. Totally unnecessary." And after a pause, "Tell me, what did you expect *me* to be like?"

"Well, I don't really know. You—you didn't come through very clearly in the letters. I can see that now." Mabaso drifted off, but Nkomo waited for the answer, riding very slowly, his mind not on the riding. The bicycle zigzagged back and forth across the road in order to stay upright.

"Well?"

"Well, for one thing, I didn't expect such a cocky little chap. I expected a more unsure of himself chap, and, well, I expected a more miserable type of chap. Your letters were often pretty miserable."

"I often feel miserable. We all do."

"Well, I don't mean that. I mean a less optimistic type of chap. You are an optimist, I can see that. And . . ." His voice trailed off again.

"My appearance?"

"Yes."

Nkomo suddenly started riding straight again, in the centre of the road. He said, "You will stop noticing it after a while." They said no more for a while.

For the last half mile to the location gate they rode in silence and Mabaso found himself thinking about the letters. Long, carefully-thought-out letters, in a clean, beautiful handwriting. Letters that were humble and polite and serious and desperate and patient all at once. Letters that reached out and explored and came back baffled and started out again. Letters that were troubled, hopeful, sometimes bitter, full of moods. That said first this, then that, then asked, What must we do? As if the answer lay in some particular arrangement of words, some advice, some formula.

He thought of the strange way the correspondence had started nine months before. How, soon after he came back from gaol, a man called and delivered the first letter, saying it had been thought better not to post it, and giving directions how to reply. The letter—written, like all the following letters, on pages torn from a school exercise book—started with the curious salutation, "Dear Friend of Africa," and went into a tortuous opening that set the theme for all the anxious, embarrassed questioning and self-questioning that followed. "Having heard of your exploits in the Defiance Campaign, and, to be more particular, of your proud exploit in leading a batch of volunteers from Heidelberg, a small town like our Nelstroom, the first small town to join the Campaign, and observing that you bear a name which shows you to belong to our Swazi people, it is to you, with your experience of struggles similar to ours, that we now turn, hoping that you will not take our overtures amiss." This letter was the only one to be signed, "Elliot Nkomo"; all the others simply ended, "Thumbs up." Later letters came through the post, but were posted in circuitous ways, from the next town, or slipped into the pages of a catalogue. And they employed a strange, round-about language, in which everything was called something else, a language that had to be read carefully and weighed up, its jokes taken seriously, its understatements brought to full size, its disguises of names and events penetrated. But soon he came to understand the language, and to believe that he could see

21

Nkomo and the others in the letters, and to write the language, too, and the act of engaging in this subtle communication brought him much closer to Nkomo than would have been the case with straightforward letters, just as prisoners who have never seen one another develop an intimate friendship by tapping out messages on the water pipe that connects their cells.

So in the letters, Du Toit, the superintendent, became " the Teacher " or " Our Pal," and when a man " had an attack of D.T.s " it meant that he was having trouble over his papers or that Du Toit was taking it out of him in some way. Ngubeni, the location spy, became " the Nose " and when he was active— " The Nose is running again." " A big rabbit hunt the other evening " meant another police raid, and " There are many mealies on the stalks now " meant that the people were becoming interested.

Mabaso spent long hours on his replies, but he was strangely helpless. He soon saw that the problems Nkomo raised were not conundrums that could be solved from long range. Nor could he give smooth assurances or encouragement, for Nkomo's letters were so frank and trusting that he could not make pretences. His letters were hard to write, and always much shorter than Nkomo's, and his feeling of defeat gave them a cold, discouraging tone. Still, the letters came regularly from Nelstroom and Mabaso began to see that Nkomo was writing them not so much to receive advice as to clear his thoughts and to put the problems down on paper. But the letters began to twine themselves around Mabaso's life in Johannesburg. The fact that he had once lived in the location gave the events a living reality for him, and in the end the letters captured him.

And when the garage closed down and his employer offered to help him get another job, Mabaso asked him to approach his friend, Dick Werdmuller, who owned the Cross-Roads Garage in Nelstroom. This employer was an unusual man. He had always been sympathetic to Mabaso—even when he went to prison for the Defiance Campaign—and he telephoned Dick Werdmuller. " I've got a wonderful boy for you, Dick. Best mechanic I ever had. You know I'm closing down, and I'd like to see this boy fixed up."

" Good. Send him out. I could use a good mechanic."

" If you take him, Dick, go careful with him. He's no ordinary boy."

" What d'you mean ? "

" Well, he's a political type of boy. I thought I'd mention it beforehand."

There was a pause, and Mabaso could picture Werdmuller weighing it up.

" Anyway, send him out. As long as he does his work and doesn't interfere with the other boys on the job, I don't care what he is."

And so, early one morning, with mixed feelings of joy and apprehension, he took the train for Nelstroom and wondered, most of the way, about that eager, persistent, worrisome school-teacher, Elliot Nkomo.

*   *   *

In a corner of the room he saw a bookcase with glass doors and he got off the bed and went over to it. He could not see the titles in the dim light, so he fetched the candle from the table and stood it on the floor between the open doors. Politics, history, economics. No fiction. The books were well kept, and there were some expensive volumes, and obviously this was Nkomo's one extravagance, for everything else in the room was shabby and poor. He opened one of the books and a sheaf of notes, written in pencil, slipped out and fell on the floor.

He was picking up the notes when Elliot Nkomo returned ; behind him was a short, stout woman in carpet slippers and a dirty apron. " This is Mother Vilakazi, our landlady," he told Mabaso. Then he said to Mother Vilakazi, " This is Mabaso of Johannesburg. He will stay with me until he can get a house, upon which he will bring his family from Johannesburg."

" You have a family ? " the landlady asked.

" Yes, a wife and a fifteen-year-old son."

" That is a small family. You like it in this location ? I mean better than Johannesburg ? "

" I don't know. I just arrived."

All this was only meant as friendly introduction, for her eyes suddenly hardened and she looked suspiciously at Elliot. "And what rent?" she asked.

"Rent? Mother Vilakazi," Elliot said in a feigned shocked voice.

"Tenants pay rent," she said firmly.

"My friend sleeps in my bed, in the same room I have always bought from you, and you say, 'What rent?'" Elliot looked slyly at Mabaso.

"Rent," she said stubbornly.

"*Double* rent, Mother Vilakazi? Really. With all that money you make poisoning the location with your concoctions! It seems that the more money you make, the more hungry for it you become."

"I know your tricks. I know your fast words, Nkomo."

"Tell me—does this space grow any bigger because my friend sleeps in it?" He winked at Mabaso, a rapid flip of eyelid.

"He does not pay for the space. He pays for the permission," she said with the same grim face.

Mabaso burst out laughing. Elliot looked up in surprise; then he became serious and accused her, "Mother Vilakazi, you have been reading my books?"

"No."

"Then where did you get that from?"

"I didn't get it," she said.

"All right, Mother, I'll pay rent," Mabaso said. "How much?"

"One pound a month. The space is paid for, so you don't pay full. One pound a month for the permission."

"And now, good Mother, how about some of your famous food?" Elliot asked. "We're hungry."

She looked at him with small, rapidly calculating eyes. "Food, too?"

"Of course. What good are starving tenants? You'll find that in the book too. You feed us food so that we can work and make money to pay your exorbitant rents."

"Food—two pounds extra."

"Now, before we decide, give us an idea of the *kinds* of food."

24

She shrugged one shoulder. "All right, no food." She started to go.

"Mother Vilakazi! Denying food . . ."

"It's all right, Mother," Mabaso said. "Two pounds for food. But bring some now. That was a hungry train I travelled in."

She waddled out showing no trace of pleasure at having bettered Elliot Nkomo.

They stretched out on the beds, and smoked and talked. They both felt light and excited, and the conversation ranged everywhere. Mabaso tried to size up Elliot, but he kept glimpsing new facets of him. He saw that he was frivolous as well as serious. Warm as well as bitter. In the letters only one side, the serious, bitter side, had come out and that was why he had gone so wrong in imagining him. And he was courageous—that explained why he had refused to mention his deformity. It was not important, it didn't matter enough to take up space in the letters. He had managed somehow to grow right out of the deformity. And yet he was afraid, vaguely afraid, and afraid also of the appalling task he had taken on himself.

"You know, Walter. I'm scared stiff of going to gaol." He was calling him "Walter" now, spontaneously and naturally, and although a man is not usually addressed by his English Christian name except by his family or his boss, it was not bad manners the way Elliot did it.

"It's not pleasant," Mabaso said. "But so many go, and we come out, and there's no disgrace about it. With so many, and the things we go there for, nobody looks down on a man who has been in gaol. It's just an unpleasantness, like a long illness."

"It's not that, Walter. You see, it's all right for you—you healthy fellows. But me? The work, the beatings, the kicks." His hand slipped down and rubbed his thigh tenderly. "Without my boots. Without a chance to rest when I want to. My trouble is that I'm scared of pain."

"I can understand that. Of course, I can see that. You must stay out of gaol. At all costs, you must avoid it."

"Do you think that possible? Do you really think that possible with our life, what we're doing?"

"No, Elliot, I don't."

But while Mabaso lay with his hands behind his head, staring gloomily at the dark ceiling, Nkomo's mood suddenly changed.

"You know, they're preparing some wonderful celebrations for when Du Toit leaves."

"When Du Toit leaves? I didn't know he was leaving. You didn't tell me that."

"For *when* he leaves. He's not leaving yet. But the people like to think of him leaving, and like to plan the celebrations. One man has promised to kill four oxen and give a feast to the whole location. One shebeen queen will supply free barberton for a whole week. The kids in my school talk of how the fireworks will look in the sky. There are lots of schemes."

"I think this is very sad, Elliot."

"It is, but it makes everyone a little less sad to think of these schemes."

"But he may never leave. Not for a long time anyway."

"Oh, there are schemes for that, too. To hurry up his leaving. Planning accidents to his car, working out how to get a snake to bite him—that kind of thing. The schemes go on till late at night. The witch doctors have some really serious schemes to give him some sickness. They throw bones and wish things on him, but the *Tokoloshi*[1] seem to be as scared of him as everybody else is. Then there are the funeral schemes. Who will organise the procession, what the choir will sing, and so on. If they ever raised funds for a coffin for Du Toit, they'd get enough for a solid gold coffin. If Du Toit died here, he'd be buried like a prince."

While they were talking, the landlady brought in the supper —two tin plates piled with stew and potatoes, each with a doorstep of bread on top : two tin cups of milkless coffee. They sat at the table and Nkomo went right on discussing the schemes for getting rid of Du Toit. It was easy to see that he got as much pleasure from them as any of the actual schemers ever did.

"People have strange dreams in this place. They come to the old *ayahs* and say, 'Last night I dreamt I saw the manager tied to an anthill. What does it mean?' or 'Tell me, *Ayah*, if one

[1]Tribal spirits.

dreams that he squashed a praying mantis, and when he looked at the squashed thing he saw it had the tiny little face of the manager, is that good or bad ? ' "

" So the people here do much wishing ? "

" Yes. But they don't wish hard enough. They wish and wish, but Du Toit is still here."

" But do you think it is only Du Toit ? Do you think it would be different with someone else ? "

" No. But he is *our* manager. We *know* him."

" You know, Elliot, these managers are all the same. They're all different—they explain it in different ways—but in the end they're all the same. Because they're doing the same job, carrying out Verwoerd's laws.[1] And if all these schemes and wishes came true and you got rid of Du Toit, you'd get Du Plooy instead, and the schemes and wishes would go on, but with a different face on the praying mantis."

" Possibly, Walter, but it's him we see. And perhaps if we had Du Plooy, he wouldn't love us so much."

" Love you ? "

" Yes, Du Toit loves us. Don't you know ? He loves us, and everything he does is for our own good. He is the father of the location—he tells us that. He is the father of the biggest family in the whole world, and all he is doing is keeping order among us, his children, and worrying about our happiness. And these laws, which make us groan and weep, why they're for our happiness too, only we're too stupid and backward to see it. You see, we're only children and we don't understand. I hope Du Plooy hates us, hates us so much it would never enter his head to try and make us happy."

Mabaso wanted to laugh but the bitter flavour of what Nkomo said subdued him. This bitterness of Nkomo's was a curious thing. It did not cloud things over as bitterness usually did, but gave them a sharp, clear outline. It had a brightness, a fine edge that found the truth unerringly. Mabaso wondered about this keen weapon of Nkomo's.

" Elliot, you never told me this. Were you active before Du Toit came? "

[1] Dr. Verwoerd, South African Minister for Native Affairs.

"No. I was lazy and inactive. And, shall I tell you? Sorry for myself. I used to crawl into myself. Come home here, read my books, sleep. Sleep too much."

"What made you—stop sleeping?"

"*Exactly* what, I don't know. There was an incident about a year ago. A small incident. There's a mad boy in this location, an awful crazy boy. His name is Tembo, and before this incident he used to wander about the location calling, ' Tembo, Tembo, Tembo, Tembo, Tembo.' We'd see him walking about searching in all the yards and calling his own name, ' Here I am,' and then go home. But he is an unpleasant crazy boy. He has filthy habits, even though he washes himself a hundred times a day. And he quarrels with everyone. He is a great nuisance but everyone puts up with him out of pity for his mother, the widow Maria Maziya. He is the only child and this sad mother calls him her baby and protects him like a baby. Now last year Du Toit said that all boys who had turned eighteen must come to the office to get passes. And this crazy little boy who had just turned eighteen went along and joined the queue. The boys who had jobs were given passes, and the others were given two-week permits to find work. The crazy boy got a permit, and you know, this is very sad, he actually went around the town trying to find a job. But he couldn't find one of course. And when he came back to get the permit renewed, Du Toit said no, and endorsed him out. Endorsed him out, Walter. Those who were there said Du Toit didn't even look up, he just put the stamp on the permit and said, ' Next.' You know, for nights after I heard about it I couldn't sleep. Don't laugh. I know what you're thinking. Yes, that's what stopped me sleeping. I don't know what got me so excited about this boy. I was so sorry for him."

"That sick boy."

"Yes. I suppose it's that. Well, I decided to go and see Du Toit, and do you know what Du Toit said? A decision has been given and it's bad to go back on a decision. I asked him if an exception couldn't be made for this boy. He turned up the Act, and wet his fingers and flipped the pages this way and that. Then he told me, ' The Act makes no allowance for insane people.' I asked him where he thought the boy would go, I lost my temper, but he didn't get angry. He put his fingers together —like this—and told me how good this law was for the location. How the idle lads are the worst element, that argument. They are the *tsotsis*.[1] They rob and attack their own people, and he said surely an intelligent fellow like me should be the first to see it. And if he didn't protect us from the *tsotsi* menace, he'd soon have the whole location up in his office complaining. I asked him if he couldn't make an exception of just this one case. He told me, 'If I make an exception of this case, I'll have to make a thousand exceptions.' So the poor lad was sent out."

"Where did he go?"

"Nobody knows. Nor how he lived. He was away for two months. Then his mother received a message and went and brought him back. He was half starved, ragged, and crazier than ever. He's still here. She hides him away."

"How does she manage that?"

"She keeps him locked in her room. But every now and then he escapes and we all go looking for him. Oh, lots of people know about him, but they don't tell Du Toit or Ngubeni. Some of the location constables know. And I'll tell you a peculiar thing. We once thought we'd better bribe them to shut up, but they wouldn't take the bribe and they shut up anyway."

"But how long can she keep on hiding him?"

"I don't know."

They drank their coffee, holding the cups with both hands around the rim. Then Mabaso began playing with the melted wax on the candle, pulling off the soft white sticks and rolling them in his fingers. "So that stopped you sleeping?"

"Yes. It was a strange thing. There were other cases, but this one caught me by the throat. First I was very depressed, then I started thinking. And then I started talking. And I found that others were thinking and also wanted to talk. About that time I started writing to you. You know, we never really formed any group. A crowd of us just grew together. You'll meet some of them to-night. So many people are thinking, and we find

[1]Young gangsters, hoodlums.

29

that somehow they are looking towards us. But we don't know what to do. Where to start. That is why we're so glad you have come."

"Don't count too much on me."

"You've had experience. You've been in it for years."

"But there's no clear way out yet."

"Still we feel better that you've come."

Mabaso was deeply moved. He felt inadequate and over-estimated and somehow very humble. He could sense something about Nkomo that was unusual even in his experience. He looked over the candle into Nkomo's face, a face pulled and beaten by suffering, but now alive with excitement. And there formed at that moment a warm love for this misshapen little man.

"Walter, what made you wake up?"

Mabaso did not answer for a while. But at last, looking into the flame of the candle, and not at Elliot, he said, "Fifteen years ago my father was kicked to death by the police. I saw it with my own eyes. I was powerless to help him. Nobody tried to help him. Since then I've been in it."

★ ★ ★

Later Elliot's friends began to arrive. Some Mabaso recognised from the letters, but with others it was more difficult, and one man, a parson, baffled him completely.

This man was the first to arrive. The Reverend Samson Shongwe was a tall, gaunt man whose threadbare, loose-hanging black garb made him look like a hungry, storm-tossed crow. He crossed the room in two gangling strides and shook Mabaso's hand with a hard bony grip. Then he stepped back and bent his arm, and held his thumb up in front of his chest. "Afrika," he said. It was a little stiff and self-conscious. Mabaso returned the salute. "*Mayebuye*—may it come," he said. He smiled at the Reverend Shongwe. The man looked good and it pleased him to see a priest among Nkomo's group. But he realised that he had not been prepared for the Reverend Shongwe, that he had not anywhere come into the letters. Perhaps he is a new man, he thought. The way he did the thumbs-up suggested he was new.

"Walter, I've already told Father Shongwe he must get you a house," Elliot said.

Mabaso looked, puzzled, from the Reverend Shongwe to Elliot.

"Is housing not a problem here?"

"Oh yes. But Father Shongwe can fix it. He will fix a house for you within a couple of months, Walter."

"Don't tease me, Elliot. How can Father Shongwe fix it?"

Elliot winked at the Reverend Shongwe. He laughed and said, "Father Shongwe has influence with Du Toit. Don't you know he is one of the good boys? He's a member of the Advisory Board. Not even an elected member. A chosen member. Du Toit has chosen him twice already."

"Are you joking, Elliot?"

"No. This is true. He *is* a member, and Du Toit *does* choose him. Father Shongwe is the most respected man in the location and Du Toit chooses him to give prestige to the Board. Du Toit is very fond of his captive parson."

"But—but——" Mabaso started a question but checked himself. For a moment he had a wild suspicion of being tricked by Elliot. But the Reverend Shongwe saw his confusion and said, "I hate it, Mabaso. I hate going there and hiding my feelings, and most of all I hate those meetings when I have to vote with Du Toit when everything in me wants to scream, 'No.' And then to hear people asking, 'What has happened to Shongwe?' But we have decided I must stay there."

"Yes," Elliot said. "He has a highly secret position with us. He puts Du Toit and Ngubeni off the scent. He tells us what's brewing. And he helps our people in many ways. He can fix up that house for you, Walter."

Mabaso smiled at the Reverend Shongwe. He felt ashamed of being so obtuse and at the same time proud of Elliot and his group for bringing off this achievement. It was a most useful achievement in a small location. And now he understood why Elliot had not risked mentioning the Reverend Shongwe in the letters, even in disguise.

While they were talking, two other men came in. Mabaso saw a young fellow, slimly built, with a keen, handsome face. He was Paul Vilakazi, no relation of the landlady. He was the treasurer.

"Vilakazi's great at selling tickets and making collections," Elliot said. "Only he is too mean with the money."

"If I gave in every time you thought of a new way of spending it, we'd always be in debt," Vilakazi said.

He was a shy boy, and for most of the evening he sat on the end of the bed, saying little and staring at Mabaso. Elliot seemed very fond of Vilakazi, and at one stage mentioned that he was a teacher at the same school, and then Mabaso saw that he was his protégé.

The man who came with Vilakazi was Saul Sibande, a short, barrel-chested man who had dressed up for the meeting. He wore a waistcoat with an enormous ancient watch chain dangling between two pockets. Sibande was a carpenter in the railway construction sheds, and a man of great influence there.

"We can count on at least eighty-six in the sheds," he told Mabaso eagerly.

"That's very good in such a short time," Mabaso said, genuinely impressed. And Elliot, unable to resist a piece of mischief, said, "Yes, exactly eighty-six. Sibande counts them over and over again."

"We have got to go on cats' feet, or it would be more," Sibande said. "If the foreman found out, they'd throw us out of the railways. And out of the location, too. So we've got to pick and choose our men carefully, only those we can trust."

Mabaso knew this type: single-minded and very tough, shrewd and practical, and one who somehow managed to draw others to him. Every large workshop had one man like this. It felt good having Sibande in the room.

Two more came in—Charles Mavuso, a reduction worker in the asbestos mines—he was an old man, toothless and wrinkled, and he coughed a lot and spat into a khaki handkerchief. And Simon Dhladla, a taxi driver. He was heavily bearded, with fat, pitted cheeks, and he looked uncomfortable in a suit that was too tight for him. Each was introduced to Mabaso, and each gave the salute. The room filled, and as there were not enough chairs, they sat on the bed or propped on the window sill, and they

32

settled down, without formality, into a meeting. In the dim candlelight it was barely possible to tell where one human form ended and another began, and persons became identified by their voices, or by the glow that lit their faces when a cigarette was drawn. They roamed over many subjects, casually, as if the meeting were one mind in reverie. The different voices came out, and returned into the darkness, and the different ideas met and mingled. And all the desires and doubts and plans and fears were there, plain to see, and slowly they merged themselves into a single new thing. Something was born. It was born in hope, for only hope could give it life, though everyone understood that its future was uncertain and fraught with danger.

At first, while Mabaso listened and was appealed to for his opinion, he again had the feeling of being inadequate, of being overestimated. The tense, concentrated misery of this location had produced these people, had forced them up and shaped them, and he felt that he must be useless to them. But after a time he saw that, in many ways, they were uncertain and at odds about what to do, in spite of a sharp appreciation of their problems and a burning desire to act. Their ideas ranged between the desperate Mau Mauism of Simon Dhladla, and the Christian pacifism of the Reverend Samson Shongwe. And as point after point came up, he began to see that there was a need for him. The years of working, organising, reading and discussing enabled him to find his way with a sure touch through the different ideas, discarding those that had been tried and rejected in other places, or seeing the clear thread in a confused thought. They needed his experience and leadership. Without him they could not have formed the organisation. And when he saw their need for him, his shyness, which was the cause of his coldness, disappeared, and he began to feel an individual warmth and pride for every person in the room.

They called themselves the Nelstroom Branch of the African National Congress, and there was something thrilling about the name, for it made them feel that they had joined hands with the hundreds of Congress organisations in other locations, in the cities and in the countryside.

Later, when the others had all gone home, Mabaso and

Nkomo lay in bed with their hands behind their heads and talked until far into the night. There was a dreamy, easy feeling between them. Just before going to sleep Mabaso said, " I'm keen for you to meet my boy, Elliot. We must see to it that he gets into your school."

" I'd like to meet him."

" He's really a bright youngster."

" I'm sure he is."

Then Mabaso felt a bit foolish talking so sentimentally about his son and the conversation drifted away and they slept.

CHAPTER THREE

IT IS ONE of the last days of the summer that has stayed too long. Children play listlessly around their kitchen doors, cattle and dogs hide in the shade. Scraps of music and snatches of voices float up out of the houses, linger for a moment in the lifeless air, and fall like stricken birds into the yards and lanes of the exhausted location. In the administration office, the sun streams in through the windows, imparting a foreign blood-warmth to wooden and metal objects, to the telephone, the papers, the curling covers of the books. It it morning but it does not feel like the start of a new day; only the end of a hot, wakeful night.

Hendrik Du Toit, his jacket off, his shirt sleeves rolled up over his biceps, sits at his desk. A line of people reaches from the desk to the door and then down the whole length of the veranda. Everyone in the line has papers in his hands. They find nothing to speak about and every half minute they all take a little shuffle forward. Grey-uniformed location clerks hurry along the veranda carrying files to and from Du Toit's office. Behind Du Toit a clerk stands at a narrow table turning up the location registers, whirring the pages and thudding the heavy black covers on the table top. Andries Gwebu, chief clerk and interpreter, stands at Du Toit's side, not merely interpreting but miraculously disposing of each case in the same process. Everything goes through him.

Du Toit works fast; a cigarette burns between his yellow fingers and he hardly ever looks up. A question, an answer, and bang with the rubber stamp. Next. Question, answer, bang. Next. The line never ends. It moves up. A segment is snapped off before the desk, moves up, another segment is snapped off, moves up. But it never grows shorter. At three in the afternoon Du Toit shuts the door, and spends the rest of the day on other work. Next morning at nine the line is there again. Day after day. The entire location is in a continuous process of coming up before Du Toit's desk. The turn for each man comes once a month, sometimes oftener, but the line is the location, reduced to a silent, shuffling human escalator. . . .

★   ★   ★

The location runs like an efficient piece of mechanism. But it was not always like that. The former superintendent, a man named Brits, neglected the location until it became a problem that oppressed the whole town. But Du Toit was a lucky find for the Nelstroom Town Council. He simply threw himself into the job of clearing up the mess, and now the lax and lazy days of Brits have gone forever. Du Toit is popular with the Council, and as a result of the proved success of his methods he is left a free hand to do pretty much as he likes in the location.

Yet the strange thing is that when he took over Brit's job, nobody thought he would be anything but a failure. His prospects in Nelstroom seemed to be poor. The way it turned out has been a surprise to everybody, and to nobody more than Du Toit himself.

Before coming to Nelstroom he had been superintendent of a big location near Johannesburg, but he had left that job under peculiar circumstances. There had been some vague trouble there, some intrigue about a cinema licence, something about being involved with a man who turned out to be a gold dealer. He was as surprised as anyone to discover that the man was a lawbreaker, but there was something not quite right in getting mixed up in it, or in pushing it beyond the point where he should have left off. But he gave an explanation and it was accepted. Everybody behaved to him exactly as before. And then, just when he was sure that the whole affair had died down, they came and asked him if he wouldn't prefer to take this job in Nelstroom that was becoming vacant. Oh no, it had nothing to do with the totally unproved allegations against him—they assured him of that. It was just that changes were being made all around. It could have been a coincidence, of course.

When Du Toit and his wife Anna came to Nelstroom, they

36

were met at the station by the mayor himself, Lourens Moolman, a man in a floppy khaki hat and a sportscoat with leather patches on the elbows. Moolman seemed delighted to see them. Talking all the time, he ushered them off the station platform towards his car ; they saw rifles and boxes of ammunition on the back seat, and the rigid carcass of an impala buck roped to the back bumper. Before taking them to their house, a red brick cottage that went with the job, Moolman drove them around the town showing them the monuments and public buildings. There was an immediate good feeling between Du Toit and Moolman. It was hardly a mingling and matching of personalities—Moolman completely swamped him, but Du Toit enjoyed being talked to and fussed over and it all gave him a warm and pleasant first impression of Nelstroom. Just before reaching the house Moolman asked, "Do you hunt ? " Du Toit said no, not very much, not since he was a youngster ; there weren't many opportunities for hunting when a man lived on the Rand and had a busy job to look after.

"Wonderful hunting here," Moolman said. "Wonderful. The season now. You must come down to the bushveld with us sometime. A-ah, I love it."

Lourens Moolman, they learnt afterwards, *was* Nelstroom. Besides being mayor, he was acting deputy sheriff and an attorney, estate agent, insurance broker, cattle auctioneer, land-owner, and part-time farmer.

Later when Hendrik Du Toit and his wife stood on the veranda of their new house and looked for the first time across the pretty town to the wooded mountains beyond, a new courage lit within them. Now at last they would be able to enjoy the easy life, the fresh air, and the warm friendships of a country town. *That*, they said, was what they had always wanted. And Du Toit squeezed his wife tight against his side and silently resolved that there would be no more mistakes. He would make his comeback in this place. Here he would wipe out the bad luck of the other place. And perhaps he would still earn the promotion that was then becoming rather overdue.

He was forty-two years old, a big man, restless, full of un-directed energy that found outlets in little movements of his

37

head, hands, and shoulders. He had pale blue eyes that popped a little and gave him an air of prowling alertness. His nose was large, not unpleasantly shaped, but heavy-looking, duller in colour than the rest of his face, as if it did not share in the system of blood circulation of his other features. He had thin sandy hair, through which one could see his freckled scalp and the silvery scar of a bullet graze that he received in a hunting accident when he was a youth. The scar ran at a right angle to the hair parting, and seen in certain lights, it had the curious effect of a white cross chalked on his head.

*   *   *

But the pleasant first impression of Nelstroom did not stay long. It did not even last beyond the next day. That second day proved to be a discouraging experience for Du Toit. It made him want to pack his things and catch the next train back, even though that would have meant throwing away the years of service he had been saving up in the way other men save up money, and giving up the pension that had been coming a little nearer every year.

Early in the morning there was a visitor, Herman Theron, the assistant town clerk. He was a sharp, foxy little man, and he came into the room with a perky strut, and without removing his hat, sat at the table and proceeded to help himself to half the Du Toits' breakfast.

"Any dirty jobs around here, who do they look for?" he asked bitterly, spearing a tomato on a fork. "Me. Last year market master. This year location manager. Anybody sick, or on leave, or beats it to another job, who do they look for? You said it—yours truly, Herman Theron."

Anna Du Toit, who was unpacking photographs and arranging them on the mantel, stiffened and glared at him in the mirror but said nothing.

"Anyway, you turned up, that's the main thing," Theron said, giving the impression that nobody in the town had thought Du Toit would really arrive.

"When did Brits leave?" Du Toit asked.

"Three weeks ago. The three longest weeks of my life.

Anyway, to-day I'll have great pleasure in handing over to you. *Great* pleasure. Couldn't stand that place."

Du Toit slowly buttered his toast, studying the operation carefully to avoid looking at Theron. He was used to people running down his job, and generally he kept quiet when they did it. But it always depressed him a little.

"What's wrong with it?" Anna Du Toit asked, looking at Theron in the mirror.

"Oh, all out there on my lonesome. Gave me the creeps."

"You mean you didn't have anyone out there with you? Didn't you have any clerks or anything?"

Theron finished his coffee first. "No. No white clerks, if that's what you mean. Oh yes, there're those blackbird clerks. But no white clerks, I'm afraid to say."

Du Toit felt a vague dismay spreading out inside him. He wondered why nobody had told him about this. It made him feel as if he had been tricked into coming to Nelstroom.

"How can a man be expected to run a whole location without any proper assistance?" Anna Du Toit asked.

Theron shrugged. "Well, there it is. Town Hall's too damn' mean with the money."

He ate and drank steadily for several minutes. Anna Du Toit stood and watched him. "How many in this location?" she asked suspiciously.

"Around twelve thousand. We're not sure, they've never been counted, but that's about the figure. That's the figure we use in the reports."

Du Toit went on eating in silence. The food had suddenly become tasteless. It wasn't the extra work—he didn't mind that. But a man was entitled to know a thing like this. If this was going to be a one-man location office, he was entitled to know it before being asked to take on the job. It might have made all the difference between taking it and turning it down.

"Well, actually that's not quite true," Theron said suddenly. It seemed to have struck him that what he said might cause mischief, and that he had better put it right. "You see . . . Well, you might as well know. We once had a housing scheme out there, but it went on the rocks, what with all that dirty

39

business with the contractors and everyone helping themselves to the money. So now the location's in debt. So it's not exactly that they are too mean. Town Hall can't afford another man out there, that's what it is."

"I see," Du Toit said thoughtfully. They all fell silent. Theron reached for an apple, bit a piece out, and examined the inside for worms. Then he ate it with muffled crackling noises.

"There's a programme all lined up for you this morning," he said with bulging cheeks. "And first on the list—Mrs. Ross. So see you all spruced up."

"Who's Mrs. Ross?" Anna Du Toit asked.

"You don't know Mrs. *Ross*?" Then Theron explained. He spoke in a curiously roundabout way, taking great care not to say too much. Obviously there was some situation between him and Mrs. Ross. She was a member of the Town Council, the only woman councillor. She was chairman of the Native Affairs Committee and therefore Du Toit's immediate boss. She was a leading Nationalist; always sat at the top table when the party big shots arrived. She could shoot like a man—in fact she carried on a rifle club where she taught the ladies how to be handy with firearms. She was a big property owner. But the great thing about her was her speeches—she could talk the back leg off a horse (this was not meant to be disparaging—it was Theron's way of describing a powerful orator).

"Sounds like someone important," Anna Du Toit said.

"Oh yes," Theron said. He paused and looked over his shoulder, then said, "Hates the sight of me."

"Hates *you*?"

"Oh, it's a long story. Finish up that coffee and let's get started."

They went into the street, but walked without speaking to each other. Theron kept greeting people but Du Toit walked with his hands in his pockets and paid no attention. He was angry. Yes, it had definitely been a trick. Now he could see that other business in an entirely different light. They *were* punishing him for it, as he had suspected all along.

But later, on thinking it over he began to feel a little better. There'll be the police fellows around, he told himself. One could

40

always go and have a chat with them. In the old place there had been a police station right next to the location office and they used to talk to each other through the window. It was a nuisance sometimes, those fellows would never let a man get on with his work. But he could see how much better it was to have them there than be left all alone in the middle of a location. Yes, perhaps it wouldn't turn out so bad.

They reached the Town Hall and Theron led the way along a dark passage to a door marked "Committee Room." Seated at the desk inside, and plainly waiting, was the Native Affairs Committee, a large woman in a purple hat, and two men each holding a brief case on his lap.

They were introduced and they all sat down. Mrs. Ross opened a folder and asked a number of questions: Age? Married? Previous experience? Previous salary? Du Toit wondered why she was treating him like an applicant who had come in answer to an advertisement, and why she was asking these questions when all the information was in the letters in front of her. But this was only a prelude to more important questions.

"I take it you're one of *our* people?"

"Oh yes. I've been in the party eleven years."

"Eleven years?" Mrs. Ross said. She seemed to be disappointed. Du Toit could almost hear them thinking, only eleven years!

"Anyway, you *are* one of *us* now," said Mrs. Ross with a bright smile. Then she told him how important she considered his job to be. "People like you are the soldiers of apartheid," she said.

While she spoke, Du Toit found himself staring at her mouth. Her lips seemed to move on their own, as if manipulated by strings, and to frame words other than those she actually used. It gave him the feeling of not quite hearing her properly, and he found himself sitting on the edge of the chair straining to catch what she said. That, and her voice, which was hoarse and overwrought, on the point of flying off, made him feel ill at ease and apprehensive.

"Now we hope you don't mind our asking, but we feel we

41

ought to know this, in view of our unfortunate experience with the last superintendent. You're not a drinking man, I take it? "

" Oh—well, no. I take a drink occasionally, that's all, but I can manage all right without it."

" You see, our last superintendent spent *too much time* at the Phoenix Hotel. To the detriment of his work."

Theron said hotly, " Mrs. Ross, that's not exactly fair. Dragging Mr. Brits——" but she turned her eyes on him and he dried up. She did not trouble to answer him. " Mr. Brits," she said, speaking exclusively to Du Toit, " spent *too much time* at the Phoenix Hotel. Oh, I know he was very popular around here, Dirk this, and Dirk that, but that's not the point. The point is he let us down. And there's been a deterioration, we can all notice it, we can see it with our own eyes. Assaults on motorists, a child run over by a drunken taxi driver, one of our ladies attacked and robbed in her own kitchen—thieving and drunkenness—criminals—actual *and* potential. . . . But oh no, Mr. Brits, what was he interested in ? . . . people are very worried . . . but some people . . . Oh, most unsatisfactory . . . riots . . . murder . . . dreadful."

Her angry voice was running through Du Toit, dragging up a trail of disturbance. And he did not know why he said it, but before he realised it the words were out. " Is it true there aren't any white clerks in this location ? " he asked. She started to riffle hastily the papers in the folder, but without looking at them. " Don't blame *us* for that, Mr. Du Toit," she said, and then in a tight voice she explained all about the housing scheme. It seemed that she had been in the right all along, but the trouble was that no one on the Council would listen to her ; that was the trouble with this Council, everyone forming factions.

Suddenly the interview was over. She looked at her watch and said " Nine-thirty ? " dived down and pulled up a leather bag from the floor, took the other smaller bag off the desk, and through a tangle of straps offered her hand to Du Toit.

" I'm sure we're going to get on very well together, Mr. Du Toit," she said. Their fingers had barely touched when she was at the door leading her committee away to the next appointment.

When Du Toit came out into the street again, he was nervous

and uneasy. Her overwrought voice was echoing in his head, her queer mouth still dancing in front of his eyes. Certain feelings that had been at rest for a long time were stirring up. An old disquiet came back—a far-off incident—a certain afternoon.

Theron was speaking. " Why she always picks on me I don't know. I'm only assistant town clerk, that's all. Not even in her department. But her trouble, she's always trying to get a crack at Moolman, and it just so happens Moolman and me are good friends. She wants to be mayor, but she never gets enough votes so she always takes it out on anyone in Moolman's crowd."

Du Toit walked on thinking about this. He wondered how this faction fight was going to work out for him. Which side would *he* land on ? He wanted to be on Moolman's side, wanted it very much, but he knew his limitations when it came to mixing with a crowd of fellows. Then, Mrs. Ross was his boss. He could see problems looming ahead.

They walked in the shade of the trees until they came to the police station, a rambling brick building with palms and a fish pond in the garden, a limp flag dangling from a pole, wooden verandas grown over with bougainvillaea, fly-screen doors, and at the back rows of corrugated iron sheds with tiny barred windows—the cells. They found the station commander, Head Constable Van der Vyver, playing billiards in the mess. Theron introduced Du Toit and Van der Vyver said, " Oh well, *I'm* getting out of here soon, personally. Getting a transfer. Still, it's quite a nice little place, Nelstroom. A bit quiet, but a nice little place. Sorry to leave it." But he was impatient to carry on playing ; his eyes kept leaving Du Toit and squinting at the balls, sizing up a shot. Then he was over the table again, swinging the cue lightly at a ball, but not touching it.

" Is there a lot of crime in this place ? " Du Toit asked.

" Well . . ." Van der Vyver said, sprawling across the table. " Nouuu . . ." He pushed out his lips and made a sound that was half voice, half whistle ; then lost himself concentrating on the shot. The balls skeltered and skidded, thumped the cushion, and came slowly to rest.

" What's that ? " Van der Vyver asked, standing up and holding his hand in the small of his back. " Oh yes—crime. No, wouldn't say there's too much here. Bit of a dead water, this place."

"I had the impression from someone I spoke to that the police are kept pretty busy here."

"No, wouldn't say that," Van der Vyver said. He was bending across the table again. Click. "A bit quiet, this place. Bit of a—bit—of—a . . ." Click. "Around fifty arrests a day, I should say—passes, liquor, that kind of stuff." Click—clunk. "Serious crime? Mmm—mmm . . . Oh, not much serious crime—not much. Circuit Court sits here for two days—that's all—judge usually plays golf on the last afternoon—drop you bastard—otherwise—the usual location stuff—the usual . . ."

Du Toit gave up trying to compete for attention with the billiard balls and walked around the room looking at shooting prizes and pictures of police rugby teams. The whole place seemed very quiet.

"No," said Van der Vyver from the table. "A dead water as far as I'm concerned." He was standing up again, chalking the cue. Du Toit went back and perched on the edge of the table.

"I'd like to know a bit more about this location," he said.

"Well, shoot."

"You say there isn't much crime there."

"Wouldn't say that."

Du Toit stared blankly at him.

"Wherever those *donders*[1] are, there's crime."

"But didn't you say it's a bit quiet here for you fellows?"

"Listen, don't blame me, blame old Brits. We rely on the location super to co-operate with us. Half the time he was never there. And when he was, he never bothered. All he had to do was pick up the phone and say, 'Got a batch for you here without passes. Got some trouble here in the location.' Then we'd go out and pick them up. But Brits used to let it all pass. Or when he did tell us, it was too late. The *donders* had run away. Why, I bet that place is crawling with unauthorised persons, dangerous weapons, liquor, stolen property. No, you'd be wrong to say there isn't much crime there."

[1]*Lit.* Thunders, but a slang term for bastard

44

" Did you say Brits had to phone *here* when he wanted the police ? "

" Yes. But days used to pass and he never phoned."

" You haven't got a branch station out there ? "

" No. This is the only station. But they're a good bunch of boys here. On their toes. You can rely on our boys here."

" But how long does it take you to get out there ? "

" About ten minutes."

" Ten minutes ? "

" Yes—you hold them for us and we come and pick them up. Takes about ten minutes in a squad car. Or, if you like, you can get your blackbird location constables to bring them in here and we handle them at this end."

Du Toit was hardly listening. *No white police in the location—* he had to say it to himself over and over to try and make it sound believable.

★   ★   ★

Theron brought one of the Council's cars out of a garage and they rode out to the location. As they travelled along the sand road, Du Toit looked at the drab houses sliding past. The place looked awful. Quite different from the old location—much poorer, much less solid-looking. At least in the old place the houses didn't look as if a good wind would flatten them out, there were some battered jacaranda trees in the streets, and a few of the streets were paved. And somehow the fact that it was part of the town, that it was possible to hear the trams and see the mine dumps and factory buildings all around, gave it a point that was absent here. This brown scab in the green valley looked unreal and abnormal, like a mistake, a bureaucratic blunder. It gave him a strange sensation, seeing it like that. It was as though for an infinitesimal moment he glimpsed another meaning to the location, then lost it as it plunged back into the dark regions of his mind.

They reached the gate and turned in and pulled up below the administration building. The building was of white-cement colour and it stood high on concrete legs, like a stilt house. It stood not only above the location, but away from it, for the

45

growth of the shantytown had been arrested about a hundred yards out, so that there was an open field between the building and the nearest houses. "They play football matches and hold their meetings here," Theron explained. Du Toit noticed a wooden dais with steps and a handrail.

They went up to the veranda. Theron unlocked the end door and kicked it open. "Your office," he said. As they went in, Du Toit felt an immediate familiarity with the room. The smell —a compound of stale sweat, insecticide, ink, and floor dust— was the smell of his old office, of all location offices. The furniture—a teak desk with a bank of boxes at one end, a tilt-back chair, green filing cabinets, a portable washstand, a water carafe on the window sill, an inventory tacked to the door— these were the same too. The desk looked curiously bare. On it were only the telephone, a block of bell buttons, and two books that he recognised as the Location Regulations and the Urban Areas Act. No papers. He could see that Theron had done very little work during the three weeks he was acting superintendent.

"Suppose I'd better show you around," Theron said briskly, and he walked about the room picking up batches of forms, cards, memo pads, and patting the blackbound books and filing cabinets. "Pass forms. Permit forms. Receipt book. Rents index. Stand register." Halfway through he stopped and came and sat with one buttock on the desk. "Oh hell, I'm just wasting my time. You know all about this stuff." He sat and tried to hard think of something else to tell Du Toit. "By the way, you got your own little joint out there," he said, jerking his thumb in the direction of the window. "Key over there." He pointed to the key hanging on a nail behind the door. Then he slid off the desk, pushed his hat from behind to straighten it, and held out his hand. Du Toit shook it and Theron clasped his other hand over Du Toit's hand and said warmly, "Well, so long Du Toit, old man. Good luck in the job."

"Are you going?" Du Toit asked, suddenly alarmed.

"Have to, old man."

"Aren't you going to introduce me to the clerks?"

"Introduce you? Oh, let's skip that to-day. They're waiting

46

for me back in town, a meeting, and I've got to run. Just call them in and introduce yourself. It'll be all right. Just tell them you're the new *baas* here."

"The location constables ? "

"Same with them. Matter of fact, I *couldn't* introduce you. I don't even know their names. Well, good luck, old man."

They shook hands.

Theron went out and down the steps and Du Toit watched his head disappear below the level of the veranda. He heard the car start and then the sound of the engine was gone too.

He sat still for a while. The place was very quiet now. Suddenly he had a desire to telephone someone—Anna ? Moolman ? He pulled the instrument towards him, but couldn't think of any real excuse for calling them. He pushed it away. He saw the block of bell buttons and pulled that in front of him. He studied it carefully, the smooth ebony slab, the five plastic buttons, one green, four white. There was a tab " Clerks " stuck across the top. The names of the clerks were written on smaller tabs opposite the buttons : Ngwenya, Maboia, Baloyi. If only there were just one white man's name, like Smit or Le Roux. . . . He thought of ringing the green bell for the chief clerk but he changed his mind. Later. He wondered about the location constables. Those cheerful black comedians. Every superintendent had his own private squad of constables drawn from the location to help him carry out administrative decisions, and every superintendent had his own special troubles with them. They had nothing to do with the ordinary police. "Constables" was a ridiculous name for them. But they had to have some name to go with their uniforms and so they were called constables. He had seen some of them standing around when he stepped out of the car with Theron. They were just standing around. They didn't come forward and salute or anything like that. Just lounged in the shade of the building and watched him arrive. From what he saw of them, they looked very shabby, uniforms dirty and slept in. They were bound to be slack under Brits, but slack always meant something more—dishonest. There was probably a huge liquor trade here. Plenty of bribery. And after liquor and bribery came everything else. Yes, with a lazy superintendent and lazy police, this place must have gone down badly. It gave one an uncomfortable feeling. It wasn't the petty crime so much, one could manage that. It was the feeling of everything being neglected and out of control. Like dry brushwood waiting for a dropped cigarette. Ten minutes did he say ? By car, that is, and provided the booms weren't down. He didn't mention that. Provided you could get to the phone and could get straight through and someone was there to answer.

He went to the window and lit a cigarette, and looked across the rooftops to the veld beyond, to the blue-green mountains beyond that. In the distance, he could see the heavy grey smoke of a train in the mountain pass. The sounds of its strenuous panting climb carried distinctly to him on the still air. That pass, he knew, led up and up to come out eventually on the plateau of the highveld. From there it was a straight, fast run to Johannesburg. He thought with bitter envy of the people in that train.

He walked up and down in front of the window, pulling hard on a cigarette. He felt a dull ache of loneliness and despair. For a moment he thought of phoning Moolman to tell him he was not taking the job. But he knew he could not do it. Not at his age. Not with his lack of training for any other kind of job. And not with so much to lose in the pension. He felt depressed and lonely, and all his disappointments were crowding in on him. He stood at the window and let his eyes take in the scene, and then he was staring with tense fury at the vast scrapyard of houses sprawling away to the railway line. The location seemed to be hugging the ground, lurking behind the haze of smoke that was only just starting to clear away.

And then there was a tightening and sharpening of the mood inside him and he was in the grip of a feeling that he knew well and that he loathed. It was the feeling that used to come to him as a boy when he had to pass the neighbourhood gang on the corner. It was the feeling that came to him often on the lonely farm where he spent his childhood : in the evenings when his father stayed late in the fields ; in the dark silent nights ; in the solitary rides on horseback to and from the farm school. It was the feeling that came to him quite suddenly one day when he was

48

going home from work and a black mob came streaming out of the location beer hall at closing time, surrounding him, pressing in on him, breathing on him ; he had fought and cursed his way out and had stood dazed and breathless until the realisation came that there was nothing hostile in the crowd.

Above all, it was the feeling of that afternoon of the riot in the mine compound. Although that happened many years ago, in his first job actually, the memory of it had never left him. He could still see every vivid detail of it. The walk with the manager into the compound to arrest the strike leaders : the argument, the sudden quarrel. Then the sudden sharp violent flare-up, the cursing and scuffling, the panic, the yelling, the crazed faces, the sour sweat smell and the blood, and the stones flying with vicious force. The manager was injured and had to spend a month in hospital ; *he* had escaped injury by running into the compound kitchen, where he crouched behind a cupboard until rescued. For weeks afterward he had to be treated for shock.

He never knew how much of it he actually saw, how much was put together later, how much was suggested by the police. But the picture of it was a complete one nevertheless, both in visual detail and in its terrifying atmosphere. Now, on this first morning in the location, the memory of that riot was echoing in his mind like a drunk man stumbling along an empty corridor.

He threw the cigarette out of the window and went back to his chair. Absently he flipped the pages of the Act and the Regulations, then pushed them to the far end of the desk. He opened the desk drawer, it was empty except for some dirty blotting paper, a half-used notebook, and some paper clips. He closed it with the palm of his hand. Then he sat and stared at the telephone again, vaguely expecting it to ring, to perform, in response to his attention.

Suddenly he pulled himself up and reached for the green books. He took a bullet-shaped ball-point pen from his pocket, and struck out Brits's name on the covers and put his own above it. He wrote his full name—Hendrik Johannes Jordaan Du Toit —signing with a vigorous flourish. He stood up and fetched the inking pad and the tray of rubber stamps from the top of a cupboard, tested them all methodically on a piece of foolscap, and arranged them in families. Then he turned to the side table and pressed the green bell button.

An undersized man, with wide shoulders and a too-large head, owl-like glasses, a collar that would not stay down, and a baggy suit, came into the room and stood before the desk.

"Your name is Andries "—Du Toit glanced at the tab next to the green button—" Gwebu ? " He spoke in the home-made kitchen language known as Fanegalo.

The clerk nodded. " *Yebbo,*" he said politely.

" I'm the new *baas* here."

The clerk bowed his head in greeting, but a trifle too low and with a faintly theatrical touch.

" Go and fetch me the book in which the money is written. I wish to work with that book."

" *Yebbo, Nkos,*" the clerk said, and went to a cupboard and brought out two leather-bound account books.

" Two books ? " Du Toit asked.

" Yes, sir." The clerk paused. " One for incoming revenue, the other for expenditure, sir," he said cheerfully, with a solemn face, and in flawless English.

CHAPTER FOUR

No two locations are alike. Each has its own problems, its own temper, its own ways of adapting to the laws and authority, its own subterfuges for defeating them. A man must get the measure of a location before he can hope to administer it properly. He must proceed slowly, feeling his way carefully into the job, for otherwise things can go terribly wrong.

At first Du Toit relied heavily on Andries Gwebu. All through the day he kept pressing the button for him. He noticed a remarkable thing about Gwebu—whenever he told him to look up some information, Gwebu would give the answer straight out of his head without referring to the books. Sometimes, for some peculiar reason, he would pretend to look it up but it was obviously a pretence because he would just turn up any page and give the answer looking straight ahead at the wall. Du Toit could not understand why he wanted to do this, but told himself it was probably just a variation of the trick, done to impress him.

This clerk was definitely some kind of genius. Du Toit had never come across a black man with such amazing brains. He often mentioned him at home to Anna and to visitors. " You should see that chief clerk I've got out there. Black as a crow and nothing to look at, but I tell you he could make rings round many of your professional accountants." The books were in a hopeless mess as a result of Brits' neglect, and the whole location had been run on Gwebu's prodigious memory. He knew the names of all the inhabitants, where they lived, how they stood with their rents and rates, and lots else about them, such as that a man had recently done six months for robbery or was living under a dead man's pass, or had let off all the rooms in his hired municipal house and had retired to his kraal on the proceeds.

Du Toit was most impressed, and he had a grudging and puzzled admiration for Gwebu. He himself used to do the same kind of thing in the old place—it came from working with the same cases and the same people every day—and he liked to put on a little act about it to impress his cronies there, but he never became as good as Gwebu at it. Yet no one would have suspected it from looking at Gwebu. He was so small and ugly and he had a dank, sour smell about him, and while with some of them who were clever you could forget what they were sometimes, you never could with Gwebu.

At first Du Toit was thankful for Gwebu's efficiency; he could not have managed without him. But after a while he realised that it was wrong to be relying so much on a clerk. It reduced his position in the office and made him feel superfluous, and even a bit foolish. He could see that he ought not to place himself in Gwebu's hands like that. And somehow it was more than a matter of prestige. He began to feel uneasy about Gwebu. There seemed to be something vaguely shifty and underhand about him. At times he even suspected Gwebu of secretly plotting against him, of working up a complicated situation merely to provide opportunities for scoring off him. There came a time when he would call for Gwebu and ask his opinion on some point, then deliberately ignore him and decide the thing his own way. But that was later on, when Du Toit had begun to acquire a feel for the job and could afford to disregard Gwebu. And when that happened, a new and curious involvement started between them.

For the first week Du Toit never went down into the location. He spent every day in the office, studying the books, questioning Gwebu, carrying on simple routine work or just tidying up. He kept saying he would go out next day, but he kept putting it off. He had developed a kind of inhibition about it. But at the end of the first week Moolman arranged for him to buy a second-hand car on easy terms, and one morning he drove past the administration building and into the location. As the car lurched over the rough, churned-up road, snowploughing a way past cows, donkeys, dray carts, boys kicking tennis balls, women carrying bundles of firewood on their heads, eyes watched him all the way.

Seen from outside, the location had a desolate and barren look, but from inside it seemed to take on extra dimensions and spring to life. The scrap materials had arranged themselves into separate units of walls, roofs, doors, and chimneys. The individual houses had touches of decoration—doors and window frames painted bright, trelliswork over gates, occasional lead-glass windows that had been rescued from some house-demolisher's rubbish dump. There were patches of gardens with sparse flowers and stunted fruit trees covered with dust. The shops, although very small—there was seldom room inside for more than three or four people—looked deceptively bigger because of the numbers of people standing around them, because of the attraction they had for other, satellite, traders who operated under the open sky on the pavement outside—tailors working at whirring sewing machines, barbers shaving clients seated on upturned candle boxes ; and because of the agitation of colour created by the flapping enamel signs for Coca-Cola, Joko Tea, Triumph Bicycles, Decca Records. There were tin churches where the bells really rang, and shanty cinemas with torn hordings advertising *King Kong* and old, old Westerns. A skyline had come up, flat, flimsy, like stage scenery, but it restored the effect of human size. And there was the distinctive feeling of a location, a kind of hum and pressure in the air, a tumult of cries, music, clatter, movement, argument, and work, a vitality generated like animal heat in the overpopulated yards and kitchens.

Du Toit watched the people in the streets carefully. He noticed that there were many more in tribal dress than he used to see in the old location. The rural and urban types seemed to be about equally mixed here. There were women in cheap, loose-fitting dresses bought in the Indian Bazaar, and women with coils of copper wire around their ankles—their breasts and navels bare, and their hair plaited and caked with red clay and hanging like the fringe of a curtain in front of their eyes. There were men in suits, men in work clothes, and men with blankets slung over their naked torsos, beads around their necks, and painted snuffboxes stuck in their pierced and stretched ear lobes. And sometimes there were tribal ornaments and European clothes on the same person. It pleased him. It was a good sign. He wanted a change from the usual kind of urban location. Everybody knows that a superintendent prefers to work with the kraal type rather than the know-all answer-back urban type.

As Du Toit drove along the streets, the location people watched him, but without looking at him. If they walked past him, their chins pointed straight ahead, but their eyes slid into the corners, following him, as they passed. Only a few greeted him. Only the children displayed their interest in him. They shouted " *M'lungu* [White man]," and ran after the car, but when he slowed down or stopped, they scampered away.

He crossed the street that marked the sudden end of the shantytown and the beginning of the housing scheme. Now the streets had become straight, the blocks regular, and it was like another town. He noticed how the air was quieter, the people better dressed, the children cleaner, the dogs fatter, as if the sameness and neatness of the little square houses had imposed a monotonous discipline on the area. It seemed dull and respectable here after the shantytown. He could see that all the life of the location went on in the shantytown.

He passed through the housing scheme and came to the old location of thatched huts, but did not drive into that part for the roads were too poor. He parked the car and looked at it from the distance. There was a smell of cattle dung and wood fires in the air, and he saw old *makhulus* with shrivelled breasts kneeling at stone mortars pounding maize. This part was like a small parcel of land lifted out of the reserve, its people, huts, trees, and rocks left undisturbed, and planted down again in the town—an exhibit at a trade fair.

After that he drove back to the office. And all the way back the furtive withdrawn eyes followed him.

*　　　*　　　*

The location continued to baffle and tease him. He was seized by a desire to get to grips with it, to master it, and he knew that until he did so he would never quell the uneasiness

54

that filled him from the moment he sat down at his desk in the morning until he climbed into his car at evening. But he did not know where to start, or even what to do. He could see that Gwebu, on whom he had banked so much at first, was becoming an obstacle. To break Gwebu's grip on the office, he tried working through the other clerks, but they were lazy and, as he soon learnt, dishonest. He shifted his attention to the location constables, futilely hoping that they might turn out to be more reliable than they looked. He sent them orders to prepare for a parade, and made it clear that all had to attend, but only seventeen of the twenty-four turned up, and nobody seemed to know what had happened to the rest. When he inspected them, he was appalled by their dirty appearance. Belts and buttons were missing, handcuffs were rusted and many had been lost, uniforms were shabby and torn. When he reprimanded them, the sergeant grinned. He saw that without new uniforms and equipment he could not even start to get discipline into the constables, and he telephoned Moolman about it. " That's not my department, you know, old man. Better ask old Tante Ross," Moolman said. And when he spoke to Mrs. Ross, she said, "Really, Mr. Du Toit, you know our financial position." He knew that there were dozens of liquor yards in the location—he saw drunks staggering about openly in the streets, and on Sundays the whole location became noisy, tipsy, and obstreperous—but the constables were quite incapable of discovering any of the yards. He knew that they were taking bribes, and he expected it, but he was shocked to find out that there was also a trade in forged documents, and that half the office clerks were involved in it. He had a number of them prosecuted, but that left him short-staffed and placed him more than ever in the hands of Gwebu. It was impossible to work properly, in the way that he felt compelled to in order to make his working day bearable. He used to sit and think about Brits, and wish he had Brits's nonchalant approach. When he had cases for the police, he could never find Van der Vyver in, and even when he left messages, the pickup van would only arrive the next day. Every location has an Advisory Board, a body of three elected and three selected location people, that is supposed to represent the location in its dealings with the superintendent and the municipality. The normal thing was for the Advisory Board to send a delegation to welcome him, and to call meetings, But the Board never came near him. He inquired from Gwebu about the Chairman of the Board, and was told it, was an old chieftain named Charles Ngubeni; he told Gwebu to bring Ngubeni up to the office, but Gwebu never got round to it.

The slackness and unreliability all around him made him feel disarmed in the location. He became irritable and began coming to the office tired out after restless nights. Nobody in the town seemed to be interested in his troubles, and what advice he received was wild and stupid. There seemed to be a silent insidious conspiracy against him, and everything only went to increase his fear of the location.

And then one morning Charles Ngubeni came unbidden into the office, and after that everything began to change.

★   ★   ★

Charles Ngubeni was the people's leader in Nelstroom. He actually called himself that, as if it were the name of an office that he held by reason of letters patent or special appointment. But nobody disputed his right to the title. He was the senior tribal headman in Nelstroom, and the Chairman of the Advisory Board, and therefore the most important inhabitant of the location, whatever he called himself. He was a vain and jealous old man, full of stiff theatrical dignity. On official occasions he would dress up in a threadbare greenish-black coat, striped pants with ragged ends, and a crumpled Homburg, and make long-winded, flowery speeches that nobody could understand. But he was a cunning and scheming old politician who for years kept the location in the palm of his hand.

The trouble was that under Brits the title of people's leader had become an empty shell. A genuine people's leader lives by trafficking in favour between the people and the superintendent. Favours for himself—the best house in the location, a dispensation to keep liquor, and favours for his friends—taxi licences, exemptions from the pass laws, meat quotas, and so on. Of course, for the favours obtained he must return favours: the superintendent expects certain services from the people's leader,

56

services of a rather special nature that are not usually spoken about outside of the four walls of the superintendent's office. There is a great balancing of favours. Leadership of the people has to be bought and continually paid for.

But Brits was not interested in favours—either way. He was not interested in the location. Not in the usual location intrigues, nor in the usual instrument for carrying them through, the Advisory Board. He arranged for the Board election every October, as the law required, and there would be a brief period of excitement while the standholders voted. Ngubeni and the same panel would be elected each year, Ngubeni on his dignified looks and past reputation, and the others on their association with him. Brits would appoint the same three nominees, and then the Advisory Board would go to sleep for another year.

So Ngubeni, although undoubtedly the people's leader in Nelstroom, was like a shopkeeper with wonderful premises but without any wares to sell. The people realised his failure, but did not blame him for it; they continued to give him the deference to which he was entitled, but they stopped coming to him with their troubles. And that made Charles Ngubeni grow more and more touchy and bad-tempered and sensitive about his position in the location.

Ngubeni realised that Du Toit's arrival must have some significance for him personally, but it took him a little while to see what it was. He listened while the location discussed and gossiped about the new man, and when there were sufficient known facts, he shrewdly weighed them up. A man comes from a big Johannesburg location to take over this little location. He is no longer young, in fact he is the oldest manager they ever had. He drives about in a cheap old car. The moment he arrives he starts putting the clerks in gaol, cleaning up the constables, and making life miserable for everybody. What could all this mean? Only that this was a manager on the way down. How would such a man treat the location? Like Brits? No. He would try to rescue himself with it.

So when Ngubeni had decided that Du Toit was a man in a somewhat similar position to his own, and that there was a chance of making common cause with him in the location, he dressed up in his Chairman's clothes and went over to the location office.

When he arrived, he found a number of people lined up, but he went straight up to the desk and said, "I wish to have a little talk with the manager."

Du Toit said, "Stand in line. Can't you see these people came ahead of you?" Then he glanced up and was startled to see a man who looked like the ambassador for one of those black Central African Republics.

"What do you want?"

Ngubeni opened his mouth, but he didn't speak. The address that he had so carefully rehearsed all the way to the office was impossible to deliver in front of all the other people in the room.

"I have come here to have a few words with the manager. I . . . I . . ." He dried up.

Du Toit said, "Well, just wait your turn," and went on filling in a yellow form, holding it firm with two fingers, and writing fast. "What's the matter, are you deaf?" he said without looking up. He handed the form across the desk and said, "Yes?" to the next man. Ngubeni stood next to the desk and looked furiously at the people in the line. They started to laugh. Their amusement stung him like a burn, and suddenly, with flashing eyes, he swung round and stalked out of the room and took his place at the end of the line.

When he finally reached the desk again, there was a line of people behind him and again it was impossible to make the carefully prepared opening.

"I wish to have a little talk with the manager."

"Yes?"

"What I have to say is for the *manager*."

"Well go ahead."

He looked about him in desperation.

"I am Charles Ngubeni," he said, putting on an extra inch of height.

Du Toit did not recall the name. He had forgotten it was the name of the man whom he had asked Gwebu to bring up to the office. He looked up, puzzled, at Andries Gwebu, who was looking at Ngubeni with a queer amused expression. Suddenly Ngubeni stepped to the side, pointed dramatically at the people who had lined up behind him, wagged his finger rapidly back and forth, and demanded, " Send these people out."

Du Toit sat up with a jerk. Now he thought it was a lunatic and was wondering how to get him out, but Gwebu said, " This is him, sir, Ngubeni. The Chairman of the Board. You *said* you wanted to interview him, sir."

" I see," Du Toit said, sitting back again but still looking a little shaken.

" You'd better see him, sir," Gwebu said, and before Du Toit could decide for himself, Gwebu turned to the people and told them, " You are now required to make yourselves scarce." He walked out behind them and tactfully closed the door.

Ngubeni sat down and gingerly placed his hat on his lap. He straightened his handkerchief. He pulled the cuffs out of his sleeves and adjusted his tie. " I welcome you on the behalf of the people of the location."

" Thank you."

" I bring you greetings."

" Thank you."

" The people are very happy to see you, sir, and they want me to tell you they are this happy, and to say welcome, and so I say, ' Welcome to Nelstroom Location.' " It came out in a rush, the last words in a loud voice. Then with the rehearsed part over, his whole body relaxed and a scheming look came into his eyes.

Du Toit watched him over the tips of his fingers. " Thank you," he said, puzzled.

" Do you know Baas Brits ? " Ngubeni asked looking keenly at Du Toit.

" No," Du Toit said, on his guard.

Ngubeni shook his head sadly.

" What was the matter with Baas Brits ? " Du Toit asked in a tone that was a warning not to run down Brits, but at the same time an invitation to tell him what *was* the matter.

Ngubeni shook his head dolefully and made clicking sounds with his tongue, conveying that the whole location had been bitterly disappointed in Brits. Then he abruptly changed the subject.

"Is the manager satisfy with everything here?" he asked with a coy look.

Du Toit narrowed his eyes. "Why, yes," he said. "Quite satisfied. Why?"

"I am not satisfy," Ngubeni said, examining the back of his hand.

"No?"

"No," Ngubeni said, turning the hand over and studying the finger tips. He waited, then said, "There are many not good things in this location. The people are too lazy and they stab each other and they steal and they do not respect the old people, they are very cheeky. The young ones—they are nothing but *tsotsis*."

"Yes?"

"Yes." There was a long pause. Then Ngubeni, speaking to the hat on his lap, said, "Maybe the manager is having a hard time in this place?"

"Why—no," Du Toit said.

"The manager he sit in this room all day long. He sit *here*. How can he know what is happening when he sit *here*, and he don't go out and talk to the people? How can he? And nobody to come and tell him what is happening all over the location." Du Toit did not answer. He rested his cheek against his fist and waited for Ngubeni. "When nobody come and tell him, it must be hard work for him," Ngubeni said, full of sympathy for all location managers and their problems.

"So?" Du Toit said.

"I am the leader of all these Swazi people. I am Chairman of the Advisory Board."

Du Toit's head was nodding slowly and rhythmically.

"*I* know what is happening. Everything. People come to me and say, Chief Ngubeni, so and so, and I say so and so, and they ask me, Chief Ngubeni, what must we do? And I say you must do so and so. All day long. That is how I know all that is happening."

"I see," Du Toit said thoughtfully. He began to draw on a scrap of paper a row of diamonds, an arrow, a ring with dots

60

inside. Ngubeni watched him, holding the hat off his knees. Then Du Toit drew a circle around all the drawings, and Ngubeni knew that the long climb was over. He stood up and said, " Well, I brought you the welcome. Now I must go, because I see you are busy."

" Sit down a minute," Du Toit said.

" But you are busy."

" Sit down."

Ngubeni sat down again. He hesitated a moment, then placed the hat on the desk.

" What did you say your name was again ? "

" Charles Ngubeni. I am the——"

" Charles, have you done this kind of work before ? "

" Oh yes. Many times."

" You sure ? "

" Oh yes."

Du Toit had a mild look in his eyes. He had grown suddenly warm towards this absurd old showman, and he gazed at him fondly. There were all the conditions here for one of those preposterous friendships such as a prisoner has for a mouse, a recluse for a child. The pale blue eyes exchanged a long look with the moist brown eyes, and that look concluded the deal.

" Charles, how much must I pay you for this ? "

" It is up to the manager. Only don't let me catch fire with the people, otherwise it is finish."

" Of course not. Will you do this alone, or are there others you can rope in ? "

" Alone. But I know others. Do you want others ? "

" We'll see. We can decide later. Now you say you are Chairman of the Advisory Board ? "

" Yes. Ten years Chairman, fifteen years member."

" Charles, I'm going to start calling your Advisory Board together again."

" Good. It was a no use under Baas Brits."

" Yes, I'm going to start calling you together every Friday afternoon. Tell this to the other members. Are they all your friends ? "

" All my friends. Everybody in this place is my friends."

" I mean—you know what I mean. Are they your *good* friends ? Are they like you ? "

" Four, yes. Two not so good."

" Anyway, remember next Friday. And at the first meeting there are a few things I want to discuss. All this climbing through the fence, for example. It's very dangerous when they do that in that part up by the train line. There'll be a serious accident one day. And besides, when they come and go through the fence like that, not through the gate, how can we ever check whether people have proper papers or not ? "

Ngubeni listened eagerly, nodding all the time.

" That is so," he agreed.

★   ★   ★

Slowly Du Toit brought in more reforms. Each involved some special problem. It took long, careful work. Slowly, too, the location began to change. Its spirit changed, slowly, like a man growing old. But Du Toit did not see it as change for the worse. He called the changes reforms, and by that he meant that they were for the benefit of the location.

Ngubeni came every evening and they talked behind closed doors. Gradually Du Toit learnt how to work with him. His information was not always reliable. It was often the wildest hearsay and Ngubeni developed a tendency to manufacture plots in order to inform on them. But Du Toit learnt how to sift out what was valuable in Ngubeni's diffuse, often spiteful, accounts. It made all the difference having Ngubeni working for him. It enabled him to feel the pulse of the location, to know what reaction to expect to his various new schemes. It not only made for sounder administration, it greatly helped put down crime, for it gave the police eyes and feelers where they never had them before. Van der Vyver had gone away on transfer, and a new man, Lieutenant Swanepoel, had taken over, and this new man was a different type from Van der Vyver, keen, energetic, a first-rate policeman.

The Advisory Board met every Friday afternoon, and Du Toit never missed a meeting. He took a keen part in the discussion, patiently debating every point. He drew the Board into everything. The Board endorsed all the reforms and then went out and explained them to the people. Du Toit and the Board got along famously.

He used to promise himself nearly every day that he would fire Gwebu, but he never did. Du Toit eventually replaced all the other clerks, but not Gwebu. His position was precarious, but the strange thing was that he managed to stay on. Gwebu infuriated Du Toit. His remarks always seemed to have a second meaning, and his face never indicated what he was thinking. And he was always playing sly hoaxes on Du Toit. He would save up obscure, deceptive-sounding words and drop them into the conversation, leaving Du Toit feeling that he had missed something he should have understood. Sometimes he pretended to understand, or believed that he did. Then he came in for heavy punishment.

" Sir, what do you intend to do with this batch of aboriginals ? " A group of labourers, recruits for the quarries, had been brought across from the railway station to have their papers endorsed, and were waiting outside on the veranda. When Gwebu asked, he happened to have an unopened package of pass forms in his hand.

" Put them on the shelf."

" Right, sir. Should I count them ? "

" Not necessary. The number's on the label."

Gwebu was always polite, flattering, and careful never to take it too far. He would stop at the point where Du Toit was suspicious but not certain what had happened, and sometimes well before that. Sometimes he would let things rest for a few days, then start using the word in the right sense, over and over again, so that Du Toit would know, but too late to say anything.

Sometimes the trick took the opposite form. Gwebu would pretend to be a fool about a subject, and encourage Du Toit to think he would get away with a statement or opinion.

" Can a man be convicted for stealing his own property ? "

" I am just a clown when it comes to legal conundrums, sir. Why do you ask, sir ? "

" There's a case on now. A man broke into his friend's house to commit a burglary, but by mistake he took a suitcase that he himself had left there a few weeks before. If you ask me, he's guilty. He had the intention to steal, and only by accident he took the wrong suitcase."

"That sounds reasonable, sir."

"Why should he get off just because he had the good luck to take the wrong suitcase? He did the act and had the intention —exactly as if he actually stole the other man's things."

"I can't argue with that, sir."

"Of course you can't. I often think I should have been a lawyer. When I see the way some of these chaps handle their cases——"

"Oh yes, sir, you would have done well in the legal profession. Regarding that case you mentioned, wasn't there a Supreme Court decision on that very point a few years ago?"

"Was there? What did it say?"

"Why, if I remember correctly, that a man can't steal from himself, sir."

It was a kind of nimble guerilla warfare, with Gwebu always skipping away to safety. It was hard to say why he did it. He often played these tricks as if there were a devil in him, as if he were driven by a reckless mischievousness.

One day Du Toit went into the next-door office while Gwebu was away. Something prompted him to open Gwebu's desk drawer. He found a box of visiting cards:

ANDRIES NATHANIEL GWEBU
BACHELOR OF ARTS
Official Interpreter

163 Oak Road,
New Location,
Nelstroom.

This was the first he knew of Gwebu's having a degree, for Gwebu never mentioned it. Again he had the feeling of being duped. He opened other drawers and found untidy heaps of books, magazines, and pamphlets: *War and Peace*, the first hundred pages grubby and manhandled, the rest crisp and clean; a cheap paper-back edition of *Darkness at Noon*; Marxist pamphlets; old copies of *Time*; a glossy-paper publication called *Gals and Gags*; a bookkeeping manual; a book on physical culture.

64

He never got rid of Gwebu, and he never really got out of his clutches. And what in the end made Gwebu irreplaceable was the discovery that he was a superb interpreter. Du Toit first saw this at the meeting to announce the new rule against climbing through the fence.

Ngubeni spoke first, and then Malooy, the bus owner, both in vernacular. Then Du Toit spoke. His short announcement was translated sentence by sentence by Gwebu. But Gwebu took wings. He made a piece of soaring oratory out of Du Toit's dull officialness. He brought the language of byelaws to life with images and metaphors. He spoke with gestures, pauses, looks, silences, and thunder. When Du Toit spoke of the danger of climbing through the fence near the railway line, Gwebu pictured it in terms of maimed children and decapitated cattle. When he warned that the pass laws would be strictly enforced, Gwebu painted a picture of a serene smiling community all happily free from the worry of arrests, and on wonderful terms with the police because they were properly documented. As with everything he said, there was a dual meaning, two images imperfectly super-imposed, leaving a shadowy outline of doubt. Darting between the legs of the hyperbole was a lively midget of sarcasm, running ahead, falling back, waiting, overtaking. When Gwebu spoke, it was always doubtful what he himself believed, and the doubt combined with the eloquence had a strangely convincing effect on his listeners. Gwebu was a great actor.

The announcement went over without trouble, thanks to Gwebu. The people stood and listened and went away. Perhaps they thought that the announcement was not meant seriously ; perhaps they thought they would be able to deal with it as they had dealt with other inconveniences, by squirming out of it some way. Or perhaps they really did think then that the new law was for the good of the location. Anyway, they stayed quiet, listened, and went away.

At that meeting Du Toit noticed a peculiar thing : everyone looked at Gwebu, and nobody at him. He didn't try to under-stand it, but it made him feel good. At later meetings he purposely played down his own part, making his speeches even more bald and official, so that Gwebu could play them up. He had an instinct that it was right to appear impersonal and anonymous when speaking to the location about new rules and regulations. He vaguely realised the importance of having someone stand between him and the audience on these occasions.

He hated Gwebu but he grew closer to him as time went by. And what started as a need for advice to avoid mistakes became a bickering, uncomfortable, involved, but indissoluble relationship. The antagonism between them was never stronger than the forces that held them together.

When Du Toit had picked his new office staff, he managed to persuade the Council to supply new uniforms for them. Boxes arrived filled with grey-black drill suits with black plastic buttons. All wore the suits except Gwebu, who received his with elegant thanks when Du Toit handed them out on an occasion that immediately developed into a ceremony, but he came to work the next day, and ever after, in his drooping slacks, baggy outsized sports jacket, and dirty green tie. Du Toit never risked taking it up with him.

When he finished with the office clerks, he started with the location constables. He dismissed the sergeant or *induna*, whose wife, he learned, was a shebeen queen. He replaced him with Isaac Gwagwa, six feet eight tall, the tallest man in the location. He chose Gwagwa purely for size and looks. He had a lean, sour face, with the skin stretched tight over the bones, and he looked tough and responsible, though actually he was quite a mild man. He was honest, though more from a kind of stubborn lack of imagination than from principle.

Next Du Toit attended to discipline. Any constable found taking bribes was kicked out and handed over to the police. It stopped open abuses, though it was not possible to judge how far the traffic was driven underground. Uniforms had to be kept clean, and boots, belts, knobkerries, handcuffs, and police whistles polished every day. After a while he managed to get the constables' uniforms changed too, from shabby, ill-fitting khaki drill into smart blue serge with brass buttons. With regular inspections the constables began to stand rigidly upright and straight in line and to answer smartly, with the comic stiffness of palace guards in an operetta.

Du Toit became very fond of Gwagwa, who never had an opinion and in an earnest, painstaking way tried to carry out every order to the letter. Gwagwa became like a lovable Great Dane around the location office.

There came a time when the tight look in Du Toit's eyes began to disappear. His sleep improved and his smoking dropped. He began to put on weight. With Ngubeni and the rehabilitated Advisory Board, Gwebu and the purged office staff, Gwagwa and the smartened-up constables, he had a protective wall around him, a system of defences that could cope with most of the foreseeable contingencies in the location. He was no longer alone in the location.

*   *   *

Mrs. Ross and the two councillors came out one morning, riding in a green Buick. She got out of the car and came up the veranda steps, delicately holding her skirt out in front with both hands. The crowd around Du Toit's door melted away and she went into the office and sat down and fanned herself with her hand. She was in a wonderfully friendly mood.

" Really, Mr. Du Toit, really," she said, nodding her head and smiling. " Really." Du Toit smiled back. This was the first time she had come out to the location, although she was always phoning him and calling him over to the Town Hall. He felt that *he* should have been saying, " Really ! " But he knew her way of congratulating people. People she congratulated were those who had done something for her, so she always acted as if she had been given a birthday surprise.

" This report," she said through the waving hand, " now what do you suggest ? "

Du Toit had not heard of any report, but he didn't want to admit it in case it was something he should have known about. He smiled again and said, " I don't know, Mrs. Ross. What do you suggest ? "

" Well I should think firstly, something *general*, the smooth way everything is running here, and of course, this is most important, a *comparison* with how it was before. Then the particular *methods*, that's the important part. Methods. How the changes were effected. That will be the interesting part, something concrete and *instructive* for other municipalities. Get the idea ? "

" Yes," Du Toit said. He frowned and asked. " By when do you want this report ? "

" Oh no, Mr. Du Toit, you're *far* too busy. I'm going to write it. This is *my* little task." She smiled brilliantly. " That's why we're here to-day. To gather the evidence. Now suppose we have a little chat of a general nature."

A leather notebook came out of her handbag, and she waited with a poised pencil. Du Toit explained. From the moment he started talking she started writing. There were some things he could not mention—for example, Ngubeni's work as informer, and there were others he was vague about. He realised, in fact, that he was by no means sure how it had all happened. But she wrote down every word he said in a kind of slapdash home-made shorthand. Then she said :

" Now the evidence of all this, Mr. Du Toit. Where should we start ? Suppose you get the clerks and constables lined up."

Du Toit got them in line on the veranda and Mrs. Ross inspected them. " Is everything all right ? " she asked, like the prisoners' friend. The uniforms looked really smart, the parade was perfect. Du Toit looked puzzled for a moment, but then he saw Gwebu standing among the onlookers crowding up the steps—in his usual slacks, sports jacket, dirty shoes.

Mrs. Ross smiled and wrote more notes.

After that they made a royal tour of the location. She counted people filling buckets and baths around the taps, and tried to work out the average per tap. She noticed the state of the roads. " Good—adequate for bicycles, horse-drawn traffic, etc." She went into a school : the children were " well fed and healthy-looking." She looked across the football field, made a note about " recreational facilities." She stopped the car, called people over, and asked, " Is everything all right ? " She interviewed a parson, a schoolteacher, a taxi driver ; noted their " cheerful respectful manners." The old location was " picturesque, an ideal way of life for a backward people." When she got back to the office, she wrote, " Whole location contented, quiet, law-abiding." She could have written it all before she started out.

68

A few weeks later Du Toit received an invitation to attend a special meeting of the Town Council. When he arrived there, he noticed how everybody was smiling at him. Mrs. Ross read her report and all could see what a fine job the Native Affairs Committee, with some assistance from Du Toit, had done in the location.

"I intend sending a copy of this report to my friend, the Minister of Native Affairs," Mrs. Ross said. "So he can see for himself how a little committee, with limited forces, can accomplish a good job of work if only it sets its mind to it."

Du Toit let it go. He had long given up trying to fight Mrs. Ross. He noticed how Moolman listened to her with a sour look on his face. Once or twice he caught Moolman's eye and they exchanged a look. When Mrs. Ross finished, one of the other members of the Native Affairs Committee stood up and announced that the Council had decided to buy Du Toit a car for use in his job.

"It gives a bad impression out there when our superintendent doesn't have a decent car. It makes them think the Council doesn't think much of its own superintendent and that gives them ideas," the councillor said.

When the meeting was over, Moolman came after Du Toit and took him by the arm. "You know, Hennie, if you think you need extra money for anything out there, I can always talk our Finance Committee into passing it. Just write straight in to us." Du Toit thought for a moment, then said, "You know I've had an idea in my mind for some time. I'd like to build a welfare centre—you know, a clinic, library, a lecture room, that kind of thing. Apart from their bioscopes, they haven't anything out there. I've been thinking about it a good deal lately, and I think it would be appreciated."

Moolman looked at him doubtfully. "Well, I suppose you know what you are about." They walked on, then Moolman turned and asked, "By the way, what about that extra clerk you wanted some time back?"

Du Toit did not answer at once. He walked on slowly, with his hands in his pockets. "No," he said at last. "I don't think I need one. I think I can manage all right." He had become

69

too fond of the location, too jealous and proud of it, and he didn't want anyone else to share in his strange involvement with it.

At the end of his first year Du Toit went away for a holiday in his new car, and Theron came back to relieve him. For those two weeks there was an air of festivity throughout the location.

CHAPTER FIVE

THERE WAS a washwoman in Nelstroom location named Mary Lukhele. She worked for three families, the Wolmaranses, the Smits, and the Beckets. Every Monday she delivered the clean laundry, wrapped in a sheet that was part of the laundry, and took away the soiled. She would make three double journeys between the location and the town, calling first on Mrs. Wolmarans who lived farthest, then on Mrs. Smit, then on Mrs. Becket. Monday was a bad day because of all the walking with the heavy bundles. But it was the day she received the pay, and the clinking of coins in the little yellow tobacco bag that she wore tied to her belt was a great help in relieving the pain in her back.

Mary Lukhele was a quarrelsome old woman. Once when another washwoman took her spot on the riverbank, she threw her into the water. She worked in her own time, with her own soap, and that spot with its smooth black rock for pounding and scrubbing, its little pool clouded with soap scum and bubbles, was hers, her workshop. She was at the river, at the same spot, every day except Mondays, when she delivered the week's wash and picked up next week's, growing more irate as the day went on. Her husband, a deliveryman for a grocery, would take a long time coming home Monday evenings, stopping at friends' houses and gossiping his way slowly through the location.

One Monday towards the end of winter Mary Lukhele loaded the bundle of laundry on her head and set out for Mrs. Becket's house as usual. There was nothing to suggest why her trip was different from all her other trips, or from all the trips of all the other washwomen. When she started out along the road, glad that it was the last trip, she had no idea that she was to become the cause of wholesale death and terror in the location and the downfall of Du Toit. Mary Lukhele bore tragedy in the bundle that she carried on her head that day. So it is important to note the day : Monday, the 10th August, 1953. A late-winter day in the middle of Du Toit's third year and in Mabaso's ninth month in the location.

She arrived at Mrs. Becket's house in the late afternoon and rang the bell on the screen door of the kitchen. Mrs. Becket came out, took the bundle inside, and counted the articles on the kitchen table. Mary Lukhele waited in the yard.

After a while Mrs. Becket kicked open the screen door and, standing on the top step, said :

" Mary, there's a collar missing."

" No, missus," Mary Lukhele said, shaking her head.

" Don't ' No ' me. There's a collar missing."

" *No*, missus. It's all there." She wagged her head and huffed her shoulders and muttered in Swazi. Mrs. Becket looked at her. " Come in here," she ordered. Mary Lukhele went up the steps into the kitchen.

" See, that one's missing. The one that goes with that shirt."

Mary Lukhele held the shirt and looked at the collars : there was no collar to match the shirt. She could not remember the collar. She slammed the shirt down on top of the pile, throwing it out of its folds.

" Then you didn't give it me. What I want with to steal your collar for ? Can I wear a collar ? "

" It's on the list. Look here—six collars. Count. Five."

" Aah—the list." She slapped it out of Mrs. Becket's hand.

" Get out of here," Mrs. Becket screamed.

" My twelve shillings," Mary Lukhele said, planting her feet on the floor.

" Clear out. You're getting no money. The shirt's ruined without the collar."

" No ? " Mary Lukhele asked. Her eyes blazed.

" No. The shirt's ruined. Go on, get out. Bring me the collar and then I'll pay you. Now get out."

" You won't pay ? " Mary Lukhele asked. She waited. Then

72

she took up the corners of the sheet and hoisted the bundle of laundry on to her back. " Where are you going ? " Mrs. Becket screamed, and tried to stop her. Mary Lukhele pushed her violently away and she crashed into the table. Mary Lukhele went down into the yard out into the street, and at that moment one of the location taxis came past. As she climbed in, she heard a police whistle shrilling in Mrs. Becket's kitchen.

She did not go to her house. She carried the bundle down to the river and sat at her spot, thinking. She knew she was in trouble. She did not know all the laws that were involved in what she had done, but she understood that it was seriously criminal and that there would be gaol in it. Her back ached and she was angry. She thought of the twelve shillings she should have received and she began swearing aloud. She thought of the two days' work : she saw the Becket's things lying stretched out, wet and soapy-smooth, on the flat rock before her—she knew every article, every patch and tear and button of the Beckets' clothes. She could picture each one. There had been no collar. Suddenly she ripped open the bundle and tossed the garments into the stream. Some stuck against the reeds and she pushed them out with a stick and she sat and watched until they had all floated away or had sunk, waterlogged. Then she got up to go home.

On the way home she heard the siren of a Flying Squad car and she followed the sound and knew that it had stopped at her house. The realisation that it had come for her took a moment to arrive, and then she sat down on the side of the road and felt the ice form inside her. She sat for a time that had no duration and at some point she knew that the Squad car had gone away again. Without listening, she heard the siren fade away in the distance.

She got up at last, and walked slowly home. She saw people she knew but did not greet them. She looked into the different yards wondering if she should stop and tell people, but took no decision and her legs went slowly along. She hoped she would see her husband gossiping in one of the yards. When she turned the last corner before her house, she stopped and her whole body froze. The police saw her the instant after she saw them. They

73

started running, the two white police in front. She turned and fled the way she had come and the police whistles and the pounding of boots brought the whole neighbourhood out. She ran with a queer, flat-footed, waddling gait, and every few yards threw up her arms and let out a scream. Suddenly she darted into a lane and into a yard, into one of the rooms and under a bed.

The police arrived the next moment and stood looking at the row of closed doors. There was already a huge crowd in the yard. It had surged in behind the police, and it made the police jittery. They kept stepping backward with their elbows out, forcing the crowd to give room.

"Where is she?" the white sergeant asked. Nobody answered.

"All right. Start here."

They searched several rooms, turning all the occupants out into the yard; at last they found her and dragged her out.

"You Mary Lukhele?" the sergeant asked, holding her by the top of her arm and shaking her. She just shook limply and said nothing.

"It's her," a black constable said.

"You're under arrest for theft and assault," the sergeant said with his face thrust into hers.

"And trespass," the white constable said.

"And trespass," the sergeant said, still gripping her arm, holding her up, and slipping the handcuffs out of his belt with his free hand.

She stood and let them do as they liked with her, but as the sergeant was about to put on the handcuffs, she suddenly came to life and lunged out and kicked him in the groin. At the same moment she wrenched free and tried to run back into the room, but the white constable kicked out and knocked her foot behind her heel and she tripped and lay flat on the ground with her arms stretched out. An ugly sound came out of the crowd. The sergeant whipped round and drew his revolver. The crowd backed and he followed it, holding the revolver against his belt. He inched the crowd back until it stood tight-packed around the

74

edges of the yard. Then he limped over to Mary Lukhele and jerked her to her feet.

"So you want to play *that* game, you black whore," he said through clenched teeth. He put the revolver back and suddenly gave her a flat blow that sounded like a board snapping. Some women screamed; he pulled the revolver again and swung round and yelled, "Shut-up you dirty Kaffirs." He turned back to Mary Lukhele and tried to put on the handcuffs. Suddenly she kicked him again in exactly the same place. He jumped away and doubled up, then slowly looked up at her, then stepped forward, and it was so fast that hardly anyone saw it, but Mary Lukhele lay unconscious on the ground, blood oozing from her mouth and chin.

There was a strange mixed shriek of protest and shock from the crowd and the sergeant sprang into the middle of the yard and bawled, "Get the hell out of this yard, you black scum. All of you. Go on. Get." But a man stepped forward and walked up to the sergeant.

"You had no right to hit a woman like that," he said.

"Don't interfere. You'll get the same."

"You had no right to assault her like that."

"Keep out of this, you black dog. Unless you want the same." The sergeant clenched his fist and held it trembling, level with his shoulder.

"Go ahead, do it," the man said, holding up his chin. The sergeant looked all around the crowd, which had slowly crept nearer. He dropped his fist.

"Get out of here or I'll arrest you."

"Well, arrest me."

"Get *out* of here. I ordered you to get out. Now get out."

The man stood still and the sergeant looked at the constable. "Arrest him," the constable said.

"And arrest me," a woman said from the crowd; she came forward with her arms out, the insides of her wrists touching.

"Arrest me," another woman said.

Two others offered to be arrested. The crowd was very tense and quiet now.

The sergeant looked down at Mary Lukhele; she was still

75

unconscious. He wondered if he had killed her. He bent down and put his hands under her armpits and tried to pull her up. He dragged her a short distance and then let her drop. The crowd watched him with sullen silence. There was blood on his tunic and hands. He put his hands on his hips and looked at the five people who were insisting on being arrested.

"Damn well I will. I'll arrest you, you black bastards."

He ordered the black constable to put on the handcuffs, and the five people offered their wrists and the handcuffs were locked on. Then the sergeant went up to the man who had stepped out first, and hooked his fingers behind the chain of the handcuffs, and jerked the man forward. He wrapped his hand round one bracelet and squeezed, using all his strength. It clicked once, and after more pressure, twice. It would not take the next notch, so the sergeant pulled the man's wrists between his knees and squeezed with both hands, so hard that the veins corded on his neck. At last, with the steel biting into the flesh, the third click came. The man made no sound, but large drops of sweat suddenly appeared all over his face as if forced through the skin by the pressure on his wrist.

"Now, you dog," the sergeant said, pushing the man away.

The sergeant placed his hand under his chin and supported his elbow with the other hand and tried to think. He had no conveyance and was wondering whether to march the prisoners through the location. He had forgotten about Mary Lukhele, but now he noticed her again. She had come round now and was sitting against the wall. But he saw that she would not be able to walk, and that, to his relief, settled it. He said to one of the black constables :

"Go and ring for a pickup."

"The office is closed."

"Then borrow a bike and go to the station."

He realised it would be a time before the pickup van came and he decided to clear the yard while they waited. But now he didn't want to do it himself. He told the white constable, "Get all these bastards outside." He watched while the crowd was shoved and jostled and herded out through the narrow entrance of the yard. It was all done in a strange silence. There was great tension in the crowd and he could feel it, but the crowd said and did nothing, and allowed itself to be moved about.

When the yard was empty, he noticed that the man with the tight handcuffs had fainted. He stood over him for a moment, then bent down, took out a key, and loosened the bracelet. Then with his boot he rolled the inert man on to his back. The white constable came back and the two of them went and sat on the step and lit cigarettes. The black constable took up guard at the entrance.

It was dark when the pickup van came. While they were loading the prisoners into the van, they saw that the crowd had waited outside and had greatly swollen. It was too dark to see how far the crowd extended, but they could feel hundreds around them, and there was a continuous sullen murmuring and a twitching restlessness. The police said nothing now, either to the crowd or to one another. They completed the loading quickly, nervously conscious of the hundreds of eyes watching them. When they finished, the black constables climbed into the back of the van and the doors were slammed, and the white policemen ran around to the cabin and climbed up, and before they were seated, the engine started and the lights went on and the van shot off with a skid, forcing a path through the crowd. As they drove round the corner, they heard booing and a sudden pandemonium behind them.

The crowd was yelling and milling about, and the noise and agitation seemed to drive it asunder, for it had suddenly grown much larger and had overflowed into the side streets. Then it began to break up, groups fragmenting off and drifting away down the streets, farther and farther, until they had spread through the location. And with them went a wave of hysteria, whose progress could be measured by the sudden rise of babbling excitement in yard after yard. For a long time the location seethed and bubbled with anger and resentment. Everyone in the location was swept up in it.

No one knew why this particular arrest had this effect. It had been harsh, but not much more so than usual, and arrests and police brutalities were known in every yard. Mary Lukhele was not specially popular in the location and everyone understood

77

that what had happened to her was the normal consequence of running away and assaulting the police. Nobody understood just why a sudden flood of savage anger swept over the location just because of Mary Lukhele's arrest.

No one knew just why the five people had come forward to be arrested, but none questioned it, and all felt that it had to be. The simple act of these people in holding out their wrists for the handcuffs was something the location had to do for Mary Lukhele, but no one could explain why. And the torture of the man in the handcuffs was something the location had to suffer, but why, no one could say. But with the doing of all these things an obstruction was removed and a flood of hate began to run through every street and every yard. And then, at one point, gangs began to roam the streets, a strange new thing for Nelstroom Location. They were youths mostly, and they formed themselves into irregular platoons and went through the streets in a curious, rhythmical, loping stride—aimlessly—from end to end of the location. And by a subtle process the location bad boys—the *tsotsis*—took control of the gangs: marched at the head and led the way and brought the others under their command. But the gangs did not interfere with anyone. They marched back and forth like caged animals in an entranced swinging unison of limbs, and their mothers and fathers and the more serious people of the location watched them with fascination, bewilderment, and a strange anxiety.

At about nine o'clock the lights of a car were seen to turn into the location gate. The car went some distance along the main road, then stopped, and the driver, a white man, rolled down the window and asked the way to Springbok Street, which was where the Lukheles lived. There was a white woman beside the driver and a white policeman in the back seat. The car drove on. Apparently the tension in the air did not penetrate into the car, for it rode in a leisurely and unagitated fashion down the middle of the main street. It turned into Springbok Street and the policeman shone a flashlight through the car window on the house numbers, and it stopped at last in front of the Lukhele's house.

There was already a crowd there, drawn by the desire to stand

78

and stare at the house where all the trouble originated. The three white people got out of the car and pushed their way along the path. The policeman rapped on the door. The crowd closed behind them, and at that moment something of its mood must have communicated itself, for the man suddenly looked back at the car in alarm, and the woman, who was shivering in a fur coat that she held high up around her head, came close to him and gripped his arm. The door opened a few inches, letting out a narrow slit of yellow light. A face appeared. There was a large number of people in the room.

"Your name Lukhele?" the policeman asked, shining the flashlight in the man's face.

"Yes."

"Hand over that washing."

"What washing?"

"Mrs. Becket's washing, you idiot. Hand it over."

"There's no washing here. All the bundles were taken out to-day."

"You sure this is the right place, Mrs. Becket?"

"Yes, I know this man. He's her husband."

"Where's that washing?"

"I tell you there's no washing."

"Don't talk like that. Who do you think you are, talking like that?"

"What's the matter? What did I say?"

"Call me 'baas' when you talk to me. Don't you know that? Baas."

"Yes, baas."

"Hand over the washing."

"I tell you there's no washing, baas. Honestly, baas, all the bundles have gone. Really, baas."

"All right, we'll see about that." He slapped the door open wide with the sole of his boot, but he took only one step into the room.

Something hit the car with a tearing, scraping crash. The policeman swung round. There was dead silence. He ran back to the car, pushing people out of his way. He examined the car and found a deep, raw dent above the back window. A shattered brick lay on the ground. He stood and held the light over it as if he had cornered a guilty criminal. Then he directed the light into the faces all around him.

"Who threw this?" he asked. Nobody spoke. The Beckets came back and climbed into the front of the car, slammed the door, then held open the back door for the policeman to come in. The policeman stood with his hand on the handle of the open door and again asked, "Who threw this?" No answer.

"The one who threw this better come forward or I'll arrest the whole damn' lot of you." His voice was nervous.

This time there was an answer. A stone came from the back of the crowd, ricocheted across the car's roof, and landed on the roof of Mary Lukhele's house. He swung round and shone the flashlight into the crowd. Impassive, expressionless faces.

"I warn you. You better not start that," he said, his lip trembling.

"Come on, get in, let's go," Becket said.

"Don't start that," the policeman said, but everyone could hear that he was frightened. He stood and shone the light about, and all could see it dancing from the trembling of his hand.

Then two stones hit the car on the farther side : they landed hard, with a sharp rat-tat, almost one sound.

"They're smashing up the car. For Christ's sake, get in," Becket yelled.

Then a dozen stones sailed over from behind the crowd, and at the same time the crowd began to draw back. The policeman gave a final desperate look around and threw himself into the car just as a stone cracked the side window. The car started with a roar and shot away with a crash of gears. A whole group of people of all ages gave chase, picking up stones as they ran and hurling them at the bouncing car. Soon the crowd thinned out and only a few boys and some excited dogs were left running, and then the car pulled out of range and the little bouncing red taillight grew rapidly smaller and finally disappeared. People stood strung out along the road, staring at the point where the taillight was last seen. Then they came back and joined the others in front of the house.

Everybody was talking. There was great excitement. But after a while the noise died down. A chill had descended on the crowd, and more and more people fell silent. Then they started to drift away, walking very soberly. Nobody said it, but all realised they had done the one unspeakable, unforgiveable thing —they had stoned the *abalungu*, the white people, and a policeman among them.

Soon the street was empty and only Aaron Lukhele and two other men who were his lodgers were left standing in front of the house. They made a quick decision. They went inside, and after a while the candles were put out. They came out again, each with a bundle of blankets under his arm, and Lukhele locked the door. The three men walked quickly away. The police would come back ; this house was cursed.

They walked through the dark streets until they came to the house of a shebeen keeper whom Lukhele knew. She answered the door, but when she saw Lukhele, the welcome disappeared from her face. She asked in a cold voice :

" What do you want here to-night, Lukhele ? "

" I want to spend some money," Lukhele told her with a forced laugh. She eyed the blankets.

" It's all finished. All drunk up. All sold." Lukhele looked past her into the room. The noise in the room told him that she was lying.

" Well, is Violet here ? "

" No. She's not here any more."

" Paulina ? "

" She's busy."

" Well, I'll come in and just sit down."

" There's no room, Lukhele." She saw the despair in his face and added, " It's been a heavy day for you, Lukhele. They took your wife and now they'll come for you. I understand your troubles. But I cannot have them looking here."

" Thank you," Lukhele said, and the three men went back into the street and stood discussing what to do. The door opened again.

" Please, Lukhele. Not here."

They moved on to the next corner and stood talking in

whispers. The three men in the empty street, each with the bundle of blankets under his arm, looked like a gang of burglars.

"What other places are there ? " one of the lodgers asked.

"They'll all be the same," Lukhele said.

"Perhaps you have some friends."

Lukhele thought for a moment, and then, without speaking, led the way to the house of a man who had once worked with him at the grocery. He led and the other two followed, and it began to annoy him that they were so helpless and so dependent on him. As if, being the landlord in the house, it was his duty to find them somewhere to stay now that the house was not available. He wished they would go away.

The whole location had now become very quiet. Occasionally they came across the remnants of a gang, tired of walking, but otherwise there were few people about. The police would return, with reinforcements ; the location was silently waiting. The anger and excitement had gone indoors. It had not gone away, only into hiding, and the chill quiet was evidence of it as much as the noise and voices had been.

They reached the friend's house, but it was in darkness. He knocked on the door. There was no answer. He knocked again, and he heard someone cough inside, but no one answered the door. He knocked again, and waited, and then tried the handle. The door was locked. He heard breathing, and smothered coughing and a sharp, angry exchange of whispers. He called out, "Let me in. This is Lukhele. Is Ngwenya there ? " But nobody answered, and at last he left and his two lodgers followed him out into the street. Suddenly he turned on them. " Have you got no friends ? "

" Yes."

" Then go to them. You're making it hard for me." They lingered and looked disappointed. " Go on. Go to your friends."

He watched them walk away and turn the corner. He stood and waited for a long time. Then an idea came to him. He hitched the blankets under his arm and he walked quickly towards New Look Location. He soon came to the neat streets and trim houses of the housing scheme and he knocked on the door of

Charles Ngubeni. The old chieftain peered at him in the darkness. Glad of a visitor at any time, Ngubeni invited him inside.

"I have come to ask you to help me, Chief," Lukhele said.

"If I am able, my son."

"You are the senior *induna*,[1] and Advisory Board Chairman, and it is to you I turn. I am in trouble."

"What do you want me to do?"

"All I want is that you let me sleep here to-night. To-morrow I'll decide what to do."

"Your name again?"

"Lukhele. I believe you knew my father well, Chief, and for his sake I am sure you will help me."

"Lukhele?" the old man frowned. "Lukhele. Is that your wife who got into trouble with the police and you who stoned the police?"

"That is my wife, but I didn't stone. All I did was to forget to call the policeman *baas*."

The old man got up and walked across the room, holding his hands behind his back. "Lukhele," he said, as if the name were a source of many memories. He gently massaged the skin under his chin. "So you want me to help you?" he said more to himself than to Lukhele. What is to be done with this? he was wondering.

"Yes. The police will come for me even though I did nothing. They will murder me."

"Murder you," the old chief repeated absently. "Murder you. I don't think they'll murder you, but I'm sorry for you, my son."

The old man tried to appear sympathetic, but his eyes had a vague and scheming look, and his words lacked all warmth.

"Then let me stay here."

"Why do you think they'll murder you? If you go quietly, they won't harm you. You're a little too excited, Lukhele."

"They will hold me responsible for the laundry and the stoning. Both. They will assault me, and quite possibly murder me. What is the matter? Don't you want me to stay here?" There was a sudden panic in his voice.

[1]Tribal headman.

83

Ngubeni rested his elbow on the shelf of the dresser and said, "Assault you," but it was an echo and the words had no meaning. Should the man be kept here and the police sent for? he was wondering. That would be one way. But who was there to send? And suppose the people found out? That would be the final finish of Charles Ngubeni. There was already too much talk mounting up and up. And suppose the police found him here before they could be informed? It would be impossible to explain.

"I have no extra beds in my house," Ngubeni said, looking away from Lukhele.

"Then I can sleep on the floor."

"It's too cold for the floor. See, it's stone and very cold. You'll become ill."

"I don't mind. Please, Chief."

"Then I'll be responsible for your illness. No, I cannot take the responsibility."

"You needn't take responsibility. I'll take it. Besides, I have blankets."

Ngubeni walked about the room again, pondering the problem. But Lukhele thought it was the problem of sleeping on the stone floor and he became exasperated that Ngubeni should make a difficulty of such a small thing.

"It's not important, the stone floor," Lukhele said, and he bent down and started to unroll the blankets. Ngubeni watched him for a moment, then became suddenly furious. He stepped forward and kicked the blankets away, sending them skidding across the room.

"I have no permit for lodgers," he said sharply. Lukhele looked up at him slowly, then wearily rolled up the blankets.

"You have made some fine speeches in your time, Chief," he said bitterly.

"You are a great Chief, Ngubeni," Lukhele said, getting to his feet. He stood with his blankets under his arm and his hand on the chair. "Where can I go?" he asked. Ngubeni gave no sign of having heard the question. Lukhele stood, reluctant to go. Ngubeni, with his elbow on the shelf, waited for him to go. There was no sound outside, but they both knew

84

that at any moment there would be the sound of cars and sirens, and the clatter of a raid. Lukhele stood, not thinking, but letting thoughts come to him, and after a while he realised that one name was going round and round in his mind. And whether it was to show Ngubeni that he didn't need him now, or whether it was the sense of relief that loosened his tongue, he said a foolish thing.

" I'm going to Mabaso's," he told Ngubeni.

Ngubeni stiffened. " Mabaso ? "

" Yes. Stay peaceful, Great Chief." And he went out.

Ngubeni watched him go, and when he heard the footsteps in the street, went and shut the door. " Mabaso," he said, and remained very thoughtful. That name again. With a faraway look in his eyes he unlaced his shoes and got ready for bed.

CHAPTER SIX

LUKHELE HURRIED back to Jubilee City and towards the house that had previously been pointed out to him as Mabaso's. As he walked, he thought about his wife Mary : he had tried to put together all the different accounts of the arrest, and although they varied greatly, they had one thing in common, that she had been injured.

He had intended to go to see her in the awaiting trial cells next morning, but now he knew that it was impossible. He had also intended to instruct a lawyer. Now he would have to make some other plans about that. Perhaps Mabaso would be able to fix it up. But should he instruct a lawyer ? Spend all that money ? Well, it was her money as much as his. But it was heartbreaking to spend the long-saved-up money on this. All their lives they had worked together, like two horses under one yoke, and now it was all gone, all in one night. What about himself ? Wouldn't he need a lawyer ? It was terrible. What had he done ? Nothing, except to forget to call the policeman *baas*. He had not thrown one stone. The others had done the stone-throwing, had even enjoyed it, but he had to pay for it with his own money. What was all this about the washing ? It was her crazy temper : he was sure about it. He knew it would get her into trouble one day. Was she badly damaged and did she perhaps need a doctor as well as a lawyer ?

He was about half a mile from Mabaso's house when he first heard the sirens. He heard them, faint and far off, and he stood and listened as the whine swelled louder. He could tell that there were two vehicles coming very fast on the road out from the town. He looked around wildly ; then ran into a lane and crouched down behind a refuse bin. He sat there for some

86

moments trying to decide what to do, but his heart was banging and he was flustered.

To reach Mabaso's house he had to cross the main street that ran through the location ; that was the same street that the police would come down on their way into the location. It's better not to try, he thought. But if he stayed there, they would find him for sure. A policeman would see him sitting out all alone in the dark, ask for his pass, see his name. Then. Caught like a flea in a comb.

He put the blankets around his legs and pulled them up to his chin. Then over his head. But he suddenly saw the futility of trying to hide under the blankets, and he got up and bundled the blankets under his arm and made a dash along the four blocks that separated him from the location main street. As he ran he heard the sirens grow louder on the road outside the location, louder then fainter as they went past up to the location gate ; then they faded right out. That meant they were turning into the gate. The sirens started up again and the cars were in the location and he found himself involved in an insane, desperate race to cross the street before the cars arrived. He made a last heart-bursting effort to reach the street, but the sirens were close by, loud now as the cars came down the street.

He finally reached the street, but the lights of the squad car caught him as he crossed, and as if the light were a hand on his shoulder, he stopped in the middle of the street, waiting, holding the blankets under his arm. He waited, blinking, as the car rushed up and skidded to a stop a few yards away.

" Hey, Kaffir, come here."

He heard nothing. He stood in the flood of light and from the car there was a sudden distorted view of the whites of his eyes as they caught the light like mirrors.

*   *   *

The raid had been late in starting that night. Lieutenant Swanepoel was away, and would only come back next morning, and the man in charge was Sergeant Ackerman, the senior sergeant. Ackerman heard the report about the arrest of Mary Lukhele and the five others and decided that the position was peculiar enough to leave to the lieutenant to handle the next morning. Ackerman was very nervous. He knew that whatever he did would be wrong. The lieutenant was always picking on him. Better to wait until the lieutenant comes back and let him handle it his own sweet way, he said. Better than taking the responsibility of going out and starting something out there to-night. It sounded ugly out there. Besides, there was the date with these girls, the hunting in this town was pretty damn' poor enough as it was, and to pass up an opportunity like that . . . They were new girls, down from Johannesburg.

One of the girls lived opposite the station and that was very convenient, for it meant that Ackerman was within call if really needed. He knew it was taking a chance, but it was a good opportunity, what with Swanepoel being away and the party taking place in a house right opposite the station. So, for one reason and another, he thought it better to leave it over until morning.

But later that night, just as the party was getting interesting, a constable came and called him over to the station, and there he heard from the jittery Sergeant Combrink about the stoning of the Beckets' car.

" We got to go out and fix these *donders*," Sergeant Combrink said.

" What, right now? " Ackerman asked.

" Yes. We got to fix them," Sergeant Combrink said. " We got to show them." Combrink was in a bad way. He didn't feel too good about letting himself be stoned out of the location. He wanted the Flying Squad to go back and put matters right for him.

" What use'll it do now ? " Ackerman asked.

" They attacked us. They all probably collecting there now in mobs, and you never know. They might take it into their heads to come here over the train line and attack the town. We got to fix them *now*."

This made the idea sound less attractive than ever to Sergeant Ackerman. " Shouldn't we get reinforcements from Withoek ? " he asked. But he imagined what Swanepoel would say if he got the whole bunch over from Withoek and it wasn't the emergency

88

that Combrink was making out. "No, can't do that without orders," he said. "Where do you think Lieutenant Swanepoel would be right now?"

"How do I know? On the train from Pretoria probably."

"Look, let's leave it till to-morrow, Karlie. Let's leave it till the lieutenant comes back. Honestly, Karlie, I'd rather do it that way. He'll be back to-morrow and the location will still be there to-morrow."

The girls had come across to the charge office and one was leaning with her elbows across Ackerman's shoulders, resting her head sideways on her hands.

"What if they come over the railway into town? What will the lieutenant say then? And we did nothing to stop it?"

"You think it's as serious as that?"

"Look, Ackerman, I was there. It's what I think. All right, if you don't want to go, you don't. You're in charge. But just remember it was I said we should fix the *donders* right here and now to-night."

"Who said I said I don't want to go? If you say it's that serious, we better go. I'm just trying to get the facts out of you, that's all." He turned to the girl. "Sorry, rabbit, we got to go on this raid."

"Aw, hell, take us with?"

"No. *Magtig*, no. You want to get us in trouble?"

"Hell, you said you'd take us on a raid, and now all of a sudden you change your mind."

"Did I? No, hell, that's impossible."

"Come on, Ackerman, we're wasting time."

"Just hang around here, rabbit. We won't be long. You just stick around. Promise?"

They brought out one of the lorries. Ten squad men with their rifles climbed in. Ackerman, the other two sergeants, and a constable climbed into Lieutenant Swanepoel's squad car. They started out, and on Ackerman's order blew the siren from the moment they left the station.

"What's the name of that one again?" Ackerman asked when they were out on the road.

"Lukhele."

" Address ? "

" 841 Springbok Street."

" Is that far inside ? "

" Why ? "

" Oh . . . Anyway, *you* know where it is." After a moment he asked, " You think any of them are armed ? "

" Maybe. I don't know."

" Is this Lukhele the only one you know who took part ? I mean didn't you get any other names ? "

" No." Then Combrink said, " I asked them all for names but they just didn't want to give it. I went up to one with my notebook and I said, ' Excuse me, before you throw that brick at Mr. Becket's Austin, would you mind letting me have your name ? "

" Aw, shut up."

They slowed down at the location gate, turned in, and drove along the location main street. All of a sudden they saw this crazy Kaffir standing right in the middle of the street holding a bundle.

" Hey, Kaffir. Come here," Ackerman bellowed through the window. He saw the scared white eyes and it reminded him of a picture of a ghost he had once seen.

" What the hell's that crazy baboon doing ? "

" Blocking up the traffic."

" Hey, Kaffir. You deaf ? *Come here*," he yelled. They saw Lukhele stand for a few seconds, then turn and run away. He dropped the blankets and ran like a startled guinea fowl, his body bent forward and his arms out, flapping like wings, and his feet pattering crazily on the road surface. For some absurd reason he ran along the centre of the street. They started the car and followed him in low gear, keeping the lights on him. " Hey, stop," Ackerman called. Lukhele ran on, and then Ackerman told the driver to pull up and gave a signal to a constable sitting in the back seat. The constable got out with his rifle and knelt beside the car. The first shot missed, but he was more careful with the second, taking his time and getting the line of the run well in the sights, and it broke Lukhele's spine just below the shoulder blades.

90

They drove up to the sprawled-out body and they all got out of the car and the constable turned the body on its back. Its eyes were open and it was not quite dead. The bullet, which had entered at a low, oblique angle, had come out below the neck and had split the chin, and the blood was just beginning to ooze out. They stood with their hands on their hips and looked, and the lorry came up, and the other men jumped over the side and joined the group around Lukhele's body. They just stood and looked and everyone waited for Ackerman, but for a while he didn't give any orders. Somehow this wasn't what they had expected. No mobs around, and this kind of killing, and right at the start of the raid ; it made them uncomfortable. Somehow it put the whole raid on a different footing. Ackerman swung round and faced Combrink.

" Well, the bastard run away, didn't he ? You saw that ? I called him to stop. You heard me, didn't you ? "

" Yes. That's true."

" Better see who he is. Look for his pass," Ackerman told the constable. He looked around at the dark houses. There was no sign of any life, but he knew that hundreds of eyes were watching through the black windows. It seemed all wrong, with the place so still, so full of echoes, and a man dead already. Well, the man run away, what could he do ? he asked himself.

The constable was on his knees going through the dead man's pockets. He found a black leather wallet with gold mounts on the corners ; it was fat with papers. He stood up and emptied them into his hand in the light of the car.

" Hmm. One of the rich ones," he said, holding up three five-pound notes.

" We watching you," one of the constables said.

" A bankbook."

" How much in it ? "

" Let me see. Jesus Christ. Three hundred and eighty-three pounds. *Jesus.*"

Ackerman whistled. " How much ? "

" Three hundred and eighty-three pounds, some change."

" Hell." They all turned and looked at the corpse of Lukhele and their eyes began to fill with respect.

" What else ? " Ackerman asked.

" Some pictures. Letters. Junk. Here's the pass. *Jesus.*"

" What's the matter ? "

" What did you say that name was ? "

" Lukhele, why ? "

" Well, this is him."

" Well, I'll be damned," Ackerman said. " Well, I'll be well and truly damned. You sure ? "

" Yes. Here, look for yourself. Same address."

" Well, I'll be absolutely absotruly buggered. We come to look for one, and the very first one we find, it turns out to be that very one. We-e-ell, no wonder he run away. Here, let me see those papers." He examined them for himself. " You right, it's him," he said, enormously relieved and very cheerful now.

" All right, *kêrels,*[1] back to the station," he said.

" To the station ? " Sergeant Combrink asked.

" Of course. We got the one we came for. Come on, *kêrels,* make it lively."

" You mean you're not going to make a raid ? Isn't that what we *came* for ? We going to go home now ? "

Sergeant Ackerman became suddenly exasperated, but took a hold on himself and stood still, thinking. The girls waiting at the station figured largely in his thoughts.

" I don't know. We can't just go round fixing them. It's all right when we're looking for someone, we've got an excuse. But we can't go round just beating everyone up. You know that. What would the lieutenant say ? "

" Can't we go and look for weapons ? "

Ackerman cursed quietly. The man was trailing him. They both knew that whatever he did would be wrong anyway, and the man was trying to get into a position where he could tell the lieutenant, " *I* wanted to raid, but he put up dozens of excuses."

" O.K., chaps," Ackerman said, trying to make it sound as if he had been in favour of it all the time. " Let's start. We'll divide into two details and remember, stick close together. Start with this street. One detail down each side."

[1] Fellows

"What about him?" the constable asked, pointing to the body of Lukhele.

"Put him on the side of the road. We'll take him to the mortuary when we come back."

The location was dark and desolate and it was like going into a captured town. The weird silence of houses full of watchful, wakeful people had an unnerving effect, and the details started out uncertainly. Suddenly there was a shrill *li-li-li-li-li* as the alarm was given by women in the nearest houses. It went off like an alarm clock, and was carried down the streets to all parts of the location, growing fainter as it travelled. They walked on, keeping close together, banging their rifle butts in unison on the ground to give themselves a feeling of solidarity. All had the shooting on their minds. They knew that the whole location had heard the shots, that many had seen the killing, and that by the special telegraph of these places the news was travelling from house to house, even though nobody could be seen in the streets. If they had gone as far as stoning a policeman earlier, they would be like a pack of wild dogs over this. Nobody liked it. It would have been different with Lieutenant Swanepoel who knew what to do, but Ackerman in charge only added to everyone's nervousness. Everyone could see that he didn't know his own mind. And it was so dark. If only there was a bit of moon so that they could see beyond the range of their flashlights.

Almost simultaneously the two details hammered on the first two doors. After a long pause the doors opened and the police went into the houses, stamping their feet, and the occupants came stumbling out to stand shivering in the street. They took a long time over the first houses, ransacking everywhere, but they found no weapons. They sent the occupants back, then turned out the houses next door. Again they found no weapons, but Ackerman found a smart new lady's coat in the wardrobe and, assuming it to be stolen, took possession of it and arrested the owner. After that they entered every second or third house. They collected some kitchen cutlery, some axes and some sticks, which could pass as dangerous weapons, and some clocks and teapots and blankets that might have been stolen property, and they rounded up about a dozen people whose papers were out

93

of order. They handcuffed them together and made them wait on a street corner while the raid went on, and as a new man was taken prisoner, he was brought back and locked on to the others. As the police left each house, they stove in a window with a rifle butt to mark the house as having been searched. But it was a halfhearted raid. None of them were in the mood. They could feel that there was something wrong, a kind of tension, and none of them wanted to stir things up. They asked for papers, examined them casually, overturned furniture, mainly because it was expected of them, but they were careful to leave a house whenever they felt that the feeling was rising too high.

They were not enjoying it, and after a time Ackerman was glad to see that the men had turned against Combrink and were with him. They started talking about getting through with it and going back to bed. At that point Ackerman would have had no trouble in calling off the raid.

But he thought, I'll show that bastard, and he decided to make a good long job of it. His night was ruined anyway.

They were near the end of the first street, and in the area of the yards, when he felt a violent thump on his shoulder. At first he thought it was a joke by one of his men, but then he saw an old rusted kitchen pot lying at his feet, and he knew he had been hit by that. "Who did that? Who did that?" he shouted in sudden panic, and swung his flashlight all around. It lit on walls and dustbins and old boxes and yard litter, and stirred up so many grotesque quivering shadows that it was impossible to distinguish anybody. While he was standing undecided and futilely waving the flashlight about, a stone hit one of his men. A moment later there was a sound of running footsteps. Two, maybe three, people were running away, somewhere out on his right. There were no proper streets here, only a maze of lanes and yards, and he did not have a plan of it in his mind, so he could not tell where they were running to. They all switched on their lights. Lights flashed and crossed everywhere, looking for the footsteps. Then a beam of light caught two figures just as they disappeared into a lane. They looked like young boys. Ackerman thought they were running toward Combrink's detail and he blew his whistle and yelled, "Combrink, catch those bastards."

"What the hell's happening?" Combrink called from a totally different direction.

Ackerman stopped, puzzled, then said to two of his men, "Go on—after them." They sprinted to the corner around which the boys had disappeared and Ackerman lit them up as they ran, but suddenly he heard footsteps running somewhere in the yard ahead of him. At the same time he heard Combrink's whistle in the yard behind. Through a gap in the houses he saw a cluster of lights. "Combrink, where the hell are you?" he shouted, and Combrink shouted back, "Here I am," but not from the direction of the lights. "Keep blowing your whistle," Ackerman shouted.

"Right. You do the same."

Ackerman tried to get his men out of the yard, blowing his whistle as he ran, but suddenly a fusillade of stones peppered them. They came in from all sides. They ducked down and ran, doubled forward; the whistle fell out of his mouth and dangled on its cord. When they had gone about twenty yards, they straightened up and he blew the whistle again, and a moment later stones came flying after them attracted by the whistle. He stopped blowing, and they all flattened against a wall. He could hear his two constables running down a nearby lane, and then change direction and run hard somewhere towards his left. "Have you caught the bastards?" he shouted. He took the men out to what he thought was the street, walking with the palms of their hands against the wall, but as they reached the end of the wall, there was a shot and a bullet whistled past him. He saw the lights again ahead, between a break in the walls, and thought it was Combrink's detail. But Combrink began blowing his whistle in the yard ahead. There were more footsteps and lights, and Ackerman realised he was running behind Combrink's detail. Another shot was fired, and then he heard one of his men screaming. He followed the lights, sure now that it was Combrink, and then he heard a sudden uproar of yelling and arguing.

He saw that one of the men who had chased the boys was lying on the ground wounded. The other was kneeling and supporting him under the armpits. Combrink was standing over him, looking guiltily into the muzzle of a revolver. " Hit in the thigh," one of the men told Ackerman as he came up.

" Hell, man, I'm sorry." Combrink was almost weeping. " I didn't know it was him. I didn't know you broke up your detail like that. I thought you were all over there." He pointed back over his shoulder. " You were shouting and blowing your whistle and I thought you were all together over there."

" Yes. You nearly killed me, too, you stupid arse," Ackerman said.

" Me ? Nearly killed you ? How come ? "

" Your first shot nearly killed me, that's all."

" My first shot ? " He stopped dead. " Was that you ? "

Ackerman shone the flashlight in his face, studied him, but said nothing.

" We better get this poor devil to hospital," he said. " Come on, chaps, carry him and go carefully." While they were lifting the wounded man, he said, " Are we all here ? " He counted the men. All were there. " Come on, let's get going."

They carried the wounded man back towards the vehicles, walking in a group around him, warily, with their guns ready. When they reached the car, they propped him in the back seat.

" A nice mess-up," Ackerman said to Combrink. " You fixed them, didn't you ? Oh yes, you certainly fixed them. All you fixed was poor old Kruger here. O.K., Karlie, you better start thinking. You got some explaining to do to the lieutenant to-morrow." They were about to drive off when a constable came to the car and said, " What about that dead Kaffir ? Shouldn't we get him to the mortuary ? "

" Oh God, yes. Load him on the lorry."

Some constables went to where they had left Lukhele, but they stood around, looking helpless, and after a few minutes one came back to the car.

" The body's gone. Somebody's taken it away."

" *What ?* "

" It's gone. Who the hell would want to take the body away ? "

" Let's get the hell out of here," Ackerman said.

96

They drove fast out of the location. They were almost back at the station when Combrink said, " You forgot one little thing in your excitement, Ackerman."

" Yes ? What's that ? " He didn't like the " *your* excitement."

" You left fifteen prisoners all nicely handcuffed standing in the street. That's all."

" Oh, my dear Jesus Christ, so I did."

" What the hell you going to tell the lieutenant about that ? " Ackerman didn't answer.

" You better go back and get them, that's what you better do. *I'm* not going. You better take a few men and go back."

Ackerman sat in heavy silence. After a while he said, " *I'm* not going either. They can kick me out of the police, but I won't go back in there to-night."

" This is the biggest balls-up of a raid I ever heard of," Combrink said.

CHAPTER SEVEN

MABASO WAS awake in bed when he heard the sirens and the shots that were fired at Lukhele. He got up and dressed and made his wife Leah and his fifteen-year-old son, Moses, do the same. He lit the lamp, but turned it very low and drew the curtains. He put on the heavy khaki overcoat that he had brought back from the war against Rommel and he buttoned the flap up under his chin. He put on the old black leather cap.

" You had better wait at Ndlovu's until we come back," he told his wife. And to his son he said, " Moses, you come with me."

Leah Mabaso went out first and ran along the street to the house of their neighbours, the Ndlovus. Walter Mabaso and his son came out and locked the door. They started walking briskly towards New Look.

" Where are we going, Father ? " Moses asked.

" First to Father Shongwe's," Mabaso said.

He was walking too fast and the boy had to run to keep at his side. He knew this trait of his father's. Whenever his mind went fast, his legs went fast too.

" What do you think the shots were, Father ? " Moses asked, out of breath.

" I wish I knew." The words had a faraway sound.

To reach the Reverend Shongwe's house they had to cross the main street, and they came within sound of the policemen's voices, but not near enough to hear what was said. They turned into a side street and turned again and walked in the shadows of a street that ran parallel to the main street. Then they heard the alarm for the raid, the high-pitched, throbbing *li-li-li-li-li* coming along the streets over the rooftops, like the cry of a supernatural messenger, and they stopped and pressed their backs to a wall. They noticed the wake of stillness that followed the alarm, the shutting of the last doors and the putting out of the last lights. They stood in the dark listening to hear which way the raid would go. Then the heavy wood and metal clunk of the rifle butts hitting the hard ground, the hammering on doors, the clatter and the voices told them, and they moved on again, walking stealthily towards Shongwe's house.

They came out to the main street again about a hundred yards ahead of the Flying Squad vehicles, and were about to cross when they heard grunts and the shuffle of feet coming towards them. They peered into the dark and saw a tangle of vague black shapes moving along close to the walls of the houses. It looked like one object, a sagging, misshapen animal with five legs. They waited behind the wall and it came past and they saw that it was a number of men carrying a body.

Mabaso recognised the face of one of the men in front. It was Charlie Nkambula, a fanatical street-corner evangelist. It took Mabaso a moment to realise that they were carrying a dead man. He let them pass, and hissed after them, " Charlie, who are you carrying ? " All four of the party turned, alarmed, then started running out of step and lugging the body. Mabaso came out to the pavement and ran a few steps, then stopped and watched them disappear into the dark. He saw black gleaming spots on the ground. He bent down and touched one and fresh blood wet his finger. Moses came and stood beside him.

" Why are they taking away the body, Father ? "

" I don't know." He stayed kneeling on one knee, thinking hard. After a moment he said, " What lunacy is this ? "

" Father, what is wrong with their taking the body ? Perhaps they are his friends."

" The police will want the body. There'll be trouble over this," he said. He looked up and asked, "That was Charlie the Preacher, wasn't it ? Did you recognise him ? "

" Yes. It was him all right, Father."

Mabaso stood up and they walked on. Who was shot ? he wondered. He could hear the sound of the raid far over to his left, the glass breaking on the ground, the silences when the

99

police went into a house, the sudden eruptions of noise when they came out. It felt safe from the police here, but they were the only people in the hushed, deserted streets and they walked noiselessly and talked in whispers.

"Why must the police have the body? If they shot the man, isn't that enough?" Moses asked.

"You're full of questions to-night. The body is evidence. They want it for the mortuary. To make a report. They like to keep charge of the evidence."

So—Charlie the Preacher, he thought. Charlie on another of his gruesome midnight expeditions. Becoming blood-mad again and raiding for corpses. But now right under the noses of the police. What was this going to lead to?

They walked on. Mabaso saw that Moses did not understand about the body being evidence, but he did not try to explain it further. He was listening to the raid noises, waiting nervously for some noise above the noise that would mean another incident. He wondered how many more events would pile up to-night. There was a strange brooding uncertainty in the air, a feeling that seeped into it from the locked-up silent fury in all the houses. The air seemed to be ready to materialise into shapes, to change its qualities, to produce live terrible things. It had become unfamiliar—unpredictable and foreign—a hostile substance. It felt strange, this consciousness of the air. For some reason he began to think of flying ants: how they wait for the moment when the ground is a certain warmth and wetness, and the air a certain humidity, and the wind the right strength and direction, and they come streaming out of the earth everywhere, all at one moment. What was there about that moment? he wondered.

Do we really know what is happening to us and why we do things? he asked himself for the hundredth time. Is this location only a great ants' nest, with everybody running around attending to his own affairs and thinking his own thoughts, but really just moving to a pattern? Just responding to the pressure of the air? As sand dunes shape themselves to the wind? A *great* ants' nest? Well, a tiny ants' nest, a minute, frantic little burrowed hole in the ground invisible from a few feet away? How big are we?

"Father, what is the matter with us?" Moses was asking.

"The matter with us? Why do you ask?"

"Father, how does it happen that the police come into everybody's houses with guns, and break things, and arrest them for nothing, and shoot people in the streets? What is the matter with us that we allow it to happen?"

Mabaso did not answer at once. The question ran through him like a sword. He saw in this childlike, unerring question all the sad history still to come. Why did we allow it to happen? And when will we stop allowing it? How much more pain and peril and bitter sacrifice is it going to take before these things could be ended? It would be this boy, boys like him who would take the brunt of it in the coming struggle, for that was how the timing was working out. But why, oh why? Did the world have no other use for this sweet brave boy than that of fighting and savage suffering?

He ran his hand over the boy's head. The prickly feel of the stiff springy hair sent a thrill of pleasure along his arm.

"There's nothing the matter with us, my son. Get that idea out of your head. All that's wrong is that when we fought for this country we had only *assegais*[1] while they had guns. And we had made war on ourselves, had bled each other, so that when *they* came we were too divided and weakened to withstand them. Now we must suffer for it. We are a conquered people—and not the first. But remember—although they conquered us, they never destroyed us. We are still here and we still outnumber them greatly.

"Is guns the answer, Father?"

"Perhaps. Perhaps one day it will have to be the answer. But meantime we have no guns and must try to find other answers. But there's one thing we must do now."

"What is that, Father?"

"Stop being so simple and trusting and so easily bamboozled. We fall for every trick they play on us—and go on doing it time after time. One other thing."

"What, Father?"

"*We* are at the heart of the answer. Whether or not there will be one depends on us. On everything we do, every minute

[1]Spears.

101

of the day. On what we become now, in this time, while there is no clear answer. If we let ourselves be crushed now, there will be no answer."

He walked a little way in silence with his hands deep in his pockets. Why was it so easy to explain now, when it had always seemed so difficult?

"Father, how much longer will it last?"

"I don't know. Nobody knows. But I believe you will see the end of it."

"And you?"

"I don't know."

He wondered about the end of it. The littered battlefield. The prodigious reconstruction. And if it came in his time, what part would there be for him. Would it not need other types of men: engineers, administrators, educators? Would not the embattled, scarred, exhausted men find themselves aliens in the world they had created?

"Father, why are the police always fighting us? Why do they make trouble over every little thing?"

"They're afraid, Moses."

"Afraid? With their guns and everything? We don't want to attack them. We just want to be left alone in peace."

"They're afraid of their thoughts, Moses. Afraid of ghosts. They can't sleep for the things they're afraid of."

"Then they are unhappy too?"

"Yes."

"I'm glad to hear that."

"They lead unhappy, cruel lives, in many ways worse than ours. There are many warm, simple things in this location that they never have. Their hate poisons their lives. Oh, they eat well and keep warm, but I don't envy them their lives." He looked down and he realised that he was feeling an embarrassment towards the boy that was entirely new to him. He walked with his eyes fixed on the ground and tried to understand this disturbance.

"Father, do all the white people hate us?"

"No. We have friends among them. And we get more every

102

day. As we stand up for ourselves we win their respect, and more and more come on our side. But you must know that the majority still hate us, and that many who don't actually hate us only withhold their hate on condition we stay poor and obedient."

They were near the Reverend Shongwe's house now. As the sounds of the raid receded behind them, they walked more slowly and became absorbed in the conversation. Mabaso was conscious of something more than words and ideas passing between them. This was a strange night. The slow chemistry that had been at work in the location was now about to take sudden effect. Substances produced by Du Toit's tyranny, which had lain inert and impotent, were now stirring. There was a ferment, and the boy was in it too. He was full of questions. In these strange circumstances—a deserted location street near midnight in the middle of a raid—his mind had suddenly filled and he was asking the important questions. And Mabaso felt a sudden pang of desolation and loneliness, for he knew that a part of his life had ended. It had ended that night, right then, when the old inquisitive playful questions gave way to the new serious questions.

"Father, why did they make us black ? "

He gave Moses a playful smack on the head. " Don't worry about that. It's a wonderful colour. It's a rich, beautiful colour. We are full of the sunshine."

He said it for the boy, because the boy needed it, but it struck him as an odd, sentimental thing to say.

*   *   *

They knocked softly on the door and the Reverend Shongwe let them in. He was still dressed. He closed the door with one hand, and they saw the Bible in his other hand, and his great bony knuckle held between the pages.

The room was steaming-hot : the coal stove had a dull red-hot spot on top and the windows were steamed over. Mabaso screwed up his eyes to get used to the light, and he saw the empty chair beside a paraffin lamp, and then, in the shadows, Mrs. Shongwe sitting motionless and silent with her hands on her lap. He looked from the Bible to the empty chair, to the upturned spectacles lying beside the lamp, and then into the Reverend Shongwe's drawn, bloodshot eyes.

"I can see you are worried, Father," he said, taking off his coat.

"Yes," the Reverend Shongwe said, as if ashamed of it. He fetched two chairs from the bedroom and set them down with a gaunt, angular movement of his long arms. "I'm glad you came, Nkosi," he said, in his deep, round voice, using the friendly, respectful patronym, as he always did with Mabaso. "I half expected that you would." His voice, like the tall, bent man himself, was too large for the tiny room.

"Father, I'm worried too. When the raid is over, I think we should call the others together."

"I was thinking the same thing."

They did not sit down. They spoke standing against the backs of the chairs and staring at the glow on the stove, and the red perspiration glistened on their faces.

"I wish it were over. I wish they'd go home and leave us alone," the Reverend Shongwe said. And Mrs. Shongwe said from her chair in the dark, "We feel terribly uneasy to-night. What's going to happen, Nkosi?"

"I hope it will calm down, Mother."

They tailed off into silence. They could feel the raid like a vague physical ache, even though it was too far away to be heard. They listened to the silence, and then they realised that there was no silence at all, and that the air was full of the furore of insects and faraway barking dogs and innumerable stirrings, and that it beat on their ears like a surf.

"What's the matter, Nkosi?" the Reverend Shongwe asked with sudden violence. "What's happening to-night? In all my time here I've never known the people to be like this."

"They're very excited."

"But stoning the police, and this business of getting themselves arrested as a protest, and the way they collect in huge crowds over the slightest thing. And the wild things they're saying. There have been arrests and raids before, but they've never reacted like this before."

"There comes a breaking point, Father."

A breaking-out point, he thought, tightening his fists around the knobs of the chair. The weather, the wind. Was it this? No. Something felt wrong. There was some deep uneasiness, a foreboding.

"Father, don't get a shock. They killed a man earlier. Did you hear those shots when they first came in the location? Well, they killed a man."

The Reverend Shongwe stared down at the table, and without turning his head, asked, "Who was it?"

"I don't know. But it's going to burst over the location when the raid's over."

"How do you know they killed someone?"

"I saw the body. But it was taken away by Charlie Nkambula and his crowd, and they ran off before I could see who it was."

The Reverend Shongwe walked to the window. He absently drew on the steamed-over glass. Suddenly he swung around.

"What's the matter with him? Is he some kind of hyena? Why does he do these things?"

"Please keep calm, Father. We need to keep our heads to-night."

"I'm sorry. What is this going to mean?" he asked with a vague, distracted movement of his hands.

"I'm sorry too. I didn't mean to jump at you."

"What will it mean?"

"It'll mean another raid when this one is over. A new kind of raid—not for liquor or passes or weapons, but for a corpse. They'll want the body. They'll take the stealing of it as some kind of defiance or insult."

At that moment a shot rang out, sharp and clear in the cold night sky and with a hard, reverberating echo. They both stiffened and the Reverend Shongwe took a deep breath. They listened without moving and then they heard the second shot, and a moment later, faintly and far away, the screams of a wounded man.

"Oh, dear God," the Reverend Shongwe said, and he sank into a chair.

Mabaso opened the door and looked up and down the street. There was a growing murmur of voices coming from the area of the raid. He stood for several minutes with his eyes straining into the dark, as if trying to see the growling uproar that was coming slowly over the rooftops. There were the sounds of people running, and suddenly a boy on a bicycle came into the street, riding furiously and ringing his bell.

"They killed a policeman, they killed a policeman," he screamed, scattering the news left and right. And then doors opened and the people poured out into the streets.

"Who killed a policeman?" they shouted after the boy.

"How was he killed?"

They stood with their hands on their hips asking each other the same questions, their breath turning to vapour in the frosty air.

"Go back inside," a tall man said, opening his arms out and sweeping a group of people back towards the pavement. "They're going to come and shoot us up now. Go back." There was a panicky rush back indoors, but a moment later people came running in from the adjoining streets ; among them was a small boy shouting :

"They shot him. It's that big one who looks like a horse."

"Who shot him?" people called from their doorsteps.

"It's that one with the face of a horse."

Mabaso watched with a frown. This puzzled him. If a policeman had been shot, why were the police not retaliating, starting at the place of the shooting, driving everyone indoors and sending a wave of quiet over the location? Where was the alarm? He stood and watched until he heard the sirens leaving the location. Then he went back inside.

"There's some funny affair going on," he told the Reverend Shongwe. He turned to the boy. "Moses, go to Dhladla's and ask him to go round in his taxi and fetch Elliot Nkomo and Paul Vilakazi and Sibande and the others and bring them straight here." He stopped and stood for a moment with his chin in his hands. "No," he said. "Tell them to be here in half an hour." He turned to Father Shongwe. "I'm going out to see what's happened. Would you like to come with me?" He paused again. "No, perhaps not."

"No, Nkosi," the Reverend Shongwe said. "I don't think

so. Du Toit is beginning to ask questions. He doesn't suspect me yet, but he's watching you."

"I don't see how we can keep it hidden much longer. But you're right about not being seen with me." He turned to Moses again. "Moses, first go and fetch Sibande and bring him here. I'll go with him."

*   *   *

Mabaso and Saul Sibande walked side by side through the seething streets. Frequently they met people who gave them the salute, and each responded in his particular style—Mabaso with a close-to-the-chest confidential salute and Sibande with an ear-high enthusiastic thumb-wagging salute. It struck Mabaso that they were getting the thumbs-up from a large number of people that night, from many who had never previously given it, and he noticed how eyes followed them wherever they went. And the old habit of the children who walked behind them saying, " Afrika," not in the form of a greeting but calling them by that name, seemed to be more pronounced that night. It is curious, he thought, how the children no longer think of " Afrika " as a country, but as the name of the movement and the people in it.

They looked a strange pair walking together : Mabaso in the sailor's cap and soldier's coat and Sibande in a Balaclava helmet and a check coat too tight for his chest but hanging down to his boots : both men equally broad and padded-looking, but one towering above the heads and the other lost in them, so that the thumbs saluted from the same level. And Mabaso silent and thoughtful, and Sibande greeting everyone and getting into eager conversation, and picking up information in one group and off-loading it again at the next in exchange for new information.

He is too excited, Mabaso told himself.

With Sibande bobbing and talking at his side, Mabaso walked in silence, listening and watching carefully. There was a confused and changeable mood in the streets, a mixture of many moods. Mabaso walked with his ear bent towards the faces in the crowd, as if testing the mood on his cheek like the heat of an iron.

It was a night of incredible events that amazed and stirred the location as nothing before had done. The realisation of all that had happened did not come at one time : it came over the location in waves, each adding something to the total amazing truth. And the location was helpless, as if in a gale, as one after another of the happenings made their impact.

The crowd seemed to form a stream that flowed in one direction, and Mabaso and Sibande allowed themselves to be carried along, and then they found themselves in the street where the abandoned prisoners were standing. The truth about the prisoners was the first to be realised, because they could be seen by everyone. The crowd milled around them. Mabaso and Sibande pushed their way through and saw the prisoners, who looked lost and somehow ashamed at having been left behind. An argument was going on.

" Are they still prisoners ? " a man asked.

" Yes, they are handcuffed. Therefore they are still prisoners."

" No, the police threw them away. They are like old clothes a man throws away. Anybody's property, but not that of the man."

Still, nobody knew what to do with fifteen people locked together by their wrists. While the crowd argued, the cast-off prisoners shivered and listened anxiously for the whine of the sirens, for everybody believed that the police would soon return for them.

" Get us loose," bellowed a man in the centre of the prisoners.

" They are still prisoners," a man insisted. " Suppose they had been locked in the cells but the police went away with the keys ? Wouldn't they still be prisoners ? "

" What difference does it make ? Get us loose."

The prisoners were beginning to freeze. Their teeth were chattering and their noses watering, and when a man raised his hand to wipe his nose, he had to pull the strange hand of his neighbour up with it.

" Where can we keep them ? "

" Let's take them to the church hall and get them some blankets."

" But how long can they stay chained up like this ? "

The crowd had closed in around the prisoners, pressing them tightly into each other's sides. There was a vast noise over their heads. The hemming in made the prisoners frightened and restless.

"Instead of all arguing here, why don't you get some tools?" a woman yelled above the voices. She was standing next to one of the prisoners, holding his imprisoned hand.

"She's right. Who can do this?"

"Cindi. Where's Cindi?" They stood on their toes and peered around, but Cindi was not in the crowd.

"Someone go and wake up Cindi."

"No," one of the prisoners said. "Let us go to Cindi. Let us get away from here."

Cindi the blacksmith lived a dozen blocks away; his smithy was at the back of his house. The prisoners pushed their way out of the crowd until they made a line, hand to hand, across the street. The crowd formed up ahead of and behind them, and a shapeless, unwieldy column began to move slowly, like a tide of lava, along the narrow street. A woman started to sing a hymn, "Lizalisi Dinga Lakho [We Go to Our Destiny]," and other voices came in, and a rich, dark sound swelled up into the night. For a while the measured, lusty singing was the dominant sound in the location. A defiant note came into the singing, and the tempo changed and the crowd fell into step. The hymn became a marching song. They were going to smash the handcuffs; the location was marching, as if in a dream, to strike off its shackles.

Sibande became suddenly restless and started to push through the people marching ahead of him. He wanted to be at the head of the column. Mabaso pulled him back, and walked on without looking at him, in step with the music. Sibande swung round to face him.

"What's the matter? What's the matter with you to-night?"

"Just stay in the crowd. They will do it all right without us."

"Are we against this? Make it clear. Are we against freeing the prisoners?"

"No. It's right to free them. But hold back for a while."

The music took hold of the crowd and led it along the streets to Cindi's place, and the crowd submitted to the rhythm of the song and marching; and these were the best moments of the night, for the crowd surrendered all its sorrows to the warm stream of music, and was left free to enjoy its dream of freedom.

After a while the marching stopped, and the singing was broken up by a burst of shouting from the people at the head of the column. Cindi was there and was opening his smithy. The crowd pressed around Cindi's house and there was another shout as the first handcuffs were broken. It took very little time to force the handcuffs. There were the sounds of hammering followed by the tinkle of chains falling on the ground, and the release of each prisoner sent another roar into the sky. And then it was over and the prisoners joined the crowd, and the jubilant crowd streamed back again into the other location streets.

Sibande and Mabaso walked among the excited people. It was like one of those midnight carnivals that take place in foreign countries. There was noise and milling about and everywhere eager, excited faces. The excitement went on by its momentum. Then there came a curious heightening in the mood ; Mabaso noticed it all around him. Now the truth about the farcical raid with its glorious ending of the police shooting each other was being slowly put together out of the rumours and scraps of eye-witness evidence. He saw how nobody would accept it at first. The truth seemed like the wildest of the rumours. And then he saw the dawning of a strange astonishment when the truth was no longer in doubt.

" It's an omen. It's the light in the sky," the witch doctors were saying.

This, coming on top of the freeing of the prisoners, caused a kind of giddy intoxication all over the location. If such things could happen, anything could happen. Miracles could happen and perhaps the long winter's night would end. Perhaps time would go back and Du Toit would leave and Brits return. Perhaps similar happenings were taking place all over the country. Would to-morrow be the new day ? Somehow the idea took root that the five people who had offered themselves for arrest were responsible for it all. Their sacrifice had made it possible : their strange but noble act had recruited mystical forces on behalf of the location, and had won this first and immediate reward. The coming of great changes seemed to be guaranteed by the support of supernatural agencies.

"It's very sad," Mabaso said to Sibande.

"What is ? "

"This talk of magical changes."

"Is it ? " Sibande said.

"It is sad in the way a hungry man dreaming of a meal is sad," he told Sibande. But he saw that Sibande did not listen or did not understand.

He stopped and watched while Sibande spoke to a group of men. There was a good feeling between the men and Sibande. Mabaso recognised some of them as Sibande's supporters in the railway sheds.

"It was the best thing that ever happened in this location," Sibande told them.

"But only one was shot," a man replied. "That was a pity. How much better if one police detail had completely shot up the other."

"Oh yes. That would have been beautiful."

"Was he killed ? " another man asked.

"No," Sibande said. "I hear he was only wounded. People who saw him being put into the car say he was still groaning."

"Perhaps he will die on the way back," the man said hopefully.

"You never know," Sibande said.

"Shooting themselves and throwing away their prisoners. Have the police come over to our side ? " another man asked.

"Perhaps they'll open the doors of the gaol to-morrow and let everyone out," Sibande said.

"Yes. Perhaps there'll be some wonderful reunions to-morrow."

Mabaso took Sibande's arm and led him away. Sibande must stop this, Mabaso said to himself. It worried him how to deal with Sibande. We need Sibande to-night, he thought, but he is going to be a big nuisance if he carries on like this.

They walked on, and Mabaso noticed the tendency of people to try to get themselves into the farcical raid in any possible way.

" My brother was among the youngsters who threw rubbish at them," a girl said.

" I know that one who was shot. He once arrested me for a pass," a man said, grinning.

The freeing of the prisoners and the comical raid were being treated as a victory by the location. And as it had been a long time since there were any victories, the location people were tasting the full joy of a triumph against the white people, and especially the white police.

" Nkosi, can't we think of a way of starting some more of these police-destroying raids ? " Sibande asked. " It will be very useful to us, you realise that ? " Mabaso did not answer.

After a while there came a subtle drop in the mood, a cooling. Mabaso could feel it, but at first he could not explain it. Then he began to see the reason in scraps of conversation and in the places where people suddenly stopped grinning and became silent and serious. The white town was still over there, sleeping, but soon to awake. There would be no to-morrow. Everybody knew it and hated knowing it and so did not mention it, but it hung over them in the way that approaching soberness and to-morrow's work hangs over a drunk man. The victory was not real. It would not last, and would be over by the morning. There was the old sour taste of disappointment, the taste of everything in the location.

Sibande stopped and joined a group listening to a talkative old man.

" They will come back," the old man said. " Mark my words, they will come back. And they will hold us responsible for their own shooting. We will be to blame for allowing them to shoot one another."

" Then maybe it will happen again. Maybe this time they'll destroy two policemen, or four," Sibande said, winning gleeful support from the crowd and turning it against the discouraging old man. Mabaso took Sibande by the arm and pulled him away. He is enjoying this too much, Mabaso said to himself. This desire to be with the crowd is Sibande's weakness. At the moment he is just a part of the crowd, not a leader ; just floating about in the crowd like a leaf on the stream. The trouble is that he is too shallow : he has the potential for leading, for people follow him, but he is too anxious to be popular. We must keep a firm hand on Sibande.

" Sibande, don't say these things."

" Why, Nkosi ? What's wrong ? "

" Sibande, it's wrong to go around stirring people up. You, in your position. It's important to calm the people to-night."

" Is it wrong for them to enjoy this ? Do you want me to talk like that old man ? "

" Yes. That's what we must do."

Sibande did not answer. He seemed to be offended. He walked sulkily beside Mabaso with his hands in his pockets. His bright little eyes looked everywhere, hungry for gossip, but he restrained himself and the brown woollen peak of his Balaclava helmet now went straight on, like a fin, among the heads of the people.

" They murdered Lukhele," they both heard a man say. They stopped, and were conscious of a drop in the noise all around them. Then they heard everyone saying it.

Mabaso had wondered why nobody seemed to know about the killing. The people living in the main street must have seen a man fall, but Mabaso concluded that they must have failed to notice the body being removed. Probably their eyes were all on the police starting the raid. And they must have thought that the man had got up and run away, and that he had been only slightly wounded. A wounded man was interesting, but it was not big enough to supplant the farcical raid and the freeing of the prisoners.

But now suddenly, as if released by a signal, as if dropped from the skies, the news of the killing had descended on the streets. It had come down everywhere at one time, and it was the full story, complete with the man's name and correct in all but one detail : how Lukhele was shot in the back while running away ; how the police ransacked his pockets and showed interest in his money ; how the bullet came out through his mouth. The one detail concerned the disappearance of the body. According to the story, it had vanished into the air.

" Who is this Lukhele ? Don't we know that name ? "
Mabaso asked.

" Yes. He has been to one of our meetings. He was beginning to show interest in us."

Eveybody was talking about Lukhele.

" Was he the husband of that woman ? "

" Yes."

" That same washwoman whom they assaulted and knocked
out, and who caused those people to volunteer for the
handcuffs ? "

" Yes. That same one. The bullet went through his body
and came out of his mouth."

" Husband and wife, are you sure ? "

" Yes, it's whole families now."

The news of Lukhele's death completely cancelled out the
raid. It gave the police a killing in exchange for a wounding,
and so turned the tables on the location. And it caused a wave
of cold frustration, a hard anger at being cheated out of the raid,
to spread through the streets. The heady excitement was still
there, but it had taken on an ominous note, and now it was
ready to be turned into new, dangerous directions.

Mabaso knew from the sensational manner of its release and
from the story about the body being spirited away that Charlie
the Preacher had launched the news. He had set it off like a
cracker in the streets, in the harebrained spectacular way that
was typical of Charlie. And Mabaso knew that somewhere in
the streets Charlie and his crowd were going around whipping
up the excitement. Mabaso looked for him, anxious to catch up
with him and stop him. But Charlie seemed to be dodging him.
Mabaso kept coming to groups which Charlie had just left ;
everywhere he could see the results of Charlie's insane work.

" Oh, I can see many new volunteers coming forward
to-night."

" Yes, it is time for more volunteers."

" I will volunteer—for anything."

" Let us volunteer for killing police and burning buildings."

" Yes, and for crossing the railway line."

" Yes, let's go into town."

114

People stood in groups discussing reckless schemes of vengeance and murder. Mabaso heard the loud, bragging voices and saw how the location desperadoes, the riffraff, and the loafers were enchanting the crowds ; how the decent people watched them, nodding their heads, fascinated.

But the groups did not move off; some instinct held them back. The schemes were too foreign, too new, and some last hesitation kept a hand on the shoulders of the crowd. And as if in an effort to overcome the last remaining inertia, there came a new note of desperation.

" Let us slit their throats."

" Let's see the blood run. Let's see if their blood looks any different from ours."

And here and there one could see knives held limply, fondly, while the bloodthirsty talk went on.

Mabaso saw and heard it all, with his nerves taut, his mouth dry, as if he were watching a child climb along a window ledge. He saw that it needed only an incident, some small encouragement, to tip the balance and turn the crowd into a mob. He cursed Charlie and all the lunatics who were stirring up the people. And he had a panicky feeling that he had left it too late, and let it grow too big, and that now it would be impossible to control it.

" It's very peculiar about the body," he heard people say.

" How could it disappear ? "

" Well, it did. They didn't take it away, and if he was in the location, somebody would have seen him."

" Well, what does it mean ? "

" What does it mean ? How do I know ? "

" Can it mean . . . ? "

It was a presposterous idea and nobody would dare say it. Could it possibly have befallen a grocer's deliveryman in Nelstroom Location, here, to-night ? It was too much to believe, but it brought back the idea of miraculous happenings. It added a wayward and uncontrollable impulsiveness to the crowd's mood, laid it open to dark, violent suggestions. Mabaso saw it in the hysteria with which women discussed it and in the way the talk swung from the miraculous disappearance to fresh extravagances

115

of revenge, and in the bemused, lost faces of those who listened to the desperate men who were taking control of the location.

The *tsotsi* gangs formed up again. And in the yards the sounds of dancing started, drums and whistles and stamping feet, sounds that used to mean enjoyment but that now filled the night with a harsh, throbbing beat, the echo of ancient wars. There were strange old chants in praise of legendary warriors and great tribal deeds. Quarrels started, and the gangs strode through the streets like caged animals and the children clung terrified to their mothers' legs. For a while the location turned its violence in on itself and it seethed inside its barbed-wire enclosure like a churning lake.

There was no accounting for this violent and instant response to Lukhele's death. The location had suffered many cruelties before and had always taken them with bitter and silent resignation. But nothing was the same in the location on this night. This was a night out of the calendar, a night out of the world. On this black, moonless night everything was enlarged, inflamed, and monstrously responsive, everything was important and effective, nothing was lost and no moments were wasted. The night had its own turbulent laws, unlike any other night.

" You see, Sibande. You see what I mean ? "

" Yes, Nkosi, I see. We've got to stop it. But how ? They won't listen to us."

" We must try, that's all."

" But they'll turn away from us. All our work will be lost. They'll think we're Du Toit's good boys."

" Well, we must risk it. A lot falls on you, Sibande."

" On me ? " Sibande looked worried.

" Yes, on you. You're the most popular among us. And you have all those fellows from the railway sheds with you. We need a solid block of support to-night. You can swing a large number on to our side."

This pleased Sibande a little, and he smiled, but after a moment the smile went away and he walked lost in thought. They walked very fast now, back towards the Reverend Shongwe's house and the meeting.

As they walked, it occurred to Mabaso that he had not seen

any of Du Toit's municipal constables out in the streets. Surely this was the time for Isaac Gwagwa and his men to be among the crowds, keeping order so as to win good marks for themselves with Du Toit. But there was no sign of the blue suits. No doubt they are doing their duty somewhere else, he thought. No doubt by staying indoors they are doing the duty of preventing the crowd from throwing municipal constables into the river. Nor were any of the great leaders to be seen—Ngubeni, Malooy, and the rest of the good boys. No doubt they were also doing their duty somewhere. Observing through windows, perhaps, and preparing a report on the whole affair, to hand to Du Toit in the morning. Maybe drawing up resolutions condemning it, to be passed by the Advisory Board at the next meeting.

As they walked, Mabaso saw how everyone looked at them and saluted them. How warmly they were received, as if it were assumed that they were going to lead the crowd in storming the town. How badly we must have worked, he thought. Is that what they look to us for ? To lead mobs ? How could they have misunderstood us so ? Perhaps we didn't make ourselves sufficiently clear. Well, that is possible because we weren't always clear even among ourselves.

No, we didn't work badly, he decided. There just wasn't enough time, that's all. If only it had come in six months' time. Or a year's time. No, there's never enough time. One is never ready.

Well, let's hope we can still do it. Nkomo will be good— he'll work like a mule : he'll enlist that section, teachers and clerks and so on. Shongwe will be good, very good, and with a wide general section—church people, the older people. However, those sections are not the trouble really. The labourers, the miners, the factory workers, they're the ones. That's why it hangs on Sibande. It won't be easy for him. It's not his style to calm people down : all his success is due to stirring them up. He won't like it. We must watch Sibande to-night. Dhladla ? Hopeless. An armchair Mau Mau. Assassinates them around the braziers, kills them off in thousands from the seat of his taxi, but he'll hang back to-night, scared stiff, neither with us nor with the crowd. Better use him as always, for the transport. Mavuso ?

117

Good, but too old and sick, and his voice too weak. Vilakazi?
A good youngster. The best youngster, but not very confident
yet. Perhaps to-night will bring Vilakazi out.

And me? Mabaso asked himself. I wish I knew. There's
been nothing for me yet, and they don't know me. And perhaps
they don't trust me. I come from Johannesburg, and am a big-
town boy, and possibly give the impression of being too slick
and scheming. And this hole-in-the-corner work has been no
good. It has kept our hands tied, our work too small, and that
is possibly why we are being misunderstood to-night.

They reached the Reverend Shongwe's house and they saw
Dhladla's taxi outside. And inside, Father Shongwe, Elliot
Nkomo, Mavuso, and Vilakazi were standing up, waiting.

CHAPTER EIGHT

"THERE'S NO time now. We must start," Mabaso said.

"But I'd like to discuss it a bit, Nkosi," Dhladla said.

"Dhladla, sometimes you've got to make up your mind. The trouble with you is you discuss it too much and never decide."

"Still, it doesn't look so clear to me to-night."

"There's no time, Dhladla."

"Well—I don't know."

"Why don't we hire the church hall and let old Dhladla have a debate about it with the *tsotsis*?" Elliot asked bitterly.

"Stop it, Elliot. We haven't time for that, either. Dhladla, if you can't make up your mind, you'd better hold back. Don't get under our feet, that's all. And keep your taxi ready: we might need it."

"No, it's all right. I don't want to hold back. Only I thought——"

"Leave it, Dhladla."

Mabaso turned to the Reverend Shongwe: "Father, the sooner you start, the better. The church people, the responsible and older people—that's your section. And keep in touch with us."

"Right, Nkosi, I'll leave now. Is it all right if Moses comes with me? I might want to send you a message."

"Yes, that's fine. Go in peace, you two."

"Stay in peace." Father Shongwe went out with Moses. When the door was closed again, Mabaso asked Vilakazi, "How soon can you get your boys together?"

"Mtembu and Makhoti have started already. There'll be a bunch of chaps waiting at the Welfare Centre. How many will turn up, though, I don't know."

" Good. But go careful with the *tsotsis*. Don't get into any fights."

" But how must we handle the *tsotsis* ? "

" The regular *tsotsis* you won't be able to do anything with. But keep as many youngsters as you can from joining them. Try and isolate the *tsotsis*. Don't fight. Keep all your boys together. And don't go into lonely places."

" You know, it strikes me that I ought to go along with Vilakazi," Sibande said.

" No, Sibande, you'll come with me."

" Don't you think Vilakazi a bit young for this work ? Don't you think he ought to have an older head along with him ? " Sibande asked.

" No, Sibande. Vilakazi and his boys are all right. Mavuso, how many of the mine fellows can you count on ? "

" About ten."

" Good. Now don't forget, if you start coughing, pack up and go home to bed."

" I won't go home to-night, Nkosi."

" Yes, if you start coughing. It's the old decision."

" Nkosi, you did say to Dhladla he could hold back if he wanted to ? " Sibande asked.

" Yes, I did. But it doesn't apply to you. Now, Elliot, what about you ? "

" Schoolmasters, washwomen, delivery boys, coal merchants, hawkers, and fortune tellers."

" Cut it out, Elliot. I think you should go with Mavuso."

" The Hospital Brigade. The old Sick-and-Lame Brigade."

" Shut up, Elliot."

" Nkosi, you told Dhladla that since it wasn't clear to him he could hold back," Sibande persisted. " Well, it's not very clear to me, either."

" Sibande, you're not going to hold back. You'll come with me. Don't you understand that this largely depends on you ? "

" On me ? I think you're exaggerating me to-night. Why do you think they'll listen to *me* ? "

" Unusual words from you, Sibande. Most unusual. What's the matter ? Feeling modest all of a sudden ? "

"Don't start that, Mabaso."

"Well, we're not going to let you out of it to-night, that's all. Get that straight. You're going to come with us if we've got to drag you along."

"What's the matter with Sibande to-night?" Vilakazi asked.

"Oh, he's suddenly become very, very modest. He suddenly feels that he has no influence in this location. Something has happened to his popularity and now he finds he has less influence than the newest bride in the location."

"You've got a sharp tongue, Mabaso. I don't like these clever jokes. I can also have an opinion."

"What's worrying you, Sibande?" Mavuso asked.

"I can't see what *use* it's going to be. What are we going to do? Tell everyone, 'Go home to bed, good people'? Talk like Ngubeni? They'll laugh at us. They'll ask us what our game is. They'll say, 'Strange goings on with Sibande and his crowd —have you heard what they're saying?—they've become spies or something.'"

"There's something in that," Mavuso said.

"No, that's not what's worrying him," Mabaso said. "He's too popular to-night, that's the trouble. You should have seen the trouble he had getting through the streets, he was so popular. He doesn't want to risk losing his vast following, that's what it is. He wants to keep on the right side of the crowd. Well, he can't do it to-night. We've got to start now. Come on, Sibande." Mabaso was at the door ready to leave.

"Mabaso, I think I can see what's worrying you," Sibande said, not moving. "Perhaps you wish *you* had my following? Is that it? Could it be jealousy, Mabaso?"

"Shut up, Sibande," Vilakazi said.

"You must be mad," Dhladla said. "I won't allow this."

"Then why does he talk like this? Why does he hit me like this?"

"Listen, Sibande," Mabaso said, coming back from the door, "I don't want to hit you, but you've got to see this. To-night it's us or the *tsotsis* and Charlie's lunatics. It's calming the crowd down or letting them be stirred up into some crazy mob action. That's what it comes down to. One or the other. And it largely

121

depends on you. If you can't see that, then what the hell are you doing here with us ? "

" I don't think you have posed it quite correctly."

" I haven't posed it correctly ? You talk like a lawyer. How would you like me to pose it ? "

" You see ? There he goes again. I mean why is that the issue ? You haven't been here long, you don't know these people like I do. They'll soon get tired of all this running around the streets. You see, they'll go home and go to bed soon. It'll all be over by the morning."

" I hope you're right, but I'm not so sure. Do you know what happened at Port Elizabeth and East London ? "

" Well, let them riot if they want to. They've got feelings. And it will make those white swine think twice before starting with this location again."

" Sibande, you're dangerous and stupid. It's a waste of time arguing with you."

" Let's leave him out of it. We're wasting time," Vilakazi said.

Sibande shrugged his shoulders. Mabaso tightened his fists, then opened them, stretching his fingers. He was angry, but he took a grip on himself and asked, " Well, what is it ? Yes or no ? "

" Well, I don't know. It's not fair to ask me yes or no."

" Yes or no ? "

" I've only heard *your* views. What about the others ? "

" If you want my view, I'd treat you as an enemy if you——" Elliot started to say.

" I'm not interested in Elliot's views. He's always agreeing with Mabaso."

" Well, my view is that you ought to come, Sibande," Vilakazi said.

" I agree with Vilakazi, and I want to say that by talking here so much you're wasting time and possibly ruining it," Mavuso said.

" What about Dhladla ? Do you agree with them, Dhladla ? "

" Yes, Sibande."

" But you said it wasn't clear."

"It's clear now," Dhladla said.

"What about Father Shongwe ? "

"Sibande, cut it out," Elliot said. "What are you trying to do ? Keep us talking here until it's all over ? "

"Well, Sibande ? " Mabaso asked.

"Do you really think I have that much influence in the location ? That I could prevent it ? "

"Yes, possibly. You and your railwaymen. Possibly you could prevent it."

"You really think that ? You really think they look to me so much ? "

"Yes, Sibande, they do," Mabaso said, keeping a restraint on himself.

"Why do you think the location looks to me rather than to you fellows ? " Sibande asked, narrowing his eyes and cocking his head.

"All right. Forget about Sibande," Mabaso said. "Come on, fellows."

"Hang on a minute," Sibande said.

Sibande thought it over. They all watched him in silence while he wrestled with it.

"Well, I hope you're right, Nkosi," he said at last.

"All right. Now let's start. We'll meet here again afterwards. Come on, Sibande."

*   *   *

They went back into the streets again—Vilakazi to join the youths who were waiting for him at the Welfare Centre, and to work at getting the youngsters away from the *tsotsi* gangs. Mavuso, weak and sick, and Elliot Nkomo, limping and tired, to go round the houses finding help among the more intelligent and sane location people. Sibande and Mabaso to rally the railwaymen, and with their aid to calm the people in the streets and get them back indoors.

When this work started, the depression that had lain heavily on Mabaso all night began to disappear. He felt the numbing doubts go and a vigour come into him, and a warmth that had the feel of the old work in the Defiance Campaign. He was working again, not merely arguing and plotting, and it was like coming out into the fresh air after being confined to a close room. He realised how frustrating the secret work had been and he felt a thrill at the knowledge that after to-night the secrecy would end. He knew now why he had hit Sibande so hard at the meeting. He had regretted it while doing it and had felt uneasy about it for a time afterward, but he saw that an instinct had made him do it and that it had been correct. If he had not done it, the others would have followed Sibande. Sibande would have won, and whatever the outcome of the night, it would have been the end of the group. It was necessary now to come out to the front and show the way. The time had come suddenly to end the quiet secret work, and when he saw this, and why he had hit at Sibande, the bitter feeling towards him disappeared ; and Sibande himself sensed it, and also something of the issue that had been decided between them. And he stopped fighting Mabaso, for that night at least, and in a cautious and strangely reticent way, worked with Mabaso.

When he found his supporters in the crowd, he simply asked them to listen to Mabaso, and left all the explaining to Mabaso. By doing this he gave the impression of backing Mabaso up, and the effect was the same as if he himself had harangued the men. After Mabaso had spoken to these people, they spread through the streets and quietly and firmly took control of the crowds. Soon there was a new current running in the location. The desperadoes had lost their moment. The danger of the riot passed, but Mabaso saw that it would revive if a new incident should occur, and particularly if the police should return to the location to take reprisals. So he worked with his ear straining to hear the distant sound of the sirens ; and the need to get the work done before the police returned gave his efforts an urgency, and a compelling power. Whenever he spoke, the people closed in and listened in silence. The crowds grew in size while he spoke. And at one stage he found himself addressing a crowd that filled the street for fifty yards ahead of him and overflowed into the side streets. He was sharp, quick, energetic, forceful : all his resources were at his command ; he worked with the deftness of being right, of being followed, and of being successful.

And his reputation swelled that night. It travelled and grew in the dark, until he emerged as the dominant person in the location. Sibande said very little. He stood alongside Mabaso with a blank withdrawn expression on his heavy face, and everyone believed that he supported Mabaso.

That night the conception of a new type of leader found its way into people's minds. Mabaso did not claim leadership, nor did anyone claim it on his behalf. But there was something about the way he worked that gave people this idea of him. There was sympathy, a respect for the worth of the location people, a refusal to blame, censure, or patronise, and most of all, a bold new way of speaking about the location's grievances. It was so different from the ways of the old cunning double-dealing leaders like Ngubeni, or of the wildcat leaders like Charlie Nkambula, who played on the people's nerves and foolishness. After the ferment of the night, after the strange experience, people turned to Mabaso with his appeal for planning, loyalty, patience, and work, and the promise only of slow, far-off rewards. It seemed as if the location came of age that night, and saw suddenly and for all time the futility of outbursts and the fraud in the work of the old types of leaders.

To bring the mood down from the heights, to say to people, "Keep your arms at your sides, your legs still, your voices down, keep calm," was not easy. Nor to deflate the crowds with the sour reminder that this was a location and they were Africans. But the sober mood returned and the people went back into their houses. The location quietened down and the streets became empty again and at last even the gangs broke up, for they had had no separate existence, being merely a product of the excitement. And when it was over, the group met again for a short while in the Reverend Shongwe's house.

"I hope it will stay quiet now," the Reverend Shongwe said.

"Yes. Let's hope so," Mabaso said. "But it could flare up again."

"I suppose so. Once these things are loosened, it's hard to keep them tied down."

"Anyway, let's hope it stays like this. Father, you and I have one more job to do. We're going to Charlie Nkambula's.

125

We mustn't let trouble boil up over that. Dhladla, would you take us in your car ? "

"With pleasure, Nkosi."

"Now, before we all go off let's say thanks to Sibande."

Sibande was standing with his hands on his hips, his short, stumpy legs apart, and his head cocked up at Mabaso. The top of the woollen Balaclava cap had fallen low over his forehead and the bottom had pushed up under his mouth, so that the little bright eyes seemed to be peering through a hatchway.

"Why don't you tell everyone how right you were and how wrong I was ? " Sibande said.

"What's the point in that ? "

"Well, I expected it. So go ahead and say it."

"Oh, leave it alone, Sibande. I thought to-night ended all this."

"Ended it ? Mabaso, I handed you the location to-night. Just understand that. So it's in order for you to say thanks to me."

"You handed me the location ? What are you talking about ? Was it yours to hand around ? I'm glad the people listened to us, but as far as I'm concerned I don't want to have any following."

"You loved it to-night, Mabaso. You know it. You loved it."

"Let's go home," Mabaso said wearily. "We all have to go to work in a few hours' time."

Mabaso and the Reverend Shongwe went in Dhladla's taxi to Charlie Nkambula's to try to find the body of Lukhele to hand to the police later in the day. The others went home.

Soon the location was stirring again. But now it was the usual stirring of early morning. From the river came the cold, stiff, and unmusical sounds of the waking birds ; from Old Look the sad lowing of cattle, and from far-off parts of the location, the wild and lonely yodelling of the awakeners. Lights came on in the kitchens and there was the clatter of pots and plates, the noise of water splashing in tin pails, and the pumping of primus stoves. Smoke wisped out of the chimneys and the smell of cooked porridge filled the air. With a jangling, night-shattering roar, the first bus started up its cold engine over at the administration building. Doors opened, braziers were poked up for a last yield of warmth from the dying coals. Then shadowy figures in caps, mufflers, and pulled-down hats came out into the streets pushing bicycles. The silent stream of cyclists making for the quarries, the asbestos mine, the railway sheds, the brickworks, the timber yards, the canning factory, and the garages started to wind its way along the dim-lit road to the town.

It was a new day but it had the sad look of all the days.

CHAPTER NINE

Du Toit parked his car in the usual place below the veranda and took the steps to his office in three agitated strides. He unlocked the door, flung it open, then banged it behind him. From these signs the clerks in the offices and those people waiting in line on the veranda knew that this was going to be a heavy day.

He took the pens and pencils out of his pocket and laid them out in the glass tray. He sat still for a moment, lost in thought, then he reached for the telephone and churned the handle. But before anyone could answer, he changed his mind and pushed the machine back to the end of the desk.

No, it was no good ringing Moolman. Moolman probably knew as much about it as he did right now; probably more. He'd have to find out all about it before ringing Moolman.

He wondered. Should I get finished with that bunch out on the veranda and leave a couple of clear hours to investigate what happened? No. That would take too long. This business had better be looked into first.

He tilted the chair back and pressed the button for Andries Gwebu. He pressed long and hard. His finger was still on the button when Gwebu came into the office. " Good morning, sir. Have a good night's rest, sir ? " Gwebu asked cheerfully.

Earlier that morning Sergeant Ackerman had phoned him at home and asked him to drop in at the station before going out to the location. Ackerman had spoken in a low voice, as if not wanting to be overheard at his end. At the police station he had found Ackerman walking around the fish pond in front of the mess. His helmet was off and his eyes were bleared and his face was puffed, red, and dirty-looking, Ackerman motioned Du Toit to stay in the car and he came out and sat next to him and told him to drive around the corner. He was very furtive. When they parked again, he told Du Toit all about the previous night. All about everything, starting with the arrest of the washwoman and ending with the shooting of Constable Kruger. It made Du Toit furious. Why had they carried out a raid without informing him first? And why, after the trouble started, hadn't they phoned to tell him about it? After all, the location was his responsibility. He would have to answer all the questions. He should have been the first to be told.

"You've got yourselves to blame," Du Toit said bitterly. "You should have called me. I could have calmed them down in a minute. They trust me and listen to me out there."

"Don't rub it in," Ackerman said.

Ackerman was very agitated. Lieutenant Swanepoel was coming back that morning and Ackerman would have to find some way of explaining the whole mess-up to him. To make things worse, Sergeant Combrink, who was gunning for Ackerman in order to grab his job, was certain to make a big thing of it to the lieutenant. It was only natural. Ackerman was in a real fix.

"You see, strictly between us and the lamppost, I had a couple of brandies last night, and then, I don't know, it felt so funny out there, and I sort of lost my head."

Du Toit could understand that. Not the brandies, but losing his head. He knew what it must have felt like out there in a hostile location, and in the middle of the night. He had a pretty good idea about that kind of thing. Still he said nothing. He wondered, though, what Ackerman was so secretive about.

"You can help me, old sport," Ackerman said, trying to make it sound casual and jovial.

"Me? How?"

"Listen." Ackerman leant close and slid his arm along the back of the seat, around but not touching Du Toit's shoulders, so close that Du Toit could see the red veins in his eyes and smell the mingled odour of stale breath and brilliantine. "Listen, do you think you could get those blackbird constables of yours to have a look round for that dead Kaffir? If we could find him, and I could sort of bang him across to the mortuary before the lieutenant comes back, well, it wouldn't look so bad then."

"Well, I don't know. I'll see what I can do," Du Toit said, turning his head.

Ackerman shifted a few inches on the seat and came still closer. "And there's another thing you can help me."

"What's that ? "

"Make out it wasn't so serious. Say you would have preferred there not to be a raid. Say that and that you would have preferred to leave it over for the lieutenant to handle. That's the best line for the lieutenant. Make out only he could have handled it properly. But it must come from you. You see, I didn't want this raid all the time, but Combrink, he wanted it, not me, and like a fool I gave in to him. Play it down. Get the idea ? "

"Yes," Du Toit said doubtfully.

"Actually, it is all quiet out there now. We sent a couple of detectives out and they report everything's quiet."

"That's one good thing, anyway."

"But there was a hell of a racket going on out there after we left last night. I never heard anything like the racket that went on. Some of our informers came over, and from what they told us, my God, we thought we were going to have a real riot on our hands out there. We haven't had much sleep, any of us. We had the Stens out, and we were waiting down by the railway line just in case they took it into their heads to come over into the town. Anyway, it's all quiet now. One more thing."

"Yes ? "

"Don't tell anyone I had these few words with you."

"O.K.," Du Toit said dully, wondering now whether it hadn't perhaps been more serious than Ackerman was making out.

Du Toit had promised nothing, but he had decided to help Ackerman if he could. There were a number of reasons for wanting to do this. One was his dislike for Swanepoel. He couldn't stand Swanepoel. Swanepoel fancied himself too much. A very important fellow Swanepoel. Oh, very. Why, he could hardly be bothered to recognise a person in the street. And always creeping up to the big shots in the town. Another reason was that he felt sorry for Ackerman : he could honestly appreciate how Ackerman must have felt out there last night. The third reason was that it was going to be necessary to make it look as though he had everything back under control in the location. Everybody was going to ask him about it and expect him to explain it all. And he would have to show that he had the whole situation in hand. To make up for not being there last night. So now with everything quiet again he didn't want Swanepoel coming along and stirring it all up by searching for that corpse and trying to rearrest those prisoners who had been left behind.

Still, as he drove out to the location, he became more and more puzzled, and then angry as he found himself at a loss to explain it all. Just why had it happened ? It wasn't the first arrest or police raid. Why had they got so hot and bothered about it ? This was a peaceful and well-run location, one of the best in the country. True, there had been no actual riot, but it had been a near thing apparently, and there had been some queer happenings. Why ? He had heard of these things happening in other locations, but he had always put it down to stupidity or mismanagement. Such things couldn't happen in his location. Not with his methods. He knew how to avoid mistakes, and if the people had grievances, why, they could come and talk to him about them. They didn't have to riot. What happened last night was very ugly. Somehow it had the feeling of being directed against him personally. Somehow he felt it as an affront by the location.

By the time he reached the office, he was irritable and depressed, and when Andries Gwebu came into the office and said cheerfully, " Good morning, sir. Have a good night's rest, sir ? " he was in no mood for that kind of sly sarcasm. So the little bastard's starting good and early this morning, he thought.

" Get out! " he shouted.

Gwebu blinked, unbelieving, through the window-pane glasses.

" What are you standing there for ? Get out."

" But you rang for me, sir."

" Can't you understand ? Get out. Go on, get out."

131

Du Toit jumped up and started to come round the desk; Gwebu turned round and flew out of the office.

Better get Ngubeni up here, Du Toit thought. Better hear what the old fox has to say about it. He went to the window and threw it rattling up, and yelled " Du-ty " without looking down at the location constables, who were sitting on the grass against the sunny wall of the building. Isaac Gwagwa, the *induna* of the constables, came round the building and up to the office. The gigantic sergeant stood in the doorway and saluted.

"Tell Chief Ngubeni I want him," Du Toit said. As Gwagwa was leaving, it suddenly struck him that Gwagwa had not reported about last night; what was more, he had not made any arrests. He had not even taken charge of the prisoners Ackerman had left behind in the street.

" COME BACK."

" Yes, sir."

" What was going on around here last night ? " He waved his hand in front of him and Gwagwa's eyes followed it around the room as if he understood Du Toit to mean that the office had been burgled, or in some way interfered with.

" Everything look all right."

" In the location, you donkey. What went on there ? "

" Oh, the police come, and——"

" Not that. I know about that. What happened afterwards ? "

" Oh, there's a big noise and shouting, sir. And you even hear singing." Gwagwa had a peculiar trick when speaking the white man's language : he could not say " I." He only knew " you," which served for both " I " and " you."

" Singing ? "

" Yes, sir. Singing and dancing and everything."

" Dancing ? "

" Yes, sir."

" Is that all ? Singing and dancing ? Are you sure that's all ? "

Gwagwa looked down and stared at his huge boots. " Yes, sir. That's all. They make a little noise, and then go to bed. You tell you everything."

" And you and the other constables ? Where were you ? "

Gwagwa ran his finger inside his collar. After a long

time he answered. " You watch a little bit, then you go to bed also."

Du Toit glared. The trick of mixing up " you " and " I " had always amused him, but now it made him suddenly furious.

" You—you—you—you—you," he heard himself spluttering. It sounded like the engine of an old water pump down on his father's farm. " Are you too stupid to learn to say 'I'?" he asked, speaking more slowly.

" Yes, sir."

" What happened to those prisoners who were left in the street ? " he asked ominously.

" What prisoners ? " Gwagwa asked in a very small voice.

Du Toit felt the skin prickle on his scalp wound. It was a sure sign that he was ready for an outburst. He controlled himself and said in a voice that just managed to keep even, " You're a liar, Isaac."

" Yes, sir."

" You know a damn' sight more about this than you want to tell me."

" Yes, sir."

" We're going to look into this, Isaac, you understand ? We're going to find out *all* about it. And God help you. Now go and fetch Chief Ngubeni. Hurry."

" Yes, sir."

Du Toit sat still for a moment, then went to the window sill and poured himself a drink of water from the earthenware carafe. Outside it was the usual scene. Everything did look quiet. There were the women around the taps, the hawkers selling roasted mealies, the children, the carts, the cows, the taxis. Everything looked calm, as if nothing at all had happened last night. That made it all the stranger. If what Ackerman said was correct, how could there be such a lack of excitement ? Were they exhausted ? They looked a bit weary, the slow way they were walking about. What kind of game were they playing ?

Now this about Gwagwa. Why hadn't the location constables done their job last night ? Were they going rotten ? That was the worst of recruiting them from their own location. The system in the police was better. You kept them circulating, so that they couldn't become too attached to any particular location. He would certainly have to deal with the location constables after this. But bad as this bunch was, was there any hope of getting any better out of this location?

He went to the desk again and started to write some correspondence, but his mind wasn't on it. What worried him most of all was the feeling of something hidden from him. It was that feeling of being baffled by the location, the same as the one he used to have in his early days at Nelstroom.

He sat and waited for Ngubeni to come. But now the idea of Ngubeni made him slightly nauseous. Ngubeni would be full of grievances and heroics. There would be a version of the events in terms of the hurt feelings and sufferings of Chief Ngubeni. He was getting tired of Ngubeni. He was beginning to see that the man was full of bluff. The man was a pest. In fact, come to think of it, what particular use had he been lately? The man was a washout. Perhaps it was time he found somebody else to replace Ngubeni.

The telephone rang. It was Ackerman, very excited.

" There's a priest fellow here from your location."

Du Toit heard Ackerman talk to someone at his end : " What's your name again ? " And he heard a muffled conversation through Ackerman's fingers held on the mouthpiece.

" Shongwe," Ackerman said, speaking into the phone again. " A priest fellow named Shongwe. And a taxi driver named Dhladla. You know what ? These two, they brought along that dead Kaffir's body. Yes, they actually turned him in. Brought him along here in a taxi. I'm banging him over to the mortuary right away."

" Shongwe ? Did you say Shongwe ? "

" Yes. You know him ? "

" Yes. How did *they* get hold of it ? "

" They won't say. They refuse to say. So I'm arresting them. They're the ones who took it away last night all right. It's obvious. I can tell from their whole demeanour. So I'm holding them on a charge of defeating the ends of justice. Concealing material evidence. And, my God, I'd like to bust their faces in for all the worry they gave me over that body."

" Shongwe ? That's funny. I never thought he'd do a thing like that."

" Funny the way they decide to bring him over here this morning."

" It *is* funny."

" Got scared, I suppose. Got scared and changed their minds. Everything quiet out there ? "

" Yes. Very quiet."

★   ★   ★

The interview with Ngubeni turned out much as Du Toit thought it would. Ngubeni did not really know much. He spoke a lot, but Du Toit could see that it was mostly gossip and hearsay, and that he was boosting and distorting what he did know so as to give himself a heroic part in it. His one point, that he had refused to harbour Lukhele—" that criminal "—he laboured until Du Toit had to tell him to keep off it. And once again he tried to warn Du Toit about Mabaso—" that agitator."

Du Toit was not impressed. He could see exactly what Ngubeni was up to : he was trying to draw attention away from his own miserable performance last night. It was not the first time Ngubeni had informed on Mabaso. Du Toit was keeping an eye on Mabaso all right. But apparently Ngubeni thought he could just go on trading on Mabaso for ever. Du Toit saw through Ngubeni—right through. Ngubeni tried to blame Mabaso for everything ; even for the stealing of Lukhele's body. That was what gave him away. The stealing had been done by Shongwe and Dhladla ; Shongwe was not the type to get mixed up with a type like Mabaso. It just showed how unreliable Ngubeni was becoming lately. Du Toit listened to Ngubeni with a tight smile and lightly touching finger tips. He soon became impatient and got rid of him.

He tried to settle down to work. He opened the door and let the people in from the veranda. He worked mechanically, without looking up and without reading the documents, knowing what each was from its colour. Ngubeni was a washout. So was Gwagwa. So was Gwebu. All were washouts. It was a disappointment, for he had tried hard to work with them, but it

135

just went to prove one thing—you couldn't rely on them. Any of them. Not even the best of them. Thank heaven it had all blown over outside. If anything had happened and he had been obliged to rely on *them* . . . ? But everything was normal now, thank heaven.

It was about ten-thirty when Mrs. Ross phoned.

" *Mr.* Du Toit, what has been going *on* out there ? " Her voice set all the screws and wires in the telephone jangling. She spoke as if the news had only just reached her. Du Toit told her that everything was quiet, that he had everything under control.

" Good God, aren't you going to *do* anything about it ? " she asked hoarsely.

" What do you mean, Mrs. Ross ? "

" Are you going to let it *rest* there ? Are you going to let them get *away* with what they did last night ? "

She said she had heard about it on the golf course and she had hurried across from the fourteenth hole to telephone from the clubhouse. Everybody at the club was very concerned, very, very deeply concerned and worried. What did he intend to do next ? Du Toit told her that he had control of the situation, was watching it carefully, and if any trouble flared up again, he would certainly know what to do.

" *I* don't think you should wait for *them* to make the next move. If you ask *me*, you're making a terrible *mistake*," she grumbled, and rang off abruptly.

Du Toit was not at all sure whether he was making a mistake or not. It seemed like common sense not to stir everything up again, but he was not sure whether he wasn't prompted by personal reasons in thinking so. Was he really scared ? Oh, nonsense. What was there to be scared of ? It was just the effect that her voice always had on him. Rattled him. He ought to take no notice. The trouble with her was she was disappointed. That was it. Disappointed because she couldn't go rearing into action, handing out revolvers to her ladies, organising women's Commandos, leading deputations to Pretoria, and giving interviews to the press. That's all it was, disappointment.

A few minutes later Lieutenant Swanepoel telephoned. He didn't give his name. That was just like him. He said, " Officer commanding Nelstroom Police speaking," and started off with dozens of questions, as if he hadn't trusted the information given by his own men and wanted to check on it.

" Seems my chaps were a little off form last night," he said. The understatement was not meant to point up the failure of last night, but to keep Du Toit out of sharing the lieutenant's contempt for the policemen involved.

" Seems so."

Du Toit said that in his opinion there was no necessity for a raid last night. They should have left it over for the lieutenant to handle. He was sure the lieutenant would have handled it properly and avoided all the trouble. It was a pity the lieutenant wasn't there to attend to it personally. Du Toit laid it on thick, hoping it would help Ackerman.

" Well, I'm here now and can handle it," Swanepoel said. His voice was full of energy, as if he couldn't wait to get started. This caught Du Toit off guard. He stammered, " W-what do you think we ought to do ? "

" Why, do it again and do it properly."

" I see," Du Toit said, and there was a long pause.

" It's up to you. Just give us the word and we'll go into action," Swanepoel said briskly.

" I was just thinking. I wonder . . . You see, everything's quiet out here now. I've got the situation completely under control. I wonder if we oughtn't to leave it alone for the time being ? "

Now Swanepoel was silent. Du Toit could hear him breathing into the telephone while he pondered what to do.

" You should tell your fellows not to start things out here without asking me first," Du Toit said, filling in the silence. " They know me and trust me out here, and I know how to handle them. It wouldn't have happened last night if they had only called me."

Swanepoel was still thinking. At last he said, " You sure ? "

" Yes. I can calm them down in a minute. *I* know how to handle them."

" No, I mean about everything being quiet out there. You think the danger's over ? "

137

"Yes, seems like it. I tell you what—if anything crops up again, I'll ring you. I'm watching it very carefully, and the first sign of anything, I'll ring you and you fellows can come out and do your stuff. How's that?" He felt bad having to refuse Swanepoel.

"Well, as you say," Swanepoel said, resigned, not convinced. Then Swanepoel added, "Councillor Ross just phoned, you know."

"Oh?"

"Yes. *She* says strong action is indicated. She says the whole town is demanding it after last night. Still, I can't advise you. You're the boss out there. I'll just tell her you said we should leave it alone."

He rang off, and Du Toit sat for a moment frowning at the telephone.

How could she, out on the golf course, know what the whole town was demanding? And what was she doing phoning Swanepoel about it? Why the hell must she stick her nose in? Why didn't she have the elementary courtesy to come out here and see for herself how everything was instead of flapping and panicking and scaring up the whole town? Well, there was one way to put a stop to this.

But Moolman was surprisingly cool when Du Toit phoned. Du Toit felt at once that something was wrong.

"Well, I don't know," Moolman said. "It was a bad affair last night. The papers haven't arrived yet, but I understand they're full of it. Front-page news about stoning the police and volunteering for arrest. Mrs. Ross thinks it's part of the Defiance Campaign. I'm inclined to agree with her."

This had not occurred to Du Toit. "But I thought that was all over," he said, and then he asked, "Mrs. Ross?"

"Yes. We've just been discussing it. You know, Hennie, *something's* got to be done. It was a shocking business last night. By the way, couldn't you have helped the police a bit last night? I understand you and your location boys kept yourselves pretty scarce."

The conversation left Du Toit with a hollow feeling. It was not merely Moolman's hostile tone, it was something deeper.

After a while it began to dawn on him that this was the first time that Moolman and Mrs. Ross had ever been on the same side about anything. On one side and, what was more, against him.

He stood up and began to pace the room. Something would have to be done all right. What? Call the police and say go ahead? No. Not that, if possible. People were already beginning to regard it as his fault. It would look as if he couldn't do his job properly, and that the police had to be brought in to fix things up for him. As if he had lost control. Why should he let people think that when it wasn't even true? Something had to be done, but not a raid. Something more constructive and positive. Something that showed a little intelligence.

Suddenly he stopped and stiffened his back, and slowly scratched his chin. Then he stalked out of the office and into Gwebu's office next door, and over to the corner where the *Government Gazettes* were stacked. He rummaged among them and found the one he wanted, a recent issue still smelling of print and bent from the wrapper. He carried it back to his office and flipped the pages, then stopped and read. Yes, there it was. He took a sheet of foolscap and a red pencil and wrote :

NOTICE

AS AND FROM TO-DAY ALL WASHWOMEN WILL BE REQUIRED TO POSSESS DAILY LABOURERS' PASSES. WILL ALL THOSE EFFECTED IMMEDIATELY COME TO THE LOCATION OFFICE TO OBTAIN THE NECESSARY REGISTRATION FORMS.

BY ORDER

H. J. J. DU TOIT

SUPERINTENDENT NELSTROOM LOCATION

He wrote it in Afrikaans and in English, and then printed, IMPORTANT. IMPORTANT, across the top and heavily underscored the two words. Now it needed to be translated into Swazi, but he did not ring for Gwebu. He wanted to think about it a bit.

Yes, this was just right. It was constructive and positive, and at the same time directly related to last night. And it was a preventive measure, not just taking revenge. The cause of all

139

the trouble last night had been the vicious woman who stole the Beckets' washing and kicked the police in their private parts. That vicious woman should never have been allowed in the location in the first place. Now, this type would be kept under control, kicked out of the location if necessary. From now on *he* would decide who were fit and proper persons to do washing. Furthermore, this would protect people's property from thieving washwomen in future. Lucky he remembered that new amendment giving local authorities the power to apply the pass laws to women.

But why only washwomen? he asked himself. What about all those shebeen queens, prostitutes, fences, all the back-yard trouble makers? Surely they should be dealt with too? Wasn't this the chance to solve the whole problem of the undesirable women in the location? Wasn't that really the location's biggest problem?

He read the *Gazette* again. Yes, this new provision was long overdue. The pass laws had for years been applied to men only, not to women, but now both could be put on the same footing. This was more logical. Without control over the women there was a huge loophole : it was impossible to run a location really properly. The women did just what they liked. They brewed drink and led immoral, lazy lives, they brawled and made mischief and talked back, and actually they were the cause of most of the trouble in the location. For a long time people had been pressing to apply the pass laws to women, but there had always been opposition on the ground that women had to keep house and look after the kids, and so could not be expected to register for employment. But they had been abusing the position : they had been using the good-housewife stunt as a cover-up for idleness, vagrancy, rackets, and crime. Well, now here was a chance to tidy up this location.

The bigger scheme now crowded the original smaller one out of his mind, and he tore the notice up and wrote another. This notice said that all women would henceforth be required to possess passes as a condition for living in the location. He simply wrote " passes " but he knew that various kinds of passes were envisaged : daily labourers' passes, for those like the washwomen who worked on different days for different people ; monthly service contracts for those in regular employment— nannies, kitchen girls, and the like ; permits to seek work for all those who would now have to give up their idle lives and find jobs in town ; exemptions for those who had bona fide reasons for not working. The exemptions would be the problem. Every-body would want them. *He* would have to decide who were bona fide housewives, old people, and invalids.

He sat back and thought of some ugly faces that he would not be seeing around the location in the near future.

He was delighted with the new scheme, and with the way he was actually turning last night's affair to advantage. He was actually using it to bring in a new reform. The location would have to accept the reform because they would see that it was in their own interests to curb the undesirable female elements ; at the same time they would realise they had brought it on them-selves. He felt very clever about what he was doing, very superior to Moolman and Mrs. Ross and Swanepoel, with their crude ideas about police raids and beating up the location out of revenge.

Then he decided that this matter was one that ought to be announced at a meeting. He knew the old trick of evading notices : there were always people turning up and saying that they hadn't seen the notice, or that they couldn't read. So now he wrote an announcement in red pencil saying that a meeting would take place on the square the next afternoon at five-thirty. That was the time when most of the location people would be coming back from work. He pinned the announcement of the meeting above the notice of the regulation. Then he rang for Andries Gwebu.

" Read this," he said.

Gwebu read it.

" Well ? " Du Toit asked eagerly.

Gwebu read it again. The whole thing, right through. " Can you say, ' Everyone not otherwise occupied at work *are* required to attend ' ? " Gwebu asked, blinking owlishly.

Du Toit breathed hard. " I don't mean that part. I mean the part about passes for women. What do you think about it ? "

Gwebu read it all again.

" Can you say, 'All those effected'? Shouldn't it be 'affected'?"

" To hell with you," Du Toit said. " Just translate it."

Gwebu wrote out the translation very carefully. He took his time over every letter and decorated the capitals with swirls and curlicues. He underlined nearly a third of the words. When he finished, he drew a daisy in the top right-hand corner. Du Toit watched him, scowling all the time. " The little bastard," he muttered. Gwebu cocked his head up and asked, " Why are you doing this, sir ? "

" Because it's time we dealt with the shebeen queens, the prostitutes—the—the undesirable female elements, that's why."

" Has this any connection with last night, sir ? "

" No." Du Toit shifted his thighs. " Yes. Of course it has. Now go and fix this notice on the board. And get the constables to line up."

" I think there'll be a very strong reaction to this, sir."

" Go and fix the notice. You heard me. Are you deaf or something ? "

Gwebu had lots more to say. He stood with a troubled, cobwebby look on his face, but after a moment he just turned and went out with the papers in his hand.

Du Toit stood at the window and watched him pin the papers on to the decaying wooden notice board that stood just inside the location gate. He was too short to reach and had to stand on a rock. There was a tight, angry look in Du Toit's face. Gwebu's baggy pants, the dirty shoes with the laces undone, the too-large head, the glasses crooked and slipping off the nose, the ancient sweater with its hole right over the stomach—these filled Du Toit with loathing. He would have to get rid of that dirty little bushman, he decided. Couldn't even trust him any more. Why was he opposing this ? Probably protecting a shebeen queen. Probably lots of them. Probably making a nice racket out of it.

He saw Gwebu come down off the rock and go around the building, and then he heard him tell Gwagwa to collect the constables together and line up. So he presumed anyway, for Gwebu spoke in vernacular. His voice was loud and cheeky, the way it sometimes went. There was a great deal of talk below the

142

window and Du Toit wondered what Gwebu was holding forth so much about.

A number of constables came back from the location streets and joined those at the building, and all formed up on the veranda. When they were properly in line, Du Toit came out. Although he was having one of his tiffs with Gwebu, he decided to use him as interpreter. He wanted to be sure that his orders would be properly understood. Du Toit warily eyed the line of constables standing against the rails of the veranda.

" Tell them there is a new law," Du Toit said to Gwebu.

" To-day is the day of a new law," Gwebu said in Swazi, starting low.

" Tell them from to-day the women must carry passes."

" And what is this new law ? Prepare yourselves. No longer will our women merely carry babies. From now on they will also carry passes." His voice was rising, taking off for a strong flight. " Yes. Our women have this day won the right to carry passes." This information was emphasised with a long, solemn look.

" All women," said Du Toit.

" Wives. Daughters. Mothers." Gwebu held his hand up, knuckles outward, and pulled his fingers down one by one. " Aunts and sisters." The five fingers shot up again. " Shebeen queens, whores, brides, nurses, schoolgirls. Desirable elements —undesirable elements. All elements. Old elements, pregnant elements, young elements with firm breasts." Down, up, down went the fingers. " Yes, this is the day for the female elements."

He spoke now with a hoarse, desperate sincerity that completely disguised the trickery of his words. He addressed the air rather than the constables. And he spoke fast to prevent Du Toit's picking up any of the words.

" Now tell them all this will be explained at a meeting to-morrow afternoon at five-thirty. A meeting for the *whole* location."

" To-morrow when the sun is *there*, there will be a meeting. A meeting of *all* the elements. Male elements, female elements. And there, at this meeting, this new privilege of the passes will be properly explained so that even the most simple-minded child will understand."

"On the square here, where we hold all our meetings," Du Toit said.

Gwebu traced the outline of the square with his finger. "Here, on this historic field."

"Tell them they must go into the location and tell everybody about the meeting and the purpose of it. They must go up and down every street. If I find any one of them missing out streets, I'll deal with him. They must take the news everywhere," Du Toit said.

Gwebu glowered and told them; "Now, brave soldiers of the Town Council, listen to your task. How are your voices? For you must take this great news on your voices down every street. Down each side of every street. Down every lane, each side, and into every yard. Down all the sides of all the yards. Into every room of the yards, and down the sides of the rooms. And in the room, down and around the sides of the tables. You must take the news everywhere. Nobody must miss this news of the meeting, and the news of the great honour of carrying passes that has to-day fallen on the female elements. And if any of you gold-buttoned eagles fail at this job, you must understand that you will burn. You will be cut short." He whipped the air in front of him with a horizontal sweep of his hand.

The constables received the onslaught with dead impassivity.

"Tell them to dismiss," Du Toit said.

"Go now. But not back to sleep at your wall. Go into the location with the message," Gwebu told them.

Most of the constables drifted out of line, but a few, including Gwagwa, stayed at attention.

"Ask them what they want."

Gwebu asked, "Have you not been told enough? What absurdity do you want to trouble us with now?"

"Sir, is it really a new law that women must carry passes?" Gwagwa asked in Afrikaans, speaking directly to Du Toit.

Du Toit answered him direct, "What's the matter with you to-day? What do you think I've just been talking about? Yes, this is a new law. Now dismiss and don't waste my time."

He turned and walked back to his door, but Gwagwa did not move. Standing stiffly at attention, he said, addressing Du Toit's back, "You don't like this new law. It is really a nonsense law." He said it with such strange plaintiveness that it did not sound like Gwagwa's voice at all.

Du Toit swung round as if struck by a stone. He walked swiftly back and glared into Gwagwa's eyes. He saw there what he had never seen before : defiance and hostility. The eyes were like assassins that come out of the dark. The two pairs of eyes bored into each other like separate independent creatures. Then suddenly the spark died in Gwagwa's eyes and a dull glazed look fell over them like a blind drawn down over a window. With an effort he pulled his eyes away from Du Toit's and stared at the ground. Du Toit felt himself stiffen and the blood rush to his face, and he felt his hand fly up and slap Gwagwa. Gwagwa took the blow without a movement, without a sound, without any change in his eyes, standing stiffly to attention.

Du Toit went back to his office and sat at his desk. He was trembling. He wished he had not struck Gwagwa ; he was sorry the moment he did it. His hand stung from the impact on the hard, bony cheek. He felt uncomfortable at having laid his hand on the man. But he could not bring himself to call Gwagwa in and say the few mollifying words that could have put everything right. He saw Gwagwa go down the steps and the constables gather around him in an excited babbling group, and then drag themselves across the field towards the location houses.

*　　　*　　　*

He slept badly that night. The day's events kept jarring him into wakefulness. When he was awake, he told himself that they were trivial incidents, and felt better. But when he drowsed back to sleep, they became monsters that terrified him. There were rings under his eyes when he came to the office next morning.

He sat in the car for a few minutes before getting out, as if he expected to be ambushed in his office. At last he got out and went up to the office, and after a while he began to see that there was nothing untoward. He had come with an uneasy fear that there would be some strange and sudden reaction to the announcement about the women's passes; he watched for signs of it, but as the morning wore on he saw that the location was taking it calmly.

The crowd outside his door was bigger than usual because so little work had been done the previous day. He worked fast and silently, and disposed of the extra-long queue before midday. Nothing happened, and he convinced himself that there would be no trouble, that the meeting would be orderly and routine, as all the others had been.

A little after midday Lieutenant Swanepoel telephoned.

" How's everything out there ? "

" Quiet."

" This meeting you're having this afternoon—do you think you'll need us ? "

" I don't think so, I can handle it."

" You sure you don't want us along ? "

" No, I don't think so. After the mess-up your fellows made last night, I think you'd all better stay away. You'd only inflame everybody. By the way, I hope you realise now how right I was the way I handled it yesterday."

" Yes, you certainly were. I admit it."

" I hope Councillor Ross admits it."

" Yes, she does. Now you quite sure you won't need us ? "

" Yes. I can manage."

" The reason I asked is we've been called out on a big stock-theft case. On one of the farms. So if you're sure you don't need us, I'm going out with a couple of my fellows on this case. Anyway, if anything develops, keep in touch with the station, and they'll keep in touch with us by radio. So long—we'll be back to-night unless we hear from you."

Du Toit went home for lunch and had a nap afterward, something he seldom did, but he was tired from lack of sleep, and in spite of the calm in the location the morning had been a strain on his nerves. He returned to the office in the middle of the afternoon.

As he got out of the car, he saw Charles Ngubeni waiting outside his door. It irritated him to see the old bore standing there in that old worn-out waiter's jacket. He thought he had just come to waste time and gossip about the meeting. But when he came nearer, he saw that there was something urgent about Ngubeni. The old man did not smile and his crumpled leather face was twitching with agitation.

They both went into the office.

" What's the matter, Charles ? "

Du Toit knew at once that Ngubeni was offended about something, for he stood halfway between the desk and the door, holding his black hat over his stomach and revolving it with his fingers.

" Yesterday, sir, the constables are shouting out a new law that women must carry passes. Is that a new law, sir ? "

" Yes, Charles."

" Sir, how can it be a new law if the Advisory Board isn't discussing it ? "

" Oh, I see. You're hurt because the Advisory Board didn't discuss it ? Well, there just wasn't time, that's all. It had to be done quick-quick."

" I thought the Board is all-a-time supposed to be discussing the business of the location. Didn't you yourself tell us that ? "

" I did, but I tell you there wasn't time."

Du Toit looked at Ngubeni's hot glistening eyes, his trembling jaw, his agitated hands—at the whole trumped-up pose of injury. Touchy as a schoolgirl, he said to himself. He wished he would go home.

" The people think it's the Advisory Board's behind this law of passes for women. They think we voted it but that we hid it from them. Now, sir, why am I here ? Let me tell you why. I am assaulted to-day." He paused to let it take effect. " Yes, me, Ngubeni, assaulted. And by women. They see me in Wildebeest Street and they scream out, ' There he is. He who wants to kill us with passes.' And they throw stones at me. Hundreds of stones. Even the children throw." He drew back his sleeve—there was a violet bruise on his forearm. He pulled up his trousers and showed a bleeding gash below the knee. " Me, Ngubeni, *induna* of the Swazi nation, stoned by women and children. How can this thing happen ? " He mopped his damp, twitching face with his handkerchief. " But the people

147

think it's the Board's behind this. They have assaulted me, not in the capacity as *induna* but in the capacity as Chairman the Advisory Board."

Du Toit's face clouded. He stared at the wounds as if they were obscene letters that had come in the mail. The sight of them suddenly drained all the life out of him. He stood up and walked out to the veranda and leaned on the rail, staring over the rooftops into the distance. Then he walked slowly back.

" When did this happen ? " he asked in a very quiet voice.

" More or less an hour ago."

" Did you report it to the location constables ? "

" Yes, sir, I report it. I report it to three of Gwagwa's constables, and I take them to Wildebeest Street. I say—arrest the women, but they don't arrest anyone. Oh no, they just smile and talk with the women. I say—go on, arrest them ; but they smile and talk nicely with the women in Wildebeest Street and they give me their back. And after a while they walk away smiling and laughing and nobody is arrested."

Du Toit squashed out his cigarette.

" Did you report this to Gwagwa ? "

" Gwagwa's gone."

" What ? "

" Yes. He and his women and his children and all his things. Gone—back to his kraal in Swaziland."

" How do you know this ? "

" Everybody know this. The whole location see him go and say to him *Hamba kahle*—go in peace. Now, sir, another thing : why they blame me for the Reverend Shongwe and Dhladla ? Why they blame the Board for that also ? "

" That ? You mean they're objecting about that, too ? "

" Yes. They roaring up about that, too."

Du Toit was in a whirl of indecision. His first thought was to cancel the meeting. But he saw at once all the difficulties of doing that. It would be impossible to explain to Mrs. Ross and Moolman, particularly after he had refused police protection. And the location would understand well enough why he had called it off. There would have to be another meeting anyway, and this time *with* police protection. But that was not all. The main difficulty was that he could not trust his own feelings. He knew that he was in a bad state of nerves, and he knew from previous occasions that when he was like this he was inclined to exaggerate things : to get enormously worried only to find out afterward that it had all been over nothing. He began to play the whole thing down. Probably there wasn't a mutiny among the constables, he told himself. Probably Ngubeni had just got mixed up in some stupid street quarrel and was twisting things, as he usually did, to make it look better for himself. As for Gwagwa's desertion, well maybe he just got homesick for his kraal and that slap yesterday finally decided him to pack up and go. And as for the location protesting about the new passes, well didn't they always protest about any new thing, only to come along afterward, when they saw that it was for their own good, and thank you for bringing it in ?

But somehow all this reasoning failed to calm him. His thoughts surged back and forth, and no single one seemed valid for more than a moment. At last, out of a welter of thoughts, he found some kind of plan.

"Charles, listen to this. I want you to go around the houses and speak nicely to people and try to get support for this new pass law. You know how to do it. And see the supporters come to the meeting—that's important. Ask some of your friends to go around with you. You'd better start right away : there isn't much time."

Ngubeni stared at him, amazed.

"You ask me to do that ? "

"Yes. You remember that time we had all the opposition to the beer raids and you explained it all so nicely to the people ? Well, it's the same idea."

Ngubeni did not answer for a while. He was breathing hard : he was stunned. At last, with stiff dignity, he said :

"Sir, Chief Ngubeni is assaulted by women of the location. You do not say, Who's the women ? You do not bring here the Flying Squad. You do not even make a notice. No, you say, Crawl around the houses like a punished dog and lick the hands of the people that put the sticks on him. Sir, I will not touch this new pass law."

149

He walked out with his back rigid, and when Du Toit called him, he refused to return. When his jerky footsteps faded into silence, Du Toit sat quite still and tried to understand what had happened with Ngubeni. He had become too dependent on Ngubeni, he thought bitterly. He should never have allowed it to develop that way. It was an absurd situation, shameful in a way. But he knew that it was useless to reproach himself, because there had been no point at which the development could have been stopped. He simply could never have managed without Ngubeni. They were partners in running the location, they were answerable for each other's liabilities. They stood or fell together.

He tried to struggle with the feeling inside him. He was full of uneasiness about the meeting. He felt jarred and unsettled, and after a moment realised that a headache was coming on. He took an aspirin out of the drawer and downed it with a drink of water from the carafe. He knew that there was nothing tangible to go on, only an idle, distorted story by Ngubeni, but he could not throw off the leaden misgiving.

He decided to drive around the location and see for himself how things looked. He did not want to go alone, so he called Gwebu to accompany him. They rode in silence. There was a prickling hostility between them. It made him uncomfortable, and he had a sudden urge to make friends with Gwebu again. But he couldn't start. He felt inhibited towards Gwebu : he couldn't trust him and was afraid to give him an opening. So they bounced and lurched along the bad roads without speaking. Occasionally they stopped at a corner and looked at the houses. Everything looked very much as it always did. But there were certain signs, and after a while Du Toit became conscious of them. Nobody was greeting him. Or Gwebu. People would see them in the car, then hurry past, as if looking at them were some kind of crime or bad luck. There was no music in any of the houses, no gramophones or mandolins. The air was dead with quiet. They could have been in the middle of the Karroo, it was so quiet. This was the time when the barefooted school-girls came home from the convent—usually they dawdled and chattered like monkeys. But now they were hurrying past, very urgent and unsmiling.

They reached the far end of Jubilee City, where there was a kind of business centre—a row of shops and a cinema. Du Toit saw a crowd outside the cinema. As the car drove along, the crowd scattered, and by the time it reached the cinema, everybody had disappeared. There was writing on the wall at the side of the cinema. That was what had drawn the crowd. Du Toit read it and he turned pale and bit his lip. There, in letters a foot high, freshly chalked and raw as a slap in the face, were the words :

WOMEN—DON'T REGISTER
RELEASE REV. SHONGWE AND DHLADLA
DOWN WITH WOMEN'S PASSES

In a different writing someone had added, DOWN WITH DU TOIT.

Du Toit stared at the obscenity for a long time. Then he put the car into gear and drove straight back to his office.

When he reached the office, he saw that people were beginning to arrive for the meeting. They were drifting across the field from the houses and taking up places below the wooden platform. It will be a big meeting, he told himself. People arriving well before the time means a big meeting.

He once again had a desire to cancel the meeting. But the same arguments prevailed against it. He decided, however, to keep the meeting short : to make the announcement and give a brief explanation of the new law, and then come home. He looked at his watch. Ten to five.

He decided to call the constables up and give them some special instructions about the meeting. He called them up to the veranda and made them line up. They looked strange without Gwagwa, like an animal that had been decapitated. It angered him, but he said nothing about Gwagwa, or about the three constables who had refused to arrest Ngubeni's attackers. That could wait until to-morrow. He gave the instructions : walk in pairs, mingle in the crowd, watch out for troublemakers, make arrests at the first sign of a disturbance, use knobkerries and handcuffs. The constables received their orders with blank faces.

He promoted the senior constable, a squat, middle-aged man named Napoleon Siponiya, to be sergeant in place of Gwagwa. Siponiya took the promotion by squeezing his shoulder blades and buttocks tightly together and staring intensely into the sky above Du Toit's head. Then Du Toit dismissed the squad and went back into his office.

He noticed that a gang of quarry labourers had arrived in the square. They were tattered and covered in white dust, having come straight from the quarry to the meeting. The square was a quarter full already, but mostly with women, who were arriving first because they had merely to walk across the field from the houses. Many had babies on their backs, under the blankets. The sun was still warm and bright, although low in the sky, and the bright blankets and headcloths of the women gave the square an effect of dazzling, agitated colour, like a country fair.

He noticed the bicycles piling up against the fence. He watched while two buses came from town and discharged their passengers straight into the crowd, like ships unloading coal. Then a procession of Zionists arrived. They were dressed in the regalia of the Sunday pilgrims—long white surplices with large blue or red crosses sewn on, front and back, leopard-skin hats, feathers, chains, and medallions ; they carried shepherds' crooks with streamers fluttering. Two in front were beating, with their palms, small barrel-like drums with the fur of the stretched skin outside ; the Zionists did not march but moved forward in a tight shuffling dance to the rhythm of the drums. The nurses from the Welfare Centre arrived in their white uniforms, and they made an antiseptic white patch in the middle of the coloured blankets and black faces. He saw a crowd of boys clamber to the top of the water tower at the far end of the field, and some constables climb after them and chase them down. The whole location would be at the meeting. Yesterday he had wanted the whole location to come, but now their eagerness to attend seemed to have some sinister meaning behind it.

He saw Charles Ngubeni, Malooy, and some other Advisory Board members arrive in one of Malooy's taxis. They parked on the road near the platform but they did not get out of the car. Then he saw Malooy reverse the car and turn it around to face the direction they had come from. Du Toit suddenly began a hasty search among the crowd for people he recognised, people he could depend on to stand with him. There were ex-Sergeant Smoke, for whom he had once arranged a pension; Sister Tembu, head nurse at the Welfare Centre, whom he had fixed up in the job; fat little Simon Ndimandi, from whom he occasionally bought jam and cigarettes; some old parsons; some hawkers and shopkeepers for whom he had wangled licences; a few others whom he had helped in different ways. Not many. He could count them easily. They looked very isolated. Except for them, the whole square was a sea of featureless grim black faces. He had never seen a location crowd quite like this. There was little noise, only a low drone of conversation like the noise of a machine buried in the ground. The high spirits that such crowds usually generated were absent, buried somewhere. It was difficult to say what was wrong with this crowd. It was not anything you could see or hear. It was something in the air rather than in the crowd itself. It was something you could feel.

His eyes fell on the telephone, then followed the wires across the room, and outside, along the poles, to the point where they merged with the road to the town.

His hand hovered for a moment, then he picked up the telephone, churned the handle, and asked the exchange to get through to the police station. " How many men have you got handy ? " he asked the constable in charge.

" There's only me and one other. The lieutenant took some fellows out to a stock-theft case. The rest are playing a match in Withoek. Is anything the matter ? "

" No, nothing's the matter. But get some men out here as quick as possible. And see they're armed."

" I thought you didn't need us. The lieutenant said you didn't need us. Most of our fellows have gone to this rugby fixture in Withoek thinking we weren't needed. I'll have to ring through to Withoek."

" Well, do it. Don't waste time."

It was not yet time to start the meeting, but the square was full and all eyes were fixed on the door of his office waiting for it to open. He could feel the weight of the eyes on the door.

Now he realised that he should have cancelled the meeting. But he knew for certain that if he went down the steps and over to his car and drove off instead of walking across to the platform, he would never again be able to show himself in the location. Or, for that matter, in the town. His heart was thumping. He put his hand up under the sweater and held it against his chest. It disgusted him to feel the sweaty, panicky palpitation. He had never believed that the fear would return. He was sure he had conquered it during his time at Nelstroom, but now it was there, like a blackmailer released from gaol and coming straight back to present the old, ugly, familiar demands.

He understood quite well the reason for the return of his fear. He understood it with a flash of insight that lit up his entire position in the location and the whole dilemma of his life. His carefully erected system of defences had suddenly, inexplicably, collapsed. He was back to that first morning in the location. He was reunited with his fear.

Some impulse made him ring for Gwebu.

"Andries, you don't really mind when I bawl at you occasionally, do you?"

"No, sir."

"You know I don't mean it. If I meant it I wouldn't have kept you here all this time. You know that?"

"Yes, sir."

"You know sometimes you're a pretty annoying little cuss yourself. Sometimes I think you make a point of rubbing me up the wrong way. Don't you now? Come on, admit it."

Gwebu looked puzzled but did not answer. Du Toit peered at him tenderly.

"Andries, I want you to interpret really well to-day. The way you can do it when you really try. I want you to put it over in a big way to-day."

"Yes, sir." Then, "Is that all, sir?"

"I've been thinking about this, and what I intend to do is to point out how it's in their own interests, this new pass law. It's simply a matter of keeping law and order. When we get rid of the undesirable female elements, this will be a better location for all concerned. That's what I want you to put across."

" Yes, sir."

" Andries, you're an intelligent chap. Tell me, why can't they see it that way ? Why are they making such an unholy rumpus about it ? "

" Do you really want my opinion, sir ? "

" Of course. Why do you think I'm asking you ? "

" Well, sir, if you want my opinion, I'll tell you. Yes, I'm going to tell you, sir. I think it's a pretty savage thing to make women take jobs in town or else get out of the location."

" WHAT ? "

" Yes, sir."

" Just what do you mean ? "

" Sir, you'll get angry if I tell you."

" No, go ahead." But now a hint of menace had come into his voice.

Gwebu took a deep breath. " Sir, it's bad enough for the men, always being stopped by police and being raided for passes in their homes at night and being arrested and sent out to the farms when they lose a job. But it'll be a hundred times worse for the women. Women's place is in the home, sir. Their place is to bring up babies and cook for their husbands. How can you expect them all to work in the town ? What if they can't get jobs ? What if there aren't enough jobs ? Are you just going to go ahead and break up half the families in the location ? "

" Just a minute, just a minute," Du Toit said with weary patience. " You've got it all wrong. This isn't meant for the ordinary decent types. This is aimed at the undesirable types. The ordinary law-abiding types will have nothing to worry about."

" The notice says all women."

" I had to word it that way. I couldn't say, ' Will all the undesirable elements come and register for passes.' "

" As far as the location knows, it's all women."

" But I'll issue exemptions. I'll investigate each case and give exemptions to the bona fide cases. There you are—that makes it clear, doesn't it ? I'm glad you raised it, because I want you to understand it yourself so you can put it over nicely at the meeting to-day. Well, if that's clear now——"

" It's not clear, sir."

" What do you mean ? " Du Toit said sharply, his patience suddenly used up. He began to see that he should never have started the discussion. But it was too late : he had given Gwebu too much encouragement. Gwebu said, " Exemption to be a wife ! Where does any man get the right to issue such a paper ? "

" What are you talking about ? "

" I mean, sir, that from now on in this location it'll not be enough for a wife to be desirable to her husband ; she will have to be desirable to you also."

" Exactly what do you mean ? I don't like that."

" I only mean this, sir ; if she is what you call an undesirable element, she'll be thrown out. That's all I mean."

" Andries, I'm sick of you. I'm sick and tired of you, of all your clever-clever showing off. I'm disappointed in you. I can see I'm wasting my time trying to be nice to you. O.K., back to your office. I'll call you when we're ready."

" You asked for my opinion, sir."

" Go on, get out, you ugly little baboon."

" Yes, sir." He turned to leave.

" Come back, Andries."

" Yes, sir."

" Forget what I said."

" Yes, sir."

" You'll do your best, won't you ? Like you can when you really try ? Won't you ? "

" Yes, sir."

Gwebu left. Du Toit placed his head on his hands and kept his eyes on his watch. He saw the minute hand move slowly round and waited until it showed exactly five-thirty.

CHAPTER TEN

He strode across the twenty yards of grass between the building and the platform, with Gwebu, half his size, running at his heels. He was conscious of thousands of eyes fixed on him like hooks. He climbed the platform steps, gripped the rail, and started at once to speak.

" This meeting has been called to tell you all about a new law for this location," he said in a harsh, impersonal voice that sounded as if he were speaking into a cave.

He stopped to let Gwebu put it into Swazi.

" This meeting has been called to tell you all about a new law for this location," Gwebu translated in a chillingly flat lifeless voice. Du Toit shot him a look. He continued :

" Now I want you to understand that this law is for the good of the whole location. The government does not make laws just to cause trouble for you. This law is like medicine : it might taste bad but it will do you good. The government is only out to help you."

Gwebu translated the baby talk, which was a kind of standard officialese for location meetings, exactly as Du Toit said it, and in a voice that made it clear that he was not associating *himself* with any such foolishness.

Du Toit frowned. " Now this law is aimed at the loafers and bad people among the location women," he said, flustered. " The law-abiding women mustn't worry. They have nothing to fear."

Gwebu rendered it, precisely and prosaically, into Swazi. The translation fluttered feebly in the air, and this had the effect of making the crowd restive. Heads were bobbing and shoulders heaving, and there was a continuous angry clicking of tongues, like twigs snapping all over the square.

"It's no good losing your tempers. It's not going to help you. I advise you to keep quiet and listen to what I have to say," Du Toit said, going red in the face.

"It's no good losing your tempers," Gwebu said weakly.

Du Toit stopped. Gwebu gave him a guilty look out of the corner of his eye. Du Toit muttered through his teeth, "I'll fix you for this." The idea came to him to try to bypass Gwebu. He began to grope about for some kind of colourful native idiom.

"The government is a lion," he said, unconsciously deepening his voice. "When it roars it must be obeyed. It's no good trying to fight the lion. But when obeyed, it will look after you and fight for *you*. So don't annoy it, that's all. Or it will bite you."

This time Gwebu made an effort. With a growl in his throat he told them the well-known old fable. But he was a lame and comical lion. There was a burst of laughter. Du Toit now lost control of himself completely and he bellowed across the square :

"Stop that. This isn't a joke. Stop that, I warn you."

The noise stopped, but Du Toit could see that the deterioration in the crowd had gone too far. He decided to get the business done with.

"Under this law the women of this location will have to carry passes from now on if they want to carry on living here."

The words seemed to hang in the air for a moment. Then a man shouted. A woman screamed. People yelled and shook their fists. A scuffle started in the middle of the crowd. He saw one of his constables stagger back with blood on his face. Then there was an uproar. It started among the people around the wounded constable, and billowed out across the square. "*Ngeke* [We won't do it]." "*Ufuna ukusibulala* [You want to kill us]," people were shouting. The whole square seethed and churned with waving arms and bobbing heads. "*Ufuna ukusibulala—bulala—bulala*"—the words dinned in his ears. Du Toit looked around for the constables. They were all standing about with their hands at their sides. He tried to attract Ngubeni's attention, hoping to appeal to him to restore quiet. Ngubeni was sitting in the taxi with his back to him and the window up. He turned away from Ngubeni and cupped his hands and yelled through them, "If you don't stop the noise, I'm closing the meeting," but his voice was drowned out. Then he noticed some men hoist a man up on their shoulders. The man held up his hands for silence and incredibly the noise began to die down. It died down slowly over the square as the man sat quite still with his arms up. When it was quiet, the man lowered his arms but he did not get down on the ground again. In a loud, clear voice he said, " Let the manager speak. When he's finished it will be our turn." He said it again, in Swazi, and then they lowered him.

Du Toit was shocked. Who was he? He peered down at the man who was standing about fifteen yards away in the thick of the crowd. He saw that he was middle-aged and bearded, tall and heavily built, and that he wore an old army overcoat with brass buttons and a black leather cap with a crumpled shield. He could see that the man was not alone, that the people around him were somehow apart from the crowd and close to the man. Then he knew it was Mabaso. He knew it more from the feeling that it could not be anyone else than from actual recognition. He had not seen much of Mabaso, although he had heard a great deal about him. But he had not heard his voice before.

The voice surprised him. It was bright and brittle, with very little accent and a quickness in finding the words. He had imagined Mabaso to be some kind of a kraal spellbinder, something like Ngubeni with a dose of witch doctor thrown in. The voice showed him to be one of those educated types. And an arrogant type at that.

He looked at the people standing around Mabaso. He recognised Sibande. Sibande was one of the location characters, a bit of a troublemaker himself; but he had never taken Sibande seriously. But it looked serious now, Sibande and Mabaso in league. There was Mavuso, too. Hadn't there been a report on him from the mine manager? All the trouble makers, collected together. *What kind of a gang was this?*

The crowd was quiet, waiting for him to continue. He looked down at Mabaso, who was pulling his overcoat straight

159

and fixing the collar on to the button. Grudgingly he took advantage of the silence that Mabaso had won for him, and in doing so, vaguely knew that he had forfeited something to Mabaso.

" So all women here will have to come up to the office and get the forms of registration. The forms will be ready next week. The registration will be done in sections and in streets. We'll start with the old location and work right down to Jubilee City, street by street. The location constables will tell you when it's the turn for your street to register."

Now it was in order to close the meeting. This was the end of the business. He looked again at Mabaso, who was standing with his arms folded. There was a faint half-smile on Mabaso's face. Oddly, he now felt a kind of gratitude towards Mabaso. The man had helped him to-day by quietening the crowd, which was more than Ngubeni and Gwebu had done ; more even than the constables, who had just stood around looking stupid. He felt a vague unwilling respect for Mabaso.

" Well, that's all. The meeting's over. You can go back to your houses."

The taxi with Ngubeni and the Board members started up immediately and drove off into the location. It left a cloud of dust behind. As Du Toit turned to leave the platform, he felt the relief come over him in a rush. He put his hand to his forehead and it came away wet with perspiration. The report for the Council—that could wait for to-morrow. *And* settling accounts with Gwebu.

" Is that what you brought us all here for ? "

He stopped, swung round. Mabaso had moved in from his previous position and was now standing about eight yards from the platform and directly in front of it. There was a hard, impudent jolt in the question that twanged on Du Toit's taut nerves. He stood and glared dumbfounded at Mabaso. Then he knew that he had no choice but to come back to the front of the platform and deal with Mabaso.

" What exactly did you say ? "

" I said is that what you brought us here for ? To hear all this talk about roaring lions and this law being like medicine for our own good ? Aren't you going to answer our questions and hear our views ? This is an important matter for us." There was no politeness or deference in Mabaso, no recognition of the fact that this was a black man addressing a white man.

Du Toit took a tight grip on himself and said stiffly to Gwebu, " Tell him if he wants to make representations, he should do it through the Advisory Board. Tell him that if he had only lived here a little longer he would know that in *this* location all representations come through the Advisory Board."

Gwebu looked helplessly at Mabaso ; with a shrug he started the futile translation, but after a few words he stopped and said, " You heard him."

" Let's not talk about the Advisory Board," Mabaso said. " Nobody here believes in it. Anyway, what has happened to your Advisory Board now ? " He pointed to the still unsettled dust that marked the route of Malooy's taxi into the location.

The people who were leaving the meeting now came back, and the crowd began to press tightly around the platform. There was a tense electric quiet. Suddenly a wave of pressure swept through the crowd, and people were thrown against the platform, striking it with their chests and shoulders. It shuddered on its rickety legs. " Get away from here. You'll smash the platform. Get away you fools." Du Toit roared, making wild scattering movements with his hands. The pressure slackened for a moment, but then there was another convulsive surge forward and a woman in a yellow blanket was heaved up and pinned by her pelvis against the wooden ledge of the platform. She gave a shriek and the crowd pulled away, and she clambered up to the floor of the platform and sat panting and sobbing and wiping her nose with her wrist. Suddenly the wall of bodies thrust against the platform again, almost forcing it off its legs. " Get away from here," Du Toit roared. Then he saw two constables stand- ing near the steps behind the platform. " Get them away," he ordered. The constables came round and shoved and heaved people away until the pressure was taken off the platform. Then he looked up and saw Mabaso standing with his arms folded and calmly waiting. It filled him with sudden fury.

" Tell him to leave the meeting immediately," he ordered in

161

a taut, quivering voice, speaking to Gwebu, but keeping his eyes fixed on Mabaso.

"Don't ask me to do that, sir, because I can't. There are a number of questions which we location people would like cleared up. And I've been asked to put them to you," Mabaso said without waiting for Gwebu to translate.

"Oh—a spokesman? Well, tell him I don't recognise him as a spokesman. Tell him that. The Advisory Board is the only spokesman I recognise. He'd better leave now if he doesn't want trouble."

Faces were pressing in under the rails of the platform, eager and expectant, like spectators around a boxing ring. All over the square the excitement was spreading. Exclamations, laughter, and bursts of shouting shot up and plunged back and travelled on hidden haphazard currents throughout the crowd, to appear again in other places. Nervousness acted as a rein on the excitement, keeping it down, but intensifying its pressure. Most of those in the square could not hear what was happening around the platform, but every shift of the tension spread instantaneously outward, as if forced through the lines of a single nervous network.

"If you don't leave immediately, I'll have you arrested for incitement."

"I'm not inciting anyone," Mabaso said, and people shouted, "*Manyela* [Hear him]—*manyela*."

"Tell them not to be misled by this man," Du Toit said grimly over the rising noise. "Tell them he will lead them into trouble, but when it comes, he will be the first to run away. He'll run like a jackal. I know these agitators." Gwebu translated it against a storm of shouts and protests.

Mabaso raised his arms. When it was quiet enough to be heard, he said :

"I'm not inciting anyone. I'm here simply to ask some questions. All I want is the opportunity to do that." And before Du Toit could reply, he said, "Please tell us, sir, must all women carry passes? What about women with babies? Old grannies? Sick women? Must they go and look for jobs? Who will cook for the men? And what if they can't get jobs—if there aren't

162

enough jobs to go round—are you going to throw them out ?
Are you going to separate wives from their husbands and
children ? And where will they live if you won't give them
passes—in the open veld like animals ? "

Du Toit heard the voice but not the questions. His hands
flew up in a flurry, and came down and gripped the rail hard,
the knuckles whitening through the purplish skin.

" Is it going to be ' *Waar's jou pas ?* '[1] every time a policeman
sees one of our location women ? " Mabaso went on, his voice
sharp, angry, and contemptuous. " Is it going to be *double* the
number of arrests and fines and imprisonments from now on ?
Are the women going to be sent to the farms too ? This is some
law. This is the worst law yet."

" I'm not going to stand here and argue with you," Du Toit
said, turning to go. " If you want to know anything come and
see me in my office."

" Oh no, sir. Don't go away. I'm not the only one who
wants to know—the whole location wants to know."

Du Toit could see that everything he said made it worse—
turned the crowd in favour of Mabaso and against him. He did
not reply. He stood with his hands on his hips and glowered at
Mabaso. At last he said menacingly, " Leave now, or there'll
be trouble."

Mabaso shook his head sadly, but made no effort to move.
The noise was rising again. " *Phendula* [answer]," a hoarse
voice arose out of the square. " *Phendula, phendula,*" the crowd
roared.

Du Toit stood with his hands on his hips, struggling to
decide. He could not answer : he could not go away. To answer
or to go, whatever he did, would be to surrender to Mabaso. To
answer—to allow himself to be questioned and ridiculed by a
location politician in front of a gloating black mob—that was
impossible. To go—and let everyone see that Mabaso had driven
him away from the meeting ! After *he* had ordered Mabaso to
leave the meeting ! No, that too was impossible.

He began a hasty search over the heads of the crowd to try
to find his location constables. He had to strain to see in the

[1] " Afrikaans. ' Where's your pass ? ' "

163

half-light. The sun was almost down now; there was a dying dark orange sunset fading into violet behind the hills. He searched carefully, but the only constables he could see were the two who had cleared the crowd away from the platform : they were tightly locked in the crowd a few yards in front of him. Peering into the gloom, he saw the others at last. They were all standing together at the far end of the square, near the houses. Most of them were crowded under the scaffolding of the water tower.

" Arrest him," Du Toit said to the nearby constables.

The constables looked at each other, and at the people jammed tight around them ; they looked determinedly away from Du Toit, pretending not to have heard.

" Go on, arrest him."

They made weak and futile attempts to free themselves, then quickly gave up and stood still again, now helplessly staring at Du Toit.

" Arrest him, or I'll have you arrested. Go on, arrest him."

They struggled and freed themselves and began to push forward towards Mabaso. People would not move out of their way and their hampered progress sent ripples of movement in different directions through the crowd, but they pushed on. For a moment there was a shocked silence all over the square.

Then a woman began to wail in a high freezing voice. The note hung quivering in the air at a point high above their heads. And then, like a flock of birds rushing up to join it, there came a wild outcry from hundreds of women. And now the men joined in, shouting, and there was pandemonium.

" *Phendula, phendula* [Answer, answer]," people shouted. " *Ngeke* [We won't do it]. *Ufuna ukusibulala* [You want to kill us]." But all words and all separate voices were swallowed up in the vast vault of noise.

Du Toit looked down at the two constables : they were being obstructed all the way on their journey to Mabaso. He looked at Mabaso—their eyes exchanged a look. The look in Du Toit's eyes asked Mabaso to restore order, but Mabaso made no move. Then he knew with a black dismay that he was in the hands of this man. He looked at the constables again. They were only a

164

few yards away from Mabaso, but a group of screaming women were preventing them getting through to him.

The noise on the square now had a desolate and bitter sound, like the cries of a defeated tribe. People were waving their arms and stamping their feet, pounding them hard into the ground in the gathering rhythm of a dance. The noise grew in violence until it reached a point when Du Toit could hear it no longer, and he was conscious only of the distorted faces and the churning mass of bodies.

The fury of the noise had a hypnotic effect on him, holding him to the rail of the platform, his eyes glued to the scene, as if he were watching it all in a cinema. He saw one of the women pull her headcloth off and wave it like a flag, and shuffle her feet in a tense entranced kind of dance. A furious torrent of Swazi words poured from her. Then she stood back, and with the swiftness of a striking snake, spat at one of the constables. He saw the silvery dribble slide down the man's face. The next moment the crowd fell back from the constables, leaving a space around them. The constables looked around in terror, and began to move backward, back towards the platform.

"Don't stop. Arrest her," Du Toit shouted above the noise.

The constables stopped retreating, like hunting dogs called to halt.

"Go on, arrest her. I order you to arrest her."

One of the constables suddenly leaped forward and seized the woman, holding both her wrists in one hand. With his free hand he unhooked the handcuffs from his belt. He tried to lock them on her, but she wrenched a hand free and slapped him in the face. He pulled back from her and his hand holding the handcuffs jerked above his head and then jerked down again, and the handcuffs doubled forward on the chain holding the two halves and struck the woman on the crown of her head. It was impossible to say if it was an accident.

The woman collapsed with a deep moan. Her blanket fell open and her heavy round breast rolled out of her blouse. Her lips oozed white froth and her eyes turned up into her head, showing the huge white undersides of her eyeballs. She writhed and moaned like a stricken animal. She flopped on to her back and the convulsions got into a rhythm and she began to roll her hips in a horrible sexual motion.

"Almighty God, she's in a fit," Du Toit screamed. From his head to his feet he was seized with horror and disgust. He stopped breathing, his head swam. He was no longer conscious of the crowd. Without knowing what he was doing, he turned and left the platform and began striding back to his office. Half-way, his legs began to run, and he climbed the veranda steps in two huge leaps. He darted into the office and collapsed, breathless, into his chair.

A moment later Andries Gwebu burst in. "What's the matter, sir, what's the matter?"

"Lock the door."

He put his head on his arms and tried to recover his breath. There was no noise from outside. There was a great chilled silence over the square. For over a minute there was no sound.

Then, like the crack of a pistol shot, a heavy jagged stone crashed through the window, spattering glass across the floor. The next instant a stone thumped against the door, splitting the panel. Two more stones flew into the room with vicious force, shattering window-panes. Then there was a bombardment of stones and other missiles. They clattered on the tin roof and thumped against the wall. Something struck the wall near the door with a hollow burst and subsided in a tinkle of glass. A length of bicycle chain came flailing into the room and landed against the farther wall.

Du Toit was kneeling below the desk on the side opposite the door. He reached up and tried to pull the telephone towards him, gripping under its base with the tips of his fingers. A stone sailed through a broken window and struck between the two bottles of ink, hurtling them across the desk like billiard balls. A bottle smashed against a picture, leaving it bristling with jagged glass splinters and swinging wildly on its hook. Then, with a flash, he was hit on the forehead, and he dropped below the desk again. He looked across the room. Gwebu was crouching against the wall right up beneath the window. He saw that this was the only safe place. He tried again to pull the telephone across the desk but the cord was too short. For a moment he remained on all fours beneath the desk. Then he crawled across the room, keeping his back very low, and crept under the window and crouched down in front of Gwebu.

There was a continuous crashing hailstorm of stones and bottles hitting the roof, and screeching along the metal and thudding against the walls and smashing windows along the length of the building. And there was a crazy furore of yelling outside.

After a while he knew that the mob had come right up below the veranda. He could tell from the greater force and more vertical direction of the stone throwing. Stones were coming up through the windows, hitting hard on the ceiling, pitting and bending the compressed cardboard. He heard the grunting and heavy breathing of people below the veranda, a different and distinct sound from the hideous yelling and the thunder of missiles.

He sat cramped down with his chin on his knees, watching the door. He waited. Any moment now. The door would burst open, they would stand there a moment, looking round in the dim light : then they would see them in the corner. Drag them out. Once out there . . .

He rubbed his eyes with his fists that smelled of the dust of the floor. The skin of his face felt stiff, paralysed, as when one is very drunk.

" Andries, get my revolver," he said in a mild voice. " In the middle drawer."

Gwebu crawled over to the desk and reached into the drawer without standing up. He crawled back across the floor, holding the revolver against his chest. Du Toit watched him, curiously detached.

" The first bastard comes in that door gets it right between the eyes," Du Toit said, clicking back the safety catch and aiming the gun very carefully at a point just beyond the edge of the door.

He was very calm now. His hand was steady, his head clear. How many could he account for ? Six, he reckoned, if he didn't waste shots. Unless they rushed him. Well, in that case, three or four. Then they'd rush him, drag him outside. He hoped unconsciousness would come quickly.

He had become very objective. It was all an adventure he had read about somewhere. He was dead calm and objective. The fear was no longer there; it had been killed along with everything else in him that had been killed. He had no feelings at all, no terror, no regret, no anger. He had eyes and ears that noted everything with a sharp, alert precision, like a recording machine, but the rest of him had gone dead. He had never felt so calm in all his life.

He thought of the most trivial things. Of his Alsatian dog, the way he retrieved a stick with his wet tongue lolling out of the side of his mouth, and his lips pulled up over the back teeth, grinning. Of the feel of his car as it loafed up a hill in third gear. Of how much he owed the Greek for cigarettes.

Gwebu was stiff with fright. His face had drained of colour and it had a look of great age. It had become a muddy, patchy, whitish grey that showed up all the blemishes in his skin. He was breathing against Du Toit's ear, and his breath had a warm and sweetish smell. His dirty sweater was dank with perspiration. He sat silent and rigid, and his knee was pressing hard into Du Toit's ribs.

" Why don't the bastards come ? " Du Toit asked. He shifted his legs to move, froglike, a few inches away from Gwebu. He put his hands to his forehead and the sticky blood that came off on to his fingers looked like tar in the murky light. Gwebu moved along too, jamming his knees back into Du Toit's body. Then it seemed as if the stone throwing was dying down. How long had it gone on—five hours ? Five minutes ? The noise outside was as loud as ever, but there were definitely fewer stones and missiles landing on the building.

Now what made this silly little bastard follow me in here ? Du Toit suddenly asked himself. The others all run away, and of them all this one sticks by me. My friend, my only friend. My educated baboon.

He caught sight of the strained putty-white face : it made him smile. Was this the same foxy little show-off he had worked with all this time ? This punctured, stinking little bag ? But whatever made him come in here? That was really funny. A white man lynched by a black mob becomes a hero, but a black man? Just another little fatality. It was really funny the way he came up in here.

Why don't the bastards come?

There was only a light patter of stones now, but the mob was still there below the veranda. There was the eerie feeling of something new being prepared. Then a wild scream of excitement tore through the air. Out of the corner of his eye he saw a pink glow high on the wall opposite the window. It rapidly spread down the wall, and on to the metal light fittings and the jagged window glass above his head. Then he saw the flames. Cautiously he pulled himself up and peered over the window ledge.

" Almighty God, they're burning my car," he screamed in a cracked, agonised voice.

It was on its side and blazing fiercely, and the mob was dancing around it. The fire reflected on the sweating faces and distended eyes, and threw gross shadows on the ceiling of the room. The abandoned dancing and high, almost musical shrieking seemed to create a scene of trees and swamp and rotting foliage, and he was a thousand miles from civilisation, a concealed spectator to a frenzied jungle ceremony.

Some women ran along the veranda, passing within a yard of him ; they took chairs out of the next office and threw them over the side, and those below pulled them apart and piled the wood on the flames. They threw down handfuls of papers, and then the filing cabinet itself. It landed with a crash and the drawers were pulled out and the old records tilted into the underside of the car. He saw a big-built woman wearing a red headcloth, step out of the crowd, and hurl a bottle of liquid at the car. As it crashed against the framework, the flames leapt up with a roar. He smelt the dense, bitter fumes of burning rubber and rexine, and he saw the windows crack and bend. It made him wince ; it was like a torture inflicted on his own body. Then there was a whoosh of flames as the petrol tank burst, and the car was consumed in a flare of light that illuminated the ground for hundreds of yards around.

169

Suddenly a volley of rifle shots rang out, fired from near by. There was a scream, "Police!" and the crowd began to scatter. By the time the lorry full of Flying Squad police came to a skidding stop alongside the burning car, the crowd of rioters had melted away. All had disappeared into the dark township. All, except two dark figures lying on the ground. Both were women. Both were dead.

CHAPTER ELEVEN

"IF YOU ask me, it's been a glorious waste of time," Sergeant Ackerman said.

Lieutenant Swanepoel said nothing. The man was really getting on his nerves. Always first out with the bright and obvious remark. Lieutenant Swanepoel took the notebook out of his breast pocket and read the entry: "Complainant: F. J. van der Rhyst. Complaint: Stock-theft. Notes: Five sheep killed (recently—*hides still soft*. Last night?) Hides left at (presumably?) scene of crime, but contents thereof removed. Interrogated farm boys (18). Searched and examined huts, also s. of c. No definite clues as to culprit(s)." He tried to write, "Lay some kind of trap for next time," but the car was lurching and the pencil went all over the page. He put the book and pencil back and buttoned down the flap of his pocket. It was true there wasn't much chance of solving this one but he didn't need this clever parakeet to tell him so.

"The bastards are getting smart," Ackerman said in a way that made him sound glad about it. "That's a new one on me —cutting out all the meat and leaving the skins. How can you identify meat?"

That was pure crap, of course. It was an old trick. Everything Ackerman said was crap. As for identification, all you did was look for signs of a recently eaten meal of mutton. But there was nothing in the pots, only dried mealie meal. And no sign of the fat anywhere. They usually kept the tails long after the meat had been eaten. But there were no tails or fat cakes. Only those hides. Besides, it was pretty definite none of those farm boys had been eating meat. You could always tell—they looked sleek and satisfied as cats.

" You should've arrested the whole damn' lot of those farm Kaffirs," Ackerman said. " Arrested them and handed them over to me. Damn' sure I'd have got confessions out of them."

" No, that would have been useless. The lieutenant is right. Best thing is to lay a trap for next time, like the lieutenant says," said Constable Roberts, looking straight ahead. He was at the steering wheel, keeping his eyes fixed on every advancing yard of the winding, churned-up farm road.

What's the matter with this idiot, Swanepoel thought. You'd have thought that after the other night he'd have the decency to keep quiet instead of bleating away like this.

" There's a story Van der Rhyst's got a couple of daughters, hot numbers," Ackerman was saying. " You know, when you said we're coming out here I sort of looked forward to it, thinking we'd meet these girls. Real hot toddies, the fellows say."

" For God's sake, can't you think of anything else ? " Lieutenant Swanepoel said irritably.

Sergeant Ackerman looked at him, surprised. " Oh, all right," he said, slumping back into the corner. The car bounced heavily in a rut, and a long strip of black lacquered hair came unstuck and fell into his face. Ackerman took out the comb that was clipped to his pocket like a fountain pen and smoothed the hair back, slowly and lovingly. He wiped off the discoloured brilliantine with the heel of his palm, wiped his hand under the seat, and replaced the comb in his pocket. A moment later the strip of hair was jerked loose again, and Ackerman took out the comb. That had been going on all through the trip—on the way out to Welgelegen, and the way back. It annoyed Swanepoel almost as much as the other thing.

Why did he have to be landed with *him* as head sergeant ?

It was a bad affair the other night. What was even worse was not settling it up next day. That was a mistake. But he let himself be talked into it. In some ways that Du Toit was as big a fool as Ackerman. It was elementary that you couldn't leave a thing like that go. Simply handing out an invitation for a repeat performance. Maybe there was something about this place. Maybe if he didn't get out of it quick he'd become as soft-headed as Du Toit and Ackerman.

Lieutenant Swanepoel's blue eyes were bloodshot at the rims. He had not been sleeping well. In the two years he had been at Nelstroom something had gone wrong with all his plans, and he was beginning to feel a bitter disenchantment with the place and everybody connected with it. His girl was in Pretoria and now she was making excuses. Now she wanted to wait until after her sister's wedding, and her letters were full of remarks like, " We've got all our lives ahead," and " The family think I'm too young to get married. I've been wondering . . ." She was cooling off. Probably there was somebody else on the scene. And there was the farce about the rugby. In Pretoria, and later in the Police Training College, he had played in good teams and had come right to the top. Now it was third-rate teams on primitive grounds, before sparse crowds that watched the matches from their cars and honked their horns for applause. Week after week he turned out against raw players whose only idea of the game was to send the opposite team to hospital. He stood a chance of being permanently injured in some quite worthless match. His game was going to hell and he was falling out of view.

" Where's that burnt-out kraal we're supposed to turn off at ? " Constable Roberts asked. " I've got a feeling we're on the wrong road."

" No, it's the right road," Swanepoel said. " I remember that clump of bluegums. The road always looks different on the way back."

" Not good for the car, all this bumping about."

He liked Roberts. Roberts was still new in the force ; only a kid, but he was the right type. Did what he was told, and had plenty of guts. Good material ; he could make something of him. There ought to be a way to get him up to sergeant quickly, so that he wouldn't have to be working with this Ackerman all the time.

" How many miles've we done? " Swanepoel asked.

" Thirteen."

" As I make it, the burnt-out kraal should be on the nineteen mark."

The trouble with Ackerman, he was too damn' light in the

head and too damn' clever for one man. Not a policeman's backside. And sex mad. A man's entitled to have his fun, but Ackerman, he'd put it in anything. Ugh—those ugly old bags! The funny thing was he could do much better, there was something about him the girls liked: he had a way with girls.

"Didn't we pass that burnt-out kraal a little way back?" Ackerman asked.

"Keep on going," Swanepoel said to Roberts.

Ackerman shrugged his shoulders and fell back into the corner. Actually, just from looking at him, you'd think he was a smart and efficient policeman. He looked good in the dark blue uniform with the gold buttons and braid, the gabardine breeches and leather leggings. The uniform gave him a kind of responsible air. It was only when he opened his mouth . . .

The road took them through a winding pass between high boulders that almost touched overhead, and then down a ravine across a small almost dry stream. Every yard was slow, tortuous going. Across the stream it was flatland for a while and they made better speed.

"Is the radio up?" Swanepoel asked, twisting round to peer out of the back window.

"It's no good putting it up. We won't hear a thing from this distance," Ackerman said.

Shut up, Swanepoel said tensely to himself. "It's down. We'd better stop," he said to Roberts. Roberts stopped the car and got out and pulled up the steel aerial that was attached to the back mudguard. All around them was the squeaking of crickets, penetrating into the car like pulsations of heat. A flock of guinea fowl which had intended to hide in the bushes while they passed now took fright at their stopping and darted frantically across the road. It was remote, untouched country, peaceful and undisturbed.

"Think I'll have a leak," said Ackerman. He opened the door and walked stiffly across the grass towards an anthill and relieved himself for a long time. Then he shook himself back into his trousers and came back to the car. They moved off again with the long flexible antenna swaying behind them like a fishing

174

rod. They caught up with some of the guinea fowl that had straggled behind the flock, and Roberts tried to run them over. They passed them and Swanepoel took out his revolver and fired two shots at them through the window, but he missed. There was nothing on the radio, only static and a loud rumbling hum. Roberts switched it off again. They were coming down into the mountain pass, out of the plateau and into the valley, and there were more trees and rocks and the air smelled warmer and sweeter. Occasionally they passed groups of kraal huts, but they did not see any people. They saw a herd of Kaffir cattle, long-horned, thin, and wild-looking, and as the car went past, the lean white tickbirds flapped up in agitation, then lazily settled down again on the backs of the cattle. For miles behind them, hanging on the lifeless air, was the dust that the car had stirred up.

Swanepoel's hands came out and waited, poised. There was a faraway look in his eyes. Suddenly his body tightened and he swung his shoulders, first one way, then the other; he swerved and then he was flying for the line. His body was functioning like a machine and there was a miraculous sense of timing and all his instincts were right. Now he was being crowded over the touchline, and he dropped the ball on to his foot and punted it to where, without looking, he knew his centre would be. Then the ball came back again in a hard, straight pass, and he took it running, and there was an exhilarating burst of speed, the opposition was left behind, and he slowed down and cantered to place the ball between the posts, dead in the middle.

He looked down and saw his clenched fist making short piston-like movements across his chest.

" . . . didn't own the farm, only managed it, a fellow named Smits," Ackerman was saying to Roberts. " It was before your and the lieutenant's time. It was somewhere round these parts. A nice-looking fellow, too."

" How'd you get to hear about it ? The thing is to get the tip-off, that's the difficult thing," Roberts said.

" This Kaffir woman was the wife of one of his boys. The boy himself came and told us. This Smits, he even gave her a ring, a gold ring, which she wore in court. He said he wanted to marry her. Can you beat that? God, he must've been hard up. Paid all the expenses for her lawyer. He was the only white man on the farm, and I suppose in a way I can understand it. It's in these circumstances these cases happen."

" What did they get ? "

" Each got two years."

There he goes again, thought Swanepoel furiously. Off on that subject again. The expert. Why don't we set up a special miscegenation squad and put him in charge ? That would be one solution. That would be the dead-right job for him, the dirty-minded goat.

" We had to trap him," Ackerman went on. " We kept watch at an empty hut at the bottom of his lands. And then one night he came along with this Kaffir woman, leading her by the hand. She was big, but nicely built, not bad-looking for a Kaffir woman. It came out in court that she was only nineteen, but I'd have sworn she was older. Anyway, they went in the hut and we looked in the window and sure enough he gave her the works. We couldn't see everything but the moon was shining, making a kind of beam of light across the hut, and each time his arse came up into this beam of moonlight. We rushed them and shone torches, and you should have seen their faces. We arrested them and took the girl to the district surgeon to take slides. You got to do that these days—you got to have medical evidence. My God, she fought like a tiger. It took five of us to hold her down while the old district surgeon did his stuff."

" I hear there's a lot of it going on on the farms," Roberts said. " More than you think. Only the difficult thing is to get the tip-off."

" Yes, you got to trap them," Ackerman said.

Swanepoel was sitting stiffly upright and his eyes were blazing. He had hold of the leather loop dangling beside the window, gripping it so hard that it crumpled in his hand.

" In Capetown, that's where it *really* goes on," Ackerman said.

" I've heard so," Roberts said.

" It's those Malay girls, the ones you can't say if they are coloured or white. A certain fellow, a pal of mine, he used to go to a certain place down by the docks. Do you know what

176

he used to do ? Look at the fingernails. Blue fingernails—send them back. That was his motto."

" I've heard that," Roberts said.

" They say when you've once had a black girl——"

" SHUT UP. BOTH of you."

They fell into gloomy silence, like children caught playing a dirty game.

*   *   *

This kind of talk infuriated Swanepoel. It rubbed on obscure inflammations deep in his mind. It sent burning particles racing through his blood stream. It was not anything he could understand or reason about, it was something that lived in the very centre of him, and that seemed to be responsible for everything he did. It made him what he was, if now he was hard, zealous, and efficient, it was that that made him so.

Often he suffered from black depressions, and when in that state he would often think about his childhood. He always thought of things in a certain order. There were the farm, the days in the fields, the ploughing, the hunting, the long journeys to and from school. The bright hot days. The smell of the dusty, denuded veld in winter. And like a cloud hovering in the sky, the loneliness. Then he would see the kitchen of the farm-house—no other part, only the kitchen. There were the black coal stove and the huge old pots and the row of cups hanging on hooks along the kitchen dresser. The whole family was there, sitting down to the evening meal—his mother, his father, his two sisters, himself. There were prayers, and they ate in a stern, forbidding silence. The loneliness and solitude of the vast veld outside hung like a weight on their spirits. Then it was years earlier and he was a small boy playing in the sand with the squatters' children who lived in the kraal at the bottom of the farm. He wore clothes and they didn't. He learnt their language and played their games. At the end of the day they went back to their pondokkies and he went back to the white farmhouse. As he walked away, he would hear their singing and laughter, and somehow it made him sad. And back in the kitchen his mother was saying, " Don't eat with your hands. White people

177

use a knife and fork. If you eat like a Kaffir, you'll grow black hands." And later, before going to bed, he was guiltily looking at his hands to see if they were becoming Kaffir hands.

"Don't talk so loud. If you talk like a Kaffir you'll get thick Kaffir lips."

And there came the day when he was forbidden to play with the squatters' children. And the day when he no longer wanted to and the day when he felt ashamed of his sin of associating with them, and when he began hating them. And they grew up together on the same farm, hating each other.

Then his father was hitching a rifle on to his shoulder before going out to the fields to investigate some trouble with the farm boys ; and he was going too, rifle in hand. And for days afterward there was his mother's choked, overwrought voice in the kitchen, berating the servants for hours on end. And later, in school, he was being told of the wars and massacres and heroes and martyrs, and he was parading with other boys in celebration of past victories, or in mournful remembrance of the black crimes of an enemy who still lived all around them.

Then it was his last year at school, and there was the day when with shock and shame, he first noticed the peculiarity about his sister. Although he had lived with the fact all his life without noticing it, he was suddenly aware that his elder sister was very dark. He and the rest of the family were as blonde as Swedes, but she had a pallid sepia complexion, with a heavy black skin blemish on her neck, and stiff black crinkled hair, and something about her features that left a nagging, horrifying doubt forever churning in his mind. Then a fury would take hold of him . . .

When he was sixteen, there was a turning point in his life. Everyone else could see it although he himself was not aware of it. The bonds holding him to his family had suddenly gone. Although he continued to live at home, it was as if he were sharing a house with strangers. There seemed to be nothing that he wanted to say to his family and nothing that he wanted to hear from them. He became secretive, solitary, and aloof. All his former friends fell away. He was sent to high school in Pretoria, but even there he found himself to be too old for his school friends. He was content to have just one friend, a boy two years his senior who was an apprentice electrician. A tightening and hardening was noticeable in him. His schoolwork made a sudden and surprising improvement, and he developed a passion for football, which he played with a grim ferocity that made him the outstanding performer in the team.

His friend had money in his pocket and took him to bars and introduced him to girls. He followed his friend as if hypnotised, and tried to imitate his way of speaking, of wearing clothes and smoking cigarettes. This boy was a particularly great talker, and his favourite subject was the races of people. He was always holding forth about Indians, Jews, Kaffirs, English-men, Greeks, and Chinese. He hated them all, in a particular order and for different reasons : Indians because they were dirty, dishonest, and bred too fast ; Jews because they were all fabulously rich and crooked and seduced Afrikaner girls ; Kaffirs because they were lazy and treacherous and were savages who had massacred the whites and would do it again, given a chance ; the English because they had stolen the land from Paul Kruger, and killed off millions of Afrikaner women and children in con-centration camps in the Boer War ; Greeks because they were dark-skinned and ran little fruit shops like Indians, yet tried to pass off as Europeans ; Chinese because they were sly and had a funny smell in their shops and were first cousins of the Indians. He disliked even certain peoples he had never come across—Japs and South Americans, for instance. The French, although he had never met any, he hated with a particular loathing because they allowed actual Negroes to dance with white girls in their cabarets. All white races, including the Afrikaners, were Europeans, but he had little time for most of the actual European races, who had become too soft and decadent. Only the Germans, first cousins of the Afrikaners, had his respect. They were tough and did not have a soft attitude about race mingling. Races became cousins to each other not for any ethnic or political reasons, but according to his own arbitrary standards of racial decency. Japs and Italians, although fighting on the same side as the Germans, were hardly cousins to them or to the Afrikaners.

There was no end to the stream of comment about other races, and it was always wrapped up with a passionate defence

179

of the Afrikaner race, which had been wronged, cheated, and misunderstood, and was still surrounded by enemies. English bishops, Gandhi and Nehru, Russia, Kaffirboeties, Roosevelt, Liberals, Anglicised Afrikaners, Oxford University, the gold mines, the Belgian Congo, the English press—there were many enemies. But the Afrikaners were the bearers of white civilisation. They were the pure white race in a sea of black savagery. So their cause would prevail, despite the enemies.

It all made a deep impression on Swanepoel. He did not have the eloquence or vehemence of his friend, or the ability to explore all the intricacies of this fascinating subject, but he listened to it with deep satisfaction. He never questioned it because it satisfied a deep thirst within him. It assuaged a longing for assurance that he was different and better than the black savages who walked about everywhere. If to do this required him to believe that he belonged to a special superior offshoot of the human race, it did not strike him as fanciful or unreasonable.

When he left school, he took a job in the Tramways Department. This was at the beginning of the war and many of his school friends were joining the Army, but he had no desire to fight an enemy who was making such a good job of his own enemies. Instead, he went with his friend to meetings of ardent and brilliant young Nationalists who saw the war as their great opportunity. They heard the promises from Berlin, and gloried in the feats of sabotage carried out by some of their members, and dreamed of the new life that would dawn when the Nazi system came to their country.

Then the war was over, and a period of gloom and disappointment set in. His job became increasingly irksome, and one day he threw it up and joined the police. There did not seem to be any particular reason for doing this, he could not remember having a debate with himself about it. He just walked out of his office one afternoon and went round to the police barracks a few blocks away. But after a few months in the recruits training school he knew that there would never be a doubt that he was in the right career. He rose rapidly in the police force. He had all the talents for a policeman. He soon learnt the tricks and wiles of the defence lawyers and how to prepare his cases so that there were no loopholes. He acquired a magical gift for extracting confessions. In all his cases, big or small, he would go after his quarry with the grim concentration of a hunter on the spoor of a big prize.

They made him a lieutenant at twenty-five. And a year later they chose him for a special training course. This was a great honour because only the best men were invited to attend this course. By then Dr. Malan had come to power and the Nationalists had won for themselves the victory that Hitler could not win for them. The programme that for so long had been only a dream of the Nationalists now became practical politics. And the need arose for tough, reliable men to carry it out. It was a strange programme, a collection of slogans taken off the banners of numerous backveld elections and elevated into a misty ideology of race and destiny. Its catchword was " *apartheid*," a word with a potent appeal to the longing for racial exclusiveness. A word with a thousand meanings and no meaning, but with a curious power to change the meaning of other words. Under apartheid the white people became the only people, and the black people the black menace ; education became an evil, and racial friendship sedition ; the Bible became the authority for imposing slavery, and world opinion became petty, malign, and of no consequence. Apartheid required strange things of people. It required queer, novel laws. And it needed a special type of policeman to enforce them.

The six months that he spent in the camp for special training were the best time of his life. He was already beginning to feel a nostalgia for those days. Those were days full of activity and interest. Breakfast in the mess with a grand bunch of boys, the cream of the force. The comradeship of belonging to a special set-apart few. Lectures and the notebooks filling up every day with the tiny, tidy handwriting ; intelligence work, military science, riot suppression, law, political theory. Novel subjects for a policeman. Out in the veld, manœuvres and gunnery practice. Lying on his belly and firing the Bren gun and mortar into the bushes. The thrill of good marksmanship. Later dismantling the pieces, holding the warm, oily, precision-engineered sections lovingly in his hands. The ride back, the

181

good dinner in the mess, the fooling around, the practical jokes, the singing, the billiards. The nights in the bungalow cramming in the precious material from the notebooks.

There were frequent visits to the camp by ministers of the government and the senior police chiefs. Everyone could see how these high personages were put in a good mood from the minute they set foot in the camp. Everything there pleased them. They spoke to the men in an easy familiar way, shook their hands warmly, and treated them as equals. They certainly added to a man's sense of importance, these visits.

He played a lot of rugby, practice in the late afternoons, matches in town at week-ends. He turned out for Police " A " and played a thrustful, alert game with just that flair for the big moment that made him a favourite with the sports reporters. His reputation as a footballer gave a kind of authority to everything else he did, and so his work and opinions made a great impression on his senior officers. He was marked for a bright future.

It was after a match in Pretoria that he met Aletta Brink. There was a party, and he saw her across the room, tall and trim in a blue costume. He went over and presented himself, and after the first few moments he was in love. She had been out of school only a year : she was immature and talkative, but he was blind to any blemishes in her. He visited her every week-end. At last they decided to get married. They fixed no date and did not have a formal engagement, but it was understood that they would marry as soon as he took up his new post after the course.

And then the course was over and they sent him to Nelstroom. The appointment was meant as a reward and a compliment, for it gave him charge of a large police area. No other officer at his age had been given such an appointment.

There was plenty to do in Nelstroom in the first few months : improve and enlarge the establishment, train new men, bring in up-to-date methods. But after that the work settled down and became routine. At first he had watched the location with great wariness, expecting it to blow up like a land mine. But nothing happened. Every day the vans came in with the usual dreary collection of cases : assault, theft, possession of liquor, pass offences, and location regulation infringements. That was all. Nothing that had the least connection with the work he had done on the course. He would scrutinise the dismal list of entries in the occurrence book and feel that he had been cheated. Nelstroom was a backwater. His reports were dull and uneventful and would never arouse the slightest interest at headquarters. The only event of any importance just had to happen when he was away from Nelstroom, and had to be so messed up by Ackerman that it was impossible to insist on going into the location to fix things up. And on top of the disappointments about his job there was the farce about the rugby and the wreck of his plans concerning Aletta Brink. He was frustrated and embittered.

*   *   *

They were about twelve miles from Nelstroom and halfway down the mountainside when they picked up the radio message. Constable Nel, who had been left in charge of the station, was calling desperately into the empty ether. ". . . Lieutenant Swanepoel. Calling Lieutenant Swanepoel. There's a riot in the location. This is Nelstroom Station calling Lieutenant Swanepoel. Can you hear, Lieutenant? There's a riot in the location."

It came through faintly. The car was too full of static and the distance over the broken country too great for the weakly-powered message.

" Stop the car," Swanepoel ordered.

He got out and took Roberts' place at the wheel and tuned the radio to get more clarity.

" Did you hear that? There's a riot among the Kaffirs. The black bastards are rioting. I knew something was up," Ackerman yelled from the back seat.

" Shut up. How the hell can we hear with all this racket going on."

Swanepoel at last got the voice more clearly. He took the microphone off its hook and held it to his mouth and slipped the button up with his thumb. There was a grim one-sided smile on his face.

" Lieutenant Swanepoel calling. I can hear you, Nelstroom. Can you hear me? This is Swanepoel."

183

" Thank God I got you, Lieutenant. There's a riot in the location. Where are you now ? "

" At Olifant's Kloof. How long's it been going on ? "

" I don't know. I just got the message. A motorist was passing the location and he brought the message."

" Is anyone killed ? "

" We think Du Toit was. He never phoned us. He was in his office but he never phoned."

" Get all the available men and get them there and see they're armed."

" They're on the way back from Withoek. I've contacted them already."

" Smash up that riot."

" Yes, sir."

" We'll go straight there. Tell the chaps to shoot and smash it up. That's the orders."

Swanepoel drove the car the rest of the way. Once he nearly overturned it skidding around a sharp corner. When they reached the tar road, he put the siren on, and went the last few miles as fast as the car could go. A few minutes before reaching the gate he heard the shots.

Swanepoel drove through the gate and stopped the car beside the lorry. Du Toit's car was still on fire ; bitter black fumes were billowing out of it. The armed police had only just climbed down from the lorry, and were standing about waiting for orders. Swanepoel saw the dead bodies lying on their faces, the blankets heaped and disarranged about their shoulders. With his boot he pushed one on to its back, and saw that the eye was blown through. Apart from these two there was no sign of any of the rioters. All had disappeared into the township. He noticed that the light was on in Du Toit's office and told Ackerman, " Put a guard at the gate. Let no one go in or out. And wait here for further orders." To Roberts he said, " Come with me," and the two of them went up the stairs to Du Toit's office.

CHAPTER TWELVE

SWANEPOEL WALKED to the window and ran his finger along the jagged edge of a broken pane. His shoulders were hunched and stiff, and his mouth was set in a hard line.

Outside the Flying Squad men were beginning to fool around. They kept bringing their rifles up and aiming them at the windows of the houses, saying " Pow " when they had the aim dead right: then dropping them hard on the ground and slapping each other's shoulders and laughing uproariously. They were becoming bored and restless. The sounds of their horseplay came into the room and unsettled the discussion.

" Do you mean to say you can't identify *any of them* ? " Swanepoel again asked.

" I've told you about Mabaso."

" We've got all that about Mabaso. We've got all that angle. I mean any of the others."

Du Toit looked at him helplessly. He was sitting at the debris-littered desk with his hands clenched and pressed between his knees. He had washed his face in the corner basin, but the blood was beginning to trickle down again, and his hair was wet and sticky.

Swanepoel looked from Du Toit to Constable Roberts, who was holding an open notebook, and shook his head in slow, sad pity. All Swanepoel wanted were some facts and names and a version of the riot that more or less agreed with his own idea of what must have happened. He wanted to go right in after them, bust in on them before they had a chance to destroy evidence and concoct alibis. But there had to be some material first, some identification of culprits and a simple framework of facts. Without that the whole thing was liable to misfire, the case collapsing in court and the accused walking clean out of it for lack of evidence.

"You see, we can't have a case with just Mabaso. Not after all this. We'd look damn' stupid if there was a case with only one accused in the dock. You see that, don't you?"

"Yes," Du Toit said glumly. He wanted to help but somehow things were not so clear now. During the riot everything had seemed perfectly clear, but now he could not get his thoughts in order. Now that the riot was over, the fright had caught up with him. He had a watery feeling in his stomach and his hand trembled so badly that the pattering of his thumb and forefinger on the desktop could be heard right across the room. He had no control over his tongue, and he kept talking about things that were no help to Swanepoel, and Swanepoel kept stopping him and saying they were irrelevant.

"We'd be a laughing stock," Swanepoel said.

"Yes, I suppose so."

Swanepoel realised that his impatience only increased Du Toit's confusion, so he conducted the interview with a tight but unsure restraint on himself. He strode restlessly about the room, but he tried to keep his voice even. His hands were like puppets, agitating the air, chasing each other, retiring to his pockets.

"Look. Let's start again. Let's carefully start again."

"Yes."

"Now here you are, addressing this meeting, and suddenly there's this first outburst of yelling and screaming."

"Yes."

"Then Mabaso is lifted up on his supporters' shoulders, and on a prearranged signal from Mabaso the crowd quietens down."

"Yes."

"This is very peculiar, you know. Why should he quieten them down? What's his motive?"

"I don't know. All I know is that he did it. And then, at that stage, the insolent bastard, what he does, he calmly gives me permission to carry on."

"You say that afterwards he made an inflammatory speech?"

"Yes. Well, questions rather."

"It doesn't matter. Inflammatory questions. Look, it's

186

perfectly obvious why he quietens them down. He suddenly remembers he wants to ask these questions. He has his instructions from his outfit, and he holds the crowd back in order to ask these inflammatory questions. That's it. He doesn't want to quieten them down, only to inflame them further. The questions are simply part of the whole plan to attack you. That's the answer."

It seemed right. Anything seemed right to Du Toit at that moment. There was a perplexed look in his face and he tried to force himself to think, but all he could remember were noises, smells, and a vast but vague commotion.

"I don't know," he said, running his fingers through his hair. "It sounds reasonable. He was definitely in control of them, and sort of directing them to—to do whatever they did."

"Right. Roberts—take this down : 'Mabaso called off the first attack in order to further inflame the crowd by asking certain inflammatory questions. Then . . .' Then he waves them on to attack you, is that right ? "

"Just a minute. Did I say that ? No, that's not quite right. Actually, after that I spoke. I even closed the meeting. We've got to get this correct, you know. It's no good putting anything down just because we're in a hurry. They're going to get hold of some lawyer or other to defend them, and then I'll be made to look a fool in the witness box for not being accurate." He wiped his face with a handkerchief, smearing a streak of blood across his forehead. A worried look came into his face. Then he said :

"Actually, it was that woman . . ." He looked away, embarrassed.

"Cross it out," Swanepoel said brusquely to Constable Roberts. The muscles in his cheek moved like hard acorns under the skin.

"That woman ? "

"Yes. It was horrible. Half naked and heaving about——"

"Please. Please, didn't we agree to leave her out of it ? She's quite irrelevant. I thought we'd agreed on that. We're talking about a prearranged attack on you—prearranged hours beforehand by means of propaganda on walls and suchlike, and

187

for the life of me I can't see what a woman having a fit has got to do with that. Just try to keep your mind on the riot. Just give me the riot."

" All right."

" Now you've closed the meeting. Take it up from there. What happens then ? "

" Well, after I closed the meeting, they attacked the platform, almost smashing it."

" I see. Stormed the platform. Right. Roberts, take down : ' They stormed the platform with such violence that they almost smashed it.' Now I want you to think very carefully. When they stormed the platform, did they have anything in their hands ? Think hard. What did you see in their hands ? "

Du Toit looked desperately around the room, as if he had been cornered, and his eyes fell on Gwebu, who was limply standing against the wall.

" I couldn't say, sir. I didn't see *anything*. I was stiff with fright, sir," Gwebu said in a startled voice.

" Think carefully," Swanepoel said to Du Toit. " Did you see anything glinting ? "

" I don't.seem to remember anything like that. It—it was too dark to see properly."

" Now think—would they have been carrying knives or razors or anything like that ? " He came and sat with one buttock on the desk ; he leaned forward and brought his face close to Du Toit's. " You see, it would be very peculiar if they were not. In these riots they always attack with dangerous weapons. It's invariable. And it would be most peculiar, if they didn't in *this* particular case, which was obviously prearranged before-hand."

" Knives and razors ? "

" Yes. Or axes or bicycle chains or iron bars—anything like that ? "

Du Toit put his head between his hands and sat still for more than a minute. Swanepoel stared at his head and there came an instant when he suddenly noticed the silvery cross made by the intersection of the hunting scar and the hair parting. He wondered why he had never noticed it before. It was like those optical puzzles that suddenly change pattern and perspective, after which it becomes impossible to see them in the old way again.

At last Du Toit looked up. His eyes were moist and bright.

"When you get that Mabaso, I hope you'll put a bullet in his head."

An impulsive drunken rage seized him, and he banged the desk drawer shut with his foot and kicked it twice viciously.

"The murderous bastards," he blurted out. "The savage bastards. After all I've done for them. I see my mistake now. My mistake was to forget that they are just savages, to try and treat them decently. Well, never again. I made a mistake but things are going to be very different around here from now on. Oh, very different. You'll see the difference, and my God, they won't know what's hit them when I'm finished with them here."

"Steady on, man. Just a minute. Roberts, take down——"

". . . I'm telling you this. You can take it down if you like. I'm going to keep a loaded Browning right here "—he thumped the desk—" here. And the first sign any bastard oversteps the mark, he's going to get it right between the eyes. Go on, write it down. Write down I'm going to shoot down the first bastard that oversteps the mark. And when I do it, you'll know where to find me, and I'd like to see any court convict me for killing vermin, that's all."

"Steady on, man. Roberts, take down : ' When they stormed the platform, they brandished knives and other dangerous implements.' Now what happened after that ? "

"After that ? Oh—yes." His rage had collapsed as startingly as it had arisen. "I think that after that Mabaso calms them down again. He holds his arms up, but standing on the ground this time, and he calms them down."

"Showing how he had complete control of them ? "

"Yes, showing just that."

"You say he had his arms up ? "

"Yes."

"Like this ? " Swanepoel raised his arms.

"Yes."

" Now did he sort of call them on like this ? " Swanepoel bent his palms slowly forward, as if beckoning to people behind him.

" Well—yes—I suppose so. I suppose you could say he was waving them on with his hands."

" That's why he had his arms up ? To wave them on or keep them back, just as he wanted ? "

" Yes."

" Roberts, got that ? Right. Now he's got them all waiting for the signal. They're all waiting, and he's there holding them in check. Then ? "

" Then he starts insulting me in front of the crowd, the cheeky black bastard. Yes, that's what he does."

" He insults you by means of these inflammatory questions ? Then ? Then they attacked you ? "

" No. No, not then."

" Well, when ? "

" No, after that I sent the two constables to arrest him, and they were pushing towards him . . ."

" Yes ? "

" And there was a lot of yelling, an awful racket, and suddenly the—the—the . . ."

He stopped and looked out of the window.

" Woman ? " Swanepoel asked.

" Yes."

Swanepoel stood with his thumbs in his belt and lifted his head up and looked all around the picture rail. He began to whistle windily and tunelessly. He walked twice across the room, slowly, thoughtfully. At last he said :

" All right. Never mind how it happened. Just try and think *who* it was carried knives and dangerous implements. Or threw stones. Or burnt the car. Just concentrate on that. And try and give me some names."

" I don't know any names. I keep telling you and you keep coming back and asking the same thing. I don't know any names. I didn't recognise any of the black pigs. How do you think it feels after an experience like that ? I wonder how you'd feel, I just wonder. How much you'd remember. It's no joke what happened to me. Maybe you think it's just a joke. I don't know any names. I don't know."

He was sitting stiffly upright, thumping his fist on the desk and looking straight at Swanepoel. Suddenly his eyes filled with tears, his head dropped on his hands, his shoulders quivered, and he sobbed like a child.

Swanepoel stood over him but did not come to his aid. He watched coldly, saying nothing. Then he went back to the window. It was night-time now, black and moonless. There were no lights in the location. The location was a black terrain of shapes and shadows, silent, lurking, waiting. There was an uncanny hovering stillness, like that which clings to the bushes in which wounded game has taken cover.

The only noise came from the Flying Squad men standing around the smouldering car and the crowd of location people who had collected on the town side of the fence. They had come home late from work or from visiting other towns and had been stopped from entering the location by the police guarding the gate. They were excited, and kept asking the Flying Squad men for details. The police were telling them tall stories about the riot and making humorous remarks about the forthcoming raid. There was a man on horseback riding up and down in front of the fence and asking cunning jocular questions to trap the police into revealing what had happened. From time to time one of the Flying Squad men would rush up to the fence and poke his rifle between the wires; when the crowd scattered, he would laugh and make a joke or borrow something, a pencil or a box of matches.

Swanepoel felt a queer kind of nervousness inside of him. There was something offensive about the location crouching in the dark like a wounded watchful animal. The nervousness was vague and ill-omened and inexplicable, but it came to him by direct communication from his adversary, by a kind of private and secret telepathy. They were waiting for each other. The feeling was nervousness, not fear, for fear in Swanepoel underwent a strange process. It travelled along a hidden subterranean route that fused and shaped it into something new, its own opposite, the grim will to go on with his duty.

191

The obstructions had been intolerable. First the reporters, some telephoning from other towns. Then Du Toit's wife, in hysteria. Then Mrs. Ross. Then Moolman. And when he had finally stopped the calls and started the interview with Du Toit, the hold-up due to the man's jittery loss of memory and self-control. The delay was like the shutting off of air. It stifled his impulse to get to grips with the location. It made him dizzy and fretful with impatience. What were they doing, plotting, over there in the dark? What was being altered during the delay? The delay was a kind of destruction, a squandering not merely of time, but of something precious and in short supply.

He thought of starting without worrying to collect any further evidence. He quickly changed his mind. That was not his method. That was Ackerman's method. It was too risky and could lead to a failure and there was not going to be any failure about this to-night. No, there was nothing to do except get to the end of this never ending interview.

He pushed up the shattered lightweight window and leaned out under it.

" You. You over there, shut up," he bellowed at the bubbling, chattering crowd on the other side of the fence. " Shut up. Stand in line and keep quiet. Sergeant Ackerman, get all those Kaffirs in line and keep them quiet."

Then he said testily to the Flying Squad men, " What's the matter with you? Have you forgotten you happen to be on duty? We can hardly hear ourselves talk in here."

He pulled his head in and came and stood in the centre of the room. He looked at Du Toit, who was now sitting and staring ahead, dazed. His eyes moved from Du Toit to Gwebu, and suddenly brightened, as if noticing Gwebu for the first time. At last, in a voice of unexpected friendliness, he said:

" You, blackbird, you saw it all. Tell us—what was the actual signal for the attack? Tell us in a few words exactly what happened."

" Sir, don't ask me. What I say wouldn't be too reliable. I was petrified. I was out of action from fright."

" Come, blackbird, just try. You can help us. You have

eyes. Why, even glasses. Tell us what you saw. Tell us who carried knives and things—who threw stones—who burnt the car."

" Sir, I wouldn't advise anyone to rely on me. I was *non compos mentis*. I was—*paralysed*."

" A-ah, to hell with you," Swanepoel said with sudden harshness. " You Kaffirs all stick together, don't you ? "

" No, sir."

" What did you say ? "

" Yes, sir."

The reply came with just too much alacrity; it puzzled Swanepoel. He did not know Gwebu. He was silent for a moment, then he turned to Du Toit.

" I've come to the conclusion that we're just wasting time. Well, what do you want me to do ? Are we going to make arrests or not ? How do you think it will look if we let them get away with *this* without arrests ? On top of that business the other night ? How do you think I'm going to explain it ? "

" I know."

" Well, what are we going to do ? "

Du Toit frowned, as if thinking, but he knew that he had nothing to suggest. But the silence prised an answer out of him, and he said :

" Arrest those location constables. If you ask me, they're in league with Mabaso. They just stood by and did nothing. They were acting very peculiar even before the meeting started. I should have seen from their . . ."

Swanepoel appeared not to have heard. At any rate he ignored it. He stood thinking, then he came and sat on the desk again.

" How about trying it another way ? Listen to me now. Just let your mind run over the events. Keep calm and just say what comes to you, without forcing it one way or the other. Try and bring back the picture of it, and just say what you see in the picture."

" All right," Du Toit said doubtfully.

" And in that picture, see if you can recognise any of the individuals."

" All right. Well, they were dancing around and burning my

193

Chev., throwing petrol on it, and chairs and papers and things. And screaming and yelling all the time."

"Roberts, take it down exactly as he says it. I don't want to interrupt him here. Now carry on."

"Well, as I said, they were burning my Chev., and if you want my opinion, that was the filthiest aspect of the whole thing. What did they want to burn my car for? Of course, that's the last car I'll ever get out of Town Hall. Why should they give me another car, run the risk again? Mind you, it's insured——"

"No, not that. Just try and confine yourself to the events of the riot."

"Well, they were burning the car. I was up in the office with Gwebu, who had come in after me. Stones were bombarding in all over the place. We were crouching below the window, which was the safest place, up here in the office. I never thought I'd come out of it alive. I had my gun ready, ready to shoot anyone who came in the door. But the cause of it? Actually, well, actually it was the—the—well, actually, it's hard to say. They all went completely berserk. Yelling like wild animals and going completely off their heads, yelling and stoning the place."

Swanepoel wiped his brow with his fingers, he raised his hands and walked to the centre of the room and said, "Stop. All right, stop. All this is completely irrelevant." He glared; then an idea came to him. "You say they were yelling. Right. Now what were they yelling? Try and remember what actual words they were yelling."

"I couldn't say what the actual words were."

"Did you hear them yelling, '*M'bulala*'? Anything like that?"

"They were yelling thousands of things."

"*M'bulala?*"

"I don't remember."

"*M'bulala—m'bulala—m'bulala?*" He pumped his fist into his hand and chanted the word in a rhythmical singsong.

"*M'bulala?*"

"Yes. Does it strike a chord?"

"Well, now you mention it, they were shouting *something bulala.*"

"There you are. I knew it. They always shout that. M'bulala means kill him."

Du Toit was about to go on, but Swanepoel held his palm up, stopping him, at the same time saying to Roberts, "Roberts, take down : ' Mabaso gave the signal and the crowd attacked, brandishing weapons as already described and screaming, "Kill him—kill him." The superintendent had no alternative but to run for his life.' " Swanepoel paused and his eyes focused on Du Toit's bleeding forehead. " ' During the attack the super-intendent received a jagged contused wound about one inch long, inflicted by a stone or sharp instrument.' By the way, you'd better get that examined by the district surgeon."

Du Toit nodded.

"I take it you agree with what we have just written ? "

"Yes," Du Toit said. He knew it was wrong, but there was a new feeling developing now, a kind of trapped helplessness. Now it was not simply the confusion and fright that had so far made it impossible for him to give a coherent version of his own. Nor even that he no longer had the strength to resist Swanepoel. A core of brutal fact was beginning to harden in the centre of his clouded impressions. His running away had been the signal for the attack. He did not consciously know it yet, but the inner knowledge of it was creeping over him, making him nervous of any further investigation of the cause of the riot and flooding him with gloom. He was completely in Swanepoel's hands. Swanepoel sensed it, for he suddenly became buoyant and said :

"You know what I'm going to do ? I'm going to pick names out of the location register and call them out, and I want you to try and see if any of these names remind you of anyone who was actually in the riot."

"All right," Du Toit said.

"Sir, may I step in here and make a suggestion ? " Gwebu asked.

"Yes, blackbird. You want to help us now ? "

"Yes, sir."

"Well, go ahead."

"Sir, the superintendent is absolutely right. They were shouting *something bulala*."

" Oh, you want to corroborate him ? Is that it ? "

" Yes, sir. They were shouting, ' *Ufuna ukusibulala.*' This means you want to kill us. Not kill *him.* ' You want to kill *us,*' is what they were shouting. That's all I wanted to suggest, sir."

Swanepoel's first reaction was to let out a guffaw. It was the result of astonishment, not amusement. Then it dawned that he had somehow been made the victim of a hoax. For a moment he did not know how to deal with it. He opened his mouth but didn't speak. He placed his hands on his hips and glared. His ferocious blue eyes searched all over Gwebu. He took a step towards Gwebu, but suddenly turned back and faced Du Toit.

" Is this Kaffir altogether sane ? "

Du Toit did not answer. Swanepoel turned to Gwebu again and stood grinding a piece of broken glass into the floor with his heel.

" All right. What exactly were they shouting ? "

" ' *Ufuna ukusibulala,*' " Gwebu said in a dry, cracked voice.

" Meaning—you want to kill us ? "

" Yes ? "

" You sure about that ? "

Gwebu gulped and nodded in one movement.

" Well, let me tell you you're a liar. Was the superintendent threatening to kill anyone ? "

" No, sir."

" Well, why should they yell, ' You want to kill us ' ? He wasn't even threatening them. I'm satisfied you're a liar. Why should they yell that ? "

Gwebu did not answer. He summoned the will to stare back at Swanepoel, then blinked both eyes at once with the sudden rapidity of a camera shutter. He looked altogether ludicrous with his baggy outsized clothes and solemn face, like a grotesque toy.

" Tell me, Kaffir, are you trying to shield anyone ? "

" No, sir."

" Well, keep out of this. You understand ? Keep your ugly nose out of this until I ask you."

Swanepoel turned to Du Toit again, but just as he was about to speak, Gwebu clutched the window sill and said, " Sir, what they meant by that was——"

" SHUT UP. I told you to keep out of this."

Then Swanepoel asked Du Toit, " How can you work with this crazy baboon ? "

" I don't know," Du Toit said. " He gives me a lot of trouble. I think I'll have to get rid of him."

" You were saying how they attacked you, yelling, ' Kill him —kill him,' and how you came up in here for safety. Now you're up here in the office. Try and remember from that point on."

" Well, I'm up here in the office and they're all down there burning the car—then some came up on the veranda."

" But not into this office ? "

" No."

" Queer, very queer."

" What they actually did, they ran into the next office."

" Oh, looking for you. I see. And before they had a chance to find you, the Flying Squad arrived, and that stopped them."

" I suppose so. The stone throwing practically stopped while they were——"

" You said blackbird comes into the office after you ? Is that what you said ? "

" Yes."

" Did he *really* come in after you ? "

" Yes he did. The only one who stood by me."

" Blackbird, you're not such a bad little Kaffir after all. Coming in here when your *baas* was in such danger. Did he *really* come *right* in here while they were attacking you ? "

" Yes, he actually did."

" Good old blackbird. Right, blackbird comes up into the office. What then ? "

" Then——"

" Blackbird, why did you do it ? "

" My legs did all the thinking for me, sir."

" Anyway, you did it, that's the important thing. Don't think it's not appreciated, what you did, even if I did shout at you a moment ago. You're not such a bad little blackbird after all."

" Sir, the reason I did it was I am the voice of the super-intendent."

" The voice of the superintendent ? I don't get that."

" Yes, sir. In the eyes of the location I am the *voice* of the superintendent. The part of the superintendent that makes the announcement. That's the reason."

" I still don't get it. But never mind, you did it, and that's the important thing, and now I can see you're not such a bad little Kaffir after all. I think we'd better put you into the report. Roberts, take down : ' Native interpreter——' What's your name ? "

" Gwebu."

" Gwebu. Pass number ? "

" A stroke C one three seven nine six."

" 'Native interpreter, that pass number, came into the office, where he offered his services to help defend the superintendent.' Right. Now, blackbird, *you* know all the people in this location. Can't you recognise any who were in the riot ? "

" Sir, my mind is a blank on that subject."

" Blackbird, are you one of Mabaso's boys ? "

" No, sir."

" Then why won't you help us ? You were pretty damn' sure about what they were shouting. Don't tell me you can't remember any of those who took part."

" No, sir. My mind is a clean sheet when it comes to the identification of individuals."

" Blackbird, if you know what's good for you—— Ah, to hell with you." He turned and stumped angrily to the window.

Gwebu went suddenly limp and he began to sweat profusely. Roberts snapped the notebook closed. Swanepoel stood with his thumbs in his belt and stared in mournful defeat out of the window. Suddenly he swung round.

" There's a whole bunch of your constables out here on the veranda. How long've they been here ? "

" I don't know. I didn't know they came back. What are they doing here ? Arrest them."

Swanepoel pondered for a moment ; then he put his head out of the window and said in a harsh voice, " All right, come in, all of you. Hurry up."

CHAPTER THIRTEEN

THERE WAS an aspect of the riot in Nelstroom that is a strange aspect of many riots—the violence is directed not so much against the superintendent as against his property. Anger boils up and overflows, but something restrains the crowd from attacking the people of the law. They take vengeance on the property of the law. They wreck buildings, burn cars, and destroy furniture. They do not kill the superintendent. In the eyes of the location, however, the location constables are not people of the law : they are property of the law, of the superintendent. And so the constables' lives were in real danger that evening : they were a target of the riot, while Du Toit was only in danger from accidents. Being location people themselves, the constables understood this perfectly.

They had come to the meeting filled with misgivings. Ever since the previous evening when they had gone around the location announcing the meeting, they had been the butt of jibes, abuse, and angry questions. They had wanted to be above this business of the women's passes but somehow they found themselves in the thick of it, on both sides, yet with both sides against them. When they heard of Gwagwa's desertion, and saw the messages chalked on the walls, and noticed the strange temper of the people, fierce quarrelling broke out among them.

When the meeting started, they walked among the crowd, in pairs and swinging their kerries, as Du Toit had ordered them to do. But when the first uproar started, they found themselves suddenly outside the crowd, as if ejected by some centrifugal process. Only one man tried to make an arrest. He went to take a woman who was shouting at Du Toit, " A curse on you by the ears of your mother." But the crowd closed in around him like the earth of a trench falling in, and somehow in the whirling of arms he was hit in the face with an empty lunch tin. That finally discouraged them all from making any effort to get back into the crowd.

The two constables whom Du Toit saw behind the platform had not gone there to be near Du Toit. Where they stood was near the gate, and from there it was an easy way out of the location. But when Du Toit called on them to clear the people away from the platform, they got stuck in the crowd, and so they were right on hand when Du Toit decided to order them to arrest Mabaso and the woman. When the stone throwing started, they were nearly murdered, for they were held responsible for the killing of the woman (she had lain still after the fit and appeared to be dead) and they were punched and kicked and their clothes were torn off them. They fought their way free and ran almost naked into the town, with a mob tailing behind them.

All the other constables stood under the water tower, watching from the distance. They could not hear what was being said, but they could read the various messages that seemed to be coming from the crowd. The crowd was like a night monster with a mind and a will of its own, and they could read its thoughts.

When Du Toit turned and ran, the message from the crowd had such a clear meaning that they, too, turned and ran. Three of them climbed up the swaying ladder to the top of the water tower, where they huddled against the iron railings until the riot was over. Two of them went into a house looking out on the square, the house of ex-Sergeant Smoke, and locked themselves in. Some reached their own houses and lay in bed in full uniform, with blankets pulled up to their chins. Others hid in the rooms of their girl friends.

Napoleon Siponiya, the *induna*, ran out of the square and into a quiet street; then he began to walk. His legs were saying, " Run," but his brain was saying, " If the people in the windows see you run, the rest of your life in Nelstroom will be misery." So he walked quickly to his house in the yard at 136 Maple Avenue. When he reached the yard he found it deserted. He sat in his front room trying to think about the trouble he was in. Then he changed out of his uniform. After a while he came out into the yard. He poked into the brazier that stood at his door and added some small coal, all the time thinking about his trouble. A number of people from the yard then came back from the meeting. They tried to catch his eye, but he avoided their look.

An old *makhulu* who lived across the yard came right up to him and peered into his face.

" Now how does it happen that the first hunting dog of the manager's hunting dogs is not attending the meeting ? " she asked mischievously, her whispered voice carrying sharply and clearly across the yard. The people of the yard came nearer and made a half-moon around the brazier.

" I was at the meeting."

" Then how is it that the *induna* of the hunting dogs is first back in the yard ? And no longer in the blue clothes ? "

Napoleon Siponiya did not answer. He poked into the brazier, absorbed by the problem of persuading the coal chips to burn.

" Could it be some lack of interest in the meeting ? And that the weather is too warm for blue suits ? "

Napoleon Siponiya flashed her a look of pure hatred. Then he planted the poker into the fire, and stood, fists on hips, facing the semicircle of people.

" I always take off my uniform when I finish my work," he said. He looked for a moment into the eyes of the old *makhulu*, but there was a wicked gleam in her eyes, and he looked away again.

" So your work is finished. They are burning down the location and your work is finished."

" He is right. His work is finished," said a woman, a young wife who was standing in a doorway holding a baby straddled across her hip. " His work is finished. To-morrow they will find a new *induna*. One that does not have the legs of a rabbit."

" This was the shortest glory I ever heard of," said the old *makhulu*. " When the sun is *there* they make him *induna*." She pointed into the western sky. " When it is *there*, they unmake him." She pointed into the ground. " Siponiya, you are a shooting star among *indunas*."

" Not only is it the end as *induna*, but they will throw him out of the constables. For running away like a rabbit," said the

201

young wife, pushing out her hip to prevent the baby slipping down.

"Ho, it is going to be bad for this yard," said another woman, one who ran a small shebeen business in one of the rooms. "Without Siponiya to take the police away, it will be raids, raids, raids. What will we do without Siponiya? For the sake of the yard, go back and defend the manager, Siponiya."

"You will be a poor man, Siponiya. From rich to poor in one night. Twenty pounds a month gone. And no more keep-quiet money from the shebeens."

"What shall we do without Siponiya to take the money every week?"

"They will throw you out of the location. And your house, which cost you eighty pounds to build, they will sell for five pounds to the new *induna*. To encourage him and punish you. You are in big trouble, Siponiya," said an old man who was the commercial wiseacre of Maple Avenue.

The taunts were intolerable. Nobody in the yard had ever before spoken to Napoleon Siponiya like that. When he walked through the yard, he was accustomed to have people stand back for him : people came out of their doors specially to greet him. His dignity demanded that he put this yapping pack of dogs to rout. But he knew that his power in the yard was really the power of the Town Council shining through him, and that as the light in a mirror goes out when the main light is put out, so now his power was gone. So he could think of nothing to say. He just stood with his hands on his hips, glaring at his tormentors.

Most of the things they were saying had already gone through his mind, but he had not expected the people to use them like *assegais* against him. He had thought that there would be more, not less, friendliness. He had vaguely believed that by running away from the meeting instead of staying and making arrests he had done something to win the approval of the people, had even made himself something of a hero. Now it seemed that the people did not appreciate his heroism. Ought he then to reverse the heroism and go back? But if he did that, Du Toit would say that the running away was cowardice, not heroism, and he would be severely punished. The going back would need much more heroism than the running away, but the people would not see it that way. They would say, " Siponiya goes back to Du Toit when the trouble is over, thereby showing his real colours as a coward." How a thing could be heroism and cowardice at the same time was a strange problem. It was too big a problem for the slow brain of Napoleon Siponiya.

He turned and went into his room. He closed the door, sat in a chair, and weighed up his position. Then he put on the uniform again. He would ask the advice of ex-Sergeant Smoke. Smoke had been in the original constables, and was a man of great wisdom. When Siponiya, spruce once more in his blue uniform, came out of his door, he was greeted with a burst of ironic congratulations.

As he walked with slow and thoughtful steps out of the yard, the old *makhulu* shouted after him, " Hurry Siponiya, hurry. There is still some rioting left. Work on what is left of the riot, and you can still save yourself."

He did not hurry. He walked slowly through the black deserted streets, his mind whirling with a problem that was too big for him. When he reached the house of ex-Sergeant Smoke, he saw that the riot was over and that the police had arrived. He darted quickly into the house so as not to be seen by the police. Inside, Smoke and the two constables who had taken refuge in his house were sitting around the table, looking as grave as undertakers.

" We are discussing the failure of the municipal constables," ex-Sergeant Smoke said. He was a burly man who still wore the uniform, but without the buttons and braid.

" I have come to discuss the same matter," said Napoleon Siponiya gravely.

" I have advised them to go back. There will be a raid now, and a chance to help in the raid and to make up for the failure. Once, many years ago, the same thing happened, there was a failure of constables ; but they took them back again. Their trouble was then, as it is now, that they could not easily find a whole new squad of constables who were any better than the existing constables."

"They will burn us," said one of the young constables.

"They will burn you if you don't go back. That is certain. They will burn you for a breach of the constables' regulations with five years in prison. The name they have for it is *mutiny*." He pronounced the important foreign word "emoot*e*ni" and delivered it tenderly, as if presenting it on a velvet cushion. "I have a good standing with the manager," Smoke went on. "Perhaps I can put in some words with him and prevent the burning."

This kind of talk made Siponiya even more unhappy and bewildered. He had not come to discuss how to achieve the lesser punishment. The problem was one of heroism and cowardice. But when he tried to put his thoughts to Smoke, the words came tumbling over each other in confusion.

"This women's passes, is it the brave thing to support that? To run away from the meeting, is that the brave or the frightened thing? You say give back support to Du Toit, but how does it look? I mean I was the *induna* this afternoon. Does it look worse to go back to Du Toit? Or to stay running away?"

"I don't understand you," Smoke said.

"I mean I was the *induna*. I ran away, it is true. But this business of the women's passes. To go back, how does that stand in regard to the opinion of the location? Or do you advise one to stay running away?"

"I don't understand you. It sounds as if you are trying to say something important, but you speak like a drunk man. But whatever you are trying to say to me, I say to you go back."

At that point the three constables who had been hiding up in the water tower came stealthily into the room and the discussion started all over again. They had seen everything : they gave a full account of the whole riot, of details that the others had not seen, and they brought in the names of many people. This made ex-Sergeant Smoke slap his thighs with joy.

"Don't worry," he told them all.

They stared, sad and puzzled, ashamed to ask what he meant in case it should be something obvious.

"Don't worry. We now have the means to bargain. It is all over. Don't worry."

Some more constables came in while Smoke was explaining how it would work. It was decided to share out the bargaining point among all the constables in the room. Smoke made them take out their notebooks ; on his instructions they each wrote down certain things.

After that they all went out into the street and walked silently across the square to the administration building. When they reached the veranda, they saw that some other constables had also decided to return. For a while they did not announce their presence to the people in the office. They stood silently on the veranda, and every now and then peered through the window. Inside Du Toit was sitting at the desk, Lieutenant Swanepoel was striding back and forth. Constable Roberts was leaning against the wall holding a notebook ; Andries Gwebu was standing with his back to the farther window. There was a storm in the face of Lieutenant Swanepoel and Du Toit kept putting his head in his hands as if trying to think. Gwebu seemed to look very small and wizened, as if he had crawled into his loose-fitting clothes to hide away. Roberts seemed to be just waiting.

★   ★   ★

When Napoleon Siponiya saw the face of Lieutenant Swanepoel in the window and heard the voice that called the constables into the room, his heart sank in dismay. The face was black with disaster and the voice had the sound of a tree cracking in a storm. That moment, when he was seen by Swanepoel, was different from all the other moments in his life. It was the sharp, clear moment from which there was no going back. Now, for the first time in all his years in the location, he found himself doubting the wisdom of ex-Sergeant Smoke.

But there was no possibility of changing his mind, and he led the way into the office, gripped in misery. He stood to attention in the corner and the other constables fell in beside him. When they had settled into line, Swanepoel stepped back to a position from where he could see them all comfortably. He spoke in a taut, menacing voice.

" So you decided to come back. Now it's all over, you come back. Well, you've committed a serious breach of regulations and we're going to have a little disciplinary inquiry. You're all under arrest."

The constables shifted their feet, swayed their heads, ran their fingers under their collars. They did not know much about the regulations but all had heard of disciplinary inquiry. The words were like the name of a sickness to them. Now there was no doubt that the returning had been a failure. There was going to be disciplinary inquiry and heavy punishment. Now they all began to see what Siponiya had seen earlier : Smoke had made a terrible mistake.

" Attention."

They stopped fidgeting and slowly pulled themselves back to attention. Their hands crept surreptitiously back to their sides.

Swanepoel suddenly pointed a finger at a man in the middle of the row.

" You. What were *you* doing during the riot ? "

The constable tried to speak. He opened his mouth, but no sound came.

" You. You heard me. Where *were* you ? "

" On duty, sir," the constable said faintly.

" On duty ? Where ? "

With the look of a man plunging from a burning building, he said, " On top of the water tower, sir."

" What the hell kind of duty were you doing up there ? "

" Observing the riot," he said. Nervously he took his notebook out of his breast pocket.

" Do you believe that ? Do you believe that rubbish ? You've arrested them. Why don't you send them back to the station and question them to-morrow ? " Du Toit said, bouncing in his chair. Swanepoel held his hand at the side of his trousers and made a flapping, patting-down movement in Du Toit's direction. Du Toit sank back into the chair.

" And *you*. Where were you ? "

" On duty, sir."

" Where ? Why do I have to drag it out of you ? "

" In Tshabalala's house."

" And you ? "

Swanepoel went right down the line ; all had been on duty ;

206

all had observed the riot. Even those constables who had not met in Smoke's house caught the idea and gave themselves vantage points around the square. When Swanepoel realised that the events had been adequately witnessed from all angles, he turned his back on the constables and spoke to Du Toit.

"This disciplinary inquiry, what do you think now?"

"Of course. The bastards ran away. Of course there must be an inquiry."

"But they were all on duty, observing the riot."

"Do you believe that? Are you going to fall for that lying rubbish?"

"But blackbird here, he also ran away. What're we going to do with him?"

"Him? I don't know. We'll see later. His position's different. He's not a constable."

"No, of course. It's different with constables."

Swanepoel turned round again and spoke to the constables.

"The position is that as constables you had no right to run away. So you understand the serious position you're in. Other people can run away, but not constables. You understand?"

He stood and looked mildly at them, but suddenly he said sternly:

"Stop grinning."

The constables had seen that the danger was past. They saw it from the tone of his voice and from the joke about other people being permitted to run away. Although Swanepoel had spoken with reference to Gwebu, they all understood that he really meant Du Toit. And with that they understood not only that the returning had been a success but the further incredible fact that Swanepoel was going to stand with them against Du Toit. This was more success than any of them had hoped for. At that moment there spread right along the line of constables a wonderful feeling of awe and respect for ex-Sergeant Smoke.

After that Swanepoel found it easy work to gather material for the raid and the court case to follow.

Constable Roberts turned to a clean page in his notebook and wrote, STONE THROWERS. He turned over a few pages and wrote, CAR OVERTURNERS. A few pages further he wrote, CAR BURNERS, and a few pages further, KNIFE AND WEAPON BRANDISHERS.

Then the names began to come in. Those who had met in Smoke's house gave names from their notebooks, the others from memory. Roberts wrote them down and Gwebu looked up the addresses in the location register. The names came in rapidly, and Swanepoel stood in the centre of the room catching them like a juggler as they were thrown at him from all angles.

After a while the supply of names slowed down. Some constables began calling out names already given by others. At first Swanepoel did not mind the repetition, for it meant a double and therefore surer identification. But a point was reached where no new names were coming in and when at the same time there was no need for further confirmation of those on the list.

Swanepoel stopped and asked Roberts to count the names in his notebook.

" Twenty-four," said Roberts.

" Only twenty-four ? " Swanepoel said to the constables. " Hundreds take part in the riot and you only identify twenty-four. This is very unsatisfactory. Are you trying to protect anyone ? "

" No, sir," the constables said in ragged chorus.

" Well, this is no good at all. Just remember I haven't promised you anything yet. I don't remember saying that your arrest has been withdrawn."

The names began to come in again. First in a trickle, then a flood. As Du Toit heard them, it occurred to him that many were vaguely familiar, reminding him of old location feuds. Some names were called out and written in the book but had to be struck out again. Somebody called Beauty Mabila, for instance. Roberts wrote it down, and Gwebu, after turning up the register, said, " Left the location last June." There was a similar case with Boy Kumalo. " Dead," said Gwebu. And with George Ncomo—" In gaol." The names of very few shebeen queens were called. This struck Du Toit as strange, since the shebeen queens had the most to lose from the new law and would have been expected to react the most violently against it.

But the constables named very few shebeen queens, and then only some minor and unpopular ones.

At one point an argument broke out between two constables. One of them said, " Solomon Ngwenya," and the other said hotly, " That's not true. You must not say Solomon Ngwenya."

" I say Solomon Ngwenya."

" Sir, I have to tell you that last month this constable lost a case against Solomon Ngwenya in the Court of the Native Commissioner."

" Solomon Ngwenya is his uncle."

" For goods sold and delivered."

" Solomon Ngwenya is his uncle and he tries to hide him."

" Better take that name out," Swanepoel said to Roberts.

If there were names that should not have been on the list, they were balanced by names that should have been there, but were omitted. All the constables had sweethearts, relatives or friends who had taken part in the riot; these names were forgotten. Sometimes, though, mistakes nearly happened—for instance, when a constable called out the name of another constable's girl friend. But they soon found a tacit method of preventing such miscarriages. The constable with the interest in the name would say, " Sir, I think there's a mistake there. I happen to know that this person was not in the location this afternoon." Or, " I happen to know that this person was sick in bed to-day." And the constable who gave the name would say, " Perhaps that is right. I'm not sure about that name."

At last there were enough names. There were names under all the categories in Roberts' notebook. The hardest list to fill was that of Knife and Weapon Brandishers. The constables had little trouble about supplying names for the other categories. They resorted to a familiar line of reasoning : if a man had an alibi, he would be able to escape punishment, and if he hadn't it meant he had been in the riot, and in that case what difference did it make whether he was actually identified or not ? But the idea of falsely putting knives and weapons into people's hands made them acutely uncomfortable. They were glumly nervous when Swanepoel mentioned knives. But their resistance to Swanepoel was low, and some broke and provided names.

There were some surprising inclusions in Roberts' notebook. One was Simon Ndimandi, the shopkeeper. Several constables identified him as being active in the riot, and one named him as carrying a knife. When Ndimandi's name was called out, Du Toit looked up sharply.

"You mean that fat little fellow who owns those shops?" he asked.

"Yes sir," the constable said confidently.

"You know him?" Swanepoel asked Du Toit.

"Yes, he owns a lot of shops. One of the richest people in the location, if not in the whole town. You know, I'd never have thought it of him. But it only shows you. You can never tell in these things." He shrugged.

About some names there was no doubt. One of these was Johanna Mandlazi, who was seen by nearly half the constables to throw stones through the office window, help overturn the car, and set it alight.

"Seems *she* had a good time to-day," Swanepoel said. "Who is she?"

"I know her," Gwebu said. "She's an old washwoman with four grown-up sons all working in the cement factory."

As nobody could possibly have had a grievance against Johanna Mandlazi, an inoffensive old woman, it was obvious that she had been correctly identified.

One of the names was supplied by Du Toit himself. It happened in this way : they were trying to pin down the identity of a woman who threw a bottle of petrol into the burning car. They established that she was a big-built woman and that she wore a red headcloth—but nobody knew her name. The description brought up a picture in Du Toit's mind of a certain shebeen queen.

"Sarah Manana," he suggested.

There was no confirmation from the constables : some looked at him as if he had done them an injury, and that convinced him that it was Sarah Manana. Sarah was huge and fat and always wore a red headcloth. She was a prosperous shebeen queen, and very impudent. Whenever she was caught and brought before the court she would plead guilty, slap the fine money down on the clerk's table, defiantly, as if paying debts in a crooked gambling game, and stomp out of court without waiting for the receipt. Du Toit thought about the woman throwing the bottle, and walking back into the crowd, and then about Sarah Manana walking contemptuously out of court. And the two walking-away figures became one. The build, the walk, and the style were all the same. And the red headcloth—that decided it. Sarah always wore a red headcloth, it was a kind of trademark.

"That definitely was Sarah Manana," Du Toit said firmly.

"Sure?"

"Sure. I'd know her a mile away."

Her name and address went into Roberts' book.

But the first name, the most important of all the names, was that of Mabaso. Even while other names were being called, Du Toit and Swanepoel both were conscious of Mabaso's name echoing in their minds. It was as if his name outweighed all the others. Although they could not have started out without the other names, it was Mabaso's name that gave the raid a feeling of importance, danger, and uniqueness.

The names were rewritten on four lists, according to addresses —one for each section of the location. Swanepoel took the lists from Roberts. The one containing Mabaso's name he folded up and stuck in his pocket.

"Come on, let's start," he said, calm now.

They all went outside and Swanepoel divided the men into four groups : one under Sergeant Ackerman, one under Sergeant Combrink, one under the Senior Constable Nel, and one under himself. He gave each group one of the lists of names, and he issued the orders briskly.

CHAPTER FOURTEEN

THE SHOTS fired by the Flying Squad echoed over the location and left behind a hushed wake, as if the bullets had wrecked a loud-speaker mechanism emitting the uproar. The rioters scattered and fled through the streets and took desperate refuge in their houses.

It needed no messages, no yard-to-yard communication for the location to know the content of the next few hours. This time the raid would be brutal and serious. It would be a raid for vengeance, to level scores not only for the riot but for the farcical raid of the other night. That was accepted. It was the price for the riot and no one questioned it. So the location prepared for a night of terror.

People tossed knives and axes into the bushes, hid away their money, emptied wallets out on beds and tables, and examined their papers to be sure that all were there and in order. They darkened their houses, drew curtains, locked doors. Strangely, most people went to bed. But not to sleep—to lie staring wide-eyed at the dark ceilings. In houses where there were children there was the extra problem of lulling their fear and making them lie quiet. Everyone prayed for the protection of darkness and silence, and dreaded that at the fatal moment some sound would draw the attention of the police to the existence of his particular house.

The riot had been a tremendous release of locked-up tension, a great soaring moment not only for those who took part, but for the whole location. The years of frustration, the accumulated resentment, the slow-hardening hatred—these combined to form an explosive mass of passion that was detonated by Du Toit's running away from the meeting. The riot was an insane, purposeless frenzy, a dangerous, reckless, foolish provocation to the police, to the whole white country, but while it lasted it was an exhilaration for everyone in the location except the few on the side of Du Toit.

But when it ended and the capacity to think and fear returned, a sombre mood of foreboding settled on the township, like a cold mist from the mountains. No voices were heard, no music played, no meals were eaten, all lamps were out, all streets were empty, all activity died. The location held its breath and waited for the raid.

★   ★   ★

In the house of Johanna Mandlazi there was bitter questioning.

"But why did you do it?" the eldest son asked. The four sons had come back from work shortly before the riot ended. They had seen their mother in the crowd around the burning car and had wanted to take her home. She had refused to come, and it had been necessary to take her by the elbows and drag her away. When they seized her, she swore and kicked, and this had saddened the sons almost as much as the sight of their mother screaming and gesticulating in front of the burning car. Later she had walked home, but sullenly, and with the four sons surrounding her like a bodyguard.

"But how does it happen that an old mother sets fire to motor-cars?"

She looked up mournfully but did not answer. She was sitting on the smooth mud-and-dung floor and holding the blankets up under her chin with both fists. Her little bark-hard feet with the crooked toes, like dried roots, stuck out to one side from under the blanket. She looked diminutive and swallowed up in the blanket, like a heap of bedding from a child's bed dropped on the floor.

"Tell us why you did it. We just want to understand."

"I don't know. A devil was inside my body."

"But you are an old mother. You are not a *tsotsi*. I can understand it from a young *tsotsi*, but not from an old *makhulu* like you."

"It was not me, I tell you. It was the devil."

213

" What if you were seen ? You will be arrested."

" Well, let them arrest me."

She clicked her tongue loudly, angrily. The sons stood all around her, towering over her, defeated, nonplussed, furious. She pulled up a corner of the blanket and wiped her nose. They could tell then that she was crying, but it was a hard, stifled, inward crying. She said in a rasping exasperated voice :

" When he said we must have passes—no, not then. I don't know."

" What if she was recognised ? " the eldest son asked the others. His name was Josiah. He was a good, sober worker and the steady rock of the family.

" We'll need a lawyer," the youngest son said.

" Who ? Who in this town would speak for anyone who burns a white man's motor-car ? "

" We'll get a lawyer from Johannesburg. Perhaps an advocate. I know one," the youngest son said. He had once been in Johannesburg and was always surprising his family with his resourcefulness and knowledge of the world.

" A lawyer will come all the way from Johannesburg ? "

" I have joined a lawyer there. I pay him ten shillings a month and he has allowed me to join him. I'll write to him and at the same time mention this advocate."

" With what money ? Just where do you think we'll get the money to bring a lawyer from Johannesburg ? "

" I have joined this lawyer, I tell you. He will come, that is the arrangement. About the fee, we will all put in for it, and for that of the advocate. It is no problem. We can start with the money Josiah has got in that post office book of his." He turned and faced his mother. " Don't worry, Mother. We'll get you a lawyer. We'll get you a very good lawyer from Johannesburg. An advocate."

Johanna Mandlazi looked up. There was a film of tears over her yellow old eyes. There was no sign that she understood or even heard what they were saying. The honour of buying her a special advocate from Johannesburg was lost on her.

" No, not when he spoke about the passes," she said. " Not then. It was when he ran away. When he turned and ran away

214

from the meeting, that was when. Then the devil came and took hold of my legs, my arms, my whole body, and made me do all these things."

She spoke sadly and quietly now. She seemed calmer now that she understood the reason. There was a silence after she spoke.

" Well, if you're arrested we'll get you this *ummeli*."[1] the youngest son said, sounding now a little less confident in the powers of a lawyer. They sat staring glumly at one another, waiting and hoping that there would be no arrest, and that if there was one it would not be too brutal. Somehow they all knew there would be one.

" They can kill me," she said with a sudden fresh outburst of vehemence. " Let them kill me."

" Keep calm, Mother."

" I will not carry a pass. I will not start now. Let them kill me."

" Stop it, Mother."

She slumped back into the blanket but stared out over the top with stiff, awkward defiance. Only her sharp little animal eyes could be seen shining over the edge of the blanket. Then they, too, disappeared, and the sons heard her crying.

After a while the crying stopped and she stood up and asked in an even voice, " What shall be done with this laundry ? "

" Don't worry about that," Josiah Mandlazi said.

" Then who will worry ? Three bundles are ready to go back, but two bundles which I fetched to-day are not ready."

" How can you worry about laundry bundles now ? "

" Don't tell me what I must worry about. Go and fetch Alemina and I will tell her where to take the laundry and to-morrow she can take back all the bundles, these here and those there."

Josiah went out to find Alemina, the orphan girl who had been adopted by all the families who lived in the yard.

The yard was empty, and cold from the absence of the coal braziers that usually stood at every door, but it was alive with the feeling of the people crowded and whispering in all the

[1]Lawyer.

215

rooms. This was one of the poorest and most overcrowded yards in the location. Josiah did not know in which room to find Alemina because she stayed in no particular place, so he knocked on the different doors in turn. As each door opened, he felt the stale, warm air gush out, and he saw the rows of blanket-wrapped forms lying on the floor.

At last he came to the room of Maria Maziya, the mother of the crazy boy who, until his trouble with Du Toit, used to walk around the location calling his own name. Since the trouble he had been kept indoors under the eyes of his mother, who now spent her whole life hiding and protecting him and preventing him from escaping. Some said that the mother was a little bit crazy too.

" She's not here. But come inside. I want to ask you something," Maria Maziya said.

When he was in and the door locked, she asked :

" Is it true that manager Du Toit was burnt to death in his car ? "

" No," he said. " It is a grandmother's rumour."

The room was occupied only by Maria and the boy. Although all the other rooms were as fully occupied as the evening bus, this room had plenty of space, for no one would share it with the boy because of his continuous singing, wild temper, and unclean habits.

" Oh, what bad luck," said the boy. He was very small for his nineteen years, monkey-sized, and he had the lugubrious old face of a clown.

" Keep quiet, Tembo," his mother said. And then to Mandlazi, " They are saying that the manager ran away from the meeting and tried to drive off in his car and they turned it over and burnt it, manager and all."

" Quite untrue. I saw the burning car and it is untrue."

" Oh, what a shame, a shame," the boy said, holding his head in his hands and rocking it violently. " But the time has come. We've made up our minds. Yes, his days are numbered." He spoke a mixture of English and Swazi. His speech was a jumble of nonsense, but nonsense with a curiously swinging literate flavour, the result of the endless hours he spent reading trash,

216

comics, advertisements, and the like, whose language he adopted and changed into his own fevered style.

His mother did not entirely understand him, but she said, " Keep quiet, Tembo. You don't know what you are saying."

" Why don't you send him to some place ? "

" There is no place. Besides, he is my son."

" He makes endless trouble for you. Is there nothing you can do ? "

" He is my baby."

" The manager is on the side of the Spies. He belongs to the Spy Ring. He has a plot to send me to gaol," the boy said in a high, excited voice. " But the law is against him. My letter to the Governor-General brought the law over to my side against him. But he's waiting. Waiting for me to make a mistake. But oh no. No more waiting."

Mandlazi saw something in the boy's hand, something with a glint on it, and when he peered closely he saw that it was a revolver. It was a heavy service-model German Luger. On the table was a polished mahogany box made to fit on a belt and carved inside to hold the shape of the gun.

" Where did he get that ? " Mandlazi asked Maria in alarm.

" I took it from a car—stole it. It's mine. I keep it here in my bed. And now the time has come to rid ourselves of this manager. We've made up our mind. And I am the one to do it. To riddle him," the boy said, pointing the gun slowly around the room.

" How long has he had it ? " Mandlazi asked.

" I don't know. I've never seen it until this minute," Maria Maziya said. There was terrible fright in her eyes.

" Give it to me. Give it at once," Mandlazi demanded, holding his hand out and taking a step towards the boy.

" You can't have it. You can't have it ! " the boy screamed. Then suddenly in a deadly cold voice, he said, " Stay still or I'll shoot." Mandlazi froze in his steps. He saw the strained wild look on the grotesque face and he knew that the boy would shoot if he came nearer. He took Maria Maziya by the arm and they both went backward out of the door into the yard. As they closed the door, they heard the boy giggling softly to himself.

" Oh, what new trouble is this ? " Maria Maziya said, without emotion, as if she had lost all capacity to suffer or wonder.

" Come, Mother," Mandlazi said. He escorted her to his own place and left her there to wait for the raid with the others of his family while he went back to find Alemina.

He found Alemina at last, and brought her back to his place. He did not hear when his mother gave her the instructions about the bundles. His mind was full only of the unhappy deranged boy alone in the dark room with that monstrous companion.

*   *   *

In the large brick-built house of Simon Ndimandi there were queer and unaccountable premonitions.

After calling at each of his three shops, slipping the cash from the till into his trousers pocket, and supervising the locking up, Simon Ndimandi had sat in his car wondering about going to the meeting. He was unhappy about the meeting—there was trouble in the air. But he was an avid gossip and the meeting exercised a powerful attraction on him. In the end he decided to go.

He drove to the square and sat in the car watching the crowd assemble. After a while he could feel that there was something provocative about the car, a big black shiny Buick. He was not popular in the location : too many people owed him money. He did not mind the lack of popularity ; in fact, he regarded it as a kind of compliment, a tribute to his wealth, but he was always careful not to let it lead to unpleasant situations. So he decided to remove the Buick from the eyes of the meeting. He drove away and parked it in the next street.

When he returned from parking the car, he took up a position at the very edge of the square. There he stood, thoughtful and uncommunicative—an onlooker. A fat, well-dressed little stranger who had just happened to stop and watch from curiosity. It was a cool day but there was perspiration around his eyes. He was feeling uncomfortable. His heart was uncomfortable, pounding and murmuring. He told himself to-morrow he would go and get another injection from the doctor.

He watched the meeting start and heard Du Toit make the

218

announcement about the passes for the women. He wondered why he was hearing Du Toit's voice and not Gwebu's, when it had always been the other way round. Then he saw that something was going on between Du Toit and a man in the audience but he was too far away to hear what it was. Feeling the tension and the danger but unable to draw himself entirely away from the scene, he crossed the road and watched from the veranda of a house. Then he noticed the location constables standing nearby, most of them clustered together under the water tower.

The sight of them made him suddenly furious. "What are you doing here? Go and help the manager," he called out. The constables looked up, startled, then turned away and looked at each other with sheepish, guilty eyes. A section of the crowd, sensing some new excitement, faced round to watch Ndimandi. He felt a sudden panic. Something told him that his safety was bound up with Du Toit's. He knew that he belonged much more with Du Toit than with this crowd, and the cowardice of the constables became a flagrant breach of a duty owed to himself as much as to Du Toit.

"Go on," he screamed. No one moved.

"Go on," he said ominously. They glared back, but did not move.

At that point his courage failed, and he stepped back into the shadows of the veranda. From where he stood, he could still see the constables. He was still furious. He could not forgive them. He took out an old envelope and began to write down their numbers. They saw him do it but did not try to hide from him. The writing of their numbers somehow transfixed them. But while he was writing, they turned and fled. It was the moment when Du Toit fled, and their fleeing was a kind of instantaneous echo in action of Du Toit's.

He stayed a moment longer and saw the first bombardment of stones rise out of the square and pound against the office building. Panting, and mopping his face, he hurried away, reached his car, and drove home.

He brushed past the group of grave-faced men with black arm-bands standing on his veranda, went into his bedroom, stepped over the legs of the black-veiled women sitting on the

219

floor, took out his heavy bunch of keys, opened his iron safe, placed the money inside, and locked the door again. Then he went into the dining-room and sat fanning himself and gasping for breath in the carved oaken chair at the head of the table.

His house was full of mourners who had come from all parts of the Transvaal for his brother-in-law's funeral, due to take place the next afternoon. A rich, warm smell of stew rose out of the huge black pots on the kitchen stove and hung in the air around the house, drawing all the children of the neighbourhood to stand clutching at the fence and gazing big-eyed at the activity. Big black old-fashioned taxis with number-plates of a variety of towns were parked at all angles in the road in front of his gate. In a lane beside the house stood the two buses that Ndimandi had hired from his friend, Hosea Malooy, to provide transport for those mourners without places in cars.

Most of the guests, being strangers to the location, had stayed away from the meeting, and were bubbling with curiosity to know the meaning of the noise that was coming over the roof-tops. Ndimandi, speaking slowly and keeping calm, in accordance with his doctor's advice, told them, up to the point when he left, namely when the stone throwing began.

" It was terrible," he said, wagging his head. Just then the rifle shots and the scream of the scattering rioters cut off the hubbub in the room.

" God help those foolish people," Ndimandi said to the silent room.

He was worried about the funeral now. Would the arrangements be able to go forward as planned ? Would the police and Du Toit not start banning things ? This riot was terrible stupidity, and it brought back to him clearly and sharply the pain of having to live in the location, caged up with people who went mad and became violent, and brought trouble to everyone, innocent and guilty, living inside the fence. What was the use of struggling to make a success of life, to acquire a bank balance and a cheque book, if he was forever to be treated like a kraal Kaffir ? What was the use of his money ? It could buy a car, some shining furniture, some suits, and regular meat with his meals, but could it get him out of the location ? Could it give him the rights of the poorest and most broken-down white man, the right to sit in a café, to own a bottle of brandy, to walk about the streets at night ? No. What was the use of money ?

His wife came in and asked if she could start serving the food. He was not hungry, but it was obvious that everyone else was. He had a sick, nervous feeling : his blood, which he could actually feel in movement ever since he had been in the doctor's hands, was racing through his arteries. " Let them eat," he said irritably and ungraciously, as if giving the signal to open the doors of a soup kitchen.

When the guests came back from the kitchen carrying plates piled high with stew and thick slices of bread, he began to feel bilious, but duty and manners demanded that he stay at the table. He thought longingly of lying down somewhere away from everybody, but realised that it was impossible because every room was full of mourners.

In the middle of the meal Hosea Malooy arrived. He came in breathlessly and looked around as if he had a burning secret and wanted everyone to leave the room. But nobody did, and someone pulled up the other carved chair and Malooy sat down face to face with Ndimandi, their pudgy knees almost touching.

" Have you heard ? " Malooy asked. He looked around the room again, then leant forward and whispered, " They attacked the superintendent. Burnt his car."

" Burnt his car ? "

" Yes. *And* the office furniture."

" Oh, terrible, terrible," said Ndimandi weakly.

" I don't get these people. Why do they act like this ? " Malooy said. He always used a kind of flattened-out slang that somehow had the effect of deadening the impact of his words. " Now the Flying Squad have pitched up and a raid will start up pretty soon."

" God help us."

While they sat facing each other, the two watch-chains dangling from their plump bellies seemed to be gossiping all on their own : lively as housewives, they bobbed with glee and swayed with astonishment at each new triviality, and showed

221

complete unconcern for the tense, hushed conversation of their owners.

"I hear there was a terrible bust-up between Du Toit and Mabaso. A real showdown. Mabaso said some shocking things," Malooy said.

"Him? Him again?"

"Yes. But he's finished after this. Done for. I don't think he has much future in the location after this, if you ask me. I'm not sorry, speaking personally. He was too full of himself, too clever. And most unfriendly. Well, I think this is the last we'll be hearing of him. Do you know that Du Toit and Ngubeni had a bust-up to-day?"

"Nugbeni? Quarrelled with Du Toit?"

"Yes. And what with Shongwe in the jug——"

"So . . ."

"Yes. It seems that you are now talking to the next chairman."

Malooy smiled and looked smugly around at all the people in the room. But Ndimandi's mind was not on Advisory Board politics.

"Did you see it all?" he asked.

"No. I left before the rough stuff started. The crowd got ugly, so I left. I did not want to get mixed up in it. But everyone is talking about it. It's everywhere." He waved his arm to take in the whole location.

Ndimandi frowned. He sucked his top lip between his teeth and bit on it. The sweat was forming in his eyesockets, but he did not wipe it away.

"You think there'll be a raid?"

"Of course."

"God help us."

"What's worrying you, Ndimandi? You weren't mixed up in it. I'm not worried. I wasn't mixed up in it. If there's any little difficulty, not that I believe there will be, why, we'll simply ask old Du Toit to straighten it out, that's all. After all, we both have a pretty good relationship with him." He gave Ndimandi a meaningful wink. "He'll stick with us. No, stop worrying, Ndimandi."

But Ndimandi could not stop worrying. He always worried,

about everything, and about this there was a deep throbbing worry right in the centre of him. There was a chilling lack of confidence both in his innocence and in Du Toit's powers of protection once the raid started, when anybody could find himself getting under the feet of the police.

"It was the fault of those constables," Ndimandi said angrily. "They should have kept order. Why didn't they keep order instead of all standing there at the back of the crowd? Anyway, I took down some of their numbers."

"That might come in pretty handy."

"Oh, why did he run away?" Ndimandi asked in an anguished voice. "That was the cause of it. It only really started up *after* he ran away."

"Yes, I heard so. It beats me why he did it."

"I saw it. The whole crowd suddenly rose up behind him, just like the sea, after he ran away. Why did he do it?"

"It was pretty dim of him. Still, they had no right to attack him and burn his valuable motor-car."

"No, they had no right to do that. And now there'll be a raid, and we're all going to catch it from the Flying Squad."

"I've told you——" Malooy started to say, but Ndimandi suddenly stood up and ran out of the room. He went to the back yard, behind the coalshed, and pressed his fingers on his tongue, and silently brought up the bile that had been lying on his stomach. After that he felt a little better.

*   *   *

Sarah Manana was told of the riot shortly before the raid began. As she walked through the location to her house, she was struck by the silence in the streets, the absence of people. She had not come through the gate and past the administration building; she had climbed through the barbed-wire fence, taking her usual short-cut across the southern corner of the location, past the Welfare Centre, the Rialto cinema, and the football ground, and in this way saved twenty minutes in reaching her house.

Walking, as always, in the middle of the street, she passed the houses of many people she knew, but she saw nobody about,

223

nobody who could satisfy her curiosity about what had happened. The houses were dark and silent and the windows lifeless and without depth, like dead men's eyes. Something is wrong to-night, she said to herself, the business will be bad to-night.

She was disappointed that there was nobody to see her return home from Withoek, for she liked to dazzle the location people with her smart clothes. Usually when she went or returned from visiting, her progress down the street was a kind of parade that left in its wake gasps and eddies of talk. Let them talk, she always said, it is good for the business.

That afternoon she had been to Withoek, the next town, for a meeting of the Good Shepherds of Zion, an enthusiastic sect whose members dressed up as pilgrims and carried the Cross through the streets on Sundays. Sarah Manana could not spare Sundays, which were her best business days, but she made up for this by becoming the committee's most energetic member and most generous donor. That day she had been to the usual Wednesday-afternoon committee meeting, and she was dressed in the manner befitting the outstanding lady of the Good Shepherds : a leopard-skin hat, like a kettledrum, with a great spray of feathers swishing up at the back ; a vivid green felt coat with fluffy collar and cuffs of yellow-dyed fur ; a red flannel blouse ; a tartan skirt, black patent leather shoes with ankle straps ; a handbag as big as a school satchel, also of leopard skin, a rope of fat artificial pearls, and a platinum wrist watch. She, indeed, had all the airs and finery of a queen that night as she walked through the township with heavy pomp, as if the streets had been specially cleared for her.

She arrived at her house and was taking out the hatpins when her next-door neighbour, Sallie Mtetwa, an old *ayah* who lived by interpreting dreams, crept in by the back door and whispered breathlessly, " They attacked the manager with stones to-night. Then they burned his beautiful car."

" Oh Lord in heaven, save us. What will happen now ? " said Sarah Manana, but not with much alarm.

" The Flying Squad people are here. There will be a raid, that's certain."

These words shot Sarah Manana into action. She had a method of preparing for police raids; practice had made her quick and skilful at following out the routine. She dashed into the yard, pulled a road-making stamp from under a mound of sacking, and pounded the earth around the edges of the yard and in certain selected places in the centre. She scattered loose dust and ashes over the hardened parts, walked on it, and kicked it up. Then she stood on the kitchen step and appraised the whole yard carefully through one eye, to be sure that the surface looked uniform. Satisfied, she swung the stamp with incredible strength over the fence into a clump of bushes ten yards away. Five feet below the smoothed-over surface were the drums of Kaffir beer, barberton, pineapple-cider, skokiaan, and other home-brewed concoctions that were the stock of her business. The police knew the trick of burying illicit liquor, and they always looked for soft and newly dug earth.

While Sarah Manana worked, Sallie Mtetwa walked after her, telling her of the riot.

"I don't think the manager was hurt," said Sallie.

"That is bad luck and also stupid," said Sarah. "What is the point of throwing stones and burning if they don't damage the manager? They will be punished anyway. Our people always do the foolish thing."

"They hurt him by making him afraid. And by burning the car."

"Not good enough."

"I don't think it was meant to be an attack on the manager. It was an attack on the municipality. An attack on the law."

"I don't understand this difference between the manager and the law."

Sarah Manana darted back into her dining-room and with great speed pulled three loose bricks out of the wall, then placed them carefully in their order on the floor. Then she walked about the house gathering various articles in her arms: packets of yeast, malt, and a bottle of methylated spirits from a shelf in the kitchen; two unlabelled bottles of brandy from her dresser drawer, a home-made galvanised iron suction pump (used for drawing the liquid out of the ground) from a cupboard in the bedroom. These she placed one by one into the cavity in the wall. She took out her purse, which contained fifty-three pounds, and put that inside, too, reaching deep into the cavity to push it into its special crevice. Then she replaced the bricks, fitted back the fragments of cement that had come away, and pulled the table against that part of the wall. Finally she set the table for dinner and placed a vase of artificial flowers in the centre.

All the while the conversation continued.

" Did you see it all—all this stoning and burning of the law ? " Sarah asked with heavy irony.

" Yes—I was there." Sallie was embarrassed. She added, " I stoned and I burned."

" Then why did you say ' They stoned ' and ' They burned ? ' Do you think I am the police that you have to pretend that you are not guilty ? " The legal phrase being one that Sarah had often heard and sometimes used, was the one that came easiest to her.

Sallie became uncomfortable and more confused ; she fingered her eyelids. " It did not seem to be *me*. Now I am sorry. But at the time everybody was doing it and I was doing it. I can hardly remember what I did. It was how he looked when he ran away from the shouting—like a leopard that cannot bite, and cannot scratch any more. And the way his long legs got quicker and quicker, and the way he sprang up the steps, like a scared old leopard climbing a tree to get away from the barking of dogs. And then we all became like dogs barking at a sick old leopard, annoying him, and pretending to want to kill him, and wanting to, but not coming close enough because we were still afraid of his claws and his strength, of the danger that was still in him. How can I tell you what made us do it ? "

" You have told me. But now the leopard is out of the tree again, and all the dogs are back in their boxes. This is a strange game you are playing with the manager."

" Sarah, if you were there you, too, would have stoned and burned."

" I do not think so. I would have laughed at the manager. I would not have become a barking dog."

226

"You would have been angry at this business of the passes for women. You would have been too angry to laugh. This business is meant for you. Now Du Toit will get you out of the location."

"I am not worried about this business of the passes," Sarah said wearily. "Not worried at all. I am too bored by it even to have attended the meeting. You'll see, Sarah Manana will be the first woman in the location to have a pass."

"You ? How will you do that ? Sarah, sometimes you talk only to make people angry." The old *ayah* was exasperated, but Sarah only laughed.

"Do you know Van der Walt, the carpenter in Nelstroom ? He will employ me and he will give me a pass. I buy much brandy from him. Oh, he cheats me—he puts water in the brandy and sells it at three times the shop price. But I buy from him. He is no worse than the others. So much do I buy that he has not made a table or chair for six months and still drives a motor car. He will be the saddest man in Nelstroom if Du Toit kicks me out of the location. So he will give me a pass. I'll pay him five pounds a month for it, and he will do it."

"It will be a strange employment where the servant pays the master."

"That is how it looks. But the white Van der Walt is really the servant of the black Sarah Manana."

Sallie Mtetwa went home then, creeping stealthily out of the back door. Sarah Manana sat in an armchair, picked up the Rand *Daily Mail*, and waited. She had nothing to fear. This was not a liquor raid anyway, and as for the other business—well, she had not been there. She had been lucky, as she was in everything. She was lucky because she was a Good Shepherd of Zion ; the Lord appreciated her work for the church and looked after her. She thought of a few cheeky pleasantries to make to the police if they should waste their time by coming to her house.

★   ★   ★

Mabaso reached his house and let himself in. He found his wife Leah and son Moses in the dining-room, sitting in the dark.

They stood up as he came in and went over to him, and he placed his arms around them. He felt a great tenderness towards them. No one spoke. They stood in the dark and he pressed them to his sides. He felt the soft, yielding flesh of his wife and the hard, wiry frame of his son and he squeezed them hard against him. At last he said :

" Leah, you must pack your things and go with Moses and hide in Father Shongwe's church. It will be empty and they'll not search there. And in the morning you must take the train back to Orlando and stay with my brother Julius." He spoke in Swazi.

He felt Leah clutch at his arm. " Why are you speaking like this ? " she asked in alarm.

" Because I don't know how it will end to-night."

" And you ? Are you going to wait here ? Why don't you come with us ? "

" No, it's not possible. Perhaps I'll not wait here, I haven't decided yet, but it's impossible for me to go with you."

They fell silent again. He could feel the sorrow in them, in the weight of their bodies against his. There seemed to be nothing to say. They understood the decision and the futility of trying to prove the opposite of what they all knew in their hearts to be inevitable. Gently he pulled her hand down and gave it a little tug in the direction of the bedroom.

" You must start now," he said.

They left his side and walked slowly into the bedroom. He crossed the room and, without removing his coat or cap, sat at the table. His cheek rested on his fist and he stared into the dark. After a while he lit the candle.

He could hear Leah and Moses moving about in the next room. He felt a deep pity for Leah. Hers had been an impossible task. What had gone wrong ? Who was to blame? He had often asked himself that, but it was not a matter for blame. Like two clocks that are allowed to run on without attention, they had drawn imperceptibly away from each other. But she had been a good wife, faithful and loyal. She had been all that most men wanted of a wife. She had not failed as a wife. She had merely been unable to match him in the strange ferment of spirit that had taken place in him. Now, with the time of parting at hand, he felt a flood of remorse and love for her.

He heard the separate sounds of his son in the next room. He knew the exact sound of the boy's step, the exact shape of his movements. The boy lived in his mind's eye, as if a part of himself, moving within him. Now he could picture the long-legged barefooted boy opening a drawer, now kneeling on the bed and packing things down into the fibre suitcase. He was filled with sorrow at the idea of parting from Leah, but he could believe it. Somehow he could not make himself believe that the time had come to part from Moses. He had always told himself that he was ready for any consequences, but he realised now that he was not ready for this one. Yet this was the one inevitable consequence. Well, now the time had come. He said it to himself again, the time had come.

They came back into the dining-room and stood waiting, unable to say good-bye. Leah had a dark heavy blanket around her shoulders, neatly folded and fixed across her bosom with a large steel safety pin. She held a paper parcel under her arm, under the blanket. Moses was wearing his old grey overcoat, too short in the sleeves to cover his raw, thick wrists, and straining on the buttons. It, too, seemed suddenly to have been outlived. The boy carried the battered yellow suitcase, the same that Mabaso had carried on his arrival at Nelstroom Station nine months before.

Mabaso went over to them and propelled them to the door.

" Moses, look after your mother."

The boy nodded. Mabaso disengaged his arm from the boy and bent forward and kissed Leah. Then he placed his hand on the boy's head, slid it down over the side of the face, and held the head firmly pressed to his side.

" Give my fond wishes to Julius. He will look after you. And try to understand why it has happened. That's all I can say. Perhaps it will work out better than we expect and you'll see me again quite soon. But be brave."

" Wouldn't it be better if we stayed here in Nelstroom to be near you ? " Leah asked.

" No, I would not like you to do that. They will make it

heavy for you here because of me. Here, take this money." He pulled the money out of his back pocket and placed it, notes and coins crumpled together, into Leah's hand.

"Now, go in peace, my wife and my son."

"Stay in peace," they said glumly.

They went out, and he heard their steps grow faint along the street as they walked towards the Reverend Shongwe's abandoned church.

Mabaso stood at the window and wondered what had delayed Elliot and the others, and whether they would come as arranged. He hoped they would be able to come, not only to discuss arrangements, but because he longed to see them, especially Elliot, once more before his arrest. He thought about the events of the last few days. How vastly everything had changed. How crowded time had been since the police came to arrest Mary Lukhele, barely fifty hours before. The location had lived a whole lifetime in that short period. Yes, he had a feeling of finality now: the great flare was burning out.

He had a sudden desire to go to the glass cupboard and look at his books. There were not many books: they occupied less than a whole shelf. But they were well cared for and there were some good books among them. His hand paused in front of Marius Fortie's book, but passed on, and he took out a fat, heavy book with thick, rough-edged pages that had been cut with a knife. The hard, rough touch of the pages had something of the terse, dry flavour of the book itself. Livingstone's *Missionary Travels in South Africa*, out of print, and like the author himself, unpopular in South Africa. He had bought it years before at a court messenger's sale, when a back-street bookseller had been sold up, and it had become one of his favourite books. He brought it to the table and idly turned the pages, glancing at the quaint, stilted engravings that gave such a warm, intimate glimpse of an Africa a hundred years ago. His eyes fell on the passages of text he had marked and on his writing in the margins. But he did not read the book. His hand played fondly with the pages, and after a while he closed the book and just sat with his hand resting on it.

Then he got up and went into the bedroom, undressed, and

changed into a heavy corduroy shirt and two sweaters, and put the overcoat back on again; for he knew that in winter the worst hardship of gaol was the seeping, bone-penetrating cold of the concrete, just as in summer it was the bugs and lice. All his people hated the cold, and Mabaso had this aversion in a marked degree.

He took an electric torch out of the drawer and placed it in his pocket. He locked the wardrobe containing his clothes and the remaining clothes of Leah and Moses. Then he took his razor, toothbrush, and a used cake of soap from the washstand, wrapped some paper around them, and placed them in his coat pocket. He would have warmth and comfort, at least while awaiting trial; he was an experienced prisoner.

He came back into the dining-room and pondered whether to wait any longer for Elliot Nkomo and the others. He wanted to leave now, for he had decided not to allow himself to be arrested in his own house. He would go to some other house, and if they found him there, good, they could arrest him; and if not, he would find some other way of getting into the cells. It was very clear to him that he would have to be arrested. But he was not going to sit and wait in his own house while they came after him, baying for his blood. All their fury aroused by the riot, all their hatred of the location would be concentrated on that visit to his house. No, it would be better to be discovered in some other place, unexpectedly, and not like a cornered animal. Or, better still, in the cell yard, mixed up among the prisoners, swept up with them in the course of the raid.

He wondered about this decision. Was he afraid? Yes, he decided, he was. Afraid of waiting while they came for him, hunting him down, afraid of being kicked and pounded, and sworn at and abused, and of the necessity of keeping his arms down and his tongue quiet, of not affording them an excuse for putting a bullet in him.

He decided to go. At any moment there would be the alarm, and then all movement in the location would be frozen. He would go to the house of a supporter named Mtetwa and wait there.

He looked around the room. He felt no sorrow at leaving

it. It was already empty, waiting for the next occupant. He tweaked out the candle and lit the electric torch and walked to the door, but there he paused and turned back and fetched the book. Then he went out, closed the door, and walked swiftly along the street.

At the corner he saw a group of people coming towards him; when they came nearer, he saw that it was Elliot Nkomo, Paul Vilakazi and Mavuso. They were making for his house. They stopped when they reached him and all moved into the shadows. There they stood and spoke in whispers.

" He refuses to come," Elliot said. Mabaso did not answer.

" We've been arguing with him all this time and he refuses," Elliot said.

" Yes, he ratted," Vilakazi said bitterly.

" He says he's resigned," Elliot said. " That's the word he used—resigned. Can you beat that? What does he think we are —a dance club? Resigned? Walter, I never came nearer to strangling a man in my life." Mabaso looked down and saw Elliot's thick, crooked fingers slowly writhe. " Sibande!" Elliot said in disgust.

" We can't talk here. It might start any moment now. I was going to Mtetwa's—let's go there."

" No, it wouldn't be fair on Mtetwa—all of us. Come to my place."

They walked to Elliot's place in silence. They went into the tiny, musk-smelling room, and Elliot bolted the door inside. They did not light a candle. All that was visible was the intermittent glow of their cigarettes. The glow-worm lights lit up parts of their faces, Mabaso's black beard, Elliot's pitted skin, Vilakazi's thin mouth, and Mavuso's hollow cheeks, and marked the places of the people in the room: Mabaso and Elliot seated on the sagging bed, Mavuso on the wooden chair, Vilakazi leaning against the window.

" He just sat there and pointed out how mistaken we've been all the time," Elliot said. " We're a danger to the struggle. We're selling the people out. And do you know what you are, Walter?"

" No. What?"

" You're a police agent."

" Did he say that ? "

" Yes—pretty well. He said, 'Are you fellows quite sure about Mabaso ?'—looking at us through those little pig eyes of his; you know the way he does it. We said, 'What do you mean?' and he said, 'Well, it's funny the way he suddenly pitches up here from nowhere and takes charge of everything and, before you know where you are, there are riots and people being killed by the police. Very funny. Who's putting him up to it ?' Oh, he sees it all very clearly now. We're ruining the struggle and you're working for the government. So he's resigned—that's a nice polite little word for ratted. Effective from to-night."

Mabaso said nothing. There was a heavy silence. Elliot said, " Don't tell me you take any notice of that rubbish ? "

" No," Mabaso said despondently. He added, " Well, we all saw it coming, didn't we ? "

" Yes, I must say I expected it after the other night."

" Yes. That's the way when they drop out. They accuse us of everything, mostly the very things they intend to start doing themselves. Anyway, let's forget him. We haven't time to waste with him. How much money have we left ? "

There was a pause before Paul Vilakazi answered. " Ninety-one pounds, eight shillings," he said, speaking reluctantly, as if being forced to divulge the whereabouts of the money to burglars.

They could not forget him. Not him, nor Father Shongwe, nor Dhladla. Their absence left the group gutted. Without their voices, their personalities, it seemed lightweight, structureless. Sibande, for all his obstinacy and egotism, had been a powerful force in the group : shrewd and determined and a performer of prodigious work. The Reverend Shongwe had been the deep, slow voice of sanity, conscience, and solemn purpose. Even Dhladla, in spite of his fireside Mau Mauism, his comic belliger-ence, and never ending objections, had occupied a place. He had been a valuable messenger and fetcher-and-carrier, and losing him made the group conscious of losing its wheels. Each had added something to the total character, each now attended like a ghost, invisibly present, silently listening.

Mabaso tried to bring the talk around to urgent matters, but

233

he could feel the drag of doing it. He could not free his own mind of the three missing persons, and especially Sibande. He was bitterly wounded by what Sibande had told Elliot. He knew that he would never forgive him—for that, or for the desertion. But he could not rid himself of a certain respect for Sibande, a certain fear for his qualities. Warped and turned against his old friends, that could become the serious new danger.

And present, too, was the knowledge that Mabaso himself would be missing from the future meetings. None of them spoke about this. It was too awkward, too disastrous. But they showed their preoccupation with it in the way they all sat facing him in the dark, listening closely to everything he said.

" The money is meant to be spent," Mabaso said briskly, trying to impart an air of business. " It's not our money, anyway. It belongs to those who gave it to us."

" I know," Vilakazi said.

" You are too mean with the money ; you love it too much," Elliot said, trying to sound cheerful.

" That's why he's such a good treasurer," Mabaso said.

" We still owe about nine pounds for the printing of tickets and hiring the hall. That leaves about eighty-two pounds," Vilakazi said, as if it gave him some kind of satisfaction to reduce the amount.

" The debts will have to wait," Mabaso said. " We'll need every penny. Even so, it won't be enough. It might bail out four or five people, that's about all. Keep it for the most serious cases—sick or old people, pregnant women. Use your discretion."

" You're right, it won't be enough," said the weak old voice of Mavuso. " We'll have to collect more, but I do not think there's enough money in the whole location to pay for this trouble."

" Yes, you'll have to start a fund," Mabaso said. " That job will fall on you—Mavuso and Vilakazi—if you're not arrested. Anyway, the time has come to rope in some of the others ; Mtetwa, he'll be all right. Makhoti and Mahlangu. Reverend Dhlamini and all those teacher fellows from Elliot's school. We won't be short of people from now on."

" Do we give receipts ? " Vilakazi asked.

" Yes, but keep names off the receipts. And make the purpose of the fund clear : for bail, to help the families that will suffer, and to pay lawyers. There'll be no hope without lawyers in a case like this. Tell them that everyone must stand together—the fortunate to help the unfortunate. The fund will help keep the people together. See them in their kitchens at night and try to keep away from the good boys and the location constables. Keep the money and receipt books hidden away. And one last thing—try to keep people's spirits up. For that you'll have to keep your own up."

" That won't be easy."

" Well, just try. Now there's a special job for Elliot. Elliot, I'm giving you a note to Abdul Carrim. You know him, the Indian who owns the store at Buffelsdrif."

He got off the bed and went to the table, clicked on the flashlight, and started to write in a school exercise book that was lying on the table. " He'll give you transport to Johannesburg, and there he'll put you in touch with certain people . . ."

He tailed off, his mind occupied with writing the note to Abdul Carrim, a man who had done good work in the Defiance Campaign.

" ' . . . Take him to Father Huddleston or Nelson Mandela or Mulvi Cachalia. Tell them of our need for sympathetic lawyers, men who will understand our troubles and hardships and help us from that motive, not from the motive of fees. We will pay what we can, but explain that we are a very poor crowd here, very much ground under. Try to get some money for us, if you can, Abdul. We need it urgently. I know how the resources are strained, but perhaps they can squeeze out a little extra for us. Perhaps some people from your Congress, some private individuals . . .' "

He wrote fast, putting it down as it came. After a while he stopped and looked up at Vilakazi and Mavuso. " Don't hang around now," he said. " Elliot will keep in touch with you. Go now, and try to find a good place to hide until the raid is over. I suggest Shongwe's church. Good luck to the fund."

They turned to go. At the door Vilakazi stopped, full of

things to say, but he checked himself and gave the thumbs-up, saying simply " Afrika."

" *Mayibuye* [May it come]," Mabaso responded, peering at them through the gloom. Then he went on writing.

They left then.

" ' . . . stay next to Nkomo in Johannesburg. Help him all you can. And please, Abdul, try to help him to get our side across. It's a wicked thing, this pass law for women, and the way it was put over on us, so sudden and brutal. You can't blame them for rioting——' "

Elliot came over to the table. " Oh no," he said, placing his hand over Mabaso's and stopping him writing. Mabaso looked up. The flashlight was lying on its side on the table, and the edge of its beam caught Elliot's face, distorting it with oblique shadows, making grotesque craters out of the skin blemishes and throwing the fat nose into monstrous relief. Mabaso saw the serious look in Elliot's eyes. He pulled his hand away.

" What's the matter ? "

" Oh no. I'd only make a mess of it. I don't know these people in Johannesburg. You know them all ; it's obvious you're the one for Johannesburg."

" Carrim will help you," Mabaso said, and wrote a few words more. Then he stopped. He looked up into Elliot's eyes again. They understood each other without the need for words. Mabaso smiled sadly and shook his head.

" Thank you, Elliot, but it's impossible."

He knew then that Elliot had the same feeling as he had.

" You've done enough for us already," Elliot said. He was breathing hard ; he was in distress and not saying all that he meant.

" No," Mabaso said. " Not after what Du Toit said : that people like me come here to make trouble, and run away, and leave the people to face it alone. It would prove Du Toit to be too right."

" But it's not running away. You can do wonderful work for us in Johannesburg."

" It would look like running away."

" But we can explain it."

" It would take too much explaining. Anyway, they'll simply come and pick me up in Johannesburg."

" It's not that—being picked up. Listen, Walter, I . . . I . . ." He stopped, embarrassed. Then he squared his shoulders. " It's just that I don't like the idea of you being in the location during the raid, that's all."

" We're all in the same boat."

" That's not true. You know it's not true," Elliot said hotly. " You know what this means, what will happen to you ; you understand all right. . . ." He was walking about the room, limping heavily in his agitation. He came to the table and placed his fists on it and peered at Mabaso. He spoke with bitter fury. " For whose benefit are you putting on this—this performance ? "

Mabaso gave Elliot a long, silent look. Then he scraped the chair round and finished writing the note. He stood up, folding the note.

" You'd better start," he said, handing Elliot the note. " Go on your bike to Carrim's ; it will take you about three hours. He will look after you from then on. Go out through the fence. If you see any lights on the road, hide by the roadside until they pass. Good luck, Elliot." He offered his hand. Elliot did not respond and did not make a move to go. Elliot was stiff and angry and he spoke now with a strange, stilted formality. " You cannot decide this by yourself. You have no right to overrule me like this."

" You're just being sentimental on my behalf. And unreasonable. Listen, Elliot, I'm going to wait here. I thought of going to Mtetwa's, but I've changed my mind. I'll be alone here. If they don't find me, then I'm going to join one of the batches of prisoners and just climb into a pickup van. They never know who they arrest and who not in these raids. Now please go, Elliot. You've got a big job to do. Don't mess it up by hanging around here arguing."

He had become suddenly irritable. He stood with his hands on his hips, waiting for Elliot to go. Elliot did not move. He bent forward and seized Elliot's hand and shook it. The arm was limp. He pushed Elliot to the door, but Elliot just stood before it, making no effort to open it. He fetched the bicycle

237

from the corner and placed Elliot's hands on the handle bars. He unlocked the door and pushed Elliot, dazed and holding the bicycle, outside. Then he came in and bolted the door again. There was a moment of silence. Then he heard the scuff of Elliot's thick boot dragging on the ground, the thud as he landed in the saddle, and the soft shush of the tyres biting into the sand. He opened the door and looked down the street. He saw the gnome-like silhouette against the starlit sky, weaving and bobbing in that strange rhythm of eccentric motion by which Elliot became united with his bicycle. Elliot was riding very fast.

Mabaso watched him turn the corner, then locked himself in the room again. Shortly after that he heard the alarm. There was a strange, unnatural intensity about the alarm this time, a shrill metallic throb of terror.

Now he waited. He heard the first distant sounds of the raid : a sudden furious barking of dogs, a sharp eruption of voices, a crash, a scream. Then silence. Then, from a different direction, running feet, a blast on a police whistle. A brief, hoarse uproar. Silence. An engine starting—stopping. Metal doors slamming. The crash of glass. Then the raid far away, in Old Look, up near the railway line. A distant shot. The first shot.

He felt calm now, waiting. The sounds of the raid, drawing nearer, like a fire burning its way slowly into the centre of the location, did not agitate him. He was resigned, prepared. He knew now what the night held for him. The blurred shapes of doubt and anxiety had moved into sharp focus, and now there was a clear knowledge in place of the vague premonition.

The wrath of the whole white country was about to break on him. No man could hope to withstand such a weight of wrath. For the crime of rioting, of startling the white country out of its illusions of peace, of stirring up its fearful nightmares, there would be terrible retribution. It would fall on the whole location, a cloudburst of hatred, but on him, the agent responsible for the riot, it would fall with concentrated fury.

Oh, he had never wanted the riot. It had been a calamity, the very antithesis of what he wanted—but who would ever understand that ? The riot had grown out of the meeting and he had been the voice of the meeting. He had stood before the crowd

238

and had allowed all the passions and feelings of the meeting to flow through him. He had personified the meeting, and therefore the sedition of challenging the white man's law. And therefore, too, the stoning of the building and the burning of the car, the attack on the visible property of the law, even though he had not wanted it and had been powerless to prevent it.

Understanding this brought him a certain composure, for it freed him from the necessity of condemning the location for the riot. He understood better now the logic of not accepting Elliot's offer. It would have been more than a confirmation of Du Toit's warning, more than desertion : it would have been to act *against* the location. In the same way as to have stopped the uproar when Du Toit refused to answer his questions would have been to aid Du Toit against the location, to assist him in imposing the new law, to have done the work that even his own constables refused to do. No, he was not prepared to work for Du Toit, to take Sibande's way out, and he felt relieved at knowing that his disappointment and disapproval of the riot would never come in issue.

He lit a cigarette and took a deep draw. His mind was steady. Idly, in the dark, he turned the pages of the book ; then he lit the flashlight and read some of the familiar passages. Or rather he let the pages remind him of their contents, for he knew them well. On a certain page there was a description of the land of the Bechuana—a land rich in pasture and woods and streams : a land of plentiful game and great cattle herds and bustling African towns and villages. That had never ceased to amaze him, for there was nothing left of it now. That part was now a waste of sand and shrub—desert. How had it happened ? How had the life been wrung out of the land ? To what crimes against nature did this shrivelling and bleaching and drying up bear witness ?

There was a strange sense of discovery in reading Livingstone's book. It was full of damning and telling surprises. It was like finding a survivor of a long-hushed-up scandal.

He turned the pages back and forth, reading at random. There were the passages dealing with the raids that the early Boers were constantly making on the neighbouring tribes.

" Plunderers," he had written in the margin. Still, everyone was doing it then, black and white. It was the way of life. But when the Boers did it, they did it in the name of Christianity ; and they raided not only for cattle, but also for children. And they spent all their time thinking of ways of harnessing the people of the tribes. Even in those days there was no end to the devices for enslaving the black population. " They have not changed much ! " Mabaso had noted. " Only they do it now under the law and on a much larger scale ! " That part of the book was full of indignation, his own in the margins and Livingstone's in the text. Commandants Potgieter and Krieger, the leaders of the newly arrived wagon nomads, had explained to Livingstone with truly magnificent effrontery, " We make the people work for us in consideration for allowing them to live in our country." " Herrenvolk in those days too ! " he had written in the margin, and Livingstone had been moved to write, " I never ceased to be most unfeignedly thankful that I was not born in a land of slaves. No one can understand the effect of the unutterable meanness of the slave system on the minds of those who, but for the strange obliquity which prevents them from feeling the degradation of not being gentlemen enough to pay for services rendered, would be equal in virtue to ourselves. Fraud becomes as natural to them as ' paying one's way ' is to the rest of mankind." He liked that passage. It seemed to contain the key to the present climate of this lunatic land. " Strange obliquity "— was it that which allowed those pleasant-looking white-bearded old farmers to grow rich on the labour of the convicts secured for them and kept in constant supply by the stifling laws and a zealous and eager police force ? Did their twisted blindness result from a life erected on fraud ?

His eyes fell on one passage and he paused. " Great peace-makers," he had written opposite it ; when he first read it he had been lost for words, and could only think of that lame annotation. " The first question put by them to strangers is respecting peace : and when they receive reports against any tribe, the case assumes all the appearances and proportions of a regular insurrection. Several measures then appear to the most mildly disposed among them as imperatively called for, and, however bloody the massacre that follows, no qualms of conscience ensue : it is a dire necessity for the sake of peace. Indeed Mr. Hendrik Potgieter most devoutly believed himself to be the great peacemaker of the country." Reading this caused him to sit up and stare into the corner. The same quick nervousness, the same inflamed fears, the same panicky impulse to rush to their rifles and put down the smallest imagined threat with a massacre, prevailed among them to-day. This very raid . . .

Yes, the angry old missionary had seen the things of a hundred years ago and had recorded them for the world, the things that had since changed and the things that had tragically remained the same. He had seen them at the beginning of the long night, and now with the night nearly over it was important to see what had happened to them. The things that had changed had changed like the land : had become hard, bitter, and angry. The things that had remained the same had changed too : had become swollen, wholesale, and all-pervading. The simple measures to obtain cattle and labour had become a vast legal network for plunder and enslavement. The simple forays of small parties of Boers against neighbouring villages had become a single continuous foray of the white country against the whole black country.

Was it true that the long night was nearly over ? He fervently believed it. In that hundred years of defeat his people had remained, had stayed on to participate in a grim, silent contest to outlive their conquerors. In that time they had changed too : nourished on pain and humiliation, they had become like that other product of the grudging soil of Africa, the gnarled, iron-hard, indestructible thorn tree, proof against all weathers and catastrophies. And now, everywhere, they were arising from the long sleep of defeat, were coming to life, were throwing off despair and helplessness, were feeling the surge of a new dream and a new value of themselves ; and that meant the end of the dark century.

He thought of Elliot riding furiously away into the night, and he smiled, for he knew that the thought came from the thought of the twisted thorn tree. He could smile because the deformity had long ceased to be painful and embarrassing to him,

241

and had even come to endear Elliot to him. Elliot would take it a little further now. Elliot had developed the qualities to take it along—until his turn came. Then there was Vilakazi; and Father Shongwe would come out one day. And there would be others, many others. More and more. Like flowers bursting into bloom in a field in spring.

A little sadly, he thought of Moses. He would be in it too. He, boys like him, would be in the centre of it. He would be cleverer, shrewder, bolder than his father; he would be more effective and he would have more allies. He would be armed with his youth, and that which had been passed on to him. And he would find the way. He was sure of that, for the dark century was ending. It saddened him to think of the life of bitter struggle and sacrifice that lay ahead for Moses. But at the same time it heartened him to know that the times ahead would give a worth to his life, and would make valid all that he himself had done, and would give a meaning to all the years of mistake and failure.

The raid noises had come nearer: the police were in the next street. He waited and heard a pickup van stop opposite a house a few doors away. Then the house was being searched and the people were standing shivering and silent in the street. The police moved on, and they went right past Elliot's door and banged on the door of a room a few yards away. He got up and went out to add himself to the group that was being loaded into the pickup van.

CHAPTER FIFTEEN

THE FOUR groups broke away and started walking towards the houses, carrying their weapons loosely, like stalking parties. Swanepoel turned suddenly and led his men off without noticing Du Toit, who had been standing behind him while he was giving the orders. Swanepoel had kept Constable Roberts in his party, and the two men walked at the head of the group, talking softly. Du Toit ran after them and fell in beside Swanepoel. Swanepoel went on talking to Roberts. As they walked, Du Toit wondered whether he had been so clever to come along on the raid. Maybe he should have gone home and called in the doctor, as Swanepoel suggested. The trouble was that after making such a big show of wanting to see the thing through, it was impossible to change his mind and go back. His head was throbbing and his legs felt weak and he was shivering with cold, although he had on his heavy overcoat, with the collar turned up around his neck and ears.

As they walked across the dry grass of the square, they moved silently and swiftly, but when they came to the houses, their steps began to ring on the hard road, and then, without a word, their pace dropped. The houses were cloaked in shadows. Shadows of dustbins and broken walls and outspanned dray carts stretched weirdly out, and took the shapes of lurking animals. Occasionally, almost under their feet, there was a sudden shifting and rustling as they disturbed a real animal, a sleeping donkey or calf. They kept stumbling into unseen potholes. The vague contours of objects, the unsure feel of the ground beneath them, and the eerie silence of houses full of people gave an uneasy feeling of walking into an ambush. Involuntarily, Du Toit gripped the revolver lying in the bottom of his coat pocket. The metal was colder than his hand, and it gave him a slight shock, as if it were an object placed in his pocket by someone else and found unexpectedly.

They stopped for a moment, and Swanepoel asked one of the black constables who had been attached to the groups as guides, to lead the way. The man came to the front and they walked on again. This was not their section, and as they walked through it they began to hurry again, moving faster and faster, until they were almost running. Their section was still some way ahead, across the main street and at the bottom half of Jubilee City. Swanepoel took the list out of his pocket and shone his light on it. The first address was Mabaso's.

Du Toit could not help peering at the houses. Occasionally he glimpsed the white-painted numbers on the doors, and each time the name of the registered occupant came instantly to his mind. He would not have recognised most of the occupants had he seen them, but he was able to make an instant association between the house numbers and the names. He even remembered how the rent stood for each house. He was able to do this every time he walked through the location, and usually he got a kick out of it, for it showed how he was able to keep the affairs of the whole location in his head. But now it annoyed him. He was doing it compulsively and he tried to stop. With an effort he kept his eyes straight ahead, and after a while he gave a little skip and fell into step with Swanepoel and Roberts. Marching in time with them lessened his desire to peer at the house numbers. He looked into Swanepoel's face. The face under the helmet was white, but not strained. It looked handsome and youthful. Swanepoel walked as if he knew exactly what he was about. The smart uniform, the leather and badges gave him an air of strength and self-confidence. Du Toit felt himself grow warm towards Swanepoel. He walked close to him and exactly in step.

But after a while his steps began to lag, and suddenly he was in the grip of a strange uneasiness. It was really strange. He looked into Swanepoel's face again, and now the feeling was altogether different. He seemed to see the man out of uniform, and that way everything was changed. His mind was back on the interview at the office. He knew now that there was something not quite right about that business. What exactly had he said there? He couldn't recall all the ins and outs of that grilling Swanepoel had put him through, but he had definitely said some things that weren't right, and had hidden some things, and there had been something not quite in order about Swanepoel up there in the office. He would have to try to put things straight the first opportunity. It wasn't going to be so simple. It made him uncomfortable thinking about the interview, and somehow it diminished his confidence in Swanepoel.

Maybe it's just my nerves, he told himself.

They came to the street where Mabaso lived, and the man who led the way slowed down. For no particular reason they began to walk warily. They reached the gate and Swanepoel asked, " Is this it ? " and the man said, " Yes, sir," and slipped away to the back of the group to join the other location constables. Swanepoel shone his light on the door and checked the number from his list. Then he drew his revolver and kicked the gate open and walked up the short cinder path. The white policemen and Du Toit followed, but the location constables stayed behind ; they had turned their backs on the house and were self-consciously blowing their noses and fingering their eyes. Swanepoel stood before the door and listened, then he hammered on the door with the butt of the revolver. The echo went crashing along the street. He waited and listened, then hammered again, then bawled, " Open up, damn you." He paused, and told Roberts, " Bust it down." Roberts tensed himself and flung his shoulder against the door, but the door was unlocked and it opened easily and Roberts lurched into the room. The others came in after him. Swanepoel stood in the centre of the room holding the flashlight in one hand and the gun in the other and waved them both about in front of him. He noticed the door leading to the bedroom and he covered it with the gun and the light simultaneously. He stood still for a moment, and then he could tell that there was no one there. He crossed the room and flung the door open. First Roberts, and then the others, came in behind him. " See who's under the bed," Swanepoel said, not expecting to find anyone, but Roberts

245

understood all right what the order meant. He heaved the loose-jointed brass bed on to its side. The mattress and blankets slid off and capsized a table and lamp. The paraffin oozed out on to the floor and under the bedclothes. "Maybe he's got ammunition and firearms or something sewn up in it," Roberts said. Swanepoel nodded. Roberts took out a knife, ripped the mattress open, and fished into the stiff coir with his hand. "No," he said after a while. "But I bet he's got it somewhere, the yellow bastard." Swanepoel noticed the wardrobe. He wrenched the door open and poked among the clothing with the revolver, shining the light on to the gun. His movements were clumsy : he had too many things in his hands. He became angry and began jabbing senselessly at the clothes with the gun and the flashlight. Then he slipped the revolver into the holster without buttoning the flap and rummaged with his hand. He felt in the pockets, found nothing, and suddenly the touch of the clothing infuriated him. He wrenched the articles off their hooks and sent them flying to all parts of the room. "Where's that dirty, stinking son of a pig ? " he muttered, speaking furiously to himself.

"He's b——— off," Roberts said. "He's yellow." Swanepoel grabbed a rifle from one of the constables, held it above his shoulder, and with a horizontal jab, smashed in the wardrobe mirror. Then he took a vicious swing at the china water jug on the washstand. It burst with a dull, wet explosion, spraying water all over the room. After that they smashed everything in the room.

They came back into the sitting-room and Swanepoel went to the bookcase, pulled out a book, and opened it with the muzzle of his gun ; then he seized handfuls of books and flung them furiously through the open front door out into the street. They wrecked the sitting-room and went into the kitchen and heaped jam, tea, paraffin, ketchup, sugar, coal, broken crockery, milk, vinegar, and bent kitchenware into a sticky, dripping pile in the middle of the floor.

Then they left.

"Where's that bastard ? We've got to get him," Swanepoel said when they were in the street again.

"Yes, we got to get that yellow bastard," Roberts said.

Du Toit was about to speak but something checked him and he walked away with his hands deep in his pockets.

*   *   *

A police car drove towards them, and the man at the wheel told Swanepoel that police reinforcements had arrived from Withoek. Swanepoel gave him some orders to convey to them.

Swanepoel was happy about the arrival of reinforcements, for they enabled him to increase the number of raiding parties and so to intensify the raid. There was no hope of searching every house, or even every second house, but the reinforcements guaranteed a more thorough comb-out of the location. Every policeman knew, without specific instructions, that the raid had other objects than the rounding up of rioters. The rounding up of rioters was the theme of the raid, as it were, but its real object was to crack down on the location, to administer a sharp deterrent, to crush it back into submission. So the whole location, and not just guilty individuals, was the target of the raid.

And so hundreds were arrested for matters that had nothing to do with the riot, or for petty technicalities, or for the way they looked, or the way they stood, or for answering back, or for not answering smartly enough, or for the misfortune of being noticed, or for having a recent bruise, or possessing a kitchen axe, or for siding with an arrested man, or for sharing a room with one, or for nothing at all. Guilt spread in all directions like an epidemic. The pickup vans roved the streets behind the raiding parties, filled up with prisoners, and sped back and forth between the location and the police cells like ambulances in the rear of a battlefield.

There was no time for niceties and inquiries. Kicks and blows took the place of language. A trail of destruction followed the police through the location.

The first man was killed in New Look Location a few minutes after the raid started. He had been drinking in a shebeen, had fallen asleep, and so had not heard of the riot. When he staggered home and saw the police standing around his house, panic took him and he ran away and they shot him.

*   *   *

Sergeant Combrink was in charge of the party that went to arrest Sarah Manana. On the way he thought about what to do. Swanepoel had given him special instructions about her. He was not to limit it to simply arresting Sarah. He was to look for petrol and also that red *doek*.[1] The lieutenant wanted that evidence to clinch the case against her. Combrink knew Sarah well : he had often arrested her in connection with liquor matters, and for a long time there had been a good feeling between them. He'd come and arrest her, and make a joke, and she'd go along, also making jokes. It was all part of the game. When arresting her, he would occasionally stay to help himself to a few snifters of her brandy. On the house. What was wrong with that ? How many times had fellows done it ? And then one day that Sarah, something got into her, and she went and told the magistrate that he'd been drinking her liquor. And laid it on thick, too. The magistrate hadn't believed her, but it had looked bad for him, and after that things had not been so good between Combrink and Sarah Manana.

His group arrived at her house and he was surprised to find the door open and the light on. He went in, and there was Sarah calmly sitting in an armchair reading the newspaper. " Hallo, Sarah," he said. He did not want to make it difficult. He hoped she'd come without any fuss, as in the old days.

Sarah gave him a slow look over the top of the newspaper.

" Ho, it's *you*," she said. She watched them all come into the room, then said to Combrink, " Has the work of the raid made you thirsty that you come in here ? " Her voice always had a kind of deep, fruity gusto, but now it was tinged with belligerence.

" Cut it out," Combrink said, reddening and looking over his shoulder at the other men in his party.

" What, no brandy to-day ? Well, this is a day. This——"

" I said cut it out," Combrink said.

" Well, if it's not brandy, what can it be ? Just a friendly visit ? " Sarah said, folding up the newspaper but not rising from the armchair. " Take a seat," she said, airily indicating the wooden chairs around the dining table. Combrink looked back again. His men had all become uncomfortable and angry, unable to understand why he was letting her make a fool of him.

[1] Headcloth

248

" Stand up," he said sharply.

Sarah pulled herself slowly out of the chair and rose to her feet. She was a good inch taller than Combrink. She was the tallest and heaviest person in the room.

" You're under arrest," Combrink said.

" Me ? What for ? You haven't even searched yet, let alone found any skokiaan, and I'm under arrest ? Is it no longer necessary to find Exhibit 1 ? "

" Keep quiet. Don't talk so much. You always talk too much," Combrink said angrily, and beginning to bluster.

" O.K.," she said. She looked hard at Combrink. Her eyes had sunk right back behind her fat, shiny cheeks. She pulled her eyes away from Combrink and looked slowly around at the other police. She was breathing heavily, her shoulders and bosom rising and subsiding in one movement.

" Now where do you keep that petrol ? " Combrink asked, fixing her with an accusing look.

" Petrol ? What do I want with petrol ? Am I a taxi driver ? "

" You know about it all right. Come on, hand it over."

" Oh, *petrol*. I see. Now I am a garage. Now you want to go somewhere and you would like some petrol. I see."

" Don't try to be clever, Sarah. I'm warning you," Combrink said, opening and closing his fists.

" O.K.," she said. She looked at the other men again. There were eight of them and they were standing in a half-circle behind Combrink. " O.K., I won't be clever."

" Well, where's it ? "

She looked hard at him. Then she took a deep breath and shrugged her shoulders in massive incomprehension and turned and walked away towards the kitchen door.

" Come back. Stand still," Combrink yelled in sudden panic. She continued to walk away. Combrink leapt after her and caught her by the arm and swung her round.

" When I say stand still, I mean stand still, you fat whore. Who do you think you are, walking away ? "

She stood with her feet planted apart and her arms hanging loosely at her sides. The folded newspaper was still in her hand. The police moved round and made a circle around her. They

249

stood shoulder to shoulder, looking at her and looking at Combrink and waiting for the order.

" Well ? " Combrink asked.

She gave him that same look again. Then she stepped forward, placed her hand on the chest of one of the police, and pushed him effortlessly and contemptuously out of the way. She walked right out of the circle of police and towards the front door.

" Catch her," Combrink yelled.

They sprang after her and pulled her back. She did not struggle but they held her tight, two on each arm.

" I'll teach you to walk away."

He slapped her hard on the face. His hand sunk into the soft flesh of her cheek and her whole face quivered with the blow. But she made no sound.

" Right, see if you can find it," Combrink said to the men, and three of them went into the kitchen and started ransacking about.

" Now maybe you'll understand we mean business. We haven't come here to fool around. You understand ? "

She glared at him with murder in her eyes. It was becoming clear to her that this was not what she had thought it was. Not one of Combrink's stunts. Not a mistake. And nothing to do with the liquor.

" Now, where's that red *doek* you were wearing ? "

" What *doek* ? "

" Are we going to start it all up again ? "

" No."

" Well, hand it over."

" O.K.," she said. She struggled to free her arms but the men held her tight. She stopped and her whole body slumped, limp and helpless, as if it were a relief not to be able to go.

" All right, let her go," Combrink told them.

She went into the bedroom and came out with an armful of headkerchiefs. She crossed the room and dropped them in a heap on the table.

" Help yourself," she said, waving her hand over them.

Combrink stared at the heap of cloths and a worried look came into his face. So many of them, all red or partly red, made him feel that something was going wrong. He had not thought of the possibility of there being a large number of red headcloths.

" Which one were you wearing ? "

" When ? "

" To-day. During the riot, you fat fool. When do you think ? "

" The riot ? "

" Yes. Don't put on an act. Which one ? "

" Did you say the riot ? "

" Yes. Come on, give it to me."

" Me ? At the riot ? You mad. You crazy. I wasn't even there." Her voice was hoarse and deep. All the fire had suddenly come back into her again.

" Don't talk like that. I'm warning you," Combrink said, a little jittery now.

" Me at the riot. What a joke ? Do you know where I was ? At, Withoek. With the Good Shepherds Committee of Withoek. Ask them. I've got twenty witnesses. Ho, you wasting you time, Mister Combrink. Go and arrest someone who was really at the riot and leave me alone. I was not even in the location."

" Is that so ? Then how do you happen to be sitting here now ? It might interest you to know that no one was allowed in after the riot."

" I came in through the fence."

" Do you hear that ? She came in through the fence."

" Yes. I always come in the fence. You think because I didn't come in the gate I was at the riot ? "

" Coming in the fence is illegal. You don't know that ? "

" Well, charge me for climbing in the fence. I was at Withoek, I tell you. Why don't you ask my witnesses ? Aah—you crazy."

" Be careful what you say, Sarah."

" I tell you I was with the Good Shepherds. Why don't you ask them ? You're all crazy-mad."

" God, listen to her. Why don't we just sling her into the pickup and stop all this arguing ? " one of the police said.

" Come on, Sarah," Combrink said, jerking his thumb towards the door. He shouted to the men in the kitchen, " Found it yet ? "

" No."

" Then never mind. We'll come back for it later." He went to the table and began to stuff all the cloths into his pockets. " Come on," he said to Sarah. He wanted to get it over with now ; he was very uneasy.

" No," she said. She was standing in the middle of the room. Her eyes were flashing. Her hands were on her hips ; she looked huge and pugnacious. Combrink looked at his men ; he was undecided. He was very nervous now.

" Who saw me at the riot ? Just tell me who ? " she demanded.

" Mr. Du Toit saw you, that's who. *He* saw you throwing petrol over his motor car."

" Du Toit ? He saw me ? That liar. If Du Toit says that, he's a liar."

" *Mister* Du Toit, you cheeky black whore."

He slapped her again, hard, on the same side of her face. For a moment she just stared as if she had felt nothing. Then her hand came slowly up and rested on her face where the slap had landed. Then she collapsed into the chair. She fingered her cheek and plucked the skin under her eye. Then she began to moan. She swayed her head and moaned in a stricken, terrifying voice.

" Shut up. Stand up."

For a moment she didn't move. Then she suddenly jerked herself out of the chair and stood up unsteadily, supporting herself with one hand on the table and holding the other over her smarting skin.

" All right, come on," Combrink said, turning towards the door.

" No."

" I see. You want to make trouble." He waited a moment, then he gave a sign to the men and they all closed in on her. One tried to grab her wrist, but she hit him on the chest with her free hand and sent him staggering. One of the other policemen tried to get his arm round her neck but she slammed him in the stomach with her elbow. They all tried to get hands on her, but she was immensely strong and elusive, and somehow they couldn't get a grip on her fat, slippery flesh. They tried to pull her down on to the floor : hands were reaching for her and dragging her down, but she managed to stay on her feet. In the struggle her arm shot up and knocked the lamp off its hook and the room was plunged into darkness. They lit flashlights, and started again, and a heaving, grunting tussle took place in the broken, swaying lights of the torches. One of the police got his hand under the collar of her blouse the same moment as she pulled away, and the blouse ripped off with a searing tear. She wore only a brassière underneath and a moment later that tore off. She fought on without stopping, her huge brown breasts writhing and floundering in the agitated lights of the torches. Somehow after that they all made for her remaining clothing, and then she was naked in the middle of the room, fighting like an animal with claws, fists, teeth, feet, elbows. No one spoke. There was a hard, sweating, panting, grunting struggle that swayed back and forth across the room, knocking over furniture, bumping into walls, and crashing them on to the floor.

Suddenly there was a shot, and she collapsed with a great deep sigh. She lay sprawled on the floor like a great old elephant felled by a hunter.

Combrink held his light towards the man who had fired the shot.

" Why did you do that ? "

" She was going to stab you. Didn't you see, she had a knife in her hand."

" My God, I didn't see. My God."

" Yes, I saw the knife gleaming in her hand. Just as she was about to stab you."

Combrink bent over her and looked at the floor around her hand. There was no knife. He asked the others to give him a hand and he turned her over and then they rolled her across the room, away from the place where she had fallen. They came back and searched the floor.

" You sure about that knife ? " Combrink asked.

" Yes. I saw it gleaming. Just as she was going to stab you."

" I don't think it was a knife. It was that watch she's wearing. I also saw it gleaming and it was definitely her watch," one of the others said.

They went over to her and shone their lights on her and saw the platinum wrist watch on her arm, the only article that had not been torn off her in the fight.

" My God," Combrink said.

" What are you going to do ? "

" Me ? We're all in this, boys."

" Yes, that's right. We better stick to that gleaming-knife story."

" I could've sworn she had a knife in her hand."

" O.K., she had a knife."

★   ★   ★

Senior Constable Nel asked, " What's that next name, you say ? "

" Ndimandi," said the constable who was holding the list. He shone his light on it again to make sure. " Yes, Simon Ndimandi."

" What Street ? "

" Hartebeest Street. Stand 7."

" Then we must've passed it. This is Impala Street," Senior Constable Nel said. At the next corner they turned back and walked briskly until they came to Hartebeest Street.

" *Now* which way ? " Nel asked, peering into the dark up and down Hartebeest Street.

" I said which WAY ? " he suddenly bellowed at the location constables, who had forgotten that they were supposed to be guides and were straggling along 'way behind the rest of the party. " This way, sir," one of the location constables said, running up. They turned right and walked downhill along Hartebeest Street, the black constable leading the way.

" Isn't he that fat little one owns all those shops ? " Nel asked. He looped the strap of his rifle around his hand and pulled it tight down on his shoulder, forcing the gun to tilt over in line with his ear.

" Yes, I think it's him."

" If it's him he's the richest Kaffir in the location. You know that ? "

254

" I thought Malooy was."

" Well, him or Malooy. Anyway, both those black *vuilgoed*[1] can buy up you and me and half the whole damn' town if they want to. Do you realise that ? You and me and nearly everyone in this damn' town except maybe Mrs. Ross."

They walked on thinking about this. Nel tugged at his bandolier to make it comfortable, wriggled his shoulders. His hand wandered down to his belt and he took the revolver out and played with it, clicking the catch on and off and spinning the barrel. Suddenly he swung round. " MOVE, you lazy Kaffirs," he yelled. The location constables ran up and began marching briskly on the heels of the white police.

" Hasn't he got high blood or low blood, something like that ? " one of the white police asked.

" Yes, I heard so," Nel said bitterly. " Spends a fortune on the quack. Thirty, forty pounds a month. Spends more just on the quack than you or me earn in a whole damn' month."

" What I can't understand is what's a type like that doing pulling a knife at the meeting ? What's he got against Du Toit ? '

" Don't ask me. That's how they are. Murder someone as easy as you or me light a cigarette."

" Yes, I suppose so."

The road dipped sharply as it approached the river. Ndimandi's house was right down near the end of the road. They were about forty yards away when they saw the vague dark shapes of the cars and buses parked around the house. " What the hell's this ? " Nel asked, slowing down and looking ahead into the dark. Nobody offered to tell him.

" God Almighty, can't anyone hear when I speak ! I asked a question."

" It's a funeral, sir," said the location constable who was leading the way.

" A funeral ? To-night ? "

" No, sir, to-morrow. They're getting ready for a funeral to-morrow."

They came up to the cars and shone their lights on the

[1]Filth.

licence plates. "My God, from *all* over," Nel said. "Here's one from Rustenburg."

"Must be a hell of a funeral," one of the policemen said.

They saw the lights of a car come down the road, and as it drew near, they saw that it was a pickup van. It stopped, its way blocked by the parked vehicles. The driver leant out. "What the hell's going on here? A wedding?"

"No, a funeral."

"Well go inside and tell those stupid bloody oxen to move these cars off the road. We can't get past."

"Yes, Lieutenant." It was the station commander from Withoek. Beside him sat one of his sergeants. Nel looked up at the house. The doors were shut and the curtains drawn, but light was leaking out of the house everywhere. "Got any prisoners in there?" Nel asked, jerking his head towards the back of the van.

"Yes, eight. Why?"

"Well, I thought you could help us, but I think we're going to need an empty van for this job."

The lieutenant craned his head out of the car window and peered up at the house. No sound came out of it, but the whole house seemed to be breathing, and to be oozing light.

"You're right," he said. "Look, I'll shoot this batch across to the cells and come straight back." He turned the van round and drove off. Nel watched him go, then turned to his men. "There's a whole bunch of them up in there, so watch out. Watch out for knives and maybe revolvers. Any funny business, look after yourselves first. That's orders."

He led his men through the gate and up the steps to the veranda. There were four white policemen in his party: only they followed him; the location constables stayed back, standing in a bunch on the pavement across the street. He stood listening, with his ear close to the door and his hand around the handle, and his men crowded close behind him. Suddenly someone inside coughed. It sounded unexpectedly loud and close, almost in their faces.

Nel flung the door open. He was blinded by the sudden light and a moment later was assailed by the warm, sickly air that

256

gushed out of the room. It took him a few seconds to recover. He held his breath and walked in warily, with his revolver drawn and held level with his chest.

All the people in the room were sitting motionless and dead-quiet, staring at the door. Their faces were glistening, and the room reeked of their sweat, and of the uneaten food on the plates that littered the table. There were only men in the room. In the mirror over the sideboard Nel caught a view of the backs of their heads, and then of his own white face and of the bullets gleaming across his chest, and of his men standing behind him.

"Stand up," he ordered, speaking as if he had an obstruction in his throat.

They all stood up in unison, like children in a classroom. About a third of them seemed to be parsons, and a quarter family elders. It seemed a little queer for a moment. It struck Nel that he had not seen so many turned-around collars and white pepper-corn beards in one place in all his life.

"Right," he said, looking slowly around the room. "Which one of you's Ndimandi?"

He did not need to be told. Ndimandi was standing in front of the carved chair, supporting himself against the table, and he had a look of such terror in his face that it was impossible to mistake him for anyone else. The other, taller, fat man who was standing beside Ndimandi was Malooy, whom Nel knew.

"You're under arrest," Nel said, turning the revolver on to Ndimandi. Ndimandi clutched at the side of the table, but otherwise he did not move. The expression on his face did not change; only the colour changed. It changed from deep brown to murky yellow, but the expression remained the same, like that of a wax effigy of himself.

Malooy took a step forward. "Look, Sergeant," he said, smiling, "I think there must be some little mistake."

"Shut up. Keep out of this, you fat pig. What're you trying to do? Obstruct the police?"

"Sergeant, Sergeant," Malooy said, coming forward with his palms spread out and smiling genially, "I'm sure there's a mistake. This man——"

257

" GET BACK."

Malooy stopped, his eyes glued on the revolver. His hands dropped to his sides, and he stepped back and stood next to Ndimandi. He was still smiling but the smile had been left stranded on his face, and it looked sick and mirthless against the cold fright that had come into his eyes.

Nel went over to him. He pushed the revolver into Malooy's soft paunch and held it there and stared into his eyes. For more than a minute he stood and stared him out, holding the revolver into the flabby body. Nobody in the room moved. Nel said, " I'm putting you under arrest, too. For obstructing the police." He spoke quietly.

Malooy said nothing.

" Stand over there," Nel said. He moved the gun on to Ndimandi. " You also."

Malooy and Ndimandi went over to the corner.

" Turn round."

They turned and faced into the corner. Nel watched them for a moment, then came back into the centre of the room. " Right," he said to the others. " Form up."

At first they did not seem to understand what he wanted ; maybe they were too stupefied by fright. They looked at him miserably, then at one another, then began to move vaguely around.

" HURRY—damn you. MOVE. HURRY. D'you think I've got all night ? Move." He grabbed a man by the shoulder and sent him hurtling across the room. " Stand there, you black dog. THERE. Go on, line up from there. ALL of you. From THERE. HERE. For God's sake, HERE." He was walking about with sharp jerky steps and his rifle was clanking up and down on his back. Sweat was pouring off his face. " MOVE, you stupid black bastards. LINE UP." His boot shot out and kicked a man who was passing in front of him. He turned to the other police. " Help me, can't you. Get these black pigs into line. GET INTO LINE. Can't you hear me ? Do you want me to bust your faces open ? " People were scurrying about, falling over each other and over the furniture. Nel was jabbing the pistol into people's ribs, forcing them into line. " You black scum, I'll teach you to listen to orders. WELL, MAKE A SECOND LINE, YOU IDIOTS."

At last they stood in two rows from wall to wall. Nel stepped back and let his eyes travel slowly along the front row. Then he waited. He seemed to be thinking. He was frowning and chewing on the inside of his lower lip.

" Where's the females ? " he asked at last, narrowing his eyes. No one answered.

" CAN'T YOU HEAR ME ? I ASKED A QUESTION."

" The women are in the back room, sir," one of the parsons answered.

" Well, BRING them here. Go on, bring them, and HURRY."

The man went out of the room into the back part of the house and came back leading the women. They were all wearing black dresses and black veils, and they came down the passage noiselessly, in single file, like a procession of ghosts.

" Here," Nel said, pointing with the revolver. They lined up facing their menfolk across the room.

" What about the kids ? " one of the policemen asked.

" What we want the kids for ? " Nel asked.

" There probably some pretty elderly kids hiding away back there if I know these bastards."

" O.K.," Nel said. He turned to the women. " Where're the kids ? "

" The children are sleeping, sir," a woman said glumly and barely audibly.

" Bring them," Nel said. " And hurry." He ordered two other women to go and help her.

The three women went into the back part of the house and returned with small babies in their arms and a group of older children tailing along behind them. " Go and see there's no kids with beards and long pants hiding under the beds," Nel said to his men, and two of them went out and started searching the back rooms.

While the babies were handed out to their mothers, the older children stood rubbing their eyes and scratching their legs and looking back and forth between their elders and the police. They had drugged looks in their faces, and their eyes were milky, as if they had not yet properly awakened from their sleep. Suddenly all the children, the babies in arms and the older children together, started to cry.

" SHUT UP," Nel shouted. " Make them shut up," he said to the mothers. They rocked the small babies against their bosoms, and held the older children under their arms, against their skirts, but it failed to pacify them. Nel became furious. " SHUT UP THAT BAWLING," he bellowed. His voice reverberated through the house. It shocked most of the older children into silence—they stood trembling and tense, but quiet —but the babies went on crying, and then Nel saw that it had been a mistake to bring them out. " All right, take the small ones back," he said, and the babies were returned to the back room. They were left there crying, and the women came back and took their places in the line.

Nel turned and faced the men.

" Passes."

While the men fished in their pockets, pulling out coloured slips of paper, reference books, tax receipts, permits, Nel walked across the room, unhitched his rifle, and handed it to one of his men. Then, wriggling his shoulders and chewing on his lip, he came back and stood before the man who was nearest the wall.

" I see. So you're from Pretoria" he said, examining the man's book.

" Yes, sir."

" Then what right you got to be in Nelstroom ? "

" I came for my cousin's funeral, sir."

" I said what *right* ? Who *told* you you can come to Nelstroom ? "

" I got a permit from the superintendent, sir."

" Let me see it."

The man handed over his visitor's permit. Nel read it, then held it up to the lamp so that the light shone through. Then he placed his foot on a chair, spread the paper out on his knee, and rubbed his thumb across the signature. He held the paper up to the light again, then held it at arm's length, cocked his head, and squinted at it through one eye.

"It's a forgery," he said, tearing the document in half.

"No sir, it's not sir, really sir. I saw the superintendent sign it, sir, really, sir," the man said, almost weeping.

"I say it's a forgery. I don't recognise the signature."

Nel placed the two halves together and tore them in half, tore the quarters in half, and so on, until the scraps were too small to hold between his fingers. Then he tossed the little bundle of confetti up into the air. "Arrest him," he said casually to one of the policemen. The man was handcuffed and taken outside.

Nel took his time examining the rest of the documents. He did not tear up all the permits, only some, as he felt like it. When a document referred to a man's wife or children, he made the wife stand forward and questioned the children about their names and ages to check whether they tallied with the information on the document. He was sharp at finding irregularities—misspelt names, illegible signatures, smudged numbers. He ordered about two-thirds of the men and a third of the women to be arrested. There were not enough handcuffs for all the prisoners, so he made them stand under guard out on the pavement. The pickup van driven by the lieutenant from Withoek had returned, and was waiting with its doors open, for Nel to come down and start the loading.

When Nel finished examining the documents, he went to the front door, faced round, and said to Ndimandi and Malooy, who were still standing in the corner, "All right. Turn round. March."

But as they started to walk towards the door, there was a scream and Ndimandi's wife ran across the room and stood with her arms out in front of her husband.

"He can't go." Her voice was shrill, almost demented. "You'll kill him. He's sick. Sick, sick, sick."

Nel's whole body stiffened. In two huge strides he was in front of her, grappling with her, trying to force her out of the way, but at the same moment Ndimandi darted away from behind her and ran squealing towards the passage that led to the back of the house. Nel let go of her and leapt at Ndimandi, tackling him football fashion and bringing him crashing to the floor.

261

Nel picked himself up and straightened his clothes and said to the remaining policemen in the room :

" O.K. Take him out."

They picked up Ndimandi by his arms and legs and carried him out face downwards, his face barely clearing the floor. He did not struggle. His body was limp, and they carried him out sagging like a rolled-up carpet.

They took him down into the street, and stood in front of the open doors of the pickup van, swinging him gently back and forth. Nel came out and said, " Throw him in," and himself lent a hand to hoist him up. They lifted him shoulder high, and then hurled him clear between the open doors of the empty van. There was a heavy crash, a searing metallic scrape, and a dull thump as his head struck the panel at the far end of the van. There was no other sound.

Now Nel had his revolver out again.

" Right. Now all of you get in." The other prisoners lined up at the back of the van and began to climb in. A number were inside, including some women, and then there was a wild shriek and they were all back at the door of the van, jumping out into the street. Two women who had been in the van were moaning and screaming and tearing at their clothes. They uttered no words, just raised a shrill hysterical uproar. The men were standing about with their hands at their sides, stunned and frozen.

Nobody dared to look inside the van. Nobody could bring himself to mention Ndimandi's name.

For a moment Nel did not know what to do. He looked helplessly at his men and made futile gestures with his arms, and then Ndimandi's wife came up behind him, and suddenly, before anybody could stop her, pulled a piece of iron pipe from behind her skirt, and, gripping it with both hands, slammed it into the side of his head. He collapsed without a sound, and lay with his head against the wheel of the van. She stood over him, with the iron pipe hanging loosely in her hand, and then she spat at him. But before the spittle ever landed, she herself was dead, shot by a policeman. There was a moment of chilled silence. And then everyone realised that a fight was on, and the stones came flying at the police the same instant as the police started shooting.

The two sides drew away from each other, the four policemen retreating up the street and the prisoners making a panicky scramble for cover behind the parked cars and buses, leaving a kind of no man's land occupied by the pickup van, with the lieutenant from Withoek and his sergeant sitting in the cabin, and Nel lying unconscious under the wheels.

Stones were hurtling over the roof of the van. The police started to advance, taking advantage of the cover afforded by the van and firing past it into the parked cars, but their fire was inhibited because of the danger of hitting the men in the van and their inability to see the target. They were about fifteen yards from the van, moving cautiously forward, when some bottles and stones were pelted at them from behind. They stopped and looked at each other, puzzled. The moment they did so there was a vicious fusillade of rocks and missiles hurled from all angles, from behind them and from the sides of the street. Then they knew that the whole situation had changed, that the fight was now not merely with the members of the funeral party, but with others who had come out of the surrounding houses and were concealed in the shadows all around them, that these new assailants were aggressive, having come out specially to attack them, and that they, the police, were in full view while their attackers were invisible. They stood back to back and fired all around them, at anything that seemed to move, or that looked like the shadow of a man. They heard sharp cries and groans, but the stone throwing did not slacken. Two of the police were hit and were bleeding and they all realised that they were outnumbered, in spite of their firearms, and that they would have to leave the street, but they did not know what to do about the men in the van, and about Nel lying unconscious under the wheels.

Suddenly the engine of the van started and the lights went on, and they realised with horror that the lieutenant was about to drive off, that he didn't know that Nel was under the wheels. One of the policemen ran forward and yelled, " For God's sake, don't move, you'll run over Nel." He reached the side of the van without being injured but there a jagged rock got him on the side of the head and he collapsed. The lieutenant and the sergeant flung the door open and jumped out, and holding the wounded man under their arms, raced through the gauntlet of flying stones back to the other police. It was impossible to rescue Nel.

The police began to retreat, walking bunched together and firing all around them, and they managed to shoot their way out of the encirclement. Then they turned and ran away up the street.

A screaming mob poured out from behind the parked cars, from behind walls and hedges, from neighbouring houses and nearby streets, and swarmed around the abandoned van. They began rocking it, working up a momentum in order to heave it over, but an argument flared up, and they stopped. Some people climbed into the van and brought out Ndimandi's body. Others lifted up Mrs. Ndimandi's body, and the two bodies were carried up into the house. Most of the members of the funeral party went with them, and they shut the door and did not return. But now there was a huge crowd in the street and they started bouncing the van again, slewing it round until it stood lengthwise in the street. Then there was a sudden, momentary unison of effort, and the van heaved lightly up and crashed over on its side.

They stood about panting and dusting their hands, and then one by one their eyes fell on Nel, and they all became silent. Nel was lying flat on his back, with his arms stretched out, snoring noisily and rolling his head violently from side to side. They stood in a ring around him, staring down at him in silence, and in the silence a taut, abrasive excitement began to run among them, and suddenly one of the women let out a shrill cry. In a moment other women joined in, and their harsh, taunting voices clawed at the men until it was no longer possible to resist their savage incitement. The rest happened very quickly. A man came out of the ring of people and stood looking down at Nel. Then he kicked him viciously in the face. Then a man carrying a heavy flat rock pushed his way forward and crashed the rock down on Nel's head. Then they swarmed all over him, kicking, stoning, clawing, and pummelling in an hysterical frenzy of revenge. Some had knives and they knelt down and crawled up and down beside the body, plunging the blades in again and again, until all that

264

remained of Nel was a limp mass of purple flesh and blood-soaked clothing.

*   *   *

Swanepoel had just entered the yard where Johanna Mandlazi lived, and was looking at the numbers on the door when he heard the shooting.

" What's that ? "

" Don't know. Sounds like trouble," Roberts said.

Swanepoel stood still and listened, undecided. He said to one of his men. " Ask them to try and pick it up on the radio." In the street outside were a pickup van and a squad car with its aerial up, and the man went out and conveyed Swanepoel's instruction to the driver of the car. But he came back after a few moments and said, " Nothing on the radio, sir."

" Funny," Swanepoel said, scratching his head.

They stood in the middle of the empty yard, listening. The shooting was taking too long, and it had an erratic and panicky sound about it that made Swanepoel sense that something was wrong. Suddenly he swung round and marched out of the yard, climbed into the squad car alongside the driver, and twisted the knobs of the radio. The rest of the group followed him out into the street. Du Toit walked a few paces behind the others, his hands deep in his pockets, his head sunk between his shoulders and buried in his coat collar. He had not spoken a word for more than half an hour. He was miserable—backsore and bone-weary, cold and exhausted, and so numbed by the shock that had at last caught up with him that he was hardly aware of what was happening around him. But a dull, instinctive stubbornness kept him tagging along. He no longer wanted to go home, nor cared how long the raid continued. It could go on for ever, and as long as it lasted, he would be in it, not taking part in it but just being present in the midst of it, as if in fulfilment of a law that required him to be a party to everything that took place in the location. It was inconceivable that the raid should go on without him.

His presence made the police uncomfortable. Only Swanepoel seemed able to ignore him. The others kept looking at him over

265

their shoulders and turning away, embarrassed. They could not understand why he insisted on trailing along at their heels when he was so obviously of no use in the raid. They could feel something of censure, hostility, in his silence and his withdrawal from the events that he himself had brought about. His attitude puzzled and discomforted them and they all wished he would go home.

He stood with his hands in his pockets and watched Swanepoel tinker impatiently with the radio. He was gripped by a black dejection, an empty, hopeless gloom.

Swanepoel angrily flicked the radio off. He sat staring at the dials in front of him. The hard nodules of muscles in his cheeks were sliding back and forth under the taut skin. He was tense. They could all feel it. For the first time during the night he showed signs of nervousness. He switched the radio on again and came out of the car.

" Go and find out what it is, and report back to me. I'll wait here," he told the driver of the pickup, and the van drove off. " Keep trying," he said to the driver of the squad car, and turned round and walked back into the yard. The others came after him.

" What are we going to do ? " Roberts asked.

" Just carry on," Swanepoel said grimly, looking straight ahead. " Just complete the arrests as planned."

But when they were back in Johanna Mandlazi's yard they realised that the shooting had finally stopped, and they were suddenly aware of something else, too. The whole location seemed to be screaming in their ears. A vast tidal wave of noise had suddenly come over the rooftops, engulfing them in an element so violently foreign to the raid that it held them gripped in terror. They stood in the middle of the yard, looking all around them and peering up at the sky above the roofs as if watching an invasion of locusts, and waiting for the strange pandemonium to translate itself into happenings that they could understand. There were people running about in the street outside, and the neighbouring yards were seething with movement, but in this yard all the people stayed inside, all the doors stayed shut, as if the presence of Swanepoel and his men immunised the yard from the general excitement, except to the extent that the noise poured into it from over the rooftops. Above the voices and shouting they could hear police whistles, engines starting hurriedly, cars racing along the streets, and from all over the location sporadic firing.

"What's happened? What's happened?" Swanepoel asked in a frightened voice.

"God, I don't know," Roberts said.

"What's——"

When he looked again, Roberts was lying on the ground, writhing and choking and clutching at his throat. Swanepoel had not even heard the shot. He stared at the agonised, writhing man, then looked up and peered slowly around the circle of black yawning doors. And then he heard a soft, high-pitched giggling. He could not tell where it came from. He stared intently around him, trying by sheer force of will to pierce the dark with his eyes. The giggling went on. It reached him with a queer acoustical effect for it seemed to come from no one place, but to seep out of the walls. And then, somehow, he knew that he was staring into a pair of eyes. One of the windows was open and the eyes were behind the lace curtain and it was more a matter of intense intuition than actual seeing, but he knew that the weird girlish giggling was coming from the open window and that his eyes were engaged with those of someone standing in the dark behind the curtain. He wanted to use his flashlight, but was afraid to in case it provided a target, and so he stood in the dark, unmoving, and staring at the spot behind the curtain, but his right hand was working furiously, taking the revolver out and preparing it for firing.

Suddenly the curtains parted and there was light enough to see the hideous monkey face, and he heard the high, excited voice, "The war has started. The day has come." And then there were three quick wild shots.

Swanepoel got the boy the instant after the third shot. The three shots hit nobody and Swanepoel realised with a pang of heartbreak that this had been no marksman, and that it was the merest fluke that Roberts had been hit. Roberts had stopped moving: he was dead. Swanepoel bent over him, and as he did

267

so, his eyes blurred with tears. He undid the strap of Roberts' rifle and pulled it away from under him, and then he stood up and took careful aim at one of the windows and fired point-blank into the room, not pausing until the magazine was empty. Then he borrowed a rifle from one of his men and did the same with that, but into another window. He did not hear the screams that came out of the rooms. When the second magazine was empty, he handed the rifle back, then bent down and raised Roberts off the ground, thrusting his shoulders under the dead man's armpit. He carried Roberts across the yard.

In the passage that led out to the street he turned and asked the men behind him, " Are we all here ? " His voice was weary.

Du Toit was not there.

" I think he cleared off," one of the men said.

The found Du Toit huddled up in the back seat of the squad car. Swanepoel did not talk to him. He propped Roberts up in the front seat between himself and the driver, and they drove off, with Du Toit sitting alone in the back. The other men followed in the pickup van.

" Back to the administration building," he told the driver. He took the transmitter off the hook, slid the button up, and spoke into the grid. " Everybody return immediately to the administration building. Everybody. Everybody return . . ."

At the administration building he saw that a number of cars and vans had already returned. A crowd of police gathered round his car and told him about the events in Hartebeest Street. Nobody knew for sure what had happened to Senior Constable Nel. Nobody held out much hope for him, but as there seemed to be some chance that he was still alive, Swanepoel sent a rescue party in one of the convoy trucks down to Hartebeest Street.

He noticed that a crowd of white civilian volunteers had gathered outside the gate. They had come in their own cars from the town and surrounding farms, but had been stopped from entering the location by the guards at the gate. They were clamouring to be let in and given a chance to go into action. They wore cartridge belts over their sports jackets and were armed with hunting rifles, shotguns, pistols, old Boer War carbines, civilian commando issue, anything that could shoot.

268

Now Swanepoel let them in and told them to wait with the police for further orders.

The rescue party returned from Hartebeest Street, and Swanepoel went over to the truck. Nel was unrecognisable, except by his lacerated, bloodstained uniform. The body was taken from the truck and laid out in the back of the pickup van. Roberts' body was taken from the car and laid alongside Nel's and the two bodies were covered with overcoats and the van started off for town.

Now all the police were back at the administration building, Swanepoel's men and the men from Withoek. They had all gathered round the van, and as it drove away, leaving an open space in their midst, they remained where they were standing, watching the red tail-light bounce away into the distance. They were very subdued. They cursed and swore revenge, but in undertones, and their faces were grim, hard, and pale. The civilians stood in a separate group, and the mood of the police communicated itself to them, and they were nervous, and as tense as coiled springs.

The night had suddenly grown quiet again. The noise from the location had inexplicably died down. There was a thin strip of moon that threw a pale silver reflection off the dew-covered low-lying rooftops, but although not a person was asleep in all those acres of houses, no sound could be heard. The location hugged the ground and drew a blanket of eerie silence over itself.

Swanepoel divided the police and civilians into four groups and gave them their orders. He spoke calmly, in a quiet voice. There were about seventy men altogether, not counting drivers and the men on guard at the gate and the building, and they climbed into the four convoy trucks. Swanepoel waited until they were all in position, then went back to his car.

Du Toit was still sitting in the back seat. Swanepoel stood and held the door handle and looked at him, but Du Toit did not even look up. The sight of Du Toit, huddled in misery in the back of his car, suddenly infuriated him. He wanted to order him to get out, to clear out of the location, and leave the police to finish the job alone. He felt a sudden surge of loathing and contempt for Du Toit, and he could barely restrain himself from

269

seizing him and throwing him out in the street. At that moment all his hatred of the location was focused on Du Toit. But he held himself in check. He said nothing and only his small savage eyes gave evidence of his thoughts. He stared at Du Toit, then impatiently opened the door, climbed in, and told the driver to start.

As they passed each of the trucks, he leant out and told the drivers to follow, and with the sirens of all the vehicles screaming full blast, he led the way down the main street back into the location.

When they reached the houses, they opened fire from both sides of the trucks, point-blank into the walls and windows. The bullets ripped easily through the flimsy sheet-iron and other scrapyard materials of the houses. They just held the guns still against the side rails, aimed down to strike at window level, and let the trucks pull the line of fire along the street. They went fast to the end of the main street, turned off, and took a circular route through the location, firing into houses all the way. A vast hubbub accompanied them, a pandemonium of blaring sirens, incessant gunfire, shrieks, shouts, roaring engines, shattering glass, and tearing metal. They came back to the main street again, then, without stopping, went right down to the end and took a zigzag route through New Look Location, firing into the white deserted-looking houses until the guns were hot in their hands. They went as far as the edge of New Look, and fired over the spruit into the grass huts of Old Look. They rode back through the centre of the location and came out again on the main street. They started out for a third trip, but about half-way down the main street Swanepoel saw an obstruction ahead. The driver slowed and they rode up to it cautiously. It was a flimsy, half-completed barricade of branches, bedsteads, chairs, dismantled fences. A number of men climbed off the trucks and quickly tore it down, tossing the debris into nearby gardens. There was no sign of the people who had built it, but the police climbed back on the trucks and stood and blazed away all around them for several minutes. Then they moved on. This time they took a route right around the edge of the location. But when they came back once more into the main street to start another trip, they were stopped by a solid, immovable, and impassable obstacle. One of Malooy's buses had been brought out from the terminus parking yard and now lay on its side, athwart the street.

Swanepoel got out of the car and stood with his hands on his hips and stared into the underside of the upturned bus. Then something told him that this was the point at which to stop. He ordered the trucks to return to the administration building. Then all the police, the civilians, and vehicles left the location.

The vehicles—trucks, pickup vans, squad cars, private sedans —rode in convoy, nose to tail, along the sand road back to the town. They did not hurry. They travelled slowly, almost wearily, as if carrying home a party of tired-out picnickers. The location heard the clatter and the engine sounds fade slowly away into the night. And then silence.

Nothing happened for quite a while. There was an interval of the weirdest silence that had ever descended on the location. An empty, desolate, gutted silence, unlike the other silences which had always been filled with breathing and whispering and the undercurrent of life. It was as if the location had at last died, as if its pulse had finally stopped.

But it slowly began to stir. People peered out from cautiously opened doorways, came into the streets, and walked up and down, stunned, dazed. Hardly anyone spoke. Nobody seemed to have grasped what had happened. Nobody understood the extent of it, the enormity of it. The dead, the wounded, the blood spreading out over linoleum and floor boards—nobody seemed to notice at first. The whimpering, the groans, the sharp crippled gasps, these, for the moment, formed part of the silence, were as yet beyond the range of comprehension. People walked up and down in the streets, sniffing the pungent cordite-laden air, picking up the still-warm cartridge shells, and walking with them in their hands, staring in horror-struck disbelief at the riddled walls of their houses, at the freaks of the gunfire—the clean round holes in windowpanes, the neat dotted lines of bullet holes sewing together brick, wood, and sheet iron. Only slowly did the understanding of it come. And with the understanding, an uncontrollable fury. It was like a great maimed buffalo first

271

recovering from the stun of the shot, then dimly sensing the leaden ache somewhere inside its huge hulk, and then, in a blind, convulsive, torrential rage, running amuck.

Nobody knew, or ever would know, all that happened in the next hour. It was too vast, too violent to be absorbed and recounted by witnesses. There were strange wild passions that had lain asleep in the seeds from immemorial times, that had survived from an ancient secret world, and these sprang alive into the air and beckoned on. Later, when the location returned to its senses, and tried to recall what it had done, it could remember that black hour only with the vague and distant blur of a dream.

It started at the abandoned pickup van in Hartebeest Street. There was a crowd standing around it ; quite a small crowd. A man set a branch alight and with it set fire to the van. The crowd watched it burn for a while. The flare drew people from the surrounding streets, and the crowd grew. They were quite subdued. They stood and watched with a kind of bemused satisfaction. Then a bigger idea took hold. Nobody seemed actually to suggest it. The idea just seemed to grow. The crowd started to move off. It moved slowly at first, then faster, faster. Soon a wild, shrilling mob was tearing through the location street, gathering numbers as it went. It came at last to the Welfare Centre. The little timber building was in darkness ; nobody stayed there at night. They forced the door and set fire to it from inside. There were methylated spirits and ether, kept for medical purposes. They used them to get the fire started. They burnt down their Welfare Centre—the only library, lecture room, and medical clinic in the whole location. They destroyed the only store of drugs and medical equipment that could have helped the people lying wounded in houses throughout the location. They were insane. They danced round the blazing building and screamed and wept. Nobody worried whether the police would return.

Some stayed to watch the Welfare Centre burn itself out ; others moved off and joined the new gangs. Other gangs had now formed up. As substances produce specific by-products in certain conditions of heat and pressure, so now the location threw

272

up a thick, evil scum. Gangs formed spontaneously in different parts of the location, and throughout the rioting they merged and separated and merged again, a continuously moving tide of violence and brutality.

A gang saw one of the location constables peeping out of his door. He was an unpopular man, being a bit too keen on pass-law enforcement. They pulled him out into the street and battered him to death. They did it quickly, systematically, without any particular hatred or frenzy. They just went to work. Some-one said the name "Ngubeni." They moved off in a long, strung-out procession to Ngubeni's house in New Look. They had stopped running now. They walked with that curious loping, swinging stride, the first thirty or so precisely in step, the others tailing after in an increasingly ragged imitation of the leaders. The leaders were mostly tough youths with thick, powerful arms and firm round pectoral muscles bulging against their tight, bright-coloured sweat shirts and jerseys. All had identical expressions on their faces—a vacant smile and entranced unseeing eyes, like the *risus* of a dead man. They carried sticks, iron bars, studded clubs, and they swung them to the taut rhythm of their dancing walk. They walked to a kind of music, a kind of breathed and whistled tempo, low and violent. They were the *tsotsis*. One could tell they were *tsotsis* by their fancy clothes, by the way they took command, and by their weird mystical unison of minds and limbs. They led the mobs. They took control of the location, and exerted a spell that drew hundreds of normally calm and sober people after them—hard-working artisans, mothers of large families, serious boys with good school records. The *tsotsis* were the incarnation of the black sinister forces that had come on this night out of the dark past. They had a kind of mystic significance, and from this came their power over the location.

The crowd that went for Ngubeni found the old chief crouched behind a wardrobe. They dragged him screaming out to the street and murdered him deftly and ruthlessly. Nobody gave any reason for it. They just snuffed his life out, coldly, almost casually. The *tsotsis* killed him, and the others swarmed over him like ravenous giant ants and ripped him apart.

Now there was a suffused yellow glow over the whole location.

A number of fires were burning simultaneously at different points. The flames licked up above the rooftops, illuminating the clouds of dense smoke that drifted heavily across the location. The fires were visible from the town, but the police did not return. It was as if the location was being given the licence to destroy itself.

In the main street the upturned bus that had finally stopped the police was blazing fiercely. Nearby, in the parking yard where Malooy kept his buses, half the fleet was on fire. Although these buses represented the only public transport between the location and the town, the mob destroyed them with glee. Black oily smoke billowed heavily out of the blazing vehicles and enclosed the whole area in a thick sour fog. The flames glinted on the moist faces of the rioters, lighting up their imbecile grins and crazed, drunken eyes.

A group of rioters broke the lock of the petrol pump that stood in the street a distance away from the burning buses, and drew petrol into cans that they fetched from the storeroom. They moved off, carrying the heavy cans on their shoulders, gaily, like peasants at a harvest festival. A crowd followed. They reached the shopping street, and stopped outside the dark locked-up cinema. They broke in and poured petrol over the seats, all across the stage, along the floor. They stood at the door and threw a burning branch inside. The whole building exploded. Some boys were killed and a number of others badly burned. But the uninjured ones formed up and loped back to the petrol pump, leaving the dead where they had fallen and the injured to crawl back home somehow. This was the only good cinema in the location. There was one other cinema, but it was half the size of this one, and it only opened rarely because the owner had no money to buy pictures. But the good cinema belonged to a white man.

They drew off more petrol, and this time went in the opposite direction along the main street, up towards the administration building. There they made a systematic job. They sprinkled petrol all through the rooms. Then they placed a can of petrol in one of the middle rooms, made a fuse of crumpled paper, soaked it in the petrol, and led it out of the door, across the veranda, to hang dangling over the side. They lit it and ran a

274

distance away. They waited, watching the flame leap eagerly along the saturated paper and dart into the door. There was a flash and a roar, a messy lateral *whoosh* rather than an explosion, and in a moment the whole building was ablaze. Most of the location turned out to see the hated administration building burn down.

But while they watched, a silent and gruesome tragedy was taking place in another part of the location. Mr. and Mrs. Bertram, a middle-aged couple who lived in the town, were driving home along the road outside the location when they saw the first fires. They stopped at the gate and wondered what the trouble was. They had a servant girl who lived in the location, and of whom they were fond, and they were worried about her safety. They drove inside to find their servant and ask her to come back home with them. They were good people. He owned a store in Nelstroom and had done the location people many kindnesses. He had a real affection for them. He spoke their language and sympathised with them and he tried to be different in his dealings with them from most of the other white people in Nelstroom. In turn he was loved by the location people.

He had always felt at ease in the location and now, driving in, did not feel that he was in any danger. They got quite far into the location without meeting anybody. Then they turned a corner, and their headlamps picked out the bobbing figures of a gang striding towards them. They stopped to let the procession go past. It did not go past. It closed in around the car. One of the leaders wrenched the car door open and dragged the man out. They held him standing up, with his arms pinioned and a hand held tight over his mouth from behind. But they left his eyes, free to see. Others pulled his wife out. There, on the roadside, they raped her. At least eighteen of them raped her. At some point she lost consciousness, but they kept on, holding her arms and shoulders pressed to the ground, and her legs in an iron grip, and one by one they vented their savagery on her inert body. Then they pulled the man on to the ground and murdered him with their feet and hands. Then they battered the last remaining spark of life out of the body of his wife.

The police did not return. The whole town was awake and

275

armed and it watched the fires grow high in the sky and slowly burn themselves out. But nobody returned to the location. There were a large number of police and civilians, heavily armed, at the railway line, and cars darted out on the road to the location to report any sign of the location people breaking out. But as long as the location spent its violence within its own boundaries, the town people preferred not to interfere. Had the rioters crossed the boundaries, there would have been a bloody battle. But they never did. They took a strange, distorted revenge on the location itself.

The riot burnt itself out, and just before sunrise the location, spent and satiated, came out of its nightmare. It lay in the cold morning light, exhausted, feebly smoking, tragic and foolish, like a battlefield.

Yet there was a pattern to all the destruction and brutality. Everything that was destroyed had a connection with the white man and his rule. The pickup van was the property of the police. The Welfare Centre was the sly, insincere smile on the face of the municipality—a hated symbol. The murdered location constable and Ngubeni were part of the machinery by which the location was ruled. The cinema was an instrument for their exploitation by the whites. The buses were the link between the location and the white town. The administration building was Du Toit.

CHAPTER SIXTEEN

Next day, at a spot on the road just outside Nelstroom, Mabaso died. His was the last life to be shed in the Nelstroom disturbances. But perhaps it was bound to end that way.

Mabaso had brought a new thing into the location—a hardness, a defiance, a resistance to being fooled by official baby talk, by the old tricks, a bold new way of speaking up—something so startling and unexpected that it swept away with dramatic suddenness Du Toit's elaborate device for maintaining white rule in the location. And by doing this he completely altered the relation between the location and the town. Du Toit lost control, and Swanepoel had to take over. Swanepoel, who could think of the location only as an enemy to be crushed, who had been trained to make war on it, who could only despise Du Toit's flabby appeasing methods—Swanepoel stepped in to apply the basic argument against the location. The confidence trick failed and the gun took over.

But as Swanepoel's attitude to the location was even more unreal than Du Toit's, he could only inflame the crisis. His actions that night had no judgment behind them ; no plan, no aim, no limit. They were merely the crude lashing out of hatred and fear. Once started, he could not stop until he had goaded the location into a frenzy that threatened to engulf himself and his men. He had had the instinct to pull out just in time— his only sensible act of the night. But his mission was a failure, worse even than Du Toit's. He had set out to crush the location back into submission. He achieved the exact opposite. And anything that served to increase the bitterness and enmity between the two towns that were doomed to live for ever chained together was an act of madness—a defeat. Yes, the night ended in mutual defeat.

But madness has a way of employing its vast cunning and demon energy towards establishing its own sanity. Facts are twisted, illusions fostered, truth destroyed to prove that the perverted is normal, the sordid

277

noble, the brutal beautiful, the guilty innocent, the coward a hero, disaster a victory—and the reverse of all these things. It was part of the madness of the white town to refuse to accept the smallest blame for anything that happened. It was unthinkable that white men could be at fault in any situation with black men. White men act from a divine purity of motive, are guided by an unassailable wisdom, and proceed majestically, with unfaltering steps, along the elevated road of their destiny.

If anything went wrong, it must have been due to some dark evil existing only in the location. If anything was done to put it right, that was merely the noble act of stamping out the evil. If blame was to be laid, there was only one place for it—the location. And the location itself, being the white man's creation and a part of his system, could only have become infected as a result of some insidious conspiracy inside it, something foreign, even to the location.

When the newspapers arrived from Johannesburg later the next day they all carried a particular version of the attack on Du Toit—that given by Swanepoel over the telephone at the start of his interview with Du Toit and Gwebu in the location office. There was the story exactly as Swanepoel had imagined it : how Du Toit was holding a peaceful routine meeting when he was attacked by a crazed mob screaming, " Kill him," and brandishing knives and other lethal weapons ; how the mob had been incited and goaded to attack by Mabaso, who was the head of a subversive organisation in the location ; how Du Toit, after vainly but courageously trying to pacify the mob, was forced to flee for his life into the office ; how the mob had burnt his car and was only prevented from burning the building with Du Toit inside by the prompt arrival of the police.

This was only a part of the news, a minor part, but it set the note for all the rest. Everything that followed the attack on Du Toit was part of the same organised terrorism. And this became the one true and official version of what happened, and it spread so fast and far afield that there was no hope of any other version overtaking or replacing it.

It stamped Mabaso in the public imagination as a desperate criminal. It satisfied the town's craving for an explanation in keeping with its notions of white infallibility, and at the same time gave it a scapegoat. Mabaso personified the location in a strange new mood ; he was the evil spirit in the location, he was the agitator behind it all. So it was

*easy to blame him for the rioting which he detested and was powerless
to prevent, for the murders and brutalities and destruction that were
perpetrated by his particular enemies, the criminal* tsotsi *element, while
he was in the cells.*

*The next day Mabaso was killed. Perhaps it would be better to
say that the wrath of the whole white country, aroused by that new thing
he brought into the location, came down on him and crushed him.*

Mabaso, who had come early into the prison yard, crouched
down near the wall and watched the space fill up. They had
brought him along in the pickup van not knowing who he was.
In the charge office they had asked for his name. He had said,
" Mabaso," but it hadn't meant anything to them. As batches
of new prisoners were let into the yard, he mingled with them
and talked to them long and earnestly.

It was not a proper prison, merely a detention centre for
awaiting-trial prisoners—convicted prisoners were sent to the
farms or to regular prisons in the big towns—and it was never
meant to hold so many. The male section had been built to take
about forty prisoners, the female about thirty, but well before
the raid was over there were hundreds in each. Each section
consisted of a large communal cell, facing, across a small paved
yard, a row of smaller cells. The two yards adjoined but were
separated by a ten-foot-high brick wall. Stretched overhead
across the wall, and then down the open side of each yard, was
a strong wire mesh. The prison was sometimes called " the cage,"
which was an apt description of it. From the yard it was possible
to see the sky through the wire, and from the street to see into
the men's yard. The women's yard faced into the private grounds
of the police station and was not visible to the public. Fixed
high up on each side of the wall was an electric bulb enclosed in
a glass bowl, from which a weak greenish light crept like mildew
down the brickwork and filtered out in a thin haze over the yard.

At first the prisoners could not get used to the crowding.
They moved about too much, became frightened, and made
excessive use of the single latrine bucket in each cell. Every now
and then a convulsive heaving would thrust people gasping and
struggling against the wall and wire. But after a time an

influence began to work among them and they settled down. They learnt to keep calm, to sit in rows, even to snatch some sleep lying wedged together. They worked out a way for husbands and wives to come up to the wall and shout messages over the top, and in the women's section a special area was kept apart for mothers with babies. Eventually they became almost cheerful, but the crowding was only made bearable by the exercise of a tight restraint, and there was a queer quicksilver moodiness among the prisoners.

Locked in the cells were some other prisoners—the normal gaol population—and as the yard filled up, orders came to open all the cell doors and allow all prisoners, old and new, to mingle.

When the people who had volunteered for the handcuffs the night of Mary Lukhele's arrest came out of their cells, everybody gazed at them in astonishment, as if they had stepped out of a tomb. It seemed so long ago that Mary Lukhele was arrested. Mary herself was not there ; she had gone to the prison hospital.

Dhladla came out, fat and lumbering, still wearing the new blue suit that he had put on to take Lukhele's body to the police station. Behind Dhladla came the Reverend Samson Shongwe. He stood at the door, looking a little dazed and lost, as if not quite sure where he was. After a moment he was recognised. People said, " Umfundisi, umfundisi," and reached hands up to touch him, and several had tears in their eyes, for he was the best-loved man in the whole location. His appearance at the door had a most moving effect on the prisoners in the yard. It made everybody feel better to see him ; it sent a wave of elation through the yard. By standing there among them he seemed to give them all an assurance that they could not be on the side of wrong and evil, and that the bad dream must therefore pass. He stood at the dark door, his lean bony forehead gleaming in the green light from the wall, his huge gaunt hands hovering distractedly in embarrassment in front of his chest, and he smiled his warm smile at the people clamouring around him. Then he saw Mabaso in the crowd, and the two men exchanged a silent greeting from deep in their eyes, and his right hand stopped moving and slowly shaped into a fist with the thumb sticking up.

" Afrika," he said, in his rich, resonant voice.

280

Mabaso and a number of others returned the salute, saying, "*Mayibuye*—may it come."

There was a pause, and then every single person in the yard jerked his thumb up and said, "*Mayibuye*—may it come." The women heard, and from over the wall came a deep contralto voice—"Afrika"; and then the whole gaol, men and women together, responded with a passionate "*Mayibuye a—a—vooo.*"

Then some of them struck up a song that used to be popular in the Defiance Campaign. It had a solemn, rousing tune, and those who had not heard it before picked it up quickly, and they rendered it with rich, luxurious harmony. And a great, clear, passionate melody swelled up out of the gaol and soared into the sky and carried over the whole town.

> *Unzima lomtwalo.*
> *Unzima lomtwalo.*
> *Unzima lomtwalo.*
> *Woyisa madoda.*

> This load is heavy.
> This load is heavy.
> This load is heavy.
> It grinds men down.

> *Vukani, mzontsundu.*
> *Vukani, mzontsundu.*
> *Vukani, mzontsundu.*
> *Silweli Afrika.*

> Awake, black hearts.
> Awake, black hearts.
> Awake, black hearts.
> Win Afrika back.

The guards rattled on the doors and yelled through the tiny iron grate, "Keep quiet. Shut up, you black swine," but the singing went on, all the louder to drown them out. "Stop that. Shut up! I order you to stop!" yelled the chief guard, who had

281

come out of his office, but they went on singing, repeating the song over and over, fashioning and improving the melody with each rendering, and nothing in the world could have stopped them then. They stopped only when they had spent themselves sufficiently of the pain in their hearts to make it bearable. The music grew softer and faded away, the last few voices stopping abruptly in the middle of a phrase, and then there was silence.

It was night-time still, and one could see the pale, cold stars overhead, and out of the side of the wire mesh the strung-out sagging lines of yellow street lamps, and intermittently the swing of car lights cutting an arc through the sky, and the bright, sharp lights wide awake in houses all over the town. It was a tense, pent-up night, too full of grim errands and nervous movement and wrought-up wakefulness, and haunted by the faint, far-off, pulsing, and persistent murmur of the location in its agony.

" I wonder if it's not better after all to be here rather than there," a voice said in the stillness.

" Perhaps."

And then silence again, and all were thinking of the terror raging over their homes. But not speaking of it, for a barrier was down, shutting each man's thoughts inside, preventing them from running amuck and animating that mass of crowded bodies into a terrible heaving panic.

Another van pulled up outside the charge office.

" How many more ? " a prisoner shouted angrily. They heard the metal doors scrape open, the steps of the new arrivals ring on the cold ground, the doors slam closed, and the van drive away.

" Let's pack round the door and stop them coming in."

" Steady on, friend."

" It's a damn' good idea, let's do it."

" Yes, why don't we do it ? "

" What ? And deny them hospitality ? No, friend, let each one of us release a little breath and make room for our new guests."

The foolish plan passed away in a joke. But they felt only hatred for the newcomers, now busy having their names and fingerprints taken in the charge office. Everybody was wondering, How many more? But although they did not know it, these were almost the last of the prisoners. The end was near.

Mabaso, Shongwe, Dhladla, and a group of their friends had taken up a place near the corner made by the dividing wall and the wall of the communal cell. They were talking softly together:

" . . . so we sat there trying to make plans and trying to cheer each other up. It was awful, Father. We missed you, both of you—so much—and—well—well, it just wasn't the same any more."

Father Shongwe did not speak. His head was bent to one side, and he was gazing far away out of the prison, as if listening to the night and not to Mabaso.

"It's ridiculous," Dhladla was saying indignantly. "How can they catch us for concealing the evidence when we *brought* the body? How can they? It's ridiculous."

"And then, on top of everything, this business of Sibande. It made us sick."

"Yes. But I must say I saw it coming. That other night . . ." Shongwe's voice drifted away, but after a moment he turned and asked fiercely, "Did he really say that, Nkosi? Did he really?"

"Yes. I could kill him."

"Please, Nkosi."

"What are we worrying about Sibande for?" one of the Congress men asked. "Why, within ten feet of us there are half a dozen fellows who can take his place."

They talked on—about the riot—Mabaso's questioning of Du Toit—Elliot's mission to Johannesburg to get hold of lawyers—Mavuso and Vilakazi's fund to bail people out and give family relief—themselves.

"Father, what do you think will happen to you and Dhladla?" Mabaso asked.

"I don't know. If only we had a lawyer we might even get off—they haven't much of a case against us. But that's impossible now. I think we're likely to get about six months each. That's what they say in there." He jerked his head in the direction of the police station. "It's not long."

"No. But in gaol it seems long."

"And you, Nkosi?"

283

"I don't know. I don't know what to expect." He said it looking away and with a vague note, but then, with a slight tremor of his voice that echoed the sudden thumping of his heart, he added, "You know, Father, I've got a funny feeling . . ."

Shongwe gave him a long, trembling look, but said nothing.

"*It's ridiculous.* I'm going to sue them for damages, the dirty Dutch pigs . . ." Dhladla was saying.

Eventually an exhausted peace descended on the prison. Bodies curled up in weird distorted heaps were dozing quietly, bathed in a chill green light, like fitful marine creatures. It was the darkest and coldest part of the night, two hours before the dawn, and there was a short while during which there were no new prisoners brought in and the gaol seemed very remote from the troubled world, like a ship adrift.

Then suddenly there was a rapid crackling of rifle fire, an abrupt heightening and sharpening of the sound coming from the location, and everybody was sitting up, awake, ears straining. They listened and heard the first outbreak of firing die down, and there came a pause, a long deathly pause, and suddenly the firing started again, louder, sharper, and more formidable now, and it lasted a long time. In the midst of it a pickup van arrived at the police station, and in the gaol they could tell from the violent shouting and cursing of the men left on duty at the station that the bodies of two policemen were being carried out of the van. The loud, murderous shooting went on, then stopped abruptly ; another pause, and just as the whole clattering convoy of trucks, vans and cars pulled up outside the station, the prisoners saw the first flames light the sky above the location.

*　　　*　　　*

They left the prisoners alone for several hours. There was a long delay, during which the sun came up and poured some thin warmth into the cage and the town started out on a crazed, demented day.

Some location constables had come across to the police station to make themselves useful, and while waiting to be given something to do they stood at the wire and told the prisoners of all that had happened in the location. They were friendly towards

284

the prisoners. They showed no enmity and were not blaming anybody. They stood with their fingers twining in the wire and their boots scuffing the sand, and they told of the death of Roberts and Nel, the shooting into houses, the murders, rape, rioting, looting and burning, all in quiet matter-of-fact voices, as if they themselves were not particularly concerned but just thought the prisoners would like to hear about it.

The prisoners listened in silence, but after a while became restless, as if not wanting to hear any more. Now it was too big. It had reached a size where everything became meaningless. They listened, it registered in their minds, and although they were aware that something had happened to add vast new dimensions to their troubles, they were too emotionally dulled to feel the impact. But what happened was that a subterranean gloom began to creep, slowly and unperceived, through the gaol.

The location constables finished their grim recital, but did not go away. They stayed around the gaol trying to be friendly. They asked to be given messages to take back to the prisoners' families and offered to arrange for food and cigarettes to be smuggled in. They seemed anxious to atone to the prisoners in some way. Whenever a white policeman came past, they pulled themselves rigidly erect and glowered furiously into the cage.

At about ten o'clock the police started the interrogations. Four teams went to work simultaneously. The sergeant came down and screamed out the names of four prisoners, two from the men's section, two from the women's. His voice had a harshness they had not met with before, even in a policeman. The four were let out of the gaol and prodded and bumped up the path into the side entrance of the police station. The door closed. Nobody in the gaol spoke.

There was a sound overhead. They looked up and saw an aeroplane, a rare sight for Nelstroom. A military plane, grey, sombre, and angry-looking. It flew slowly around the town, then climbed high, turned on its side, hung in space for a moment, and swooped down in the direction of the location. It was lost to sight, then scooped itself up and went far away down the valley. It stayed there a little while, in the same position, but just growing smaller to the eye. But then it was coming back, and was right back over the location, flying low, out of sight, but with a reverberating roar of engines. It did it once again, then once again, then went away. It did not drop any bombs or fire its guns, as everyone expected. It just flew back and forth, very low, several times over the location, then flew away.

After about fifteen minutes the four prisoners came back out of the side door of the station. From one corner of the men's yard it was just possible to see them coming down the steps. Two of them had handcuffs on, but the other two had their hands free. The handcuffed ones were put into a pickup van to be driven to Withoek, where it had been decided to send all those found to be directly implicated in the rioting. The other two, a man and a woman, were escorted back to the gaol and let in again. The man's eyes had a glassy look, and he was staggering. He collapsed in a corner and lay gasping, his chest heaving painfully.

The sergeant put his face to the iron grate and screamed out four more names. The four prisoners were taken out, like fish pulled out of a tank, and were pushed and joggled up the path into the police station.

While the names were being called, Father Shongwe sat bolt upright, his hand held tight around Mabaso's. When the prisoners were led away, he said, " Well, it's pretty definite that they don't know you're here. It's amazing."

" Yes, it seems so. It's a common name."

" They must be so sure you've escaped that it hasn't occurred to them to look for you in here."

" They'll find out soon enough. Let's see what's wrong with this fellow."

They pushed their way through to the distressed man, but while they stood over him, he recovered and pulled himself into a sitting position. He said that they had wanted a confession from him, and that to help him make up his mind they had put his head into a gas mask with the air tube stopped up by a cork. But an enormous noise arose in his head and he collapsed before making up his mind.

" It's an old trick," Mabaso told Father Shongwe. " It leaves no mark. Without marks to show it's hard for a fellow to repudiate a confession."

"It disgusts me," Father Shongwe said.

After a while the second group of prisoners came out. They had been dealt with more quickly. All were handcuffed and put in the van for Withoek. Four more were fished out.

From early morning white civilians passing in the street outside had stopped to look into the seething cage. Now an excited crowd had collected. They were restless and sullen-looking and some of them were drunk. These were the white town's *tsotsis*.

One man carrying a rifle was walking rapidly up and down and saying in a hoarse bull voice, "This is it, boys. We got to defend our women." A continuous angry murmuring came from the crowd.

One man took long, careful aim with his rifle into the cage, moving the weapon minutely along as he followed a particular prisoner in the sights. Suddenly he jerked the rifle up and sent a bullet whistling over the top of the gaol.

"Now I know," Father Shongwe said, standing near the wire and glaring with cold contempt at the bobbing, excited crowd. "Now I've seen it for myself—a lynch mob."

Two weak-legged staring prisoners were let back into the cage. The sergeant's hoarse, ugly voice came through the grating again. This time he called six names. They were speeding up the interrogation.

There was a sudden bustle of activity in the vicinity of the police station. A farmers' commando, bristling with guns, came riding up on horseback. A lorry arrived, packed with police reinforcements from another town, the men carrying rifles topped with bayonets. A lorry loaded with heavily armed police set out for the location.

Shongwe tensely watched through the wire. Then he turned and made his way back to his place in the corner. Mabaso watched him. He noticed the strained, worried look. Shongwe sat down, and after a while looked up and asked Mabaso to come and join him. Mabaso went over and sat next to him. Shongwe did not speak at once. After a while he asked, "What has happened to Leah and Moses ? " But that was not what he wanted to say. Mabaso told him about the plans he had made for them. They sat a little while without talking. Suddenly Shongwe said vehemently, " This is terrible, Nkosi, this suspense." Mabaso said nothing; his hands hung loosely between his knees and he traced with his finger an invisible design on the patch of concrete between his feet.

" Nkosi, why did you do it ? I've never heard of such a thing—giving yourself up ! "

Mabaso said, " It just had to be, Father." Then after a pause he said, " But I'm not sorry. Don't worry about me."

Shongwe put his hand on Mabaso's knee and shook it and tried to smile. He said, " No, I'm not worried." But after a moment he added, " Well, it's not that. Not your arrest. I don't mean that. Everybody here "—he looked around the yard— " we're all under arrest. What I mean is if they can do that to these poor fellows "—he indicated some of the men who had been nearly asphyxiated—" these fellows, whom they haven't even got any evidence against, when it comes—when——" He found it impossible to say.

Mabaso said, " Father, don't worry about me." He tried to say something else, but everything he thought of sounded foolish or heroic or put on. He sat for a moment, then squeezed Father Shongwe's hand and got up and went away. He had been over it in his mind a dozen times and it was all settled for him, but he could not cope with Father Shongwe's sorrow.

From the prison yard it was possible to see only a small sector of the town outside—a few yards of the side wall of the police station, a triangle of lawn, the edge of the fish pond, a brief stretch of the street, some trees, a small segment of sky. Yet every part of that space was involved in the wrought-up vengeful fury that had seized the town. And the town itself was merely the centre of a whirlwind of wrath that had swept over the whole country. Over the radios that the prisoners could hear faintly playing in the cars parked in the street came appeals for calm issued by government Ministers and police chiefs, so phrased as to keep the hysteria at boiling point, and promises

288

of help on the way, as though Nelstroom were a beleaguered garrison, and public announcements of the orders to police to shoot to kill at the first sign of a revival of trouble, and threats to the whole black population—a reckless spate of inflammatory violence that was, at the same time, a cunning distortion and an evil exploitation for political purposes of the happenings. And the waves of fury and fear that radiated out from Nelstroom were mirrored back, inflamed and intensified.

And in the gaol the menace pressed down like a black hail cloud, darkening the sky and charging the air with an ominous pressure. An unbearable struggle went on in every prisoner—a struggle between the need to keep calm, to hold on to the mood of stubborn resignation which had become instinct among his people in times of great trial, as a particular behaviour pattern fastens itself to a species of animal, and an alarm, a clawing, clutching dread that had come suddenly alive, like a nest of spiders brought prematurely to spawn by exposure in the cage. For many it was an impossible torment. None of them were able to speak of it, but it could be seen deep in their eyes, and in a sudden glazed loneliness and detachment and limp withdrawal that came over them and made them seem like birds dropping off to sleep on the perch in a crowded aviary.

It made many wish that their interrogation was over, and that the result of it would be to be sent to Withoek, whatever that might entail. The spirit had been good during the night, but now, after the news of the dreadful happenings in the location, and the suspense of waiting for names to be called, and the terrible tension mounting around the police station, and the exhaustion, and the growing hunger, it had gone grey and desolate.

And then a strange thing happened. Father Shongwe, who was sitting on the stone step leading into the cell, started to sing " Unzima Lomtwalo " again. He started by singing to himself, but soon his voice swelled out, deep, confident, and sad. He took the song quite a long way on his own. Everybody turned to him, surprised, but he went on singing. His eyes were closed, and his face was caught in a far-away smile, and he caressed the song with such personal tenderness that he might have been all alone under a tree on the mountainside. Soon some other voices came in, then more and more. There was a timidity at first, but suddenly they threw off all restraint and the music just burst out into the sky, and the whole gaol, from both sides of the wall, was singing the song with a crashing, tumultuous, ringing defiance. They stood up and placed arms around each other's shoulders, and they looked up into the sky, many with tears glistening on their cheeks, and each one gave of his whole soul and surrendered himself to the wild rush of music.

The white people in the vicinity of the prison went crazy. The mob on the street outside began screaming and hurling stones against the wire. The newly arrived policemen ran across to the gaol and banged on the wire with their rifles and yelled, " Shut up ! Keep quiet. Shut up, you bastards ! Where do you think you are ? " But their voices went hoarse trying to hurl themselves against that mighty tower of music. The farmers' commando and all the police officers, including Swanepoel, came out of the station and stood around the cage yelling, " Shut up. Keep quiet, you black pigs. SHUT UP, SHUT UP, SHUT UP ! " But no one inside heard.

But after a while the police and even the mob outside stopped shouting and gesticulating, and a queer kind of discomfort came over them, such as comes to a man who mistakes a shadow for a burglar, and they just stood around with their hands on their hips, not looking at one another. They wanted to go away then, but something held them listening. Buried deep in the impassioned song was a strange secret, a power to reach into the hearts even of their torturers. The police stood listening until it was finished, and then, without a word to the prisoners, turned round and marched back to the police station. And among the mob in the street there were many who suddenly found that they had better things to do than hang around watching a lot of Kaffir prisoners in a cage, and they sauntered away, leaving only the most violent and clamorous of them standing at the fence.

It was a small triumph, so insignificant that none of the white people saw it as such. But there are times when the power of small, commonplace things can be miraculous. A few degrees of warmth can save a man's life. A tiny light on the shore can guide a ship through the storm. This was such a case. This small victory reminded the prisoners that they were alive. It gave them back the right to breathe, to feel the sun's rays, to widen their shoulders and to feel in their veins that surge that was carrying them through the long night into the future.

*   *   *

It was strange that they did not call out Mabaso's name. But it was, as Father Shongwe said, that they simply never thought of looking for him in the gaol. They had broadcast his description and cars were being stopped and train compartments searched in towns all over the eastern Transvaal. They just assumed he had escaped and they carried on the interrogation of the other prisoners with a hollow, disappointed feeling, as if by his escape the location had managed to secure a victory after all. The name was right there in the charge book, but it was a common Swazi name and it meant nothing to them. And it so happened that in the random picking of names for interrogation Mabaso's name was passed over time after time.

In the gaol, prisoners began to listen with tense interest, not only for their own name, but for Mabaso's. They all knew that he was a special case. The whole prison became interested in the queer fateful game that Mabaso and the police appeared to be playing, unwittingly, with one another.

The interrogations had by now sifted out many prisoners to send to Withoek, and there was more space in the yard, enough to stretch out on the floor and have some comfort at last. Some food—fish and potato chips wrapped in newspaper, hunks of bread, oranges—had found its way into the gaol. Somehow, in spite of the long-drawn-out terror of the interrogations, there was less tension now.

Mabaso undid the buttons of his overcoat, pulled open his lumber jacket, and sprawled flat on his back in the sun. He tugged his battered black cap away from under his head, pushed the inside up with his fist, and placed it over his face. The sun thawed the odours out of it and he found himself savouring the warm personal smell of sweat and leather. He crossed his feet and from under the cap studied with one eye the large yellow shoe that reared up, and imagined he saw faces in it. Then he pulled the comb out of his pocket and with both eyes closed, and breathing into the cap, he combed his beard. A great calm had come over him.

Everything was as it had to be. There was no other way. There were no regrets. It was right that he had spoken up to Du Toit. He had not caused the attack on Du Toit but it was right that if people were going to be arrested for it, he should be among them. Not simply to prove Du Toit wrong, to make a show of proving that his kind of people did not run away. Something deeper than that. To show the location that in times of trouble—— No, not to show anything. It was right because that's where he wanted to be, where he had to be, where, unless his whole life was to be made meaningless, he could only be.

Sometimes an experience befalls a people that affects them for all the future. Even though it befalls only a small number of the people, even though it might destroy that number, its impact spreads out and it lives on for ever among all the people. It makes the next experience a little different, and becomes a part of the next experience, and so on, and thus it survives to help shape the day that finally brings an end to all the grief and strife. In this kind of experience nothing is lost. Nothing is wasted. Nothing is given or suffered in vain.

Well, that's another way of saying the same thing, Mabaso thought. If this belongs to me, then I'm a part of the experience and cannot hope to escape from it. A part, but not in the sense of something tossed helplessly about by the events. In the dynamic, organic sense. In the sense that the events and I respond to each other and help to make each other. The very character of this experience has been affected by the presence in it of me and Shongwe and people like us. Perhaps out of all this pain will come that bright new thing : perhaps this is the pain of bursting out. Maybe I can say that I helped it along a little, helped by applying a little strength at the right point.

What they will do with it when it comes—who can say ? Perhaps they will even betray it, as people have betrayed so many of the revolutions of history. But that belongs in the future. It is not important now. What is important is to give them the chance. There is only one direction.

He could not think of anything to add to that. The warmth of the sun made him drowsy, and he lay with his hands behind his head and enjoyed the feel of the warmth seeping through his clothing.

They learned that he was there eventually. It was shortly after midday. Nobody ever knew how they learnt it. Perhaps there was an informer in the yard : or perhaps a prisoner blurted it out during an interrogation in order to take the pressure off himself. But about half a dozen policemen led by Lieutenant Swanepoel himself came into the yard and called out Mabaso's name. Some other prisoners had to wake him to tell him he was wanted. He sat up, looked around, then stood to his feet. He gave the thumbs-up salute, almost jauntily, to the Reverend Shongwe and then to the rest of the yard, and walked out. The police escorted him without talking, and without touching him. He was not in the police station for long. There was no need for an interrogation ; it was decided to send him straightaway to Withoek. Meantime the news that it was Mabaso had spread to the crowd in the street. The police put Mabaso into a pickup van all by himself, and the journey started. The crowd in the street rushed for their cars and followed the van.

It appeared that a little way outside Nelstroom the van had a breakdown and it was necessary to open the door to get to the tools. Mabaso, it seemed, jumped out and tried to escape. That was how he came to be shot a number of times in the back.

Or so they said.

CHAPTER SEVENTEEN

AFTER THE raid they dropped Du Toit off at his house. Without a word, he got out of the car and climbed the steps up to the veranda. He found the lights on, and Anna, his wife, waiting up for him. She guided him into the room and helped him out of his overcoat, and he flopped into the armchair without speaking. Anna watched him anxiously, then went into the hall to telephone the doctor. He bent forward, unlaced his shoes, prised them off with his toes, and sank back into the depth of the chair. His whole body ached.

Anna came back from the hall and went into the kitchen to make coffee. Through the open door she kept asking, " Are you all right ? " " Are you sure you're all right ? " And he answered, " Yes, there's nothing serious. Just knocked out," and, " Yes, I'm all right."

That was the only conversation they had. She did not speak, nor did he tell her, about the happenings in the location. Neither of them wanted to open up that calamitous subject, with its endless, unanswerable questions.

Anna brought the coffee, and he gulped it greedily, but it scalded the inside of his cold, parched mouth and slopped on to his shirt. He drank the rest in nervous little sips, holding the saucer trembling against his chest.

Every few seconds he looked up and gazed about him. The room seemed fantastically strange after the dark, churning violence of the location. The lights had a brilliance that bored into his eyeballs and made every object stand out with a fierce, knife-edged aggressiveness. The portraits on the wall looked startled and frostbitten. The pattern on the linoleum had a dazzling sharpness that seemed to raise it off the floor. The quietness itself had a stark, hair-raising quality that brought up small, intense sounds—the ticking of the clock, the whirr of the refrigerator, the hum of insects. The cream walls, the polished mirror, the gleaming table top, the ornaments standing up straight on the mantelpiece—all looked as if seized in a lunacy of cleanliness and good behaviour. He had the sensation of seeing everything afresh, from unusual angles, as if he had become a cat or a beetle.

He finished the coffee and put the cup down on the table. His hands shook and the cup rattled in the saucer. His hands and feet were numb, and he kept feeling little tremors of cold run up his back. To get some warmth into his limbs, he rubbed his hands together, his feet together, simultaneously, like a fly washing itself. He did it vigorously for a minute or so, then the movement died out of him and he sat with his elbows on his knees, staring into the fire, and his big, popping blue eyes, usually so inquisitive and alert, were now mild and liquid—defeated.

The doctor arrived and tended to his head wound, and gave him an injection. He undressed in a daze and climbed into bed, and after a while he fell into a heavy, troubled sleep, which lasted through the following day and night. And during all that time he writhed and groaned and in his disturbed mind relived the whole experience, but in a monstrously agonised, bizarre re-enactment of it that played out every incident on his raw nerves and flesh. His mind twisted and seethed in a terrifying chaos of swirling scenes, scenes that merged in strange, fearful relationships, wisped apart, evaporated, and rematerialised, with everything overlaid by a colouring of vicious enmity towards himself. His ears rang to a continuous pandemonium of crashing and smashing, stones thundering on iron, mobs screeching, hoarse commands, car engines roaring, blaring sirens, thumping boots, and rifles, blows, kicks, screams, the harsh staccato bark of gunfire and the whine, whistle, and slap of bullets. In shuddering fear he found himself dragged back once more into that empty yard, with the weird girlish giggling coming out of the walls; saw again Roberts writhing on the ground, the blood-soaked, limp body of Nel being moved from the truck to the pickup van;

felt himself mesmerised and humiliated once again by the bearded man in a khaki coat hoisted above the crowd and holding his arms up for silence; heard the questions dinning into him, he sitting at the littered desk, his face washed but not dried, and Swanepoel pounding him with the relentless questions; saw himself walking and peering at house numbers, foolishly, guiltily, as if searching for something; sitting huddled in the back of Swanepoel's car, standing speechless on the platform in front of the screaming meeting, trying to decide whether to stay or go; slipping into step with Swanepoel and Roberts, and suddenly feeling his steps go languid and tired, and no longer in rhythm with them; and that recurrent theme, that persistant horror obtruding into everything, that disgusting half-naked, white-eyed, mouth-foaming woman heaving and arching in front of him as if in the act of sex; and himself running away. And the huge *WHY*? the feverish search for reasons, the anxious scrutiny of everything to find a common factor that would explain it all. And then at one point a vast discordant jangling of bells, bells that swelled to overwhelming size, then shrunk smaller, smaller, smaller into one tiny quivering point of light; and after that a long period of blackness.

He did not so much awake as focus himself slowly back into his surroundings. He lay still for a long time staring at the ceiling. The sun was streaming in through the window, slanting across the bed and thickening the air where it shone with dancing dust. His body felt like a landscape that had been battered by a storm. He lay still, aware that a cataclysmic nightmare had raged inside him, but feeling its terrifying atmosphere and details receding from him. His face felt sticky with dried sweat, his pyjamas were dishevelled and stale, and there was a sour smell about him, but he felt in his exhausted limbs and unwashed skin some vague intimation of comfort.

*   *   *

There were some newspapers lying heaped on the table beside his bed, but for a long time he did not read them. They frightened him. He saw the headlines and pictures quivering on the page, clamouring to be read, but the papers had about them something

296

of the deranged, unreal quality of his nightmare, and he could not bring himself to pick them up. Anna sat on the bed and told him of what happened after he left the location. She spoke quietly, solicitously, as if she were visiting him in hospital. His mind reeled. Did I start all that? he kept asking himself. He felt like the man who shouts into a valley and loosens an avalanche that buries dozens of villages.

Later he dressed and wandered moodily about the house. Anna kept coming up to him, slipping her arm around his waist and walking along with him a little way. She was full of warmth and affection for him. She purred around him as if glad of the opportunity to show that she was standing loyally at his side.

"There's nothing to blame yourself for," she told him. "Everybody understands." Yet he felt a vague estrangement from her. He wanted to tell her that he could not face going back to the location, but he knew it would distress her. Only here, in Nelstroom, had their life at last settled down. He felt uncomfortable about her sympathy, as if he were getting it under false pretences.

They went out to the veranda and he placed his arm around her shoulders and squeezed her tightly to his side, and together they gazed out over the pretty wooded town. It reminded him of that first day in Nelstroom when Moolman brought them back from the station and they stood together like this, on this spot, looking out across the town for the first time. He pictured himself as being much younger then—more hair, slimmer, straighter. He remembered bitterly how keen he had been to make a success of the new job. Well, nobody could say he hadn't tried.

What exactly happened? God, what an explosion. And all over a missing collar in some stinking washgirl's bundle of laundry.

The town looked the same as usual, as if nothing at all had happened. He saw some neighbours watering their gardens, housewives shaking carpets out over the sides of their stoeps : people were walking in the streets carrying briefcases and parcels, cars sped by on their way through to the bushveld : there was an ox wagon laden with peaches creaking slowly past the front

297

of the house : some children playing about on bicycles. The town had put on a great big air of innocence.

The scene in front of him blurred out, and he found himself thinking of the raid again, and of how when walking with Swanepoel and Roberts in the location, his steps suddenly lagged and he had that queer feeling about Swanepoel, and looking into his face, suddenly saw him out of uniform. It was a strange moment, one of the strangest in his life. He remembered the awful feeling it gave him. He knew then that something had collapsed between himself and the police. Yet he had said nothing, and had gone on walking, keeping close to Swanepoel, sticking right on his heels because he knew then that if he got left behind in that location, he would have been murdered—flip—like that, and not a person in the whole place would have lifted a finger to help him. So loved and appreciated was he by those black bastards he'd slaved himself to death over, trying to run their dirty location on decent lines for them. And so all the time he kept on walking close to the police, although resenting them and they resenting him, and he had the terrible feeling of being a kind of spy among them. What a strange situation for a white man to get into. . . .

He felt restless, he had an urge to work. He disengaged his arm from Anna and went inside. He took some paper out of the sideboard drawer and sat down with it at the table. He wrote, REPORT ON RIOT IN NELSTROOM LOCATION, and underscored it heavily three times. Below that he wrote, " (1) Immediate Causes," and halfway down the page, " (2) Contributing Factors." But then his hand went limp and he sat and stared at the paper for a long time. Eventually he got up and stood looking out of the window. He found himself thinking of his car longingly. He could imagine it standing out there in the drive, just below the window, the chromium shone up with Silvo, the tyres blackened with boot polish, the whole car agleam as it used to look every Sunday morning when he finished working on it. It felt like Sunday somehow.

Suddenly he had an idea, and he went out to the garage, pulled the tin box of carpenter's tools out from under the workbench, and dragged it into the kitchen. Then he went into the

298

pantry and stood with his hand on his chin, contemplating the shelves. With sudden bustle, he cleared everything from the top shelf, ripped off the half-rotted oilcloth, prised the shelf off its brackets, and carried it into the kitchen. Holding it firm across a chair with his knee, he began to saw it in half. But the wood was tough, and after a few minutes he gave up. He propped the half-sawn plank against the wall, the saw next to it, and went into the bedroom and lay down on the bed.

He lay on his back for a while, thinking, but then he reached out and picked up one of the papers. The first thing he saw was his own picture—reproduced from that same photograph that had been standing on the dining-room dresser. " Courageous Superintendent," the caption read. He read on eagerly. The small print below the caption described how he had held the infuriated mob at bay until shortly before the police arrived. This startled him a little. Then he smiled. He'd never thought of it that way. He'd been blaming himself for the way things had gone, and now here they were praising him for what he did ! He closed his eyes and tried to visualise what had actually happened. He began to wonder whether he did not in fact hold the crowd in check during that crucial period when the police were on the way to the location. Everything was so mixed up anyway, who could say what the facts really were ?

He read further, but as he did so his pleasure began to disappear.

The riot took up nearly the whole front page : there were so many incidents. Reading about them was a dizzying experience. His eyes would read one thing, but his mind would recall the events as he saw them, so that there was a kind of double vision, like seeing an object through badly focused binoculars. Things were left out, things made up, things cunningly rearranged so as to throw all the blame on the location and emphasise the courage and restraint of the police and officials.

At first he thought it was just careless or hurried reporting, and it annoyed him. " Where'd they get that from ? " he said out loud at one point, sitting bolt upright in the bed.

Then he realised that it all had a familiar flavour. He saw it quite clearly, and it made him feel suddenly depressed. It

299

sounded just like his interrogation by Swanepoel in the location office immediately after the breakup of the meeting. It had the same kind of pattern as the questions Swanepoel had put to him and the answers that had eventually been squeezed out of him. Yes, it was easy to see whose hand was behind those newspaper stories.

He wondered what he was going to do about that statement he had given to Swanepoel. He remembered that even while the interrogation was going on, he had realised that something was wrong, he was not speaking the truth, and that he had a vague intention of correcting it later. And he remembered how, during the raid, it had worried him, and he had made a firm resolve to put it right the first opportunity. Now that same worry was back again, but increased by the knowledge that he would pretty soon have to make up his mind finally whether he was going to tell Swanepoel he was backing out of certain things in the statement.

He sat staring at the wall, wondering how he was going to broach it with Swanepoel, but then after a few minutes he shrugged his shoulders and said, " Oh, Jesus, it must be my nerves."

He took up the paper again, nervous and disturbed now. That part about the rape of Mrs. Bertram and the murder of her and her husband shocked him. As he read it he felt a stinging sensation under his eyelids. Anna had told him about it and it had upset him then, but now a hard ball of pain welled up inside him. He knew that couple well. The thing was they were *friends* of the location. He used to hear talk about them around the office and nobody had a bad word to say against them. God, what a way to die. That poor woman. It was bad enough those two constables being murdered, terrible, but somehow it wasn't the same thing. That was like being killed in warfare, in a way. But what happened to Mr. and Mrs. Bertram had something very ugly and evil about it. What crazy, hideous thing had run loose in the location that night ?

Was there any such thing as a *friend* of the location ? Could a white man be one, that is ? He used to call *himself* that. At all those early meetings, when he was bringing in the new

300

reforms. That, and sometimes "father of the location." He meant it, too. He always had quite a fondness for the place : it sort of grew on you. It wasn't always easy to get a response, of course, and you had to keep your distance, make sure that you always did things justly, fairly, and without favouritism. Maybe that put up a kind of barrier between you and them, made it hard to get on real terms with them. Still, there was something about the place, and the people, too. They were warm and simple, like children, and working out there among them, you couldn't help taking a certain liking to them. That was the trouble about this job. It made you peculiar. It filled you with ideas you had to keep your mouth shut about, else your friends would start wondering about you. What a job ! Was there any other job like it in the whole world ?

But suddenly he became very tense. " A-ah, to hell with them ! " he said fiercely. " Friend or enemy, they murder you just the same. As they did to Mr. and Mrs. Bertram. As they tried to do to me."

He went on reading, and came to the part about the murder of Ngubeni. He stiffened. Anna had not told him about it. The news was buried far down in the report and handled in only two sentences. " Among those killed was Charles Ngubeni, a Swazi headman and the Chairman of the Advisory Board. A crowd of rioters dragged him out of his house and killed him in the street." The news left him aghast. It chilled him more even than the news about the Bertrams had. " Good God," he kept saying. He read it over and over. The picture came back of that last time when Ngubeni walked out of the office, full of hurt feelings. He remembered the stiff, angry back and the sound of his jerky footsteps disappearing down the veranda steps. He had grown tired of Ngubeni, had come to see him as a bit of a fraud, but now he couldn't bring himself to think of him like that. He thought of all the discussions behind closed doors, all the intrigues, all the Board meetings, all the times they had stood together on the platform at public meetings, all the work they had done together. They had been very close to each other. It had been, in fact, some queer kind of partnership for running the location. . . .

301

He sat thinking about Ngubeni for a long time. He knew then how close to him, personally, it had come.

He just could not understand the whole affair. There was something unnatural and disturbing and uncanny about it. What made the location suddenly blow up in his face like this? Up till the time they arrested that washgirl there wasn't a sign, not the smallest clue, that anything was going wrong. Everything had been running so smoothly, and suddenly, out of the blue sky, *this*. And all the time he had been going out there, working in that office alone, surrounded by them, unaware that there was a bomb ticking away under his feet. How could he have been so wrong in sizing up the location? How could he have made such a mistake? What was there about the location that made it become like a vicious poisonous animal and turn on everyone, friend and enemy alike? Had he ever really understood that place?

Maybe the trouble was he had the wrong attitude to the location—building them that Welfare Centre, extending the town's veterinary services for their animals, putting in all those extra water-taps and dustbins—oh dozens of things. Trying to win their goodwill! Maybe that was wrong, and maybe Swanepoel's outlook was right after all. To hell with goodwill—crack down on them and keep them in their place, and the first sign of any funny business, let them have it, hard.

He was smoking now, puffing absently on the cigarette and blowing out clouds of smoke. His eyes had a blank, distant look. He knew now that it was his problem, a problem that had become vital to him. There was an answer, somewhere, but it seemed to be just out of his reach. It had nothing to do with his outlook. It was absurd that the harsher you were, the less you did for them, the more they liked it, the better they behaved, and the *safer* it was for you. It didn't make sense. Anyway, he could never have Swanepoel's outlook. The way the police acted that night shocked him, the enjoyment they got out of it, until things went wrong, revolted him. No, he could never be like that. True, he had said all kinds of violent things up there in the office, but that was just nerves and fright. And this business had not exactly increased his love for those location Kaffirs, but even so he couldn't suddenly change into a Swanepoel. Maybe it was the job itself. Maybe the answer lay in the kind of work a man did out there. It was a dirty job—weren't people always saying that, anyway ? You sat in that stinking place and the dirt seeped into you. You went home at night and the dirt stuck to you, went home on you. *They* said it was a dirty job because you were mixing with black Kaffirs all day long. But maybe it really was a dirty job. In a real sense. An unnatural job. Yes, somehow unnatural. That was why all sorts of terrible, unexpected things happened in that job. That was why you were always trying to explain things, thrashing around for answers and never finding them. The job seemed to go against the grain, somehow.

He just knew that it was all over now. He could not see himself sitting at that desk, in that location, again. Something had snapped between him and the police. Something had snapped between him and the job. And there was something else, too, that he didn't like to contemplate.

He got off the bed and went into the kitchen, where Anna was preparing lunch. He placed his hand on her shoulder and said, " Anna, I've made up my mind about something." He intended to tell her that he had decided not to go back to the location. It would be a blow for her, but he hoped that when he had given her all the reasons, she would see it his way. But at the last moment the reasons deserted him. Instead his mind was suddenly filled with all the reasons for staying on—the fact that he was too old to start looking for private employment, that he would lose his pension, that by walking out of this job he would make it impossible to get back into this work again, the only kind of work he really knew, and despite all his dilemmas, loved. Anna looked up at him, waiting. He was blushing. Then he took his hand away and said, " Oh, it's nothing important. I'll tell you another time." He went into the dining-room and played the radio.

Late that afternoon Swanepoel came to visit him. He arrived in his squad car, polished and new-looking again, and he mounted the steps with a swish of gabardine and squeak of leather. He looked fine : uniform spruce, and his face pink, shaved, and even plump-looking, as if he were just back from a holiday. He was friendly and cheerful. With the tension of the raid gone, he seemed ready to forgive Du Toit and to treat him like an old comrade-in-arms. He called him " old fellow," and " old sport," though, as was usual with him, he did not address him by name.

" When do you think you'll be back in circulation again, old sport ? "

" I don't know. A few days, I think. I'm seeing my doctor to-night and I'll hear what he has to say."

" Well, don't leave it too long. We've got work to do."

He carried a thick cardboard folder tied up with green tape, but he seemed to be in no hurry to open it.

" Yes, we're not wasting any time. We're setting up a police station in the location right now. Been sanctioned already. They're giving us about a dozen new men for it."

" Yes ? "

" Yes. So you can stop worrying about this kind of thing happening again. We'll be there to watch the bastards from now on, day and night. Just let them start trouble again—just let them ! " Du Toit didn't look impressed. " Who'll be in charge out there ? " he asked.

" I will, old sport—for the time being. You, me—and your new assistant."

" New assistant ? "

" Yes. You're getting a white man to work under you. About time, too. I don't know how you stood it alone for so long.

" But where are we going to work ? There's no building— no records—nothing."

" That's being taken care of. The're putting up a prefab place while the rebuilding is going on." He paused, then he said, " It's a nuisance about the records, of course, but that'll sort itself out."

Du Toit listened without enthusiasm. He wanted to say one sentence to Swanepoel : " I'm not going back ! " But somehow he couldn't get it out. Swanepoel talked on cheerfully, full of eagerness to get started again, and there came a point when the opportunity for telling Swanepoel just evaporated.

At last Swanepoel went to the table and opened up the cardboard folder. " Your statement," he said, handing Du Toit a wad of foolscap pages stapled together at the corner. " Had it typed out. Copy for you, copy for us, copy for the Attorney General, copy for the Minister. He's got his already. Phoned us and asked for it." He was very brisk and businesslike, much more the lawyer than the policeman now.

Du Toit took the document and read the first paragraph slowly. He dropped his eyes and read some sentences near the bottom of the page, then flipped over the pages and read passages at random. His heart was beating wildly. It was his statement, all right : as extracted from him under Swanepoel's grilling in the location office. Taken out of Roberts' notebook and put into sentences, but all there, exactly as he had been browbeaten into making it. It seemed incredible that Swanepoel should produce it now, a betrayal, an act of blackmail.

" Sign here," Swanepoel said, holding the last page flat on the table and offering Du Toit a fountain pen with its cap on the back.

" Just a minute. Let me read it properly."

" Oh ? " Then, " Well, go ahead."

While Du Toit read painfully slowly through the statement, Swanepoel walked around the room picking ornaments off the mantelpiece and examining them, staring up at the pictures, and gazing out of the window. Du Toit had his own pen out and he was making Xs all down the margin. Swanepoel watched him through narrowing eyes.

" Of course, you know the whole case depends on your statement," Swanepoel said in a deadly level voice. Du Toit looked up, but said nothing, and went on reading.

" And the Minister's got it already. So's the press. . . ."

Du Toit read right to the end, then looked up.

" O.K.? " Swanepoel asked, walking over to him.

" How about leaving it with me a little while ? I'd like to think over it when I've got a little more time," Du Toit said, breathing hard.

Swanepoel looked searchingly at him, then suddenly smiled. " O.K.," he said. " It's important, so perhaps you'd better go over it carefully. You mustn't sign anything you're not sure about, old fellow. I'll pick it up in the morning."

Swanepoel left.

After about five minutes Du Toit stood up and put on his coat. He went out for a walk. He did not see where he went, but he found himself down in the park, walking round and round the footpaths. His hands were thrust deep into his pockets, and his lips were moving. He was talking to himself: What's the matter with me? Am I mad? Why am I doing this? For them? A lot of bloodthirsty black Kaffirs who'd murder me the first chance? I must be crazy. Why don't I just sign? Why not just sign and be finished with it? What do I stand to get out of this? Nothing. Not a damn' thing. Not a single damn' thing.

Yet . . . Yet—there was something. . . .

It was dark when he got home. He was still undecided. He glanced at the document still lying on the table where he had left it. It looked loathsome to him. Several times he went to the table in order to sign, simply to get rid of it, but there was a hard ball of resistance, a crass pigheadedness that refused to let him do it.

He wanted to discuss it with Anna. Several times he was on the point of raising it, but he knew it would be hopeless. She wouldn't understand. He didn't even know how to state the problem to her. It wasn't just a question of keeping one's mouth shut while Swanepoel put over a lot of lies about the riot, or even of actively supporting Swanepoel. That was a moral problem, but it was right there in front of you, you could tackle it and come to a decision about it. This other problem had something buried deep inside it. This afternoon when he had gone over the whole thing in his mind he felt he had come near to the problem, but somehow it had remained just out of his reach. He tried again to come to grips with it. It was too shadowy, too big for him.

He ate his supper glumly. Anna tried to make conversation but soon gave up. They finished the meal in silence. He drank only half his coffee, then left the table and sat in the armchair. He felt himself grow tensely angry with Swanepoel. The man seemed to be hovering over him, clouding his thoughts, oppressing him, hemming him in.

Then, quite suddenly, he saw it before him. The thought,

306

ready-made and explicit, was standing up in the front of his mind as if it had been there a long time. Swanepoel did not come to the location to save him from the mob. Swanepoel didn't care a damn about him. He didn't raid the location to track down and arrest the rioters. Or to restore law and order. No, all this was merely an excuse to let loose an orgy of murder and cruelty against the location. All the evil that flooded the location that night poured out of Swanepoel himself. *Swanepoel did not represent law and order : he represented crime and violence.*

It staggered him to realise it. It took him a few moments to get used to the shocking notion. He stood up and walked slowly over to the window. He gazed outside with unseeing eyes. Then he began pacing the room slowly, his hands clasped behind his back. Anna watched him with a worried look. She sighed, and took out her knitting, but every few moments looked up and followed him with her eyes. He did not see her.

Now he understood what happened when suddenly during the raid everything felt changed between himself and the police. That was the moment when he knew that he could never belong with them, the point of separation between him and them.

And now he understood a further thing, and why he had kept it hidden from himself. He, himself, was little better than the police. His job made them allies. Both carried out the same work, merely with different methods. They stood for the same things. They had the same aim : to keep the location in Suppression. And that made him as guilty as Swanepoel—his accomplice, jointly responsible with him, in the same way as the person who acts as a lookout and keeps the car running while his friends murder a man inside a shop is guilty of the crime of the whole gang. His job made him a *daily* accomplice of the police—but more, he aided and abetted them that particular night by supplying lies and excuses to help them carry out their dirty work. He was an accessory for Swanepoel by helping him cover up his crimes under the guise of legal police action.

He felt suddenly nauseated with himself. Yes, this was a dirty job, all right, a filthy job. This was the kind of thing it dragged a man into. Filth—the kind that goes right through you and into your bones. How can any self-respecting man allow himself

307

to do this work? Only by lying to himself, deluding himself, by building up a smoke-screen of fake philanthropy, by becoming a fraud. Well, the riot had done one thing, it had stripped him down so that he could see himself in his true light now. And he was covered in the accumulated dirt of that job. No, he was no hero the other night.

One thing was certain now. Nothing would make him sign that statement. Swanepoel could go to hell. He felt relieved at making the decision at last.

But that night, for some reason, he had difficulty in going off to sleep. In the quiet of the night all the strange aspects of what he was doing crowded into his mind. He felt like a man lost in dangerous, unexplored country. The decision began to assume strange and frightening proportions. The logic of it did not grow weaker: it became even more formidable and convincing, but it was the logic of a lunatic. He went to sleep eventually, but the relief at having decided had left him.

When morning came, he felt nervous and exhausted. He sat on the edge of the bed and went over it all again. It was not only the question of losing the job and the chance of getting a similar job. There was also the question of falling out with everybody in Nelstroom—they'd think him some kind of a traitor. Of falling out with the Party. Of having it follow him wherever he went. Of making a deliberate act against his own people. Still, in the daylight, he could see clearly that the decision was right, whatever it involved for him. It was the only course for an honest man. That strange plodding obstinacy of his came into play and kept him anchored to his decision.

He got dressed and just wandered around the house, waiting. He still did not know how he was going to say it to Swanepoel, and he felt a little sick at the thought of the interview. Swanepoel came shortly after ten o'clock. He bounced up the veranda steps and rapped a cocky tattoo on the door. Dut Toit let him in, and then for some strange reason gave him a friendly slap on the shoulder. Swanepoel looked at him, a little startled, then led the way into the dining-room.

"Have you got it, old man?" he asked.

Du Toit didn't answer. He took out a packet of cigarettes

308

and offered one. Swanepoel accepted and Du Toit took one and then very carefully he lit both cigarettes. His hand was shaking.

"I meant to tell you—if there's anything you want to add to it, it's not too late to put it in. Did anything strike you when you were reading over it?"

Du Toit did not look at him. He suddenly got up and went into the kitchen and asked Anna to make some coffee. He stood with his palm on the kitchen table, watching her as she filled the kettle. He lingered while she laid the cups out on the tray. At last he dragged himself back into the dining-room. As he walked in he saw that Swanepoel had found the statement, which had been lying on the mantelpiece, and was holding it in his hand.

Swanepoel said, "Oh. I see you've left it exactly as we drew it up. I take it it's O.K. like this, then?"

Du Toit evaded his look.

"What's the matter?" Swanepoel asked. Du Toit was standing with his elbow on the dresser, drumming his fingers.

"I said what's the matter? Can't you hear me?"

Du Toit slowly turned to him and caught the full charge of ice-blue venom from his eyes. And in one moment all the limp helplessness that had made him such an easy prey to Swanepoel during the interrogation in the office overwhelmed him.

"No, nothing's the matter," he said, barely audibly.

"Well, let's just sign it. I've got work to do," Swanepoel said, taking his fountain pen out and fixing the cap on the back. He walked across the room, held the document down on the dresser with the last page open, and handed Du Toit the pen.

Du Toit took it and, with a trembling hand, signed.

*   *   *

When Swanepoel left, Du Toit went and sat at the table. He felt stunned, as if he had been involved in a street mishap. Everything had been set, his course planned, and suddenly he was sent flying and it was all over. His first reaction was a disbelief that he had actually signed: it seemed so unreal. But then a kind of uneasy peace came over him.

He decided to take a walk out to the location and see how things looked out there. *That* was settled, anyway: he was going back. Maybe it was best after all. Maybe it *was* only nerves—shock—and he had been seeing things in an unbalanced way. Anyway, now it was all settled, he was going back to work and in some queer way it made him feel much better. He would start work to-morrow and meantime take a look around the place to-day just to see how the land lay.

He put on his hat and coat and walked slowly along the pavement in the direction of the location. People greeted him, and he smiled back but avoided getting into conversation. He came to Potgieter Street and walked right to the end, and was passing the Cross Roads Garage when he saw Dick Werdmuller, the proprietor, sitting in the little glass box where he took in the petrol money. Dick shouted to him as he went past, and came out to the pavement. His leathery old face was wrinkled in a smile, and he shook hands warmly with Du Toit.

" Where you going, Mr. Du Toit ? "

" Out to the location," Du Toit told him.

" Well, for God's sake, take a car."

They went into the garage. " How's this old rickshaw do ? Not very dandy but its only a few miles out. Sorry can't let you have my car, but the wife's using it. Still, this will do. Tell me, Mr. Du Toit, that was a pretty terrible business the other night ? "

Du Toit said, " It certainly was."

" You know, one of my boys was mixed up in it. Seems he was the ringleader. You know, I'd never believe it of him. He was such a good worker around here. Best mechanic I ever had. And then, on top of everything, the bloody fool tries to escape and gets himself shot. You know, Mr. Du Toit, it broke my heart when I heard about that. I really liked that boy. Did you know him ? "

" Not very well."

" Well, I wonder, that's all. . . . They say he was at the back of it all, but somehow I can't help wondering . . . You know how it is, when you know a boy and find him reliable and well liked all round, well, you ask yourself—could he do a thing like that ? This whole business has upset me. I just can't help thinking about that boy. You know what I think ? He just had too many ideas in his head, too much spirit, as they say. But he wasn't no agitator."

" Yes. He seemed to be very well educated," Du Toit said.

" He certainly was. He knew words you or I never heard of. I'm telling you this, Mr. Du Toit, even though you were the victim of it the other night, because I think you ought to know how he struck me, that boy. Fair's fair. Maybe you don't like me talking like this ? " He stopped and looked at Du Toit with his trembling, worried old eyes.

Du Toit felt that Dick expected him to be angry. He didn't know what to say. " No, it's all right," he said.

Dick went on, " What's he want to try and escape for ? Why'd he do that ? If he wanted money for a lawyer or anything, why, I'd have put it up for him. I hope you don't mind me speaking to you like this, but it keeps going round in my mind. Anyway, I've decided to do something. Want to know what ? "

" What, Mr. Werdmuller ? "

" I'm giving twenty pounds to that boy's family. He was a good worker here and, well, I feel I owe it to his family."

Du Toit was in the car now, starting it up. " You'd better watch out, Mr. Werdmuller," he said, " how you talk—in this town."

He drove slowly out to the location. He thought with puzzled interest about Dick Werdmuller. So even *he* fell for him. What was there about that Kaffir ? God, he'd never met one like that. Still, old Dickie'd better look out how he talked, otherwise pretty soon he'd find himself minus customers.

When he reached the location gates he found a number of policemen armed with Sten guns standing about. All those going in or out had to show credentials. They recognised Du Toit and let him pass, but he pulled up at the other side of the gate. Just inside the wire a number of workmen were busy hammering up the temporary structure that Swanepoel had spoken about. Ahead of him was the gutted administration building. It still stood propped up on its concrete legs, but the roof had collapsed inside and he could see the sky through the windows. The veranda had burnt completely away, the walls were black, and a whole area around the building was strewn

311

with burnt wreckage and charred paper. A stiff, acrid smell still hung in the air. It had been a devastating fire. The building had been destroyed with a thoroughness that drove home the finality of the collapse of all the things that had once held him to the location.

He started the car up again and went about twenty yards, then turned back and asked one of the policemen to accompany him. A young blond man climbed in, holding his gun gingerly, and they went slowly down the main street.

Houses on both sides of the street looked deserted, as if they had been hastily evacuated : windows were boarded up : doors swung loosely on single hinges : roofs sagged where pillars or masonry had crumbled under them. Furniture was strewn about in the gardens. He noticed the neat, straight lines of bullet holes joining house to house to house.

There was a tight expression around his mouth. He did not speak to the young policeman sitting beside him. The pattern that had dominated his behaviour during the raid was coming into play again. He passed two trucks laden with armed police coming up the street in the opposite direction : the location was being heavily patrolled. Some of the men greeted him, but he did not return the greeting. He had a destination, and drove grimly on towards it.

They came to the overturned bus, lying across the street in a pool of glass and charred horsehair. He had to ride on to the pavement to squeeze past it. A little distance farther on he came to Malooy's bus yard, strewn with the black carcases of buses, like some dry-land Pearl Harbour. He turned into the shopping street and saw that half a block of shops had burnt down with the cinema.

There were people in the streets but they walked with an unreal air, as if the streets had no existence for them. Nobody greeted him. He felt eyes following him as he went past, but when he turned his head, the eyes disappeared into the landscape. He heard a babble of noise, turned a corner in that direction, and saw a crowd of women drawing water from a street tap. The moment they saw him they froze into silence : stood immobile with paraffin tins of water balanced on their heads, stayed in the

312

act of bending over the tap, or tying the cloth that held a baby on the back—until he went past, when the tableau melted once more into activity. He felt the hostility of the whole location in the air all around him. It pressed on him, a silent, freezing, invisible encirclement of hate.

He came at last to the Welfare Centre : or rather to the plot on which it had once stood. Apart from the chimney, now grotesquely tall and teetering, there was nothing that stood more than a foot above the ground. From the charred brickwork foundation it was possible to see where the different rooms had been, but the rest of the timber building was completely incinerated.

He came out of the car and stood with his hands on his hips and stared at the ashes of his best gift to the location. Its destruction had an element of mockery, a gross, insulting spitefulness aimed directly at him. He looked at it and felt himself become furious. Suddenly he turned away from the policeman and blew his nose hard several times into his handkerchief. Then he turned and said quietly, " Come on, let's go."

He drove back to the gate. Again, all the way, hidden hostile eyes followed him, and he drew an area of silence along with him through the location.

At the gate he let the policeman out and then switched the engine off and sat in the car. He lit a cigarette and drew deep, trying to conquer the fluttering in his stomach.

Sergeant Ackerman was at the gate. He came over to the car and said, " That interpreter boy of yours, he heard you were here. He wants to speak to you."

" Where's he ? "

" I told him to wait there." He pointed to a tree about thirty yards away. Among the crowd standing under it Du Toit could see Gwebu's squat, untidy figure and his eyeglasses reflecting two blank flashes of sunlight.

" O.K. I'll see him," Du Toit said.

Ackerman put two fingers to his mouth and let out a piercing whistle, then waved his arm from the shoulder and yelled, " Hey, you, Kleinbooi, come here." Gwebu ran across the grass and stopped a few yards from the car.

"This him?" Ackerman asked Du Toit.

"Yes."

"O.K.," Ackerman said, nodding to Gwebu, and Gwebu walked up to the side of the car.

Gwebu looked more slovenly than ever before. He still wore the grey sweater with a large unravelling hole in the middle and the dirty striped shirt that he had worn on the night of the riot. The shirt had blood spots on it—his own blood, Du Toit realised with a slight shock, flecked off him while they were crouched together under the window. Gwebu had washed neither himself nor his clothes since the night of the riot.

Gwebu stood at the window of the car. "Sir, they didn't shout, 'M'bulala,'" he said. "They shouted, 'Ufuna ukusi bulala'—'You want to kill us'—a very different thing. Lieutenant Swanepoel's got it wrong, sir." He spoke very earnestly. This had obviously become his particular agony.

Du Toit looked coldly at him. "I don't want to discuss that with you," he said.

Gwebu looked surprised. "But, sir, it's important. I think we've got to do . . ."

"I said I don't want to discuss it. Is that clear?"

"Yes, sir."

"You wanted to speak to me?"

"Yes, sir."

"Well, what's it?"

"No, nothing, sir. Nothing." He stepped back and bobbed his head—a little bow. "Well, I'll be running along now."

He looked hard at Gwebu. The dirt, the smell of him, and the sudden cowering manner added to his irritation. Then he remembered how Gwebu had shared the ordeal with him, and began to feel sorry for speaking harshly to him.

"Andries?"

"Yes, sir?"

"Just tell me one thing—why did you run into the office with me like that?"

"I don't know, sir."

"You *must* know. What was in your mind? Was it that you wanted to stick by me? Was that it?"

"As I said, sir, I don't know. I couldn't say why I did it. My legs did the thinking for me, sir."

"I see," Du Toit said, his tone changing. He added sourly, "Anyway, you looked damn' funny under the window like that. You should have seen yourself—your face. I'll always remember how you looked that night."

"I hope it will give you amusement for many years to come, sir," Gwebu said without a flicker on his face.

"Stop that!"

"Yes, sir."

"We're starting to-morrow." He was curt and businesslike now. "You'd better meet me and we'll decide how we're going to get everything organised again. How're we going to do it—with—without the building, the records. . . .?" He waved his hand impatiently in front of him. "Anyway, I'll see you here at the gate. Nine o'clock sharp."

He put the car into gear and accelerated the engine, but Gwebu stepped forward and stood right against the door.

"Don't go yet, sir. Do you know they're going to be *defended*?"

"That so?" Du Toit said, frowning. He disengaged the gear, but left the engine running.

"Yes, sir. A big Q.C. from Johannesburg is coming out here to defend the case—and I'm not going to say the crowd threatened to kill you. Not to *that* man, sir. He's too clever—he'll twist me all around, and I've got to tell the truth."

"*What* man?" Du Toit said, switching off the engine.

"Gerald Bramley, Q.C., sir."

Du Toit narrowed his eyes and looked hard at Gwebu. Was this one of his old tricks? If this was true it had all the sound of bad news. Gerald Bramley was one of the most famous of the lawyers, a spectacular court man and a ferocious cross-examiner. The thought of having to back up that statement in court, with Gerald Bramley on the opposing side, had chilling implications.

"I don't believe you!" he said in a dry voice. "How'll they ever pay him?"

"He's doing it for nothing, sir, that's the strange part. He sometimes takes these cases for nothing. When there's a matter of *principle* involved, or when something seems worth while fighting."

"Who approached him?" Du Toit asked.

"Oh, I don't know. Some people here."

"Which people? Who's behind all this?"

"Oh, some crowd." Gwebu looked soberly at Du Toit and added, "You know, sir, this little affair has united the whole location."

"How? What d'you mean 'united'?"

"Oh—just *united* them. You know, made them all stand together."

"I know what the word means. I want to know in what way. *How* united? Who's *doing* it?"

"Oh, I don't know, sir.. I don't get mixed up in these things."

Du Toit felt exasperated. He looked at Gwebu, who stared back with that blank, owl-like expression. There was the old prickly tension between them. He saw that Gwebu wouldn't be drawn, that it was useless to try to take it further. It was the same old Gwebu—the sniper concealed behind an innocent-looking brick wall. This time he had planted in Du Toit's mind a neat little nest of worries. What did it mean about them being united? And how did they manage to get Bramley? Who *was* behind it all? There was something very funny here.

He had a feeling of utter hopelessness. He looked at Gwebu searchingly. Only *him* left now—Ngubeni murdered, Gwagwa gone, the whole force of location constables become useless. Start all over again? With this! From here? He looked out of the car window—his eyes travelled past the gutted administration building, down the main street with its shattered houses, down as far as the overturned bus, then back in a sweep over the jigsaw huddle of rooftops. There was a strange, twisting, smoky light over the location, a wild, drunken sign in the sky.

No, Swanepoel had not solved any problems. The location had more problems now than at any previous time. Different problems, angrier, uglier, sharper. Swanepoel would have done everybody a favour if he had stayed out of the location that night.

He decided to go home now. He'd had enough for one day. He turned the key again, but Gwebu didn't seem to want to let him go. He stood looking into the car, and there was that trace of a glint in his eyes that meant that something new was coming up.

"You remember, sir, that time with Lieutenant Swanepoel there was some talk about Sarah Manana, the shebeen queen? Someone identified her, if you remember."

"I identified her."

"Yes, sir. You identified her. Well, you know she was shot?"

"Yes. She tried to stab a policeman, so I heard."

"Well, that's not true, sir. She didn't try to stab anybody. They never found any knife on her or near her."

"How do you know this?" Du Toit asked sharply.

"There's an old *ayah* who lives in her yard. This woman saw and heard everything—there was no knife."

Du Toit had become very serious.

Gwebu went on. "Furthermore, she was not at the riot. She was at a church meeting in Withoek. She came back after the riot was over, but climbed through the fence, and so consequently did not see the police at the gate. And, sir, the whole location knows you identified her. That old *ayah* woman has seen to that."

"If this one of your jokes, I'll kill you."

"Let's go down to Sessabie Street, sir."

"Why?"

"Please, sir, let's go down. Then you'll see for yourself."

"All right then." Gwebu came round and sat in the car. Du Toit started the engine and they shot away with a jerk. "I don't believe it," he said a number of times. They went down to the far end of Jubilee City, twisting and winding along the crooked streets. At last they turned into Sessabie Street, and then, almost before they knew it, they found themselves in the midst of a crowd of several hundred people who had collected in front of Sarah Manana's house. There had been wailing and

317

singing and beating of drums, but the moment the car turned the corner, the crowd became silent. Among the crowd were a number of Sunday pilgrims, location Zionists of various sects. They were clad in full regalia—white ankle-length surplices, with large red, green, or blue crosses sewn on front and back, mitre hats, medallions, chains, ropes, and feathers. They stood holding beribboned shepherd's crooks, crucifixes, fur-covered tub-like drums, banners, and musical instruments, and stared as if at an apparition into the car.

"There are her witnesses, sir," Gwebu said. His voice was trembling. "They were with her at Withoek. Would you like to ask them some questions ? "

"What are they *doing* here ? "

"This was to have been her funeral, sir. But the police took the body away, so they're holding a service outside her house. Mrs. Manana was very popular with the church, sir."

He looked out and saw that the crowd was standing right round the car, but at a distance away, as if in superstitious fear of coming too near. All their eyes were on him, and he could feel, from the weight of their looks and silence, almost like a physical experience, the single thought that was in each of their minds—that he had caused Sarah's death.

"Go on, ask them, sir," Gwebu said, frightened too, but unable to stop himself taking this revenge on Du Toit.

"Shut up," Du Toit said, turning his head swiftly to him, then back to the crowd. He saw some people having a whispered consultation. Their faces were agitated but grim. He watched them, wondering what they were going to do.

His heart was pounding. He put his hand up under his sweater and felt the sickly, clammy palpitation in his chest.

He did not take his eyes off them. He saw them nod to each other and then a tall, burly man, one of the Zionist priests, started to walk towards the car. As he walked, the crowd surged after him. Du Toit leant out and shouted, " Keep away from the car ! " The man stopped, the crowd with him. Then he came forward again, and the crowd followed.

The numbing fear that he knew so well, and that he loathed ; that had never left him during all his time in Nelstroom but had merely been lulled, disguised, or concealed from time to time; that had shaped all his actions in the location, now returned stark, chill, and paralysing.

The man came up and placed his hand on the door handle. " Mr. Manager . . ." he started to say.

Du Toit thought he was trying to open the door and he put his arm outside and slapped the man's hand away. Then he started the engine, and blowing the hooter loud and hard, drove the car forward, forcing people to get out of the way as best they could. His head was swimming. He could not think.

He went through the crowd, and then before picking up speed, took a last look in the rearview mirror. He saw the crowd standing tight-packed right across the street, muttering and angry.

He let the clutch out too suddenly, and the car shot forward with a jolt. He turned the next corner, but skidded round so crazily that the car almost overturned. He drove much too fast, blowing the hooter furiously and bouncing and bumping the car with bad handling. Fowls, dogs, and children scattered before him in a squawking, squealing panic. He drove through the back streets of Jubilee City stirring up so much noise and excitement that half the location came out of their houses to see what the trouble was. As he passed he left behind him eddies of wild, babbling talk.

He dropped Gwebu off at the gate and sped into town. He left the car at the Cross-Roads Garage, and without even going in to speak to Werdmuller, strode back to his house.

He tried to think of how he would explain it to Anna.

He found Anna sitting in the dining-room, knitting. He stood at the door with his hands on his hips. She looked up and smiled. He felt a sudden tenderness and sorrow for her, and he went over to her. He put his hand under her chin, turned her face up, and kissed her. Then he took a deep breath and said :

" Let's start packing."

" WHAT ? "

He tried to explain—not about his fear, but about all the reasons that had been in his mind when he thought he was not going to sign the statement. It just didn't make sense. He gave up, and went to the garage and brought back some cardboard

319

containers that had been used to bring their things to Nelstroom. Anna was sobbing. He went over to her and kissed her wet face. She gave him a long, bewildered look, with eyes drowned in tears. Then a sad smile broke through. She squeezed his hand and stood up, gathered the pictures off the mantelpiece, and stacked them in a pile on the table.

THE END

SECOND CHANCE PRESS, Sagaponack, New York 11962

All titles come in $15.95 cloth editions and $7.95 trade paper editions unless otherwise noted.

Bloom, Harry. TRANSVAAL EPISODE. "Fiery and admirable, with power, passion and a controlled savagery that makes it uncomfortable but fascinating reading." *London Daily Telegraph.*

Broun, Heywood Hale. A STUDIED MADNESS. "The most ruefully articulate, inside book on the American Theater in years." *John Barkham.* "A highly entertaining memoir that could be mistaken for a novel." *Milwaukee Journal.*

Conrad, Earl. GULF STREAM NORTH. "A graphic recounting of five days at sea. The crew is black, the captain white, but all are bound together in the mystique and commerce of fishing. A first class reissue." *San Diego Union.*

Degenhard, William. THE REGULATORS. "This six hundred page novel to end all novels about Dan Shays will not let you down. In manages to endow the uprising known as Shays Rebellion with all the sweep of a minor epic." *New York Times.* (cloth) ... $22.50 (paper) ... $11.95

deJong, Dola. THE FIELD. "An overwhelming tragedy of refugees escaping Europe during World War II, this novel can tell us more about history than do books of history themselves." *St. Louis Globe Democrat.*

Goodman, Mitchell. THE END OF IT. "A classic of American literature; the single American masterpiece about the Second World War." *The Nation* "Philosophical, poetic, it says something new about war." *Norman Mailer.*

Levy, Alan. SO MANY HEROES. "Alan Levy lived through the Russian-led invasion of Czechoslovakia in 1968 and has written about it with an intimacy of detail and emotion that transcends mere journalistic reporting. A large book about a tiny nation's hope and tragedy." *Newsweek.*

Lortz, Richard. LOVERS LIVING, LOVERS DEAD. "The sort of subtle menace last evinced in Henry James' *The Turn of the Screw.* This portrait of innocence corrupted should keep a vast readership in its terrifying grasp." *San Diego Union.*

Lortz, Richard. THE VALDEPEÑAS. "The story begins with a seemingly realistic depiction of a group of vacationers summering off the coast of Spain . . . then becomes progressively surrealistic. Suspense builds to a chaotic ending making this a one-sitting, hard-to-put-down book." *Library Journal.*

O'Neal, Charles. THREE WISHES FOR JAMIE. "A humerous, sensitive love story with adventure, laughter, tears and a sprinkling of Irish folklore." *Los Angeles Times.*

Salas, Floyd. TATTOO THE WICKED CROSS. "An extraordinarily evocative novel set on a California Juvenile prison farm. One of the best and most important first novels published during the last ten years." *Saturday Review.*

Schuman, Julian. CHINA: AN UNCENSORED LOOK. "It is appropriate, timely and fortunate for those who wish to know how it was in China during the momentous years from 1948 through 1953 that the *Second Chance Press* has reprinted this book. Its time has come." *Foreign Service Journal.*

Shepard, Martin. FRITZ. The definitive biography of the founder of Gestalt Therapy. "A masterful yet loving portrait that goes far beyond biography, offering a Fritz Perls to whom few, if any, were privy." *Psychology Today.*

Singer, Loren: THE PARALLAX VIEW. "A tidy, taut and stylish thriller that functions as a political chiller as well! Breathbating suspense." *New York Magazine.*

Stern, Richard: "A brilliant fusing of the themes of a father's attempt to understand and exonerate his son with a plot of wartime espionage." *Richard Ellmann* "Brilliant . . . authentic . . . exciting." *Commonweal.*